Readers love ARIEL TACHNA's
Partnership in Blood novels

"I absolutely love this series."
—Romance Junkies

"I've thoroughly enjoyed the premise for these books and the characters, and recommend them to any reader who enjoys paranormal fantasy; especially those involving vampires, wizards and magic."
— Literary Nymphs Reviews

"…an amazingly well written series that I know that paranormal romantics will enjoy."
—Night Owl Reviews

"[Reparation in Blood] is action packed and full of fascinating and amazing characters. A worthwhile read and fitting end to the series."
—Bitten by Books

"This series is definitely for anyone looking for a new twist on Vampires, and who likes a bit of angst and a bit of adventure mixed into their romance."
—Dark Diva Reviews

"Ariel Tachna has created a truly original version of the vampire archetype…"
—Steve Williams, Suite 101

http://www.dreamspinnerpress.com

Perilous Partnership

A Partnership in Blood Novel

ARIEL TACHNA

Dreamspinner Press

Published by
DREAMSPINNER PRESS

5032 Capital Circle SW, Suite 2, PMB# 279, Tallahassee, FL 32305-7886 USA
http://www.dreamspinnerpress.com/

Perilous Partnership
© 2014 Ariel Tachna.

Cover Art
© 2010 DWS Photography.
cerberuspic@gmail.com
Cover content is for illustrative purposes only and any person depicted on the cover is a model.

ISBN: 978-1-63216-668-5
Digital ISBN: 978-1-63216-669-2
Library of Congress Control Number: 2014950197
Second Edition October 2014
First Edition published by Dreamspinner Press, October 2010

Printed in the United States of America
∞
This paper meets the requirements of
ANSI/NISO Z39.48-1992 (Permanence of Paper).

To Nicki and Emmet, who worked overtime for this one.

Prologue

"MESDAMES ET messieurs, it is with much emotion that I stand before you today for the last time as the général of the Milice de Sorcellerie," Marcel said, his voice hoarse as he regarded the press corps he had faced so many times. "As we speak, the Milice is being officially dismantled and its operatives returned to civilian life once again. To those who have served with me these past two years, I say thank you. We owe our survival as a society to your dedication and sacrifice. For those who will be welcoming them back into your offices and your lives, remember what they have gone through and be patient with them. Many of them are wounded in body and spirit. Many of them have suffered great loss. Some of them have also welcomed vampires into their lives, forming partnerships that will extend beyond the Milice and affect them in ways we are only beginning to understand. Those men and women have suffered and sacrificed as well, and they deserve your respect and your open-mindedness. I can't order you to accept them, but I would ask that you give them the same chance you would give any new person of importance in your friends' and colleagues' lives. They have earned that at the very least.

"As I return to private life myself, I begin to feel my age," Marcel continued. "Unlike most of the wizards I commanded during the war, I am not a young man anymore. I've spent the last sixty years in public service to the wizarding community and to France as a whole. I'm tired, mesdames et messieurs. So once the Milice is completely decommissioned, I will be retiring from my other public roles as well. L'ANS will pass into the able hands of a younger generation as we move forward into this new reality where vampires are an acknowledged, valued segment of the magical community and of society as a whole. It gives me great pleasure to introduce to you the new head of l'ANS, whose experience, ingenuity, and dedication will help usher in a new age in the world of magic: Raymond Payet." In the wings, Raymond glanced at Jean for reassurance one last time before stepping onto the dais and joining Marcel at the podium. When the polite applause died down, Raymond focused on the cameras, knowing his true audience was not the journalists assembled in front of him but the people watching at home and the ones who would read about it in the paper the next day. "Thank you, Marcel, for the kind introduction," he began, clearing his throat to be heard more effectively. He and Jean had spent hours preparing for this moment, writing and rewriting his speech, examining every nuance to make sure he said exactly what he wanted to say, nothing more, nothing less.

When silence returned to the room, Raymond continued. "Today is a new beginning for l'ANS in many different ways. For some years now, l'Association Nationale de Sorcellerie has been synonymous in many minds with wizards. And while we certainly fall within the purview of l'ANS, we represent one small portion of the magical realm. We are doers of magic, calling on an intrinsic ability to create extrinsic effects, but we are hardly the full extent of magical creatures. L'ANS must become more than just a society of wizards. We must become the voice for all magical beings, mortal, immortal, living or undead. We must usher in a new era of equality that acknowledges and celebrates our similarities and our differences.

"Some of you, both here and at home, are asking yourselves right now what you could possibly have in common with some creature of the night, some shapeshifter or faerie or goblin or troll. The answer will vary from person to person, from race to race, but every one of you who has ever married, promising to love your spouse until death do you part, has something in common with one vampire who will have one partner, one lover, one source of blood for as long as that person remains alive. Every one of you who has lost a spouse has something in common with another vampire who buried his Avoué four hundred years ago and still mourns his loss, and with the oldest vampire in Paris who still mourns his Avoué fifteen hundred years later. Every one of you who has held a child you love in your arms has something in common with the werewolves, who celebrate every new birth because they happen so rarely. You may think you have nothing in common with the so-called lesser magical races, but I tell you now: you're wrong. As we move forward, l'ANS has expanded its mission to protect and speak for not only the wizarding community, but the magical community as a whole.

"The alliance that allowed the Milice de Sorcellerie to win the war against Serrier has formally ended, along with the war itself and the Milice, but the need for magic has not disappeared. One of the reasons the alliance was so vital was that it freed wizards to attend again to the necessary task of maintaining the magical equilibrium that allows our world to exist. Imagine our delight then when we discovered that the very making of the alliance contributed far more effectively than anything we wizards could do on our own. The link between vampire and wizard has become more than a military tool. It creates a magical connection in profound, lasting ways that we still do not fully understand. That, too, will be one of the new roles of l'ANS: researching the partnership bonds so that we can use them to their fullest potential and properly prepare any vampire or wizard who wishes to participate for all the repercussions.

"In 1944, we recognized the right of all citizens to vote, regardless of gender, guaranteeing women equal protection under the law. We stand now at another historic moment, having given vampires that same protection. No longer will they be subject to discrimination because of their nature. No longer will they have to hide who they are for fear of being cast out of their homes or having their businesses destroyed. I am not naïve. I know it will take more than just the passing of the equal rights legislation for attitudes to change. However, as the new head of l'ANS, I pledge the full support of the organization—financial, legal, and moral—to seeing that legislation become a reality for every vampire, just as we already work tirelessly to address issues related to the wizarding community. Discrimination, in any form, cannot be allowed to exist. We fought a war to keep that very thing from happening. We cannot ignore bigotry from those who do not choose to attempt an overthrow of the government in order to air their grievances.

"As much as we all would like to pretend otherwise, Serrier struck a chord with enough wizards to carry out a rebellion that lasted for two years. While I deplore the methods he used in his attempt to effectuate change, I understand why his propaganda resonated with some wizards. So I say now to those disaffected within society: I welcome dialogue with each and every one of you. The only way we can avoid a repeat of this terrible war is by addressing the underlying reasons behind it. Serrier was a megalomaniac whose madness cost him his life and his reforms. While we are well rid of him, we must be proactive and seek ways to avoid a recurrence, not only of the war, but of the grievances that led to it. Already, I have spoken with the President about revisiting the laws concerning dark magic. Knowledge is never evil. It is how that knowledge is used that determines whether something is good or evil. It is the intent behind a spell that determines whether it is in fact dark magic, not the spell itself.

"Finally, as the new head of l'ANS, I intend to push for an increase in education and outreach services with the intention of avoiding situations like far too many I heard of from wizards who sided with Serrier, where young wizards, teenagers often, were persecuted much as the vampires have been because they were different. Magic is not something to be beaten out of children. Nor is it something to be feared. Rather, it is a gift to be nurtured and trained so that it can be used to the benefit of society. Wizard or vampire, werewolf or faerie, the magical races are a part of this world for a reason. We are a part of this country and it is time everyone recognized that, ourselves included.

"Mesdames et messieurs, thank you for your time and attention. We have a long road ahead of us, but we have taken those first, all important steps. Bonsoir."

The reporters shouted questions after him, but Raymond paid them no attention. He simply walked off the dais, through the wings of the auditorium, and into Jean's waiting arms.

"Whatever the future brings," Jean murmured in Raymond's ear, "I'll always support your position as head of l'ANS. In le jeu des Cours, in Parlement, within l'ANS, or in the media."

Raymond's joyful laughter echoed off the walls. He had trouble believing how far they had come. Only yesterday, when Marcel had made his announcement to l'ANS, Raymond had received a standing ovation from the wizards who had fought with the Milice, a show of support Raymond would not have believed possible a few months ago. And he had the vampires—this vampire—to thank for that. He hooked his arm through Jean's. "Let's go home."

Chapter 1

One year later

RAYMOND DUCKED inside his apartment building, cursing the rain that dripped down the back of his neck despite his ensorcelled coat, which was supposed to protect him from the weather. He really needed a coat with a hood.

Either that, or he needed to adjust the wards on his and Jean's apartment to let him displace himself directly inside rather than having to walk through them. He'd been telling himself to do that for over a year, but something always seemed to take precedence. Like convincing the world he didn't have the same megalomaniac tendencies that had possessed Serrier, despite having sided with the dark wizard at the very beginning of the rebellion. He had told Marcel making him head of l'ANS was a mistake, but Marcel had not listened. Raymond was glad of that most days. He enjoyed the work, enjoyed the challenges of addressing all the changes brought about by the alliance and the war and the equal rights legislation. He could have done without the bureaucracy, but he figured it was a part of any job, and at least he had the clout to cut through a lot of it. Not as much as Marcel, but far more than he had expected when he agreed to take the job. It helped that no one knew, even now, exactly what to expect from....

"Jean." The arms around his waist could belong to no other, if only because the wards wouldn't let anyone else through without his express permission. He and Jean had debated that point extensively, but in the end, they'd agreed that making any exception set a precedent for other exceptions, and neither of them could afford to be at risk. Nor did they want people, friend or foe, dropping by at all hours of the day and night. Marcel had maintained a true open-door policy, both at his office and at home, but while Raymond was willing to offer that consideration at work, he had no desire to share the home he and Jean were building with unexpected callers.

"How was your day?" Raymond asked, turning in Jean's embrace. They kept the same hours, having adjusted their schedules to allow both wizards and vampires access to their assistance, but they rarely saw each other for more than a few minutes while they were working unless they scheduled a meeting. The days of spending their entire shift together had ended with the war.

"Long," Jean replied, his lips resting against the side of Raymond's neck, making the wizard hope Jean would ask to feed tonight. It had been three days, and Raymond still missed the intimacy of the near-constant feeding. He knew it had been a product of the situation, not something they could maintain in the long term. That seemed to make no difference to his need, particularly when their schedules kept Jean from feeding every night.

"Mine too," Raymond agreed, arms going around Jean's slender waist, still amazed even after a year at his lover's deceptive appearance. Jean did not look strong enough to hurt a fly, yet Raymond had watched him throw a grown man across the street without straining. He closed his eyes as he breathed in the spicy scent of Jean's cologne, wondering if he dared leave his news until morning. It might not stop Jean from feeding, but it would certainly kill any more romantic thoughts.

Jean sighed, kissing Raymond's neck and lifting his head. "We have a problem."

Raymond echoed his sigh. "I'm guessing it's the same problem that landed on my desk today. Paul Charlot and his partner?"

Jean nodded. "You'd think all our warnings would keep people from forming partnerships unsupervised, but from what Guillemin told me, neither one is happy with the bond."

"Merde," Raymond groaned. "Paul said the same thing. All people need to do is look at Alain and Orlando or Sebastien and Thierry or any of the other partnerships that formed during the war to see there's more to the bond than simply protection from daylight and a boost to the wizard's power."

Jean shrugged. "Vampires see the brand on Alain's neck and look no further than that for an explanation of Orlando's behavior."

"I'll buy that for Orlando and Alain," Raymond allowed, thinking about the instant attraction and almost equally immediate bond between Jean's best friend and Raymond's second-in-command. "The Aveu de Sang puts them in a class by themselves, but Thierry doesn't have a mark. Mathieu doesn't. I don't."

Jean laughed. "You're the president of l'ANS. I'm chef de la Cour. Thierry is a past master at hiding what he feels behind his mask of strategist, and the others aren't nearly as much in the public eye. We see it because we know to look for it and because our ties to the other ex-combatants act as a sort of pass into their confidence. You know what they're feeling without having to be told, and so you see the little signs outsiders miss."

Raymond could see Jean's point. He hardly advertised the fact that he came home every night to the bed and arms of the chef de la Cour. People who knew them realized it, but a wizard who had spent the war anywhere but in Paris might not. Paul, the wizard who had been waiting for him when he arrived at three o'clock that afternoon—he worked from three to one in the morning so he would be available to vampires who were still confined by daylight—had not even been a member of l'ANS during the war, having only come into his magical abilities six months ago. Raymond did not know his partner, Guillemin, to know why the vampire had disregarded all the warnings. Unless the lure of being protected from sunlight by his partner's blood was sufficient to override his common sense. "There's got to be a better way to deal with this."

"There is," Jean reminded him, seeing the concern and frustration on his lover's handsome face. He reached up and smoothed the worry lines from the wizard's forehead, feeling once again the attraction that had little to do with the short dark hair, strong features, and beautiful body and everything to do with the strength of character that lay beneath the surface. "It just keeps taking second place to everything else we're trying to accomplish."

L'Institut Marcel Chavinier. Raymond's dream and the ultimate tribute to his mentor, the man whose brilliance and courage had led to the founding of the alliance and the creation of the partnerships that had won the war and continued to define the lives of so many. "We aren't ready to go forward with it yet."

"Why not?" Jean asked seriously. "What's really holding us back?"

Raymond laughed bitterly. "Time? Money? Curriculum? Faculty? The hundred other things requiring our time?"

Jean nodded his understanding. "I'm not used to being subject to the whims of the Parlement and the rest of the world. I've ruled my own Cour for so long that I'm used to setting my agenda and ignoring everything else. I know it isn't that simple, but we've got two men whose lives have been turned upside down."

"No more or less than ours were a year ago." Raymond had not wanted a partner, much less a lover and had fought the bond between them tooth and nail. Thankfully, he had failed spectacularly.

"No," Jean agreed, "but we were fighting a war, ready to make sacrifices in order to win. For most of us, the resulting partnerships weren't sacrifices at all, but do you really think Adèle wouldn't undo her bond if she could?"

"I know she would," Raymond replied, thinking ruefully of the most heinous case of incompatibility he had witnessed among partners. Paul and Guillemin might not be happy with the far-reaching influences of the bond on their lives, but he doubted it could compare to the kind of misery Adèle and her partner Jude had inflicted on each other before the decommissioning of the Milice de Sorcellerie had allowed her to leave Paris and her partner as well. As far as he knew, they had not seen each other in over a year. The scholar in him wondered if the bond had broken in that time or if it merely lay dormant, waiting for them to be together again. His own need for Jean had in no way lessened, but they lived in constant proximity and Jean fed from him regularly. Even when those feedings did not include making love, they were some of the most intimate moments of Raymond's life. When Jean did make love to him with his body as well as his fangs, nothing else could compare. "Do you think we need to ignore the agenda we've laid out and focus entirely on l'Institut?"

"I think if we don't, we're going to have more and more problems like the one we have now. That isn't fair to our people, yours or mine," Jean clarified. "We've worked hard to establish l'ANS as a voice for wizards, vampires, and other magical creatures alike. We can't afford to lose the faith of our own people, because then we'll have no credibility with anyone else."

Jean's words made sense, a reminder to Raymond that he did not have to navigate the minefield of public life alone. His partner—his lover—was a past master at le jeu des Cours, the subtle vampire game of power and position that governed so much of their interactions with each other. As a chef de la Cour, a leader of the vampires, Jean had lived under constant scrutiny since taking on that role in Paris almost four hundred years earlier. If anyone could help Raymond balance all the demands on his time, it would be Jean. "Then the question is how to explain the change in priorities."

"No, the question is who to leave in charge of other priorities while we focus on l'Institut," Jean corrected. "Alain and Orlando can take over some of the legislative work. Thierry would spell us both into next week if we did that to him, but he can do some of the outreach work you've been doing yourself. He's good with people. Let him take over the education campaign. Fabienne can easily handle the complaints that come in, separating out the ones you need to deal with from the ones anyone in l'ANS can handle. At this point, she probably knows the drill as well as you do."

Raymond had to admit the truth of that statement. His secretary, a paired vampire, had proven herself a genius at organization, handling the bulk of Raymond's correspondence and paperwork with an ease he envied. Being a vampire, she kept him from doing anything that might cause Jean to lose face in le jeu des Cours and helped explain issues relating to vampire culture. Meanwhile, having a partner gave her an equal sensitivity to wizards and their concerns. Her partner spent his working hours with the task force that maintained the equilibrium of the elemental magic. "I could leave Mathieu in charge of the magical balance. He already does all the work. He could make the decisions instead of waiting for me to tell him where to focus."

"That's the spirit," Jean encouraged. "It's getting late. Have you had dinner yet?"

"I had a dinner meeting tonight," Raymond confirmed with a yawn.

"Then it's bedtime," Jean declared. "We'll take tomorrow to look at everything we have going on and decide how to delegate it. By the end of the week, we should be able to devote ourselves completely to l'Institut."

Raymond nodded his agreement. "I need a bath first," he amended. "I couldn't get warm today."

The chill did not bother Jean the way it did mortals, but he was not opposed to having his lover wet and naked.

"I'll join you," he proposed, urging Raymond down the hall into the generous-sized bathroom—generous by Parisian standards, anyway. The white claw foot tub was, like most everything in Jean's apartment, himself included, a remnant of a bygone era, but it was big enough for both men, and the hot water heater was efficient. Jean turned on the taps before turning his attention to his lover, his hands skimming efficiently over Raymond's clothes, buttons and zippers yielding to their expertise. In moments he had his lover naked for his delectation.

Raymond let him, a fact that always warmed Jean's heart, the memory of his partner fighting their bond still vivid in his mind for all that over a year had passed. Raymond's self-mastery was phenomenal, which made the knowledge that he accepted Jean's touch, Jean's bite, all the headier. Jean had not seduced his lover into their relationship, because his lover was proof against such machinations. He was there, in Jean's apartment, Jean's bed, Jean's life, because he had chosen to be. Jean was pretty sure that made him the luckiest man on the planet. His lips lingered on the scar that followed Raymond's spine, a vivid reminder of the past. Raymond would say it was a reminder of his fallibility in falling for Serrier's propaganda at the beginning of the rebellion, l'émeute des Sorciers, as it had come to be called. Jean disagreed, though he knew he would never convince Raymond of his point of view. He saw it instead as a mark of bravery. Despite the scar on his back and all it represented, Raymond had defected, fought against Serrier, and seen him brought low. To Jean's knowledge, only two other wizards alive bore similar marks. The others had met their end in the final battle. As he always did when Jean saw the scar, he traced its length with his tongue. He did not actually expect his saliva to heal that mark as it healed the bites from his feeding, but that did not dissuade him from his ritual. If nothing else, Raymond needed the reminder that Jean did not view the cicatrix as a mark of shame.

Raymond's eyes closed as a gasp escaped his lips, the same reaction he had every time Jean's mouth found the livid line on his back. He kept thinking he would grow accustomed to his lover's insistence on touching his mark of Cain, but even after a year, it still took him aback that anyone would want to lavish attention on his disfigurement. Jean had never hesitated, not from the first time he had seen it, both of them engorged with power from the Piège-Pouvoir they had undertaken to clean up an outburst of wild magic. He shivered as Jean's tongue slid lower, all thought of anything but his lover fleeing in the wake of the hot wet muscle drifting across his buttocks. "I thought we were going to take a bath," he murmured.

"We will," Jean promised, "but I hope that isn't all we're going to do."

Raymond's body reacted predictably, his cock hardening, the rest of him melting with heat. He would have sagged if Jean's hands had not caught him. As it was, his legs trembled as Jean's tongue worked its way into his crease. He leaned forward, bracing his hands on the sink, wondering if this would be the time when Jean's fangs pierced the sensitive skin of his buttocks. He had begged Jean repeatedly to stop protecting him from the feel of his fangs, but the vampire had yet to yield. Jean's lips closed over his entrance, sucking eagerly at his flesh, and Raymond pushed back against him, needing more, deeper, harder. Jean complied as if reading Raymond's mind, his tongue pushing its way inside, hot and agile and driving Raymond wild. His head fell forward onto his hands, little moans escaping his lips. "Jean!"

"In the tub," Jean ordered, pulling back and divesting himself quickly. "Don't worry, I'll take care of you."

Raymond considered begging again, but ultimately he needed a bath—although he was certainly no longer cold! They might as well combine both bath and sex. He stepped into the tub, turning back to watch as Jean's body came the rest of the way into view. Long and slender, he managed to be commanding even when naked, sending a thrill through Raymond as he anticipated giving in to the quietly imposing presence.

Jean joined him in the tub, looming over Raymond's reclining form. Kneeling down so he straddled his lover's hips, he took a moment to stroke his hands down the planes of Raymond's chest, enjoying the way the hard muscles jumped beneath his fingers. When Raymond tipped his head back, Jean leaned down and nipped lightly at the line of the wizard's jaw.

"Please," Raymond whispered.

"You don't have to beg," Jean assured him. "I want it as much as you do."

Raymond doubted that was possible, but protesting gained him nothing. Instead, he let his head fall all the way back against the edge of the tub, offering the full length of his neck for his lover's mark. Jean did not hesitate to accept the offer, his tongue sliding across Raymond's skin before his fangs penetrated, delving deep. Raymond arched up, his body seeking more contact with his lover's.

Jean obliged, bearing down against Raymond's cock, the erotic frottage enough to have both of them moaning. It took only minutes before they were both desperate for release. Jean slipped his hand between their bodies, closing it around both cocks, the additional pressure enough to trigger their mutual climax.

Licking delicately at Raymond's skin, Jean lifted his head and kissed his lover tenderly.

"Did you take enough?" Raymond asked lazily.

"More than enough," Jean assured him. "Let's finish your bath and go to bed. We have a lot to do tomorrow."

Raymond nodded, reaching automatically for the shampoo. He bathed quickly, the lure of lying in bed beside his lover enough to push him past his sex-induced lethargy.

Jean helped him dry off and led him into the bedroom, pushing aside the black brocade curtains that enclosed the four-poster bed. Raymond all but collapsed onto the dark sheets, reaching up and drawing Jean down beside him.

"Sleep well," Jean murmured, giving Raymond a final kiss.

Raymond pulled Jean closer as sleep overtook him, needing the consolation of holding his lover close. Jean moved willingly, watching as the lines of stress and worry slowly faded from Raymond's brow. Smiling, he pressed a light kiss to the corner of his lover's lips and settled in to enjoy the hours spent in his wizard's arms.

Chapter 2

"WE NEED a place away from Paris," Raymond declared as he and Jean discussed plans for l'Institut. They had spent the earlier part of their day, far earlier than they usually went in to work, figuring out how to redistribute their responsibilities. Once they decided to do it and explained the reasons to the people gaining new roles, everyone had pitched in willingly to help. Now they needed to find a suitable location.

"Why?" Jean asked. "We don't want it to seem like we're hiding anything."

"For a couple of reasons," Raymond said. "First of all, I'd rather not bankrupt l'ANS by trying to buy a big enough place in Paris, even if we could find one. Money aside, though, we don't want the students or the researchers at l'Institut under constant scrutiny. Yes, we dealt with it because we had a war going on and what else were we supposed to do? But that certainly doesn't mean it was easy making all the adjustments the partnerships have required while in the spotlight the way we were. I think the school will be less vulnerable away from the capital as well, especially if we can find somewhere truly in the country—in le Morvan or in Auvergne or perhaps in Franche-Comté. The isolation would allow us to protect the location and the students more effectively."

Jean chuckled. "Serrier's dead, Raymond. He can't come trouble our pursuits anymore."

Raymond shrugged. "That doesn't mean there aren't people who would like to see us fail on a variety of fronts. We're political targets at the very least, and the right wing would welcome a public misstep on our part simply because we represent magical creatures of every kind. Serrier's active supporters were all rounded up after the war thanks to Eric and Vincent, but no amount of military intelligence can read into people's hearts. We have no way of knowing how many sympathizers remain who would love to see our new venture fail simply because it advances an agenda counter to theirs."

"I'm not that naïve," Jean reminded Raymond. "I know all about political agendas. I also know what secrecy can do to the appearance of any undertaking. You've worked hard to open l'ANS to more races than ever before. I don't want that threatened by someone suspicious of what we're doing at l'Institut simply because it's under wraps."

"Let's compromise," Raymond proposed, seeing the logic in Jean's words. "If you can find a location within the city that will house l'Institut and isn't outrageously priced, I'll take a look at it. If you can't, we'll look farther afield."

"Fair enough," Jean agreed. "That way, too, we can say we couldn't find anything in the capital if we end up in the provinces."

"Regardless of where we end up basing l'Institut, I'd like to have Adèle help with the security. She might have buried herself away in le Morvan, but few wizards know more about protective spells than she does," Raymond declared.

"Will she come back to the city if l'Institut is here?" Jean worried aloud.

Raymond shrugged. "For Marcel, she would have. I don't know if she will for us, but it can't hurt to ask."

"Damn Leighton for his insensitivity," Jean muttered.

"You know Adèle was almost as bad," Raymond reminded him, thinking of the explosive relationship between the sultry wizard and her antiquated partner.

"She reacted to him badly," Jean agreed, "but I don't think she would have started their fight if he hadn't insisted on treating her like dirt. He has to stop living in the sixteenth century."

"I don't know what else we can do to him that Adèle hasn't already done by sequestering herself in the country and ending their partnership," Raymond said, shaking his head. "You can't force someone to change their attitude."

"I wish I knew how they were dealing with the separation," Jean commented. "It would give us something to tell Paul and Guillemin, if nothing else."

Raymond snorted softly. "I don't know whether to thank those two for forcing our hand with l'Institut or kick their sorry arses for not listening to everything we've said about the partnerships since the war ended."

"Kick them now, thank them later," Jean proposed. "They certainly deserve it for being irresponsible."

Raymond shook his head in frustration. "We don't even know if it really is irresponsibility or if something in the wizards and vampires senses a potential partner even before the first bite."

"All the more reason to start our research as quickly as possible," Jean insisted. "We can't afford not to have these answers."

"Then find me a building we can afford to buy," Raymond said.

A WEEK later Jean had no choice but to admit defeat. "Everything that's available is either half the size we need or ten times what we can afford."

"I did warn you," Raymond said with a laugh, reaching for Jean's hand and pulling him down onto the wizard's lap. "I've been doing a little searching, and I think I've found the perfect spot."

"Where?" Jean asked.

"In le Morvan, not far from where Adèle lives," Raymond replied. "It's an abandoned monastery, so there are plenty of rooms where students could stay as well as rooms we could use as classrooms or to conduct our research. It will need some work, and not all of it magical, but the price is perfect, and the setup sounds ideal."

"Then I guess we need to take a trip to le Morvan," Jean declared.

"We have a meeting with the realtor tomorrow morning," Raymond replied. "She's expecting us at eleven."

"You are far too efficient," Jean teased. "Whatever am I going to do with you?"

Raymond grinned. "Keep me?"

"Absolutely," Jean declared, eyes flashing with passion and possessiveness. He managed to rein in his instincts most of the time, so he doubted Raymond knew exactly how hard he fought each day to let his lover out of his sight. That the war had ended and their enemies had been captured or killed mattered not at all. His instincts jangled the entire time he and Raymond were apart. "But that wasn't what I meant."

"It doesn't matter anyway," Raymond laughed. "Fabienne made all the arrangements. If you're doing something with anyone, it should be her."

Jean laughed in turn, thinking of the dark-skinned vampire's partner. Mathieu might not be as powerful a wizard as Raymond was, but that did not mean he wanted to start a fight. "Mathieu might have something to say about that."

Raymond might have something to say about that too, for all that he had made the suggestion jokingly. He tamped down the surge of jealousy, reminding himself that Jean had given him no reason to doubt him and many reasons to trust. It was his own insecurity that made him wonder why Jean would want him, not anything Jean had said or done. On the contrary. Jean was assiduous in telling Raymond exactly how much he appreciated the wizard. Raymond just had trouble believing it. Not wanting to seem needy, he laughed with Jean. "We could take them."

Raymond must not have done as good a job hiding his reaction as he thought, because Jean pulled him into a hard embrace, kissing him thoroughly, leaving no doubt where his interests lay.

"I don't want them," Jean growled, releasing Raymond's lips only long enough to speak. He captured them again, manhandling Raymond backward until his hips hit his desk. He swallowed Raymond's moan, hands flying over the wizard's body as he pushed and pulled at his lover's clothes. He didn't bother trying to remove them. He only needed access to certain parts of Raymond's body anyway.

Raymond gasped again as Jean's hands burrowed beneath his shirt and into his trousers, finding all his sensitive spots and exploiting them mercilessly. His vampire had two distinct personalities inside his handsome exterior, and Raymond still could not always predict which one would surface at any given moment. He was not sure what had set Jean off this time, but since his lover always left him completely sated either way, he was not about to complain. He simply leaned back against the desk and gave himself over to Jean's mastery.

The inherent surrender in Raymond's posture fired Jean's blood. He tore open his trousers and spat in his palm, smearing the saliva over his rigid cock. Without prompting, Raymond turned, offering his bare backside to his lover. Jean stepped forward, his cock burrowing into the welcoming furrow between Raymond's cheeks. He grabbed Raymond's shoulders, lifting him into a more upright position so he could reach the curve of his lover's neck with his fangs. Teeth and cock pierced the wizard simultaneously, winning a hoarse shout from Raymond's throat. Jean smiled as hot blood rushed over his tongue, hoping Fabienne was at her desk and would hear the sounds they were making. Rationally, he knew she had no interest in his lover, nor did Raymond have any in her, but the feelings surging within him had no grounding in rationality. They were as primitive, as primal as the magic that had maintained Jean's existence for over a millennium.

Raymond spared a second's thought for the press conference he had to attend that afternoon and the marks on his neck that wouldn't be healed by then. He could heal them himself or ask another wizard to do that, but he would not. He never had, refusing to act as if his relationship with Jean shamed him in any way. They generally took pains not to flaunt the personal side of their relationship so as not to call into question the professional side, but this would not be the first time Raymond had arrived at a public appearance with a fresh bite mark on his neck. Raymond hoped no one would comment on it. He would hate to have to hex anyone.

Then Jean's cock hit his sweet spot and Raymond could not think anymore, the delicious pressure blanking his mind completely. He never remembered to tell Jean later, but he cherished that as much as any other part of their lovemaking. An academic and historian by nature, his mind was never a quiet place, except when Jean stole all thought, all breath this way. "More," he whispered, not averse to begging if it got him what he wanted.

It always got him what he wanted.

Jean's hips moved faster, harder, striving for that extra millimeter of connection as he sucked more deeply on Raymond's neck. He plundered the tender flesh for the nourishment of his body—but far more importantly, for the nourishment of his soul. Raymond's blood always tasted sweet, but it usually had an underlying savor to it, the little piece of himself that Raymond held back, that gave him his extraordinary control, even in the midst of sex; but every once in a while, everything would click together and Raymond's mind would surrender. It was Jean's Holy Grail, that moment when he tasted true abandon in his lover's blood. Knowing he had achieved it now, with Fabienne on the other side of the door and a press conference in an hour and all the work they needed to do looming over them, sent Jean's passion spiraling out of control. Reaching around Raymond, he sought his lover's shaft, pumping it in time with his pistoning hips. It took only moments before Raymond found his release, the contractions rippling through his passage enough to trigger Jean's orgasm as well.

Some minutes later, as their pulses steadied and their breathing eased, Jean carefully extracted his fangs, licking tenderly along the line of Raymond's throat to speed the healing of the torn skin as much as his saliva could do. "That's still going to be there tonight, no matter how many times I lick it," he warned Raymond.

"And you are oh so bothered by that fact," Raymond teased, hearing the note of satisfaction in Jean's voice.

"I'm not bothered by it at all," Jean replied lazily. "I've never felt constrained to hide what we are to each other, on any level. I usually do a better job of respecting your concerns though."

"You know that if we were anyone other than the chef de la Cour and the president of l'ANS, I'd proclaim it from the housetops," Raymond declared, straightening so he could turn in Jean's arms. He rued the loss of their intimate connection, but he needed to see Jean's face, needed Jean to see his face so Jean would see how serious he was. "I don't want to hide that you're my lover. I've never wanted that, but when proclaiming it could hurt our political agenda and choosing to be discreet allows us to function effectively, the good outweighs the subterfuge. I choose not to volunteer information, and so far no one has dared to ask me outright."

"And if they did?" Jean asked, muscles tensing.

"I wouldn't deny it," Raymond promised, kissing Jean heedless of the blood still staining his lips. "I'm not ashamed of you or of us. I simply choose not to flaunt it."

"Usually."

Raymond lifted a hand to his neck, feeling the incisions left by Jean's fangs. "Usually," he agreed. "You normally leave marks where no one else can see them, so it isn't an issue of hiding or flaunting anything."

Only because Raymond worried so about appearances and their impact on the political agenda of l'ANS. Jean did not know if that kind of tension could break the partnership bond between them, but he knew enough of personal relationships to know that constant arguments would make their lives hell. It was a small enough concession to make when he got Raymond and his tireless hard work against discrimination in the bargain. Either way, discussing it further would only annoy him and probably Raymond as well.

"What's on the agenda for the press conference tonight?" Jean asked, changing the subject.

"Announcing the new responsibilities we've delegated and unveiling the timeline for l'Institut," Raymond replied. "Nothing groundbreaking as far as I can foresee."

"Do you want me to be there?"

Raymond shrugged. "Only if you want. I'd think you could find some more enjoyable way to use your time."

He probably could, but that would mean letting Raymond out of his sight. The fresh bites made that marginally easier, but nothing made it easy. He made a mental note to ask one of the other paired vampires if he had the same problem. Not Orlando; the Aveu de Sang skewed everything about his relationship with Alain. Sebastien, perhaps, although Jean had still not completely assimilated the sudden cessation in tension between them after nearly four hundred years of misunderstanding. "I have a few things to take care of, but I'll see you before the conference starts."

Raymond smiled. He always offered to let Jean skip the tedious question-and-answer sessions. The vampire always refused. "Then I'll see you at seven."

Jean leaned in for one more quick kiss, his sensitive nose catching the smell of sex still surrounding Raymond. "Take a shower before then or everyone in the room will know I did more than bite you."

Raymond laughed and incanted a quick cleaning spell. "Better?"

It was not better at all as far as Jean was concerned. He was tempted to start all over again so Raymond would stay covered in his scent, but he would have to be satisfied with seeing the imprint of his fangs on Raymond's neck instead. "I think I like you the other way."

Raymond shook his head at Jean's grumbling. "Get out of here. Some of us have work to do."

Jean laughed as he left Raymond's office, but the questions raised by his sudden jealousy lingered. He wandered past the office Sebastien and Thierry shared, but the door was shut, and the light was off. He did not want to have this conversation over the phone, and he did not have time to take the train all the way out to Versailles and back before the press conference. His feet carried him out of l'ANS headquarters and halfway to Sang Froid before he even realized where he was going. Once he did, he sped up, hoping Angélique would be in and have time to talk. She had been a friend for many long years, as in touch with her vampire nature as any vampire he had ever known. If anyone could help him make sense of his feelings, it would be Angélique.

Arriving in Montmartre, he smiled to see the improvements to the exterior of Sang Froid in the year since the passage of the equality legislation that had allowed vampire business owners to come out of hiding. Where once the entrance had been nondescript, not attempting to draw attention to itself, now the entrance had an elegant sign proclaiming the name of the business. Where once Jean would have slipped across the square clinging to the shadows, now he walked openly to the door, not worrying someone would see him and wonder about the nature of his visit.

"Jean!" Angélique said, surprise and delight clear in her voice at the sight of the chef de la Cour. "What are you doing here? I know you don't need the services of my employees."

Jean laughed. "You never know, Angélique. Raymond could have decided he's done with me."

Angélique rolled eyes. "You don't expect me to believe that. I can smell the blood and sex on you, mon cher. You're as besotted with him as ever."

Jean nodded. "That's why I'm here, actually. I seem to fall more in love with him every day, to the point that I have trouble letting him out of my sight. If we were simply Raymond and Jean, that might not be a problem, but we're also president of l'ANS and chef de la Cour."

Angélique nodded. "Come into my parlor," she said with a wink, leading Jean toward the room she used as an office. Only the escritoire against one wall gave any indication of the functional purpose of the room. Beyond that, the room could have been the boudoir of any high-class Middle Eastern courtesan, a reminder of her origins. Jean had often wondered how Angélique's partner had adjusted to her past. "What brought this on? You've been chef de la Cour for almost four hundred years. I realize Raymond's position is newer, but he doesn't strike me as someone whose head would be turned by the spotlight."

"It isn't that," Jean said. "He is one of the most down-to-earth people I know. He keeps insisting we need to be discreet about the depth of our personal relationship because of the nature of our public personas. I know he's right, but it goes against everything I am. I want to declare him to the Cour as my Consort. I want to give him that security and have it for myself, but I can't. No one would care who my Consort was if it were anyone else, but I don't have a different partner. I have Raymond."

"Do you really want a different partner?" Angélique asked.

"No! Mon Dieu, non!" Jean exclaimed. "I can't imagine being with anyone else this way, not when I can have him. If, God forbid, he had not survived the war, perhaps I would have considered finding someone else, but he is as much a part of me as my hand."

"Or your cock?" Angélique teased.

Jean flushed, something he swore he had overcome centuries ago. He could hardly deny it, though. "Or that. The point is that I don't want anyone else. I have to learn to live with the partner I have, with all that entails. And at the moment, letting him out of my sight is nearly impossible, which makes doing our jobs difficult."

"So what do you need from me, besides someone to listen to you vent?"

"I need to know if I'm the only one feeling this way. We haven't made the announcement yet, but we're going forward with a research institute to try to understand the partnership bonds. If I'm the only one feeling this way, then I'll just have to learn to live with it—but if I'm not, we need to address that as we begin our research and as we prepare other wizards and vampires to take partners," Jean explained.

Angélique smiled. "You aren't the only one, and you're doing far better than many. You wouldn't believe the number of vampires who have come to visit me, hoping the taste of someone else's blood would help them put things back in perspective. It has yet to work."

"Who?" Jean asked, worried now about the stability of the Cour.

Angélique shook her head. "I don't share information about my customers. You know that. It's one of the reasons you always felt safe coming here before you met Raymond. I won't jeopardize my business without a legal order requiring I share those records. I will tell you that most of them left with the intention of making things work with their partners since they couldn't rid themselves of the need for them. And I don't have to tell you who doesn't feel that way."

"Leighton."

"You'll want to do something about him, Jean. I don't know what the solution is, but he's a loose cannon, and that isn't good for the Cour, with or without l'ANS," Angélique warned.

Jean nodded. "I just wish I had an idea. Maybe our research will help us find a solution. I know he made his own bed with the way he treated Adèle, but I can imagine how I would feel if Raymond suddenly pushed me out of his life. It doesn't excuse Jude's behavior, then or now, but I feel sorry for him."

"Well, stop," Angélique ordered. "I worked with him and his partner, and *I* wanted to slap him more than once. Her restraint in not killing him was phenomenal."

"No, they just fucked each other over by fucking each other silly," Jean said with a sigh. "I'll talk to Raymond. He wants Adèle to help with security for l'Institut. Maybe something can be done as we move forward, some spell or potion or something to either help Leighton control himself or to help her find a way to tolerate him."

Chapter 3

THE TRIP to le Morvan, the heavily wooded region southeast of Paris between the capital and Dijon, would have taken three hours by car—if either of them had owned one—and nearly that long by train, given the remoteness of the town nearest the abandoned monastery. Raymond had a simpler solution, transporting himself there and having Mathieu send Jean after him. With the disbanding of the Milice de Sorcellerie, the magical arm of the French military, after the war, most wizards had stopped carrying their repères, since they no longer needed a link to the locator map that had allowed Marcel to keep track of his operatives while they were on patrol. Raymond had insisted they move the map to l'ANS headquarters in case of any future need, and he still carried his repère religiously, making it a matter of a quick spell for Mathieu to send Jean to join him. He thought again, as he had done countless times since the partnerships formed, how much easier it would be if a wizard's magic worked on his partner—but while he had no explanation for the limitation, neither could he deny its reality. The repère and the locator map assured a solution as long as another wizard was around, for himself or for any other paired wizard who needed it.

"Monsieur Payet," the real estate agent said, coming up and shaking Raymond's hand. "It's an honor to finally meet you face to face. I thought you said monsieur Bellaiche would be—" She broke off when Jean appeared at Raymond's side. "Oh."

Raymond chuckled. "Magic is a wonderful thing, madame Prost. Jean, this is madame Prost, our real estate agent."

"Madame." Jean offered his hand. The woman visibly steeled herself as she took it, giving Raymond another reason to chuckle, but Jean behaved himself, and the woman relaxed.

"You said you're interested in the monastery outside of Dommartin. You do realize it's been sitting empty for ten years."

"We're aware of the state it's probably in," Raymond assured her. "We're more interested in the amount of space it would afford us than the condition it's currently in. We have the means to see to the necessary repairs."

"If you're sure," madame Prost replied. "I have my car. It's about a thirty-minute drive unless you'd rather...."

Raymond smiled. "Taking your car is fine, madame. Magic is a wonderful thing, but even it has its limits. You can tell us about the area as we go. I know le Morvan only by reputation. I've never had the occasion to visit."

"The regional park was founded in 1970," madame Prost explained, "to protect the unique biodiversity of the region. It's a nature preserve that also celebrates the rich cultural heritage of the area. From Roman times, it's been a center of thermal baths. Autun was built around that time and is a wonderful example of Roman city planning. Of course, Dommartin is much smaller and much more recent, but it goes to show the depth of history in the region."

"Are you aware at all of the magical history of the region?" Jean asked. As they drove through the thick forest, he thought he could sense magical resonances, a sensitivity he had developed somewhat since the beginning of his partnership with Raymond. He did not expect to find another locus the way they had at Notre-Dame—if only because there should only be four, each aligned with one of the elemental powers—and with the identification of the cathedral as a locus, four had been pinpointed already.

"No, that's not an area I can advise you on," the real estate agent apologized. "I wouldn't even know who to ask."

"I would," Raymond said. "Not by name, but if we decide we like the monastery, Jean, Adèle can probably get us in touch with some of the local wizards and perhaps even some of the other races as well. Does Autun have a Cour? Your counterpart there might be of some help as well."

The look on Jean's face suggested he doubted that statement's accuracy, but he held his tongue in front of the realtor. She did not need to realize there was dissension among the Cours. Raymond caught the look, however, and filed the question away for later. If establishing l'Institut in Dommartin would create problems for Jean, he needed to know that before they committed to buying the monastery. Not that he was planning on signing papers today. They had far too many issues to address before they made that kind of decision.

"We'd do better to ask my colleague in Dijon or in Auxerre," Jean said. "It has been a number of years since I've had any contact with the chef de la Cour autunoise." He rather wanted to keep it that way, though he knew it would not be possible if the monastery in Dommartin worked out as a site for l'Institut.

"Dijon is a two-hour drive, and Auxerre is one and a half hours away," madame Prost supplied helpfully. "Autun is only about forty-five minutes."

"How far away is Château-Chinon?" Raymond asked, far more concerned about the proximity of friendly wizards than friendly vampires at this point. Having Adèle within arm's reach would simplify their lives immensely.

"Oh, not far at all," madame Prost replied. "Perhaps ten minutes. Probably not even that, honestly, if you want the town itself. Château-Chinon-Campagne is a little farther, another two or three kilometers perhaps."

Raymond and Jean shared a glance and a smile. Perfect. "We have a former colleague from the Milice de Sorcellerie who works in Château-Chinon-Ville," Raymond explained. "Having her close will make settling in easier, should we decide to purchase the monastery."

"You didn't say why you were interested in it," madame Prost probed lightly.

"No, we didn't," Jean agreed, deliberately not elaborating.

Madame Prost seemed a little shocked by the abruptness of the answer, but she let the matter drop as she pulled off the main road onto the narrow track that led north out of Dommartin toward l'étang de l'Île. "The monastery is just over this hill."

The monastery, when it came into sight, was not large as such installations went, but in addition to the chapel, it had several buildings, all in the typical yellow limestone of the region. The buildings were laid out in a large rectangle, leaving a central open area originally for outdoor activity or perhaps as a pen for livestock. Either way, with a little attention to landscaping, it would provide a lovely terrace and garden for those who enjoyed such pleasures.

Madame Prost produced the key to the largest of the buildings, ushering them inside the shadowed interior. Jean breathed a soft sigh of relief. He had fed from Raymond the day before, so the sun posed no threat to him, but a thousand years of survival instincts telling him to shun sunlight were hard to cast off in only a year with his partner.

"The monastery is not actually in the parc naturel," madame Prost was saying when Jean relaxed enough to mentally rejoin the conversation, "so you shouldn't have any problem with permits for any changes you want to make. It wasn't interesting enough historically or architecturally to end up on any of the landmark registers either."

"All to our good fortune," Raymond said, looking around and mentally assigning functions to the different spaces. The réfectoire would serve as a dining hall, of course. The monks' cells could be turned into private rooms—small ones, but hopefully the people who were there as students would only stay for a week or two, and they could take out a few walls to make larger rooms for the researchers and faculty who would be staying for longer stretches of time. "Is it heated?"

"The previous owners had plans to open it as an auberge, but they ran out of money before they could finish the renovations," madame Prost said. "They installed radiators in some of the areas, but not all."

Raymond nodded, internally debating the logistics of completing the heating system versus asking the wizards to maintain the temperature in whatever spaces they were using. That would work for their rooms and for the public areas but not for the rooms the vampires slept in. He would have to think more on that. "What about electricity?"

"They did that first," the real estate agent replied. "The main complex has electricity and running water. I believe they also installed electricity in the grange, but with no plumbing fixtures, it doesn't have water."

Raymond nodded and moved deeper into the abbey, opening doors and letting his imagination run wild. The scriptorium could be one classroom, the salle capitulaire another. As he kept walking, he found the infirmary, the chauffoir, the apothecary, even the old laundry room, all of which could be converted into meeting space, office space, laboratories. Eyes alight, he turned to face Jean, hoping to see the same enthusiasm on his partner's face. Jean's expression was composed as always, but Raymond saw a smile playing around the corners of his mouth. "Could we see the other buildings?"

"Of course," madame Prost said, leading them back out into the weak winter sunshine.

A quick tour of the grange, obviously used for keeping animals and tools, revealed holes in the roof and in one wall, but the rest of the structure seemed sound. Raymond wished Thierry were there, but he could always arrange another visit before they signed the contract. The purchase would be "as is," since the previous owners had defaulted on their loan and the property was currently owned by a bank, but at least they would know what they were getting into before they made their own purchase. The other two buildings, the hostellerie that had been used to welcome guests when the abbey was active, and the abbot's lodging, were in somewhat better shape, but even they would need work after ten years of standing empty.

The air was fresh, though, as Raymond moved to the center of the cloister and breathed deeply. "Will you excuse us for a moment, madame Prost?" he asked, not wanting to share the privacy of this ritual with an outsider.

The real estate agent looked startled, but she stepped out of their line of sight without protest.

"What do you think?" Raymond asked Jean softly.

"It's perfect, and you know it," Jean said in an equally hushed tone. "It needs work, but the setting, the buildings, are ideal. We won't find anything better."

"That's what I thought," Raymond agreed. "Let me check the magical resonances. We'll need to have Thierry, Alain, and Adèle come visit as well. I'm adept enough to check at a surface level to make sure nothing is amiss, but I would prefer to have them check more thoroughly before we commit. Most places have a natural affinity with one element more than the others, but occasionally we'll find a location with no affinity for one element at all, and for this kind of endeavor, we need all four elements in some degree."

"A phone call would be enough to get Thierry and Alain here now," Jean commented. "If Adèle is on duty, that might be a little more complicated for her."

"Let me see what I can feel first," Raymond said, closing his eyes and stretching his magical senses to the natural world around him. Air stirred his hair lightly in response to his call, the eddies warming at his command. He breathed deeply, letting the energy of the atmosphere fill him. With a nod, he sank to his knees, threading his fingers through the tall, winter-brown grass until he reached the earth beneath their feet. Sluggish with the cold, it responded slowly to his less-than-practiced touch, but eventually Raymond could feel a tremor of magical current. He would definitely have Thierry verify his assessment, though, because their undertaking would become more complicated if the stagnation he felt was from more than just the season. Fire leapt to his fingertips instantly. The small lake that he could barely see through the stand of leafless trees drew his attention finally.

"Walk with me?" he asked Jean, turning his head to meet his partner's eyes.

Anywhere you want to go, Jean replied silently, a nod of his head all the answer Raymond needed. They made their way down to the shore of the pond. As Raymond knelt and dipped his fingers in the icy water, Jean looked up and down the water's edge. The pond had a stream at each end, although he could not tell if it was natural or man-made. More concerning, from a security standpoint, was the collection of houses he could see across the expanse of water. They would have to discuss that with Adèle, if she agreed to undertake the security precautions for l'Institut. With no barrier to keep people out, only common courtesy would stop their neighbors from coming to investigate what they were doing. In his experience, the novelty of new neighbors would overrule common courtesy for the first few months at least.

Like the soil, the water in the pond was slow to respond to the touch of Raymond's magic. Here, with the element of his own affinity, he could diagnose the cause in a way he had not been able to with the earth. In the heart of a sleepy backwater, an area with deep history but little activity, the elements knew as little about magic as about modernity. In Paris, the Seine responded to Raymond's magic like a welcoming lover, but here the elements were more hesitant. Patiently, wooing the strength of the pond like he would woo a reluctant lover, Raymond stretched his magic over the surface of the basin, exploring its depths as he offered himself for inspection as well. Slowly the lake awoke, sharing with him its secrets and its inherent power. It was no locus, but it would provide a well of energy for him to plumb when his own resources grew thin. As he started to draw back, he felt Jean's hand on his shoulder. That brought a smile to his face, a subtle reminder that his resources would never be stretched as thin as they were before the alliance that united him with his partner. Jean's fangs would see to that.

Lifting his fingers from the water and blowing on them to warm them, Raymond turned to Jean. "I still want Thierry at least to come test the earth, but I managed to get a minimal response even from that, and I have the least affinity there. Unless he finds something I missed, I see nothing to hold us back."

"I don't like the open lakefront," Jean confided. "It seems like an unprotected front."

"Were you not the one, a few weeks ago, telling me the war was over?" Raymond teased.

Jean shrugged. "And you pointed out, quite rightly, that while the war was over, we remain political targets because of everything l'ANS stands for and because some people will never see vampires as anything other than evil."

"Don't say never," Raymond insisted. "It may take time for us to make the equality legislation a reality for everyone, but we'll keep working until it is. As for the lakefront, Adèle should be able to secure that for us. It will take a group of wizards working in concert to secure the perimeter of the property, but it can be done. You remember the wards Marcel had in place on Milice headquarters."

Jean nodded. "I didn't know if that kind of magic could be applied on open spaces."

Raymond smiled. "We'll have to provide anchor points, but yes, it can be applied across an open space as long as it has something concrete to act as a limit."

"Do you want to call Thierry now or come back later?"

Raymond considered the question. "Let's do it now. Do you mind telling the realtor we'll be a few more minutes? Now that we've decided to do this, I want it underway as swiftly as possible." He pulled out his cell phone and dialed Thierry's office number as Jean walked away to talk to madame Prost.

"Noyer."

"Bonjour, Sebastien. It's Raymond. Is Thierry around?"

"Hold on a moment. Let me get him."

Raymond waited for a moment until Thierry answered. "Bonjour, Raymond. What can I do for you?"

Raymond smiled at the question, thinking how far they had come in the past year. Before the alliance Thierry had not trusted Raymond at all, and now he greeted him like an old friend. "I need your magical expertise, if you can spare me fifteen minutes of your time," he said. "Jean and I are at a potential site for l'Institut, and I need you to check on the elemental power. It felt a little off to me, but I had the same reaction at first from the water, only to find it was disuse rather than absence. I don't have the skill to check the earth the same way."

"Do you have your repère?" Thierry asked.

"Yes."

"I'll be there in a few minutes."

"Wear your coat," Raymond warned. "It's considerably colder here than in the capital. The air smells like snow, although the sky is clear."

"Do you need Alain to come too?"

"Only if he wants to," Raymond replied. "The wind came immediately to my call."

"He's right here. I'll ask." Raymond could hear Thierry's voice followed by Alain's muffled reply. "He says he'd like to see it. We'll be there in a moment."

Before Raymond could end the call and pocket his phone, four figures appeared a short distance away. He chuckled, thinking he should have known Orlando and Sebastien would not be left out of the adventure.

"It's beautiful!" Orlando said before the others could speak. "So peaceful!"

"It was a monastery," Jean replied with a chuckle, returning from speaking with the realtor in time to hear Orlando's comment. He answered Raymond's silent question with a quick nod. "They built with the idea of natural beauty and silence drawing the monks' thoughts and lives to God."

"I can see why they chose this spot."

"Do you want me to check up closer to the buildings or is here good enough?" Thierry asked Raymond.

"Does it matter?" Raymond replied. "If you get one response here, is there a chance it will be significantly different a few hundred meters away?" Water did not work that way, any point in a given body of water as powerful as any other, but earth was trickier, the combination of minerals, the depth of the bedrock, even the kind of stone all combining to make a difference not always apparent to the naked eye. The vintners of the region were quick to point out how little it took to make a difference in their wines. Perhaps the same was true for the earth's magical properties.

"Not usually," Thierry replied. "And even if it is, the shore is hardly too far to walk if someone needs that stronger boost." He knelt where he was, spreading his palms flat against the stones that formed the beach, closing his eyes as he let his power stretch. He felt the initial lethargy Raymond had described, but as he delved deeper, he sensed a solidity that would support any magical endeavor. Opening his eyes, he stood, dusting his hands together. "There's nothing exceptional about the place, but it's solid. The power of the earth probably won't add strength to our endeavors, but it will support anything we do here."

"The same is true of the air," Alain added. "Perhaps even a little more so. In the country like this, with none of the pollution from cars and factories, its purity could be a source of energy."

Raymond smiled. He had suspected as much from his own explorations, but just as Thierry was aligned with the earth, Alain's affinity for air gave him even greater insight. "Then unless anyone has a concern I haven't addressed, I think the time has come to negotiate."

Jean rubbed his hands together. "And that is where I come in."

Chapter 4

RAYMOND WAS still shaking his head hours later when he and Jean returned home after the visit to the abbey and the subsequent negotiations. "I can't believe you convinced the bank's representative to come that far down on the price."

Jean chuckled. "They aren't earning any money on a piece of property sitting empty and falling into disrepair, a fact the bank officer was well aware of. Since we agreed to take the loan through his bank, he had a choice between making a sale and earning interest on a sizeable sum or letting the offer pass and going back to earning nothing on a piece of property that decreases in value with each passing month."

"Are you sure taking the loan was a good idea?" Raymond asked. "We can afford the price you negotiated without it."

Jean shook his head. "And here I thought I'd taught you something this year. There are no penalties for paying off the loan early. I'm sure you heard me verify that before we signed."

Raymond nodded.

"Then it's really quite simple. When we get the mortgage book, we send the full amount of the loan in the first month. Yes, we'll have to pay one month's interest, but that's still substantially less than the original asking price, and there's nothing the bank can do about it. We'll have the property. They'll have the principal back, and we'll be free and clear of the loan."

"You are something else," Raymond marveled. "I think I'm glad you decided to side with us."

Jean laughed. "As if there was another side to consider. Orlando didn't know when he met Alain in the cemetery that I'd already decided to accept the alliance almost regardless of the terms because I could see the way the wind was blowing with Serrier, so he negotiated a fair bargain. He still has no real sense of le jeu des Cours despite being my protégé for over a century, and now that he has Alain, he's outside of that. His Aveu de Sang puts him in a class by himself as far as vampire society is concerned."

"Is Sebastien in that same class?" Raymond asked, curious about the bond that united Alain and Orlando so that Orlando could only feed from his partner without being physically ill. Sebastien had made the same vow to a man long since dead.

"Yes and no," Jean replied, not at all comfortable with the subject. The past year had changed many things, but even knowing the truth of those long-ago events did not lessen Jean's feelings of betrayal. "It should have then, but Sebastien's Aveu de Sang came about under rather odd circumstances. He made his Aveu de Sang with a man most of the other vampires considered already pledged to someone else. Not magically, and not truly even verbally, but everyone except the man himself considered it understood. When Sebastien arrived and within a matter of weeks had seemingly stolen the man from another vampire, a high-ranking vampire, the Cour shunned him despite the Aveu de Sang. He didn't truly rejoin the Cour until the day the alliance formed in the Gare de Lyon. I don't know how much you remember of that morning or whether you would have noticed the details, not knowing the whole story, but Sebastien wasn't actually invited. I was very careful to invite only my 'friends' to the gathering, and Sebastien definitely didn't number among them. Monsieur Lombard told him about it and insisted he make an appearance. In hindsight I'm glad he did. His help with Orlando as the Aveu de Sang grew and strengthened was invaluable, not to mention the rest of his help in the war effort."

Raymond remembered the incident not because of Jean's reaction to it—he had still been fighting their partnership then, convinced the alliance would fail and the vampires would be the death of them all—but because Sebastien's arrival had coincided with Thierry's explosion of temper, and the resulting collision of magic and vampire had revealed a much simpler and faster way of finding paired vampires and wizards than the trial-and-error tasting they had done before. Thierry's magic should have at least knocked Sebastien to the floor, but Sebastien had shaken it off like it was nothing. That was their first inkling that a wizard's magic would not work on his partner.

Far more telling than the memory and Jean's neutral description of it was the expression on Jean's face. "So if Sebastien didn't steal your lover from you, what actually happened?"

"I never said he was my lover," Jean said, eyes widening as he looked at his partner in surprise.

Raymond smiled and pulled Jean into a tender embrace. "I may not have your skills at le jeu des Cours, but je ne suis pas né de la dernière pluie. The fact that you chose not to mention a single name except Sebastien's in your recounting gave you away. And don't tell me you've forgotten the names of the people involved. I've lived with you for a year now. I know how sharp your memory is."

Caught, Jean gave in. "According to Sebastien he met Thibaut soon after he arrived in Paris. Thibaut offered his neck and his body and pushed for an Aveu de Sang within days. Sebastien had no reason to refuse, not realizing until much later that Thibaut had been my lover for over a year and had not broken things off with me before making the Aveu de Sang with him. I thought he had stolen Thibaut when in fact Thibaut betrayed me."

And you have not let anyone close since, Raymond thought, knowing not to speak the words of pity aloud. Jean would never accept them. He considered urging his partner to feed, but Jean would read his emotions in his blood as clearly as if he had spoken aloud. Deciding another course of action was in order, he nuzzled along the line of Jean's jaw, pleased beyond words when his lover's head fell back. Whether he topped or bottomed, Jean usually took control of their lovemaking, a situation Raymond found perfectly acceptable most of the time. Tonight, however, Jean needed to be loved instead.

Raymond nipped softly at the smooth skin of Jean's neck, knowing the hint of teeth would titillate his lover as little else. Perhaps it was because feeding was such a part of sex for the vampires, and even more for him and Jean because of their partnership bond. It might not be an Aveu de Sang, but Raymond did not think his life could be any more fully entwined with that of the man in his arms. Backing Jean toward the bedroom, he continued his amorous assault, not sure how long Jean would continue to let him lead.

They waltzed through the door into the inner sanctum of the apartment, the one room Jean would allow no one but the two of them to enter. Even the woman who came once a week to clean did not venture over the sill of this door. The windows and volets were shut against the cold night, enclosing them in a sumptuous cocoon. The plush rug was thick beneath their feet as they stepped from the bare tiles of the rest of the house into their haven. Raymond toed off his shoes and socks, his feet sinking into the deep pile of the Persian rug. Against him, he could feel Jean doing the same.

The dark walls, covered in silk wallpaper, absorbed the little bit of light that filtered in from the other room, leaving both men cast in deep shadows. Raymond slowly undressed Jean, lingering over each bit of pale flesh as it was revealed, stroking, licking, even biting, determined to erase all thoughts of the past from his lover's mind. When Jean was finally naked, Raymond nudged him onto the bed, the black brocade curtains coming loose with a quick tug of the ties to enclose the bed in complete darkness. Raymond did not need light to make love to the vampire beneath him, though the darkness required him to use his other senses instead. He could have summoned light with a whispered spell, but he did not want anything to take his focus away from the task at hand.

Without his eyes to guide him, Raymond felt his other senses sharpen. The silk of the sheets, always soft against his skin, was suddenly another caress. Every falter in Jean's breathing sent a new bolt of desire down Raymond's spine. The scent of arousal curled around his nose, urging him to add to it. He stroked Jean's erection, feeling the dampness at its tip. Wanting to taste, he shifted unerringly until he could close his lips around the mushroomed head, his tongue pushing back the foreskin, seeking the familiar, salty flavor that exploded in his mouth. Jean's hips bucked up, pushing the thick shaft deeper into Raymond's mouth. He compensated by adjusting the angle so the head slid down his throat. At the same time, he slid one hand beneath Jean's body, cupping his hand around his lover's slim ass.

"Please," Jean whispered above him. "Touch me."

He almost asked Jean what he thought Raymond was doing, but that would have meant lifting his head and losing the delicious taste of his lover. Besides, he knew what Jean meant even if his request had been vague. Releasing his grip for a moment, he slid his hand up Jean's body, palm up. Seconds later, Jean placed their lube in his upturned hand. With a smile, Raymond squirted some on his fingers and slid them home. The moan that escaped Jean's throat brought another grin as Raymond lavished dual attentions on his vampire. Finding Jean's prostate, he settled in for a long, thorough massage. His own arousal nagged at him, but he found it easy to ignore in favor of giving Jean what he needed.

Beneath him, Jean writhed uncontrollably, gasping and panting with each pass of Raymond's fingers over his sensitive node. "Raymond, s'il te plaît."

Lifting his head finally, Raymond peered through the darkness as if he could see his lover and make out the expression on the vampire's face. "What do you need, Jean? Tell me."

Jean bit back the words that wanted to come. He had decided a year ago not to pressure Raymond with declarations of any kind, acting on his emotions for his reluctant partner without ever putting them into words. "Inside me," he said instead.

Raymond wiggled his fingers, wringing another deep groan from Jean.

"Don't be dense. I want your cock inside me. Now."

Raymond obliged, moving between Jean's willingly parted legs so he could lower himself onto his lover's body, taking a moment to kiss the softness of Jean's lips, his tongue ghosting across the tips of Jean's fangs, before moving back to position himself at Jean's entrance. He slicked himself quickly, rocking his way slowly inside, taking care to lift Jean's hips onto his thighs so the tip of his cock would nudge his lover's prostate with every pass. If Jean's desperate thrashing was any indication, Raymond had succeeded. Once he had them positioned the way he wanted, the wizard leaned forward again, rejoining their lips as well. They never spoke of love, but Raymond fully intended to make love to Jean, not merely fuck him through the mattress. He knew his own heart even if he had never worked up the courage to speak it aloud. Surely Jean knew, as often as he fed from Raymond.

Long moments passed as they strove together for release, the darkness enshrouding them, giving them these private moments to be Raymond and Jean rather than the president of l'ANS and the chef de la Cour parisienne. They took full advantage of it, wrapping around each other like they never intended to let go. When they finally reached the limits of their control, they shattered together—Jean's fangs piercing Raymond's tongue, the hot rush of blood surprising both of them and sending Jean over the edge as he tasted the unmistakable emotions. He almost spoke his heart then. But even though Raymond shared Jean's feelings, Jean knew the wizard wasn't ready to talk about them or even admit to having them. Jean could afford to be patient. Declaration or not, he and Raymond were clearly building a life together. That was all that mattered.

In the aftermath, Raymond cradled Jean against his shoulder. "That's going to hurt when I have my coffee in the morning," he joked.

In reply, Jean pulled Raymond's head to his, their lips meeting. He sucked Raymond's tongue into his mouth, laving the wounds carefully and thoroughly enough to have Raymond moaning against him again. "That will help. I'll be glad to do it again in the morning."

Raymond chuckled. "I'll take you up on that. Now, tell me what the story is with the chef de la Cour in Autun."

Jean rolled his eyes, though he knew Raymond could not see him. "He's another reactionary. I haven't talked to him in probably twenty years, but our last meeting did not go well. Each Cour is independent, but we do have some contact with each other, and as a rule, we try to maintain amicable ties at least. You never know when one of us might need something only another chef de la Cour can provide. Think about Luc Cabalet and his contribution to the war."

Raymond remembered the chef de la Cour amiénoise well. He had arrived, demanding an explanation from Jean, only to find himself partnered with one of the few wizards Raymond would not have wanted to face in a fight. While the posturing between the two vampires had been obvious even to an outsider, they had set their differences aside to fight a common enemy. "But the chef de la Cour in Autun doesn't maintain those ties?"

"Not at all. Every few years the chefs de la Cour will gather to discuss matters that affect us all. He stormed out twenty years ago and has not returned. As far as I know, he tolerates the chefs de la Cour from Dijon and Auxerre because they're his nearest neighbors, but only when he has no other choice. I don't think he'll challenge our undertakings in Dommartin, but we shouldn't expect any help from him."

"What did you disagree about?" Raymond asked.

"Does it really matter?"

"I don't know," Raymond replied, "but the fact that you won't tell me makes me think it was more important than you want to let on. I'm not asking as the president of l'ANS. I'm asking as your lover. I promised to support you in any way I could before I knew what Marcel had in store for me. That promise still holds, except it's even more vital now that I have a public role as well. I don't want to do anything through ignorance that would make life more difficult for you."

Jean nodded. "And I appreciate that, but it's a moot point now even if he agrees to have anything to do with us."

"Jean."

"Raymond."

Jean's tone mimicked Raymond's exasperation so perfectly that the wizard laughed. "All right, I won't pressure you to tell me, but promise me you will tell me if it becomes relevant again. I meant what I said about not wanting to cause you to lose face."

"I know, and I appreciate it," Jean said. "Now, you should get some sleep. Tomorrow will be a busy day. We have to start figuring out what repairs need to be done to the abbey and how soon we can make it habitable. We don't have to have everything finished before we start, but we'll need the basics covered."

Raymond smiled and kissed Jean lightly. "I think you're more excited about this than I am."

Jean chuckled. "It's been a long time since I've had a project of this scope to oversee. And don't tell me you aren't interested in the results of the research we'll be able to do. I know you're as fascinated by how and why the partnership bonds work as I am."

Raymond could hardly deny it when that had been one of the major reasons for establishing l'Institut in the first place. "There will be more than enough work for both of us, I'm sure."

Chapter 5

"YOU'RE LATE."

Raymond met Jean's eyes with a smothered grin. The wizard they had arranged to meet was as stunningly beautiful and as caustically impatient as ever. "We had an emergency come up at the last minute, and even though we delegated it to someone else, we still had to decide who to call on."

Jean nudged Raymond's side as he walked past him, approaching Adèle with a smile and a courtly bow over her hand. Her current garb—heavy hiking boots, jeans, a fisherman's sweater, and a heavy coat—might bear no resemblance to the chic attire she had worn when they had first met in Paris and he had imagined she might be the partner for him. If anything, though, she was even more attractive this way for being more genuine than she had been then. "Forgive our tardiness?"

Adèle rolled her eyes, having been on the receiving end of Jean's suave charm more than once. She was woman enough to appreciate it even as she reminded herself that Jean and Raymond were far more than colleagues. The fading bite marks she could see above Raymond's collar proclaimed them to be paired, and while Adèle knew her experience with her own partner was atypical, she also knew how hard the bond between a pair drove them toward each other. She would bet a year's salary they were lovers. She felt a pang for what might have been if her blood had been compatible with some other vampire instead of her antiquated, self-important bastard of a partner. "Marcel had no idea what he was doing, putting you two in charge. You're a potent team."

Jean chuckled. "That's exactly why he did it, my dear. Because nobody can resist us both at once."

And that was God's own truth as far as Adèle could see. She had sworn to stay as far away from l'ANS and politics as possible after she returned to le Morvan at the end of the war, her temporary assignment with the Gendarmerie Nationale to gather up any remaining agents notwithstanding, and she had kept that promise for eleven months. It had only taken one phone call from Raymond to make her break it. Granted, the request required her to drive all of fifteen minutes from her sleepy village of Château-Chinon, but that was not the point. "What do you need me to do? You weren't very clear on the phone."

"You're standing outside the gate to the newly founded Institut Marcel Chavinier," Raymond said proudly, his hand sweeping wide to encompass the monastery and the surrounding grounds. "Inside these walls we will study magic, especially the magic that binds our races together, and we will use what we learn to help prepare vampires and wizards for the creation of a partnership bond instead of having people stumbling into them with no idea of the repercussions of such a relationship." He laughed ruefully, his voice taking on a less bombastic tone as he continued. "Obviously it needs some work first, but our biggest concern, both now and in the future, will be the security of the complex. We haven't received any threats yet, but you know how the right wing loves to complain about everything we do."

Adèle nodded, hiding her flinch at Raymond's choice of words. She knew all about the repercussions of the partnership bonds. She barely managed to keep from rubbing the scar on her left breast, the two puncture wounds from her partner's fangs a reminder of all the reasons to resist the pull of their bond. "Unless you were planning on turning it into something like a hotel, you'd want security of some sort. Take me around. Let me see what you have in mind so I can figure out the best options."

"Inside or outside first?" Raymond asked. He knew where he would start if he were doing the wards, but Adèle knew more about the kinds of wards they would need than any other wizard in France. He would trust her judgment.

"Outside," Adèle replied. "I'll start here at the door and work my way around the perimeter, but I want to walk it first and see where my grounding points will be. I imagine you'll want the wards to include at least some of the grounds."

"Yes, especially down to the lake," Raymond said. "Thierry and Alain checked their elements and fire sprang right to my fingertips when I called it, but I could only draw on the water when I went down to the shore."

"Do you want the barriers to go out into the lake at all?"

Raymond frowned. "We don't own the lake, just the lakeside property. If people want to swim later, they'll do so at their own risk. I don't want people wandering in out of curiosity that way, that's all."

"Which answers my next question," Adèle said with a smile. "You want barriers to keep people from getting in without permission rather than wards to hold off spells."

"Do you really think we need that kind of ward?" Jean asked. "We aren't anticipating any resistance within l'ANS or from nonaffiliated wizards, unless you know something we don't."

Adèle shook her head. "No. I just wanted to make sure you didn't know something *I* don't. I'm not exactly high on the list of people with access to classified information these days."

"You could probably name the job you wanted and get it," Raymond reminded her. "Sarraute was impressed with the job you did helping his officers round up the remaining dissidents after the war."

"But that would mean moving to Paris, and my home is here," Adèle said. "I lived there during the war, but this is where I belong. There's just something about the freshness of the air. Can't you smell the difference? And even in the summer, when it's miserably hot in the capital, there's a cool breeze here."

Jean could not help but wonder how much of Adèle's insistence on staying in le Morvan came from Leighton's presence in Paris, but he did not bring it up. She was entitled to her privacy, and he had no idea what he would gain by forcing her to admit it anyway.

"Well, obviously this is the entrance," Raymond said, letting the conversation slide away from Adèle's personal life and back to business. She had always been a private one, and he had no desire to make her uncomfortable. "This is the one place where people need to be able to approach the building directly, because we may have unexpected visitors. Other than that, you can put the wards at whatever distance you think is best."

Adèle nodded again, running her hand over the frame of the door, calculating how best to provide the security Raymond wanted. "Okay, the door will be pretty straightforward, and the walls provide an easy delineation of 'inside' and 'outside' as far as my magic is concerned. Do you want them to extend beyond the edge of the walls on this side at all?"

Raymond had not gotten that far in his thoughts, so they walked along the outer wall of the complex to the corner. "Not all of this is exterior wall," Adèle commented as they walked. "Some of this is actually part of buildings."

"That was fairly typical," Jean said. "To save on money and labor, the monks built the individual buildings along the periphery of the abbey and then filled in between them with an outside wall to limit access to the interior."

Adèle looked up, surprised. "How did you know that?"

"Because I helped build one in Paris before I was turned," Jean revealed, fingering the rosary in his pocket given to him by Père Emmanuel, his spiritual advisor. Even before Raymond had turned it into his repère, he kept it with him most of the time. Now he kept it with him always, knowing Raymond could always use it to find him.

"You were a monk?" Adèle asked incredulously.

Raymond snorted as Jean shook his head. "No, but I was in the seminary. It was a different time, and if you weren't born into the aristocracy—and sometimes even if you were—your choices were a lot more limited than they are now. I could enter the seminary or I could starve. It wasn't a hard choice. At least as a priest, I would be assured of a roof over my head and something in my belly until the Vikings came. Then everyone starved regardless of their class. I was turned about six months before my ordination would have taken place."

"Yes, but poverty, chastity, and all that? I just don't see it," Adèle laughed. "I guess I don't have to see it."

"The Church was different then too," Jean reminded her. "Poverty, yes, because everyone was poor then, even the king because the Vikings raided every summer, but while I wouldn't have been able to marry, I knew very few priests who were actually celibate. They simply didn't talk about it, and they gave their lovers enough perks that the lovers didn't either."

Adèle just shook her head. "If you say so. So, Raymond, have you decided where you want the wards to stop?"

Raymond smiled at the abrupt change of subject, but he had grown used to Adèle's ways. "Here along the approach from the road, I think it should go at least to the tree line, maybe a little inside. We want people to come to the front gate, not go searching for a side entrance."

Adèle mentally calculated distances as they rounded the far corner of the wall and started down the side toward the lake. "You'll want to get those walls patched quickly," she warned as they walked past a place where the stones had tumbled inward, leaving an unintended entrance into the cloister.

"That's first on my list," Raymond assured her. "I think we should follow the outer walls and then continue all the way down to the lake. That way the entire area behind the abbey will be protected for any kind of outdoor activities people want to undertake."

"Pétanque?" Jean teased.

"Football," Adèle and Raymond said in unison, sending all three of them into peals of laughter.

"Mon Dieu, it feels good to laugh like this," Raymond said after they calmed down. "I think you're right about being away from Paris, Adèle. I can feel my stress disappearing just standing here. My feet are freezing, but my stress is going."

"I have an idea of what needs to be done out here," Adèle said, looking down at Raymond's thin loafers. "Go inside and think about what you want done in there. I'll find you when I'm done outside."

Raymond tucked his hands under his arms as the wind picked up a little and took her advice. The inside of the building was only marginally warmer, the heat having been turned off to save energy, but at least they were out of the breeze.

"I thought your coat was spelled to keep you warm."

"It is," Raymond said, "but I didn't spell my shoes. My coat only goes to my knees." He murmured another incantation, and the foyer to the abbey warmed up slightly. "I don't even know where to start."

"With a floor plan of the building," Jean said. "Then we can start looking at how we want to distribute space, and from there we can set our priorities. We need an office."

"*An* office?" Raymond grinned at his lover.

"An office," Jean repeated. "We may have to maintain certain appearances in the public sphere, but l'Institut isn't public. If we need to meet with someone from outside our respective communities, we can do that in Paris. We don't need to hide here."

Raymond was not sure he agreed, but it was not worth the discussion. "Okay, a headmaster's office, then. It would make sense to use the abbot's quarters for that. Surely he had some sort of an office or receiving room."

"It would depend on when the abbey was built and who his guests were," Jean replied. "There would have been an hostellerie for distinguished guests, another one for visiting monks, and a third one for the poor, although it doesn't look like all three of those survived or possibly were ever built here. I'm not sure how many distinguished guests made it this far into the wilderness. He would have had space in his lodging as well, if you don't mind our office being in a separate building."

"For now, I think I'd rather it be over here where we can oversee everything," Raymond replied after a moment's thought. "Besides, that way we can focus on getting this building usable first. Later, once we're up and running and can focus on the other buildings, we can always move the office."

"Then it's simply a question of choosing one of the copyists' chambers and making it our office," Jean said. "It won't be a large room, but it will be larger than your old office in Milice headquarters."

"That wasn't an office," Raymond said with a laugh. "That was a broom closet, and it was far, far away from everyone who wanted to pretend I didn't exist."

"I have very fond memories of that broom closet," Jean said, his voice dropping in pitch as he remembered the hours spent in the cluttered room, racing against time to find answers and sneaking a few minutes for a quick feeding or fumble in the dark. He did not miss the fear that had been so prevalent in those days, but he sometimes missed the freedom of being out of the limelight.

"Raymond?"

Adèle's voice startled them out of their reminiscing. "Yes?"

"I've done the majority of the wards, but the one across the lakefront is a larger distance than I can handle on my own," Adèle explained. "Do you have time to give me a hand?"

"Of course," Raymond said, rubbing his hands together before he put his gloves back on. "We can finish up the interior planning later. We don't want you to have to make an extra trip."

"It's only a fifteen-minute drive," Adèle reminded him. "I didn't even bother using a displacement spell. Besides, the wards will need to be adjusted as you expand the number of buildings you're using and the number of people you want to admit without question, so it's not like I won't be back again, probably fairly often at first."

Raymond and Jean followed her back outside and down to the lake. "The wards on either side end at the two oak trees. The problem is connecting them with a barrier strong enough to do the job."

"What do you need from me?" Raymond asked.

"All the power you can give me," Adèle replied.

Without waiting to be asked, Jean reached for Raymond's hand, folding up the edge of his coat sleeve and easing down the cuff of his glove to bare the wizard's wrist. Raymond glanced at him in surprise, but Jean simply smiled and lifted the smooth skin to his lips, licking it once before biting down deeply. He did not need to feed in earnest, but the connection between them would augment Raymond's energy exponentially. Of all the wards on the property, Jean wanted this one to be the strongest.

Raymond focused his magic, pushing the energy outward to Adèle, who harnessed it and made swift work of the spell. Even concentrating as he was on keeping control of the stronger surge of power, Raymond did not miss the flicker of sadness that crossed Adèle's face at the sight of Jean feeding from his wrist. He did not want to break her concentration by asking about it now, but he resolved to check on how she was doing without her partner as soon as they returned inside.

With the influx of magical energy from Raymond—Adèle forcefully repressed the wayward thought that if she had a partner she could stand to be around, she would not have needed his help in the first place—it took only a matter of minutes to finish the wards. "Thank you," she said when she released control of Raymond's magic back to him.

"Come inside for a few minutes," Raymond said as Jean released his fangs' hold and licked the small punctures to heal them. "It's cold out here and you're flushed from it."

Adèle shrugged. "I'm used to it."

"Come inside anyway. I'd like to talk to you, if Jean will excuse us for a bit."

Jean looked surprised, but he nodded. "I want to check on the abbot's lodge to see if there's suitable space for an office."

Raymond recognized the offer for what it was, since they had already decided to have their office in the main building for now, which just made him appreciate his lover all the more. "Shall we go inside?"

Adèle followed Raymond without comment, but he could see her tensing. "How are you doing, Adèle?"

"I'm well," Adèle replied automatically. "I told you that on the phone when you first called."

"Now tell me the rest of it," Raymond pressed. "Are you still feeling the tug of the partnership bond?"

"I told Marcel a year ago I want nothing to do with that salaud," Adèle spat. "I haven't seen or heard anything since then to change my mind."

"You still aren't answering my question," Raymond said quietly, afraid that in itself was his answer.

"What do you want me to say?" Adèle retorted. "That I still dream of him at night? That I've caught myself comparing every man I've slept with since then to him? That if he walked in here right now I don't know whether I'd slap him or throw myself at him?"

"I don't *want* you to say any of those things," Raymond replied, "but if that's what you're feeling, I'd rather know so I can try to help you than be kept unaware."

"I'm fine. I stay down here and I ignore the pull when it gets bad and I go on with my life. If you find a cure for my affliction, I won't say no, but until then, I'm fine practicing avoidance," Adèle said. She caught her fingers trailing over the scar, though she knew Raymond could not see it beneath the layers of clothing. She had asked a friend to heal the rest of the marks her partner had left on her body, but she had left that one as a reminder of what he had done— could do—to her. Without it, she feared she would forget and give in to the lure of the partnership bond. "No one can come inside without your permission at this point. I'll come back once you're ready to open l'Institut to set the privacy wards and whatever else you need."

Before Raymond could protest or ask another question, she had disappeared.

"Merde," Raymond muttered. It seemed avoidance was not the solution he had hoped it would be.

Chapter 6

"ALAIN, ORLANDO, Thierry, Sebastien, thank you for joining us," Raymond said as the four men came into his and Jean's apartment. "I hope you don't mind that we're meeting here rather than at l'ANS offices. This is much more comfortable."

"Indeed," Sebastien said, looking around the apartment. His tense past with Jean meant that this was his first visit. His eyes grew wider with each new antique he sighted. It seemed the entire apartment could have been taken from a museum. "Are all of these originals?"

"That would be a question for Jean," Raymond replied, "but I believe they are. It's quite a collection."

"Certes," Sebastien agreed.

"You mentioned having something to discuss," Thierry interjected.

"And we will," Raymond promised, "but we can act like civilized men. Would you care for an aperitif? Alain, something for you?"

"We'll open a bottle of champagne," Jean interrupted before Alain could reply. "We are celebrating, after all."

"Champagne is fine," Alain said. "What are we celebrating?"

"The imminent opening of l'Institut Marcel Chavinier, of course," Raymond said. "The sale of the property went through, and Adèle has already done the first layer of wards. We've even solicited bids from companies for the work that can't be done magically. I can repair a hole in a wall. I can't install a new heating system."

The other two wizards nodded, well aware that their knowledge of any given subject limited their magic's effectiveness. Jean returned a moment later with a bottle of champagne and six flutes. He popped the cork with sophisticated ease and poured a taste into one glass. Raymond tasted it and approved, so Jean poured the others, distributing them to their guests.

"To the success of l'Institut Marcel Chavinier," Raymond said, lifting his glass. The others followed suit and drank the toast.

"Dinner won't be ready for another hour," Raymond said when they had completed the toast. "I thought we could discuss business now and then enjoy a meal among friends."

The comment brought a smile to all six faces. Prior to the formation of the alliance, Jean and Orlando had already been friends, as had Thierry and Alain, but the third wizard and the third vampire had been complete outcasts. "What a difference a year makes," Thierry chuckled with a nod toward Raymond.

"What a difference a war makes," Jean agreed. "Have a seat and we'll get our business out of the way."

They moved toward the seating area in the salon, the group devolving into three couples as they chose their seats. Alain and Orlando sat on one divan, Thierry and Sebastien on the other, while Jean and Raymond chose the armchairs on either side of a huge marble fireplace that crackled appealingly.

"Until the bids come in, we can't do a lot on the physical side of opening l'Institut," Raymond explained when everyone was settled, "but we can begin to work on both the educational and research aspects. The building is essential, of course, but it does us no good without a purpose."

"The number of partnerships forming has decreased significantly since the war ended because the desperation that drove us to bond no longer applies, but out of curiosity, stupidity, or some other motivation, some people still go searching for their partners. Sometimes that doesn't end well," Jean continued. "If both partners enter the bond aware of what it entails and willing to make that commitment, then everything is fine."

"But we still only barely understand what the commitment entails," Sebastien said with a shake of his head. "We had no idea what we were doing when we formed our partnerships at the beginning of the alliance."

"And that's where the research comes in," Raymond explained. "We're hoping established pairs will be willing to help with that, both in terms of sharing their experiences and possibly in letting us conduct some experiments. Nothing that would damage the bond, but to help us determine how long certain effects last, that sort of thing. And this is where we need your help. We need to catalogue what we know, for the educational side—and what we don't know, so we can outline the research component."

"What we do know," Orlando began. "We know that between partners, the wizard's blood protects the vampire from sunlight for a period of time, depending on when the vampire last fed and how much he took."

"And we know that while the vampire feeds, the wizard's power increases significantly," Alain added.

Raymond nodded as they spoke, jotting down notes in a pad on the table next to him.

"We know a wizard's magic doesn't work on his partner," Thierry said with a wink for Sebastien.

"And that the bond forms from the first taste of the partner's blood," Sebastien continued.

"Does it, though?" Raymond disagreed. "The first taste is enough to establish the partnership and to protect the vampire from sunlight, but does the deeper bond, the one that draws the partners together, really form that quickly?"

"Yes," Alain and Orlando said immediately.

"When we first met," Orlando went on, "there was nothing between us, no alliance, no knowledge of the protection from sunlight, nothing but the taste of Alain's blood in my mouth."

"And the feel of Orlando's fangs in my wrist."

"But you remember what it was like, Jean. I couldn't stop thinking about him and talking about him," Orlando continued. "When we met the next night, the compulsion to reach for his hand again was nearly overwhelming. If he had rejected me, maybe I would have recovered from it, but from the moment he offered his wrist that second time, there was no going back. Not for me."

"Nor for me," Alain agreed. "I talked to Marcel that night, trying to figure out what was going on, if somehow Orlando had enchanted me. Marcel assured me that wasn't possible—because if it were, vampires wouldn't be in the situation they were in."

"What about you, Thierry?" Raymond asked.

"The day before we met at the Gare de Lyon to search for partners, I buried my wife—who was killed in an ambush—the night you followed Orlando, and I followed Alain to their second meeting," Thierry reminded everyone. "I'd decided to do whatever it took to bring down Serrier, even if it meant a brand on my neck to match the one on Alain's. The burst of magic that hit Sebastien got away from me because I was so frustrated at not having found one. I was so focused on finding a partner that I would have agreed to anything once I had one. Whatever that meant."

"I wasn't sure I wanted to be there either," Sebastien added, "given my shaky position within the Cour, but that first bite was all it took. I knew Thierry was grieving from the moment I tasted his blood, so I didn't press for anything more than a functional partnership, but the fascination was there."

"Perhaps my distrust of the situation skewed my reactions," Raymond mused aloud, "because I certainly did not want to be partnered with any vampire. We won't have that problem this time around. No one will be obliged to form a partnership. Since we can use magic to identify partners instead of blood, if the partners meet and decide they don't want to continue, they should be able to walk away, at least before the first exchange of blood."

"What else do we know?" Jean asked.

"We know that the bond forms based on some sort of magical compatibility and not on any existing preferences on the part of the people involved," Thierry said. "I never had any interest in men before Sebastien. Honestly, I still don't have any interest in men, just in Sebastien. It's something to consider, since all the pairings I know well have gone beyond the alliance and become personal. Intimate."

"There were a few who seemed to drift apart after Serrier's defeat," Raymond said, "but they are people who went back to other jobs after the war. Many of the wizards aren't even still in Paris, so I don't know what their status is now."

"What about Adèle?" Alain asked.

"Adèle has not seen her partner in a year, but the bond is still there," Raymond said. "She confirmed it when we saw her in Dommartin. She's resisting, but the bond is still there. Another reason to provide a time and space for partners to get acquainted before they bond. I don't imagine it took long for Adèle to realize she was mismatched."

"That's what I don't understand," Orlando said. "I know I'm not very smart, but I don't understand how something like that could happen. Why, when most of the partnerships are seamless, did two such incompatible people match?"

"Don't put yourself down," Alain and Jean said simultaneously, making them both laugh. "There's a difference between intelligence and education," Jean continued. "And while you might not have studied arcane lore the way Raymond or I have, that doesn't mean you aren't intelligent. Besides, we don't understand it anymore than you do."

"It's one of the things we need to add to the research agenda," Raymond said. "We need to understand why pairings form so we can help advise people on their options. Monsieur Lombard posited that the elemental magic wouldn't make a mistake, but that doesn't mean it takes everything into consideration. I mean, what would have happened if Thierry's wife had still been alive? Or Alain's ex-wife, for that matter?"

"Did any partnerships form where one of the partners already had a lover or spouse?" Sebastien asked. "I didn't know anyone well enough when we started to be aware if any of them had established relationships."

"Not that I was ever aware of," Raymond said.

"Me either," Jean agreed, "which is interesting in and of itself. An individual's personal preferences don't matter, but their personal commitments do?"

Raymond sighed. "More questions and still no answers."

"So let's focus on the questions," Thierry proposed. "After all, they're far more numerous than the answers."

"Why does it all work?" Orlando said immediately.

The wizards laughed. "That may be the one thing we'll never be able to answer," Raymond admitted. "We can usually learn to predict magical outcomes, but we can't always explain why they work the way they do. For example, a lot of spells can be cast in modern French, but they work best in old French, except that nobody speaks old French anymore, and minor mispronunciations keep the spell from working as well as it used to because of it. Nobody knows why, but we know it does."

"Does the age of the vampire affect the bond?" Sebastien threw out. "It affects so much else in our existence. It would seem logical that it could affect this as well."

"Certainly to hear Magali talk about the final battle between Marcel and Serrier, when monsieur Lombard bit Marcel, he stripped through Serrier's wards like a hot knife through butter," Raymond agreed. "Of course, that's pairing the most powerful wizard of our time with the oldest known vampire in France. I suspect the differences will usually be more subtle than that."

"Probably," Jean agreed, "but there's also the inherent strength of the wizard. Monsieur Lombard's age combined with Marcel's power. Either one alone would have made an impact, but not as much as the combination."

"Could that be part of what influences the creation of the bonds?" Alain wondered aloud. "Some relationship between the age of the vampire and the strength of the wizard? You and Jean are another perfect example of that."

"It's certainly something we can investigate," Raymond agreed, making a note on his pad. "What else?"

"How often can a vampire feed from his partner without weakening the wizard?" Jean asked immediately. "Alain and Orlando don't count because the Aveu de Sang protects Alain, but I shouldn't have been able to feed as often as I did during the war, and yet I did without any harm to you."

"I noticed the same thing," Sebastien said. "I don't feed as often now as I did then—nor do I need to feed as often as I did before we formed the partnership—but I don't ever get the sense that I'm weakening Thierry by taking what I need."

"Nor do I feel weakened by his feeding," Thierry confirmed.

"Got it," Raymond said.

"On a purely practical level, we know that a vampire feeding from his partner helps maintain the magical equilibrium. How widespread is that effect?" Thierry asked. "Does Sebastien feeding from me here help address an imbalance in Tahiti, or do we need partnerships scattered throughout the world for it to be an effective way to address the issue? Half the world or more still doesn't believe magical disequilibrium is even a real phenomenon."

"We don't *need* them at all now that the war is over and we can do our jobs again, but certainly the job of maintaining balance has grown easier over the past year," Raymond replied. "I've noted that as well."

"Obviously this isn't an issue for us at this point, but can the partnerships function on a blood level without having to spill over to a sexual level?" Alain asked. "We didn't know what we were getting into. I wouldn't change things between Orlando and myself, but that's asking a lot of a wizard or a vampire to take on a lover as well as a partner. It was a lot during the war, but we had the necessity of winning the war as a reason to accept things we might have otherwise questioned."

"Which begs the question of whether the personal side of the relationship affects the magical side," Raymond added. "Would a partnership predicated purely on an exchange of blood have the same power as one that has a more personal component? My guess is that while it might be possible, the more complete the relationship, the more powerful the bond, and the more powerful the effects. We saw that when we first realized that the exchange of blood could affect the magical balance. It worked when it was just feeding, but it worked even better when the couple started having sex too."

No one asked who the couple was. It didn't matter, and some things were best left private.

"What else?"

"You mentioned geography in terms of the magical equilibrium, but what about in terms of finding partners in the first place?" Thierry asked. "Most of us found our partners here in Paris, and even those who didn't found their partners nearby, like Magali and Luc in Amiens. At the time, I was too thrilled to have the help against Serrier to question it, but does it seem a little simplistic to you?"

"What are you suggesting? That we have different partners somewhere else who we won't ever meet?" Orlando scoffed. "I don't buy that."

"You probably don't," Thierry allowed, thinking about how far Orlando had come since the early days of the alliance, "except think about how unlikely it was for you to trust Alain the way you did. I'm not saying you misjudged him, because you obviously didn't. But everyone commented on it at the time. You'd gone from being almost a complete loner to having an Avoué in a matter of days. Hell, almost a matter of hours."

"It's not unheard of for a vampire to form an attachment that quickly," Sebastien said, thinking of his own Avoué, dead nearly four hundred years, "because we can sense so much about a person from the blood we drink. Yes, Orlando had more reason than most to be distrustful, but that doesn't change the fact that he could sense Alain's basic trustworthiness from the first time he bit him."

"That doesn't answer the question of proximity, though," Thierry insisted. "If we took one of the wizards or vampires whose partner didn't survive the war somewhere else, would we find a new partner for that person?"

"Again, it's a question we can research," Raymond said. "There's also the question of whether those people would want a new partner. Many of them have drifted off my radar since the end of the war."

The timer buzzed in the kitchen, interrupting their conversation. "Excuse me a moment." Raymond rose and disappeared into the other room. He reappeared a few minutes later with a large Limoges soup crock in hand. "Dinner is ready. We have bœuf bourgignon and steamed asparagus, if Jean will be so kind as to get it from the kitchen. We can continue the conversation as we eat if you have other things to add."

Jean went to get the asparagus while everyone else moved to the table. "It smells delicious," Alain commented. "Shall I pour the wine?"

"Thank you," Raymond said as he ladled the thick stew into bowls for the wizards. "Orlando, Sebastien, you are welcome to some if you wish. Jean told me it doesn't hurt you to eat even if it doesn't provide any nourishment. Don't feel obliged, though. I live with a vampire, so I'm used to him sitting with me while I eat."

Both vampires demurred, although they did each take a glass of wine.

"What I want to know," Thierry said as Jean came back in and the three wizards began to eat, "is how you and Jean plan to do everything that needs to be done by yourselves. This is a major undertaking."

"We aren't going to start everything at once," Raymond replied. "We'll start the education program first, since it won't require as much work or as much space. As space is ready, we'll get the research component underway."

"I repeat. That's too much work for two people. At least let me help oversee the repairs. I probably can't do anything about the research, but I know stone. I can help find the safest areas of the building, the ones that need the least repairs, so the repairmen can work more efficiently," Thierry proposed.

"I didn't want to ask," Raymond said. "L'Institut isn't going to be a small commitment, and this isn't the Milice anymore. You're entitled to a private life and time off and—"

"And what you're doing there will be good for all of us," Thierry interrupted. "No, none of us want out of our bonds, but how many times have I heard you say that knowledge is never evil and something everyone can benefit from? Let us help you, Raymond. Alain and me, but also everyone else. I think if you asked for volunteers, you'd be amazed at the response."

"Who among the wizards are you thinking would be good candidates for the school aspect?" Alain asked. "I can start talking to people to see what kind of interest there is."

"People who use magic as part of their professional lives," Raymond said immediately. "They're the ones who would benefit most directly from having a partner, because they're the ones who may be limited at times because of their own abilities or strength. Having a partner would help them in concrete and immediate ways."

"So wizards attached to the medical community, the military, and law enforcement, as well as the wizards within l'ANS who deal with the magical equilibrium and don't already have partners," Alain enumerated. "Anyone else?"

"Probably, but that's a good place to start. I hope once word gets out, people will come to us instead of us having to seek out candidates," Raymond said.

"We can only hope."

Chapter 7

"I DON'T think I've ever seen such an incredible collection of antiques outside of a museum," Thierry said as he, Sebastien, Alain, and Orlando left Jean and Raymond's apartment.

"I haven't seen such an incredible collection inside most museums," Alain agreed with a shake of his head.

"Jean has had more than twelve lifetimes to collect it," Orlando reminded them, slipping his hand into Alain's now that they were no longer in their employers' home. "Maybe even more, if you consider the average lifespan when he was changed. He was changed sometime before the fall of 911, because he should have died in the Viking invasions that ended with the Traité de Saint-Clair-sur-Epte when Rollon became Duke of Normandy."

"Oh là là," Thierry said, whistling under his breath. "I knew he was old, but I didn't know he was that old!"

"You'd never know to look at him," Alain agreed, dancing away from Orlando's poking fingers. "Just because I have your brand on my neck doesn't mean I'm blind."

"You two are so married," Thierry said as he rolled his eyes.

"And you're not?" Alain retorted. "Seems to me I remember listening to a discussion recently of the relative merits of an apartment in town and a house in the banlieue."

"It was a valid discussion," Thierry defended. "You were the one who kept asking me what we were still doing in Aleth's house in Versailles."

"How's the settling in going?" Orlando asked Sebastien, deliberately cutting off the incipient bickering. He had been around Alain and Thierry long enough to know better than to let them start trading insults. He had other plans for the evening—plans that did not involve his lover's best friend.

"It's a bit of a challenge going from two apartments and a house to one apartment, even if it's larger than either of the original apartments," Sebastien replied, "but we're making progress. We put Thierry's apartment on the market last week, and mine should be ready to go in less than a month. The house is the biggest problem, because we have to figure out what to do with the furniture and things we can't use."

"There's always the Secours catholique," Orlando suggested. "I know that's who Jean has given things to in the past when he's found a more unique piece to replace something mundane."

"He has mundane things?" Sebastien quipped.

Orlando laughed. "Not in the salon, no, but I know he was still looking for some pieces to complete his kitchen and bedroom. Not that I've seen the inside of his bedroom. He doesn't let anyone in there. Well, except Raymond, I guess."

All four of them laughed at that. "I hope he lets Raymond in," Alain said.

"I'm quite sure he does," Orlando said. "I've known him for over a hundred years, and I've never seen him as relaxed as he was tonight, even when it was just the two of us. Whatever there is between them, it's good for him."

"For both of them," Thierry said, "because I could say the same about Raymond. He's still trying to take on too much at once, but it isn't because he's looking for an excuse to hide anymore. It's because suddenly he feels like he can take on the world. At least that's the way it looks to me."

"I'd agree with that." Alain felt exactly the way he suspected Raymond did. "It's like he's come into his own this year, with the new responsibilities."

"So how are we going to make sure they don't burn themselves out?" Sebastien asked. "I don't know who the Cour would devolve to in Jean's absence, but I don't particularly care to find out. He's ushered in a new era for us, and I want to see where he can take us."

"We start by making sure they get back to Paris at night so they can sleep in their own bed," Alain said. "We can take turns casting the displacement spells on Jean. I don't see Raymond staying at the abbey without him."

"Just make sure you tell Jean before you cast the spell," Orlando requested. "If you suggest it as a way to make sure Raymond takes care of himself, he'll go along with it, but you don't want to be on the receiving end of Jean's temper if you take that kind of decision out of his hands."

They reached the subway stop, stamping their tickets and descending into the warmth of the station out of the cold winter night. They had several stops along the same line before Sebastien and Thierry had to change trains to head north to their new home. "I guess we're about to get better acquainted with le Morvan," Thierry said as they waited for the train to arrive. "I've never been one for the country, but I like a challenge."

"Is that why you're still with Sebastien?" Alain joked. "Something new and different?"

Thierry shot Alain a dirty look. "No," he said, his voice tight as he reached for Sebastien's hand. "Something worth keeping."

"I know," Alain said, all teasing gone from his voice. "You know I know."

Thierry glared at him a moment longer and then let it go. "Between the three of us, you, me, and Raymond, we have three of the four elements covered. I know Raymond mentioned getting Adèle to help with the wards, but she probably has the most restrictive job of any of us. We need someone else to help with fire." He still hesitated to suggest the most logical choice. Despite having learned the truth of Eric's apparent defection to Serrier's camp, Thierry was not entirely sure Alain was ready to work with the man again.

"David," Alain said, his voice betraying his lack of enthusiasm, "but we couldn't count on his partner being free to help him for anything big."

"Not to mention that he can be a self-righteous prick at times," Thierry agreed. "We could ask... Eric."

"We could," Alain replied slowly, "although he doesn't have a partner."

"Not a vampire one," Thierry agreed, "but we learned the art of boosting each other's strength before we knew what our partners could do for our magic. Just because Vincent isn't a vampire doesn't mean he can't help. If he wants to."

Alain's face tightened even more at the mention of the former dark wizard. He had mostly forgiven Eric for his part in Orlando's capture during the war, but even a year later, the mere thought of the four days Orlando had been missing and the hell he had gone through at Serrier's hands was a physical ache in Alain's heart. "If Raymond wants him around, I won't say no."

Orlando squeezed Alain's hand gently. "I'm here because of them too. Don't forget that part."

Alain smiled wryly. "I won't. You won't let me."

Thierry and Sebastien exchanged an amused glance. Orlando had started a campaign almost the moment he awoke from his starvation-induced coma to mend fences between Alain and Eric. Thierry doubted their friendship would ever go back to the way it was before the war, but he continued to believe they could find a new balance. "This is our stop," he said, looking up as the train pulled into the station. "We'll see you tomorrow at the office. We can go out to the abbey from there."

"Bonne soirée," Orlando and Alain said as the other two exited the train, leaving them alone in the car.

When no one got on from the platform, Orlando turned to Alain with a mischievous grin. "Lock the door."

Alain's eyes widened slightly as he lifted his hand to cast a spell on the sliding doors. "Don't distract me too much. We'll miss our stop."

Orlando laughed as he pulled Alain into his arms, his lips sliding over the brand on Alain's neck as he pressed Alain against the wall of the Métro car. "Like it would be the first time."

Alain did not reply. He could not, with Orlando's fangs slipping beneath his skin. From the first time Orlando had bitten him, on a cold October night over a year before in the Père Lachaise cemetery, the feeling of those sharp canines sliding beneath his skin had sent him reeling with a sensation far too sexual for logic. In the intervening time, he had stopped registering the pinch of pain. His only reaction now was to beg for more. Knowing his mind would not function well enough to form words, he settled for sliding his fingers into

Orlando's dark hair, massaging his vampire's scalp as Orlando sucked life-giving blood through the brand that bound them together.

Alain's eyes closed as he focused on the mental bond that had developed between them as well, the wave of love and desire he felt from Orlando only adding to his own need. He worked a hand between their bodies. When his fingers found the hard bulge in his lover's trousers, he stroked along its length, tantalizing Orlando as Orlando's fangs tantalized him. Immediately Orlando's hands closed over his ass, pulling Alain closer as he rocked against the wizard's hand and groin, an erotic dance with only one end in mind: orgasm.

Alain moved his hand, letting their bodies rub together, and sought instead the hem of Orlando's sweater, sliding beneath it in search of sensitive flesh. The smooth skin of Orlando's back gave way to the smoother skin of his chest as Alain sought the vampire's nipples, tweaking them the way he knew his lover liked best. The surge of Orlando's reaction caused an answering jerk in Alain's cock. He could feel the dampness increasing as they rubbed together harder and faster, his breath sawing in and out of his chest. He needed to climax like he needed to breathe, but he needed Orlando to come first.

Trying to speed that moment along, Alain slid his other hand into the back of Orlando's trousers. Orlando bucked harder against him as Alain cupped the firm curve of the vampire's buttocks. Though Alain had grown used to the freedom of touching Orlando this way, he never forgot to be grateful for the love and trust it implied. *Come for me.*

The bond created between them by their Aveu de Sang did not allow for the transfer of actual thoughts, but Alain had learned that the emotions behind the words often carried through with almost equal effect. This time was no exception. Almost immediately, Orlando shuddered against him, the rush of heat through their clothes enough to trigger Alain's climax as well.

After a moment Orlando lifted his head, licking at wounds that would be healed by morning—one of the side benefits of the Aveu de Sang. "And look," the vampire murmured. "We didn't even miss our stop. Let's go home. I haven't gotten enough of you yet."

Alain grinned. That was another benefit. Orlando's fangs in his neck and the power of the bond between them gave him an almost immediate recovery time.

RAYMOND LOOKED around the kitchen, making sure he had finished cleaning up everything from dinner. He could have sped up the process with a wave of his hand, but while he trusted his magical acumen, he did not want to take any risk with Jean's collection. Some of the pieces were originals from the late eighteenth century, and Raymond had no idea how they would react to magic. He had learned relatively early in his wizarding life that some objects, due to their chemical composition or some other factor for which he had no explanation, interacted explosively with otherwise harmless spells. His shields would protect him from any backlash, but he did not want to have to explain to his lover how he had broken a one-of-a-kind piece.

Deciding everything was rearranged to his satisfaction, he refilled his wine and went in search of his missing lover. He found Jean on the small balcony that overlooked the Faubourg St-Honoré. "I think tonight went well. They had a lot of good suggestions."

"They did," Jean agreed, opening his arms and pulling Raymond to stand beside him. Raymond went willingly, murmuring a warming spell since he had not put on his coat. "They are competent wizards and good men."

Raymond nodded. "I always knew they were competent wizards. It's taken some time for me to come to appreciate them as individuals."

Jean remembered the tension from early in the alliance when Alain and Thierry, along with most of the Milice, had distrusted Raymond because of his past. "You never really told me what happened back then. Why you sided with Serrier. Were you always on the fringes?"

Raymond shrugged, not entirely comfortable talking about his past. "We're of an age, the three of us, at least now. Alain and Thierry are a couple of years older than I am, though by the time we all came to Paris and became involved with l'ANS, it wasn't enough to matter, but they were already friends. Best friends. And I wasn't very socially adept. I preferred my books to people. I realize now how wrong I was, but at the time, I was convinced they wouldn't know what to do with a book if I shoved one in their faces. So I got my job teaching history and researching the origins of various spells and the logic behind them, while Alain and Thierry worked for Marcel in a variety of capacities. They each married. Alain had his son. They added a third to their friendship, Eric, with his wife and kids. And I studied. Then Serrier came along. You have to understand that his rhetoric didn't start out as an attempt to overthrow the government. He came on the scene talking about the laws restricting dark magic and arguing that magic wasn't light or dark in and of itself but rather in its application. Blood magic, sex magic, even the *Abbatoire*, he argued, could be used for good as well as for evil. For someone like me— obsessed with the past and the uses that various spells had been put to over time as well as the evolution of society's opinion on those spells—his ideas were pure brilliance. I was thoroughly taken in, completely dazzled."

"What happened?" Jean asked. "That certainly wasn't the rhetoric he was spouting by the time Marcel asked for the vampires' aid."

"He got frustrated," Raymond replied. "The Parlement wasn't interested in even entertaining his propositions. Marcel had other issues on his agenda and so didn't use his political pull to try to get the attention of the députés. Serrier said if they wouldn't pay attention to us, we had to demand their attention. He was a persuasive speaker. A powerful speaker, and he had an audience who was tired of feeling dictated to by nonwizards. We followed him. Wrongly, I can see now, but at the time, I was blinded by the sense of purpose he instilled in us. We were going to change the world for the better."

Jean nodded. "I've heard that a few times in my existence. It never ends well. Lafayette, Robespierre, Napoléon, Les Trois Glorieuses, Napoléon III... I could go on. Revolutions begin with the highest of intentions and end in chaos far more often than they end in success, at least in France."

"When Serrier's protests turned violent, I started questioning his position," Raymond went on, "and when he went from violence to outright cruelty, I switched sides. But by then I already had the scar on my back and a reputation. It was mostly unfounded, but that didn't matter. Marcel believed me, but everyone else watched me constantly, sure I was there to spy for Serrier or to undermine the Milice. There wasn't anything I could say or do to convince them otherwise, so I didn't even try. I moved into the garret where I lived when we met and hid from the world so Serrier couldn't find me. And I did everything I could to make sure he failed."

"Which he did, thanks to you."

Raymond shrugged, uncomfortable with the praise. "Monsieur Lombard killed him, not me or anything I thought to do."

"Monsieur Lombard might have killed him, but I was there too, if you remember. I watched you fight, and I watched you constantly seeking new and better ways to bring him down," Jean insisted. "Marcel was right to choose you as his successor. Dinner tonight proved that once again, if you needed more proof."

"How so?" Raymond asked, surprised by the assertion.

"You talked about Alain and Thierry as part of the wider Milice when you talked about your detractors after you defected, but I was there too. I know they were your *biggest* detractors, or at least your highest placed ones," Jean said. "They worked with you when Marcel ordered, but they'd have been just as happy to see you in hell as to have your help. Tonight they came to dinner at your invitation, sat and discussed plans for l'Institut with you, drank your wine, and did all the things friends do. Not simply colleagues. Friends. You may not have been thinking in those terms when you invited them here instead of convening a meeting in your office, and they may not have been thinking that way when they accepted, but I've had over a millennium to observe people. Those were your friends—our friends—sitting around our table tonight, and they'll work all the harder on l'Institut because of it."

Chapter 8

"WHERE DO you want me to start?" Thierry asked Raymond as soon as they arrived at Dommartin the next morning. Alain and Orlando had not arrived, but Thierry was not sure they would come out yet given Alain's complete lack of sensitivity where earth was concerned.

"The first concern is making sure the main building is sound," Raymond said. "Even if we don't renovate all the rooms immediately, I need to know if any areas are dangerous."

"I can do that. I'll reinforce anything I can, of course, but this isn't Notre-Dame. There isn't a source of magical power here to support my efforts like there was there."

"Notre-Dame is unique in many ways," Raymond agreed. "Information is enough for now. Even if we end up doing a portion of the repairs magically, we don't have to do it all at once."

"I'll get started then," Thierry said.

"I'll make sure you aren't disturbed in case you need Sebastien's help." Raymond had learned quickly how intimate an act vampires considered feeding. While that stricture had relaxed somewhat as vampires grew more accustomed to feeding from their partners during magical rituals, Raymond saw no reason to push their limits unnecessarily.

"As if I would let him try it without me," Sebastien growled. "I'm not taking any chances on losing him."

"I told you—"

"And I told you," Sebastien interrupted. "We'll mark anywhere that's unsafe."

Raymond just shook his head and marveled again at the difference a year had made for all of them. Maybe Jean was right and they were even becoming friends. Certainly Thierry would never have carried on this kind of conversation in Raymond's hearing during the war.

Inside, Thierry turned on Sebastien. "That was one time, in the midst of a panicked situation." He still shuddered a little to think how close he had come to losing himself in the earth as he searched for Orlando immediately after his capture. "It won't happen today because I'm not as invested in getting immediate results, the risks be damned."

"I'm still going to bite you while you work," Sebastien insisted. "If nothing else, it's a more efficient use of time and effort."

Thierry could hardly argue with that, so he let it go. "I guess it's a good thing you weren't hungry last night."

"I'll always be hungry for you," Sebastien replied, moving to stand behind Thierry. The wizard reached out for the exterior wall of the main building and began chanting. As Sebastien felt the rising power—something he had been unable to do until after their experience at Notre-Dame—he slid his arms around Thierry's waist, letting his lover lean back against him, and pulled Thierry's scarf and collar aside to access warm, smooth skin. Thierry shivered in his arms as Sebastien licked the spot in preparation for his bite. To Sebastien's continued delight, the rhythmic chanting faltered when his fangs met flesh, piercing deeply. The soft moan that escaped Thierry's lips went straight to Sebastien's groin, leaving him in no doubt that he would be finding a dark corner to lure his wizard into at some point during the day. For now though, he sucked gently and let Thierry work.

The stones of the abbey had none of the sentience that had so shocked Thierry at Notre-Dame and that had made the cathedral such a hot spot during the last days of the war, but Thierry could still sense their age as he sent tendrils of energy through the walls, testing cohesion, seeking weak spots. Each time he found one, he marked it with a magical flare for later attention, preferring to do a full scan of the building before addressing his concerns. Sebastien moved with him as he went from room to room, his fangs a constant reminder of his presence, a stabilizing force that allowed Thierry's mind and magic to meld with the stones without fear. He would not go too deep because Sebastien would be there to draw him back.

Even with Sebastien's help, Thierry could feel the drain on his power as they neared the réfectoire, the last room in the building. "I think that's enough for today," he said as he flagged the eastern corner of the room. "There is no reason to push my limits over this. We're not fighting a war this time."

"Thank God." Sebastien gave a final lick to the incisions on Thierry's neck and spun the wizard in his arms, kissing him fiercely, his fangs scoring Thierry's tongue. "Do any of those doors on the monks' cells lock?"

Thierry grinned. "I can make them lock."

"Let's go."

They backtracked through the hall to the nearest cell, Thierry checking as they stumbled into the room to make sure he had not flagged it as needing repair. He had no desire to slam up against a wall only to have it crumble around them. A flick of his wand locked the door, his concentration too shattered by Sebastien's hands flying over his body for him to manage even the little bit of wandless magic Alain had managed to teach him since the war ended. The slim length of oak clattered to the ground as all thought but getting Sebastien naked as quickly as possible flew out of Thierry's head. The room they were in had a narrow cot in it, probably left over from the monastery era.

Thierry gave no thought to the dust that rose from beneath his hands as his palms landed on the thin mattress. His only care was the strong fingers pressing against his opening.

Strong, *slick* fingers.

"You brought lube?" Thierry gasped.

"You were going to be working," Sebastien replied as if it was the most obvious thing in the world. "Of course I brought lube."

Thierry wanted to make some comment about the presumption of that statement—but Sebastien's fingers found his gland, working over it mercilessly, and all Thierry could do was gasp and try not to come on the spot. Even though Sebastien's bite had been practical in nature, the sensation of his lover's fangs moving beneath his skin could never be anything but purely sexual, and the work they had done in the monastery constituted one long hour of foreplay. Thierry had come to terms with his reaction to Sebastien's bite during his recovery from the Rite d'équilibrage on Samhain the year before and never looked back. He might not have a brand on his neck to match Alain's, but he belonged to his vampire, body and soul.

"Now," he begged, needing more than fingers inside him. Sebastien complied immediately, the head of his cock pushing past the outer ring. Thierry braced for a long, fast stroke, sure Sebastien was as desperate as he was, but it didn't come. Instead, Sebastien took his time, sliding inside Thierry's body centimeter by centimeter until the tip of his erection prodded directly against Thierry's sweet spot.

"Putain," the wizard gasped. "Sebastien!"

"None of that," Sebastien scolded. "Let me love you properly."

Thierry's head fell forward, his forehead hitting the mattress as Sebastien nudged his prostate with every pass, each thrust sending a zing through his body and a spurt of fluid out of his already leaking cock. He enjoyed sex with Sebastien in any form, but he thought this might be his favorite, his lover behind him, driving into him, every bump against his gland its own miniature orgasm. The depth of Sebastien's movements never changed, unerringly driving Thierry wild, but the speed increased as desperation grew.

"Now," Sebastien ordered, his hand sliding beneath Thierry to grip the wizard's cock and pull on it masterfully.

The touch and the husky word probably would have been enough by themselves, but the feeling of Sebastien's other hand pushing his shirt up under his arms and the sudden pinch of the vampire's fangs next to his spine finished Thierry off. His cock twitched heavily as his orgasm rushed through him, leaving him trembling through the aftermath as Sebastien drove into him deep and hard in search of his own release.

Seconds later, Thierry felt the heat inside him that could only come from his lover, accompanied by a tender lick over the marks on his back. Strong arms came around him, pulling him up so he sat on his knees, leaning back against Sebastien's strong, slender chest. "I love you."

Sebastien pressed a kiss to the smooth skin behind Thierry's ear. "Love you too." His hands wandered possessively over Thierry's half-naked body, lingering in all his favorite spots: the curve of Thierry's hip, the expanse of his chest, the heavy sac. Even more than that, he loved the way Thierry rested trustingly in his arms, their bodies still joined.

"WHAT ARE you doing?" Jean asked, coming up to where Raymond stood in the weak winter sunlight in the middle of the cloister.

"Trying to imagine what it will look like in a few months," Raymond replied, "with flowers starting to bloom and students and researchers walking the halls, bringing it to life again. Trying to envision the steps to get it there."

"Rome wasn't built in a day," Jean reminded him gently. "We've already made a start. Thierry is doing his part, and we'll have bids by the end of the week for the repair work. Then it will be a question of overseeing that and taking care of details. It will all come together before you know it."

"That's what I'm worried about," Raymond admitted. "I want to be here, not in the offices of l'ANS, and I don't know how long I'll be able to delegate enough responsibilities to give l'Institut the attention it deserves. I'm afraid I'm going to have to choose, and I don't know which one is the right choice. I believe in l'Institut and what we'll be doing here, but I also know Marcel chose me as his successor because I understood Serrier's appeal while still rejecting his methods. I need to give the rest of our agenda the attention it deserves as well, or l'ANS will lose credibility."

"Let's not borrow trouble," Jean suggested gently. "For the moment, the immediate needs of l'ANS are in the capable hands of your staff, so you can give l'Institut the push it needs to get it started. Once it's established, you can still be involved with the research without running everything here. Name a headmaster or a director, whatever title you want to use, to run the daily affairs, and stay on the Board of Directors so you're involved in the big decisions. Everyone wins."

"We—all the partnered vampires and wizards who are willing—will be the subjects of the research as much as the source of the questions. We won't be able to be uninvolved."

"There you go," Jean said with a smile. "So tell me what you see."

Raymond turned full circle around the cloister, eyes alighting on each of the buildings. "The main building will be the hub, I think," he began. "Classrooms, living quarters for those who choose to stay here, either for classes or for research. The Hostellerie can be more of a hotel, for people who come for a night or two, where the monks' cells will be the longer-term lodging. The grange can be converted into a gymnasium and the old church into a lecture hall."

"Don't," Jean asked, the words out before he could stop them. "I know it was decommissioned when it was first sold off, but even if it means you don't restore it, don't turn it into something it isn't."

Mentally recalculating, Raymond walked toward the grange. "It would take more work, but we could convert the grange into a lecture hall, especially if we don't have the expense of converting the chapel right away. I've never been a devout man. I forget that you are."

"I think Père Emmanuel would have a few things to say about the state of my devotion," Jean said with a laugh, "but I am devout in my own way. I appreciate the consideration."

Raymond bit back the offer that sprang to his lips of permanent consideration. They had gone through this more than once as they debated the issues of their private versus public lives. They would gain nothing by going through it again, nor could they afford to forget the spotlight that shone on both of them and the enemies who would take advantage of any perceived weakness or improprieties. He settled for smiling. "I'm glad it was something I could do for you. Shall we go see what Thierry has found?"

Going inside, they found all the signs of Thierry's passage, his magical markers bright against the pale stone, but no sign of the wizard himself or of his partner.

"We knew it would need work," Jean reminded Raymond as the wizard's face grew more dejected with each marker they found.

"I'd hoped it wouldn't need this much work," Raymond sighed. "I may need to adjust my vision to summer rather than spring."

"What other wizards besides Thierry could you call for help? Who else has an affinity to earth?"

"Magali, if she and Luc will come from Amiens again. Vincent, Eric's lover. Hugues Fouquet, Alain's lieutenant from the war. Marcel, if he will come out of retirement. Monique, but her prison term will not be up for another few months. Earth is the rarest affinity." Raymond racked his brain for other options. "I could perhaps send out a call for anyone who might be able to help even if they aren't active in l'ANS. We could compensate them for their time, within reason."

"Magali, Thierry, and Marcel have partners, which would augment their effectiveness," Jean reminded Raymond. "If monsieur Lombard will consent to help as well."

"And Vincent has Eric to help him as he works with earth. Wizards can also augment each other, as we do in the Rite d'équilibrage, or as we did to help Adèle with the wards. It might not be the same increase a vampire gives his partner, but it is still an increase."

"We could offer our power to Vincent to channel as well," Jean said. "As long as he can handle the influx, other wizards could provide the magical power."

Raymond chuckled. "It sounds like we need an old-fashioned wine harvest. One long weekend, everyone who can come pitching in. We'll provide shelter and food. They'll provide the magic, channeled through those with an affinity to earth."

"It works for the vintners. It will work for us."

Feeling considerably better, Raymond returned to the entrance of the main building, cataloguing the markers with a purpose now. "Thierry used different signatures in different places. We'll have to ask him what the difference is when he turns up again, but at least we'll have a sorted list."

"Speak of the devil," Jean murmured as Sebastien and Thierry appeared at the other end of the hall. Jean coughed to hide the smile he could not stifle at the glazed look in Thierry's eyes and the smug satisfaction on Sebastien's face. As they drew nearer, the unmistakable smell of sex assailed his senses.

"Thierry, Sebastien, I was looking for you," Raymond exclaimed, apparently oblivious to the signs that were so obvious to Jean. "What do the different marking spells indicate?"

"How dangerous the area is," Thierry said. "Yellow indicates places that need repair but aren't in any danger of collapsing. Orange is for places that need serious repair but can probably be put off for a few months. Red is for the areas that need repair before anyone can safely use that space or go near that area."

Looking around, Jean was pleased to see far more yellow and orange marks than red, at least in this section. "Is the rest of the building in pretty much the same shape as this area?"

"For the most part," Thierry replied. "A lot of the entrance here and some of the living quarters were obviously restored before the building was abandoned. There are a few sections where it doesn't look like anything had been done for fifty years, and those sections are more dangerous. That said, they're all grouped together in one wing, so you could just close the wing until later."

"Is it stable enough for us to take a look?" Raymond asked.

Thierry frowned. "Probably, but don't touch anything. Some of the walls are held together by a wish and a prayer."

Jean's frown matched Thierry's as they walked down the corridor that led to the restricted wing. He could see the large red marker at the juncture of the two corridors, and every instinct he had told him to stop Raymond from walking down that hall, but the others proceeded without hesitation. Jean told himself to stop being irrational, but the presentiment did not fade as they walked farther down the passageway, Thierry giving a running commentary of what rooms were on the other side of the various doors and what state each one was in. When they reached the far end, Jean gave in to his nerves, pulling Raymond with him out the far door and into the open air. "Close that entire wing," he said urgently. "Don't even bother repairing it. Just close it completely."

"What?" Raymond asked, surprised. "Why?"

"I can't explain why," Jean admitted, "but you shouldn't go there. It's dangerous."

"Jean—"

Jean shook his head. "Please. At least do it until we can get stonemasons and enough wizards to shore it up. And some kind of ritual cleansing. I don't know what happened in that hallway, but it feels... malevolent."

"Jean, relax," Raymond urged, seeing the looks of growing concern on Thierry's and Sebastien's faces. "We'll make sure it's repaired properly before we let anyone use that wing. It's not like we have students beating down the door to get in."

"Give it time," Thierry said with a laugh, trying to lighten the suddenly somber turn of the conversation. "Once wizards, and especially vampires, realize what they can gain from partnerships, they'll be lining up outside."

Chapter 9

"DO YOU really think people will want to form partnerships now that the war is over?" Raymond asked Thierry later that afternoon when the four men had returned to l'ANS offices in Paris.

"I thought that was the whole point of l'Institut," Thierry said, confusion on his face.

"It is and it isn't," Raymond explained. "It is because people are stumbling into partnerships they aren't prepared to manage and then want out when it's too late, but I expect at least some people to go through the education portion and then decide not to seek a partner. The research will be important in terms of the magical equilibrium and any other effects on that kind of fundamental level, but even most of that is more to help those of us already living with partnerships to understand what's happened to us rather than because I actually expect most of the findings to make a difference in the grander scheme of things."

Thierry mulled that over for a few minutes. "I can't speak for anyone else," he said finally, "but I know what I feel when I'm with Sebastien. I know what I feel when he bites me, but even just being with him. There's a sense of being complete, not just personally, but magically, for the first time. Can wizards exist and function and even live happy, fulfilled lives without a vampire by their side? Undoubtedly, because we've been doing it for as long as there have been wizards, but a part of me also recognizes that I would only live a happy, fulfilled life without a partner if I didn't know what I was missing. I'd be willing to bet that I'm a stronger wizard now, even without Sebastien biting me, than I was before the partnerships formed, simply because we have our bond. Certainly I'd never managed any kind of wandless magic before the war began. I can only do rudimentary things now, but that's still a quantifiable change in my abilities from before our partnership. I can only imagine what Alain feels with the Aveu de Sang." He kept his voice level and masked the disappointment he still sometimes felt at knowing he would never have that level of relationship with his lover—but Sebastien had already had an Avoué, and that magic only worked once. "I've wondered occasionally if the Aveu de Sang wasn't intended to bind vampires and wizards specifically. I mean, a wizard had to have created the spell at some point, even if it is something a vampire now does without needing a wizard for it to work. Have you not noticed some increase in your power too?"

Raymond shrugged. "Wizards naturally grow in power, especially after times of great use. It's like developing any other muscle in your body. If you work it hard enough, it will get stronger."

"But you can lose that too, right?" Thierry asked. "I mean, I can see us all gaining in power during the war because we used magic constantly, even for things we might not have otherwise, because time was so critical that any shortcut was welcome. I don't use my abilities nearly as often now as I did then, yet I don't feel any weakening, and I'm fairly sure I'm even stronger now than at the end of the war."

Raymond tipped his head to one side, clearly considering the hypothesis. "Did you ever do a dépistage-pouvoir scan before the war started to see how strong you were?"

"Soon after I first arrived at l'ANS," Thierry replied. "Would the change from then give us valid results? That was probably fifteen years ago."

"It won't be an ironclad result," Raymond agreed, "but we have enough models predicting growth under various circumstances for us to see if you exceed that. And it gives us a baseline now to see if the effect continues later. We may not be able to accurately compare your strength now to what it was three years ago at the beginning of the war, but if we do one now, we can definitely see if you've had significant growth this time next year. A lot of the studies we'll end up doing at l'Institut will be longitudinal. There won't be a single, magically straightforward answer to most of our questions. If there were, people would have discovered it years ago."

"Is this an easy scan to administer?" Jean asked.

"Reasonably so," Raymond replied. "It takes a couple of hours and requires a wizard to do magical tasks that become more challenging as the test goes on. Each new task requires more magical output to complete. Where a wizard breaks down, for lack of a better expression, determines the rating from the scan. Why?"

"Because it seems to me like a good baseline to have—both for the wizards who have partners, for our research, and also for the wizards coming into the program, so we can track their improvements over time," Jean said. "Thierry just said he didn't know how useful his old scan would be. That's fine, because we certainly didn't know what we were doing when we started the alliance. But we do know now, somewhat anyway, and it would be ludicrous to start this kind of program without all the initial information we need to determine the eventual success of the applicants."

"The results don't generally change over a year or two either," Thierry said, "so if they have a recent scan, we could probably use that."

Raymond shook his head. "No, if we're going to conduct reliable research, we need truly accurate starting data. A year ago we had just finished a war, and two years ago we were in the middle of one. People's ratings could potentially have changed significantly in that time. We can afford to do this correctly."

"When would you want to do the scan?" Thierry asked.

"Not today," Raymond said. "You've already expended a considerable amount of magic today, and that could skew your results. The other thing is that since we don't know how long feeding affects a wizard's ability, we should probably not do the scan within at least twelve hours of Sebastien feeding from you. Think of it as the magical equivalent of fasting before getting blood work done at the doctor's office."

"We could schedule it for tomorrow," Thierry said. "Sebastien fed while I was working today, so he won't be at risk."

"You know, there's something we didn't mention last night at dinner that could also be relevant," Jean said suddenly. "Orlando mentioned, the first night he met Alain, that he'd only taken a few mouthfuls but he felt as energized as if he'd drained a man dry. The effect didn't last as long as a full feeding, but it could still be something to look into. Is a vampire strengthened by feeding from a wizard, and specifically from his partner, the same way a wizard is strengthened by that feeding?"

"That's research you'll have to do on the new partners," Sebastien said flatly. "Orlando may be the only vampire with an Aveu de Sang, but I don't see you finding many partnered vampires volunteering to drink someone else's blood."

"No, probably not," Jean agreed. "Angélique said she'd had a few customers convinced they were imagining how much better their partners' blood tasted until they actually tasted blood from one of her employees. We could test the vampires as they enter the program and again after they find a partner."

"And again somewhat later to see if the effect is cumulative or if it's a one-time boost," Raymond added. "Thierry, I imagine you're tired from your exertions today, so we'll let you get some rest. I'll get the scan arranged for tomorrow morning at nine. Twelve hours with no feeding."

"I'm not twelve," Thierry reminded Raymond. "I can restrain myself."

"We'll see you in the morning then. I'll come in to oversee it myself so there aren't any surprises or glitches. With all the time spent on l'Institut recently, I'm not keeping normal office hours anyway," Raymond said.

"And the world hasn't come to an end yet?" Thierry teased, laughing when he saw the shocked look on Raymond's face. "Sorry. I didn't mean to overstep my bounds."

"No, you didn't," Raymond hastened to say. "I was just surprised. You say things like that to Alain all the time, but this may be the first time you've ever joked around like that with me."

Thierry flushed. "I guess I'm getting used to you being around all the time."

He left the office before Raymond could reply to that, Sebastien trailing behind him. Jean turned to Raymond and grinned. "I told you they were becoming your friends."

Raymond shrugged. "Let's go visit Marcel. I haven't seen him in a while, and I'd like to let him know what's going on with l'Institut and see if maybe he'd like to come help with the repairs."

Jean glanced at the clock. "He won't be awake yet. The last time I talked to Mireille, she said he's become almost as nocturnal as a vampire. He spends the evenings with monsieur Lombard at Le Saulnier café and the early morning hours playing chess with him in front of the fireplace in the library. She still hunts for monsieur Lombard, so whatever is going on, it isn't a feeding partnership, but they've apparently become great friends."

"We could go by Le Saulnier or by monsieur Lombard's house, I suppose," Raymond said. "Monsieur Lombard might have some insights as well, or at least a longer view of things. Not that yours isn't quite long as well, but another thousand years of experience is nothing to scoff at."

Jean shrugged. "There comes a point where there is nothing new under the sun or moon, I'm afraid, or at least I thought that way until I met you. I suppose that just goes to prove that there's always something new to learn or experience."

"And that's all the more reason to talk to monsieur Lombard," Raymond agreed. "He might see something that hasn't occurred to us because we're too close to it. It starts getting dark around five. If we go to Le Saulnier around six-thirty, they will have time to settle in for the evening and have a drink or two, not that it would affect monsieur Lombard."

"If we're going to stay up talking with them half the night, you should rest while you can," Jean said.

Raymond smiled at his lover, touched by the way Jean never let him overextend himself. Raymond supposed some people might find it overbearing, but having been on his own from an early age, he appreciated the tangible sign of Jean's affection for him. The vampire might never love him, but he did care about him, and that was enough for now.

"I don't imagine you'll let me rest here."

Jean's snort was all the answer Raymond needed. "If you 'rest' here, you'll end up feeling obliged to answer the hundred emails Fabienne forwarded to you since yesterday or see any of the twenty people probably waiting for you outside your office. We'll go home and you'll sleep in our bed." *Where you belong.*

THE AUSTERE nineteenth-century façade of l'Hôtel-Dieu on île de la Cité belied the miracles of modern technology and magical medicine that resided within. Alain hoped the wizarding doctors at the center of the city's public hospital system would be interested in the benefits a partnership with a vampire could provide them. The director of the hospital, despite not being a wizard himself, was certainly interested when Alain had explained the increase in strength and ability he had experienced with Orlando at his side. The director had even agreed to allow a paid leave of absence to any doctors who decided to participate in the educational seminars once l'Institut was ready. Now Alain just had to convince the wizards.

"Alain, what are you doing here?" Maurice Fortin, one of the doctors who had joined the Milice de Sorcellerie as part of its medical corps, asked as he walked into the break room.

Alain rose from his seat and shook the other man's hand warmly. "Doing a bit of work for l'ANS today."

"What new scheme has Raymond cooked up?" Maurice grinned as he gestured for Alain to sit again. "Do you want coffee? I need it to get through the day most days."

"Yes, please," Alain said, waiting while the doctor poured them both a cup of coffee and joined Alain at the small table. "I would think this would be easy after working with the Milice for two years."

"The injuries and illnesses aren't as severe," Maurice replied, "but they're a lot more constant. During the war, if a battle wasn't going on, I might not get a new patient for days. Here, it feels like I get new patients every few minutes. It wouldn't be as bad if I didn't work in the ER, but that's where my skills can do the most good."

"Magical or medical or both?" Alain asked.

"Both," Maurice said. "I can stop an injury from bleeding out with magic even if I have to repair the damage with sutures or send the patient on to a specialist for whatever kind of treatment he needs."

"Are you magically drained as well as physically tired?" Alain inquired.

"Why are you asking?" Maurice said. "I mean, I don't mind answering your questions, but you didn't come here to check on my health."

"No, I didn't," Alain admitted. "L'ANS is starting a new education and outreach program designed to help prepare wizards and vampires who might be interested in forming partnerships like we did during the alliance. The war is over, but the benefits have continued."

"What kind of benefits? I mean, I remember the vampires' feeding helped their partners heal more quickly, but that doesn't help me deal with my patients," Maurice said.

"No, the healing aspect only works between partners, but having a partner could help you with some of the magical drain," Alain said. "We know for a fact that having your partner feed as you're doing magic increases your power and decreases your fatigue afterward, and we suspect that the effects of long-term feeding are cumulative, so that your abilities actually increase over time even when your partner isn't feeding."

"And Raymond thinks people will go for this?" Maurice asked.

"Why wouldn't they?" Alain retorted. "The increase in power is exponential."

"Because you have to let a vampire bite you," Maurice replied.

"I hadn't pegged you as xenophobic."

"I'm not," Maurice said immediately, "but that's a lot to ask."

"It's very little to ask," Alain disagreed. "Just think about it. L'Institut Marcel Chavinier isn't open yet, but you'd be a good candidate when it does."

"How long are you talking about for this 'program'?" Maurice asked.

"I don't know yet," Alain said, "but I've already talked to the director of the hospital, and he's willing to give people the time off to participate. And there's no requirement—or guarantee for that matter—that you find a partner at the end of the program. It's all about educating people so they can decide if they want to have a partner."

"I'll think about it," Maurice said, his tone somewhat grudging.

"Will you at least tell anyone you know who might be interested about it?" Alain requested. "Even if you decide not to go forward with it, someone else might."

Maurice nodded and finished his coffee. "I can do that. My break's over. I've got to get back to work."

Alain let him go. He wished he had received a more enthusiastic response, but while he believed to the depths of his being that no one who embraced a partnership fully would ever regret it, he also had the example of Adèle and Jude to remind him that some partnerships simply could not function. He must have been projecting his doubts or frustrations, because a sudden wave of reassurance and love came through his bond with Orlando, bringing a smile to his face.

Over the next three hours, Alain had similar conversations with the other wizarding doctors who came through the lounge, explaining the program Raymond was trying to create, justifying the need for the partnerships, and generally doing everything he could to convince people to give the program a chance.

He got varying reactions, from downright scornful to guardedly interested. Not what he had hoped for as he arrived at the hospital that morning, but better than he had feared after Maurice's dismissive reaction. Glancing at his watch, he turned in his visitor's badge at the hospital and went on to his next stop: the directeur-général of the Gendarmerie Nationale, Guy Sarraute.

An aide ushered Alain into a Spartan office, far plainer than the wizard would have expected for such a highly placed figure. He offered his hand to the older man sitting behind the desk, still obviously fit despite his thinning hair and lightly lined face. "Monsieur le directeur-général, thank you for agreeing to see me."

"Monsieur Magnier," the officer replied, shaking Alain's hand. "Please, have a seat and tell me what brings one of the heroes of l'émeute des Sorciers to see me."

Alain took a seat across the desk from the other man and tried to decide how to begin. "We learned a lot of things during the war," Alain began, "as you well know. One of those things we learned, or at least began to learn, is the incredible symbiosis that can exist between a vampire and wizard. We think that symbiosis could be of use to people who use magic as part of their professional lives, especially in situations where that use could tax their abilities at times."

"That's a very pretty speech," Sarraute said with a cocked eyebrow. "Now cut the bullshit and say it in French, not jargon."

Alain laughed in surprise and settled in to bargain.

Chapter 10

"STOP PACING," Jean ordered Raymond as Raymond did his best to wear a hole in the rug of his office.

"I think better when I pace," Raymond muttered.

"Yes, but you're driving me crazy. Think out loud so I can help you figure things out," Jean insisted.

"I don't even know where to begin. Thierry's results on the dépistage-pouvoir scan are far higher than any model predicts that they should be, even with the amount of magic he did during the war," Raymond began, "so that's a definite positive. The effects of the partnerships clearly are cumulative, which is another benefit we can point out as we're discussing it with interested wizards. I'm a little surprised at how great the increase was, but there could be a variety of other factors contributing to that—use, Thierry finally growing into his natural abilities, which weren't fully tapped before the war began, or perhaps physical and emotional maturity since his last scan."

"So why do you seem concerned about it?"

"Because I can't explain it," Raymond admitted. "You know how I am. I need to understand the how and why of things. I'm far more perplexed by our conversation with Marcel and monsieur Lombard. Watching them together, listening to Mireille talk about the time they spend together—they act like any set of committed partners, but unless they're lying to us, monsieur Lombard hasn't tasted Marcel's blood since the final battle against Serrier. Either they're partners or they aren't. This doesn't make sense!"

"Every time we've had a discussion about anything related to magic, you have said Marcel is an exceptional wizard and that the regular rules seem not to apply to him," Jean reminded his partner. "Monsieur Lombard is nearly twice my age, the oldest vampire in Paris, probably in France, maybe in an even wider sphere. Judging anything about vampires by his example is the height of folly. So could it be possible that they simply make their own rules?"

Raymond snorted inelegantly. "You said it yourself. The regular rules don't apply where Marcel is concerned, but if he—if they—can resist the partnership bond, then others can too."

"Besides their age and power, what makes them unique?" Jean said.

"I don't know where to start," Raymond said. "Monsieur Lombard recognized Marcel as his partner instantly, but he only asked to feed enough to protect himself from the rising sun as we went inside after Serrier. He fed again, we were told, to help Marcel when he was hit with a spell and then to help him break through Serrier's wards around his hiding spot. So that's a total of three bites."

"All functional ones as well," Jean added. "He wasn't feeding because he was hungry or because there was something irresistible about Marcel's blood. He bit Marcel to protect himself and then to protect and empower Marcel. Could that have an impact?"

"Merde, Jean, anything could have an impact at this point," Raymond said with a deep sigh. "It's worth noting, I suppose. Is it a distinction you would make?"

Jean thought back over the earliest days of his relationship with Raymond. "At first, it was very much about the protection from the sunlight," he said after a moment. "But by the time we went to La Réunion to help after the typhoon, it had become more than that. Soon after the alliance began, I went to visit Karine." He still flinched at the thought of his sometimes lover, who had fallen into Serrier's hands and been brutally tortured before she was killed. "I fed from her then, but not after. I went to see her once after that, but she wasn't home, so I ended up feeding from you for nourishment as well as protection. And then the night of the Piège-Pouvoir, I saw the flowers I'd left outside her door and came to you."

Raymond smiled even though he knew Jean still felt guilty that he had not searched for Karine that night. The dangerous and powerful ritual to trap the wild magic that had escaped when Thierry lost control of the balancing ritual the day before had left them glutted with power, shattering the self-imposed control both he and Jean had maintained on the boundaries of their partnership until that night. "The first night we made love."

"The night I asked you to give me a chance as a lover, not just as a partner," Jean agreed. *The night I fell in love.* "Up until that night, for all the reasons we've already talked about, we were benefiting from the partnership without letting the bond become personal. So we managed to do what Marcel and monsieur Lombard have done."

Raymond stopped his pacing and turned to face Jean. "Did we really? Or did we simply fight it as long as we could?"

"Did you want more than a utilitarian partnership before that night?" Jean asked, surprised. "I thought…."

Raymond shrugged. "I don't know if I *wanted* it, but I knew I could have more if I just gave in. I'd always been alone, but especially in the two years prior to that. The lure of having someone of my own was powerful indeed. Marcel and monsieur Lombard seem to have given each other that aspect of the partnerships without giving in to the magical side. We tried to do the opposite. Unsuccessfully."

"Were we unsuccessful, though, or did we choose to change our minds?" Jean pressed. "Yes, I came to you for release that night, but if you had turned me away, I would have gone." He was not sure he could walk away anymore, but that night he still could have, if Raymond had resisted his pleas.

"I don't know," Raymond admitted. "If you hadn't come to my apartment, I would have hunkered down and found a way to deal with the influx of power and the need for release and the fear of being alone, because that's what I do—what I did. I doubt I would ever have come to you because I wouldn't have let myself, but I couldn't say no that night. I needed you too much."

"So what does that tell us?" Jean asked, trying to pick apart his memories and separate his desires from his choices.

"It tells us we're no closer to having an answer than we were yesterday," Raymond said with a sigh. "Nothing makes sense."

"Does it have to?" Jean asked seriously. "I know you want to understand—I'm the same way—but personal desire aside, does the magic that governs our lives have to make sense? Does it have to be predictable?"

"I've never known it not to be," Raymond said. "I suppose that isn't a guarantee, but I've always been able to find a pattern even when I can't find an explanation. I may not know why things work, but I can generally predict how they will work. With the partnerships, I have yet to find that balance."

"Then we'll keep looking. What time is Marcel coming to see l'Institut?"

Raymond smiled inwardly at the decisive change of subject. Jean would discuss options and theories with him as long as it was productive to do so, but he would never let Raymond wallow in self-pity. Yet another reason their partnership was the bedrock of his new life.

"He said he'd be here around two and we could go from there. Thierry and Sebastien and Vincent and Eric will be there as well," Raymond replied. "I wasn't able to reach Hugues Fouquet, so it may just be the three wizards and Sebastien plus us."

"We'll use the time and energy we have and go from there," Jean replied philosophically. "We don't have to finish all the repairs in one day."

"Even with the entire strength of the Milice, wizards and vampires alike, I'm not sure we could do everything in one day," Raymond joked. "Too few adepts where earth is concerned, if nothing else. Thierry worked miracles at Notre-Dame with only Sebastien's aid, but that was more because Notre-Dame proved to be one of the four magical loci than because of Thierry and Sebastien. Even with the assistance Sebastien can provide and the assistance we can provide Marcel or Vincent, this will be slow going. I'll be happy if we completely stabilize the entryway today."

"I obviously have no idea the kind of work this will entail," Jean said with a grin. "Every time I've seen you do magic, you cast a spell and it's done."

"This isn't just a question of casting a spell," Raymond replied. "Thierry could explain it better than I can because he actually makes it work. When we were at Notre-Dame that night, I could tell the cathedral was damaged by the spells Aguiraud and his wizards cast, but all I could do was cast spells to brace the walls. As you said, cast a spell and it's done. Thierry was actually able to repair the damage to the stones. To mend them on an elemental level. I think it's one of the reasons why the affinity with earth is so rare. My affinity with water lets me move water, but water is water. If it's displaced, by its very nature, it finds its own again, seeping down into the aquifer until it joins the water system again. When Alain stirs the air, he moves it around, but it remains whole. Adèle or Eric might create fire to devour something, but the fire is complete and integral in and of itself. Earth, though, can be formed, melded, and separated in ways the other elements can't. I can take a stone and shatter it into pieces that can be glued back together, but they'll still be separate pieces. A wizard with a true affinity to earth can do more than glue them back together. He or she can create them anew, but it's a slow, difficult, power-heavy task. That's why I was so concerned about leaving Thierry to see to the cathedral alone, even though I knew I couldn't do more than I'd done."

Jean nodded slowly, his respect for Marcel and Thierry increasing. He didn't know Vincent well, his late defection from Serrier's camp and his role in Orlando's capture keeping him from being comfortable with a greater degree of involvement in l'ANS. He suspected Eric would have preferred more, but the former spy's loyalty to his lover kept him from pushing. Jean didn't know the whole story behind Eric's placement as Marcel's spy, but he had heard enough from Orlando to know that significant tension still existed between Eric and his former friends, Alain and Thierry. Hopefully that wouldn't be a problem.

"Does Thierry know Eric and Vincent will be there?"

"He said he didn't have a problem with it," Raymond replied. "I can't be perceived as playing favorites, so I didn't ask him until after Vincent had agreed to help, but Thierry didn't even blink, as if he'd expected it."

"He has to be aware how rare his affinity is and of other wizards who share it," Jean mused. "He probably expected it even if he didn't suggest it."

Raymond nodded. "We have an hour until everyone gets here. I should check with Fabienne about the outreach campaign in the provinces. We were supposed to have new materials to send out to the local chapters of l'ANS for distribution to various youth organizations, hoping to find and mentor young wizards as soon as their magical abilities begin to emerge. I've been so busy with l'Institut that I'm not sure I've talked to her since we closed on the monastery. I can't keep neglecting the rest of our agenda."

"Check in with her now," Jean said, "but I'd be willing to bet it's all taken care of and everything is ready to go or indeed has already been sent. You don't have to run everything yourself."

Raymond stuck his head out of his office. "Fabienne, are the new outreach materials ready to send out?"

"They went out yesterday," Fabienne said, her lacquered nails clicking over her keyboard. "There's a memo on your desk about it, along with some things that need your signature. The memos are just to keep you informed, but if you could find time to sign a few things, it would make it a lot easier to keep the organization running while you're getting l'Institut set up."

"I don't pay you enough," Raymond said.

"No, you don't, but if you did, you wouldn't have money for anything else," Fabienne joked back. "We will all benefit from what you're doing with l'Institut, and once it's functioning, it won't need as much of your time. We all understand that."

"I'm pretty sure I don't deserve you," Raymond told her.

She smiled. "Maybe not, but we deserve you."

Inside Raymond's office, Jean didn't try to hide his smile. Raymond would eventually learn to believe in himself. He left Raymond to his signatures and went to check on his own inbox. It probably wouldn't be as full as Raymond's, but he had responsibilities of his own.

AT PRECISELY two o'clock, Jean returned to Raymond's office to find Marcel, Thierry, and Sebastien already inside. "Good afternoon, gentlemen," he said as he walked inside. "Are we ready to go?"

"We're just waiting for Vincent and Eric," Raymond said, "but if you want to go ahead with Thierry, Marcel and Sebastien, I can wait for them. Thierry has been there before. He can take Jean and guide Marcel with Sebastien."

"Are you sure you don't mind?" Thierry asked.

"No, go ahead," Raymond insisted. "The sooner you get there, the sooner we can get to work."

"This is quite the compound you have here," Marcel observed when he and Jean arrived in Dommartin a few minutes later.

"It still needs a lot of work," Jean demurred, "but it will be a fitting tribute to a true visionary."

"Oh, my boy, you keep telling yourself that. I was a desperate man in an untenable position. Nothing more."

Jean knew better than that, but he also knew better than to contradict Marcel. "Let me show you around. I know most of what Raymond intends."

"I'd love a tour."

Jean escorted Marcel across the cloister and into the main building. "This will be the primary focus of l'Institut, both the research and the school. We'll start the repairs with this area. Thierry can tell you better what needs to be done, or you can probably tell yourself. We'll use the old cells either for lodging or offices, and the other areas will be classroom and research space."

"Has Raymond thought about naming a director yet?" Marcel asked.

"He's torn," Jean confided. "He wants to do it himself, but he knows he's needed in Paris as well, and he doesn't see how he can do both."

"He probably can't," Marcel said. "I know how much work it is to run l'ANS. I did it for years. And he's started several new initiatives on top of maintaining the existing ones."

"He was checking on a new outreach program this morning," Jean recounted. "And all upset because he hadn't had time for it this past week. I don't know how to help him."

"Make sure he surrounds himself with competent people, and don't let him spend more than a reasonable amount of time working," Marcel advised. "We aren't fighting a war anymore. If something doesn't get done today, it will get done tomorrow. Other than maintaining the magical equilibrium, nothing he is doing is time sensitive."

"I think he would disagree with you on that."

"I know he would, but I'm just an old man. You're his partner. His lover. You have ways of taking care of him and making sure he rests that aren't open to me. Don't be afraid to use them."

Jean laughed. "I'll remember that. There are the others. I imagine Raymond is eager to get started."

They walked back to where the other wizards stood, just inside the main doorway to the abbey. "Where shall we start?" Marcel asked, his voice jovial.

"Here at the entrance," Raymond said. "I think we should secure this area, then work deeper into the building. Once we have a few areas safe, we can start bringing people in to remodel and prepare the space for its future uses."

"How do you propose to do this?" Vincent asked. "I haven't done any work on an elemental level in a long time, and I'm not sure I've ever done the kind of repair work we'll need to do here."

"Thierry and Sebastien will work together," Raymond replied. "Thierry is familiar with what needs to be done. Sebastien will augment his abilities. I hoped Eric would be able to supplement you, and Jean and I could help Marcel."

"As much as I appreciate you wanting to let me work with Vincent," Eric interrupted, "that probably isn't the smartest use of our resources. Yes, I can boost Vincent's strength, but I'm not a vampire and we don't have your kind of partnership. You and your partner could add far more to Vincent's abilities, and Marcel is so powerful on his own that he can do more alone. Let me work with him, and you work with Vincent."

Raymond looked at the big, bald wizard. "I don't have a problem with that if Vincent doesn't."

"Thank you. Not everyone wants to work with someone who bears Serrier's mark."

Raymond swore he could feel Serrier's spell cutting down his back again at Vincent's words. "I can hardly criticize you for that when I bear the same scar."

"You just came to your senses long before I did."

Raymond shrugged. "You came to your senses too, and you saved at least two lives in the process. I can't force others to accept you, but you don't need to question where you stand with me."

"Someone will have to remind me how to do this."

"Give me your hand," Marcel said. "I'll help you once, and then once you remember, you can go from there. Don't feel like you have to do as much as Thierry or as me. Any repair you do is one closer to being done."

Vincent held out his hand. Marcel placed it on the wall next to one of Thierry's markers and began a soft incantation, guiding Vincent's magic through the process of repairing a fissure in the stone.

"Now you try it."

Vincent repeated the spell Marcel had used on the next weak spot, struggling a little to recreate the magical melding. He started to despair when he felt a surge of unfamiliar strength. Suddenly the solution seemed simple, and he completed the repair in three heartbeats.

"Was that you?" Vincent asked, turning to Raymond.

Raymond nodded. "You looked like you were struggling. I can't do what you do with the stone, but I can add strength. There's no reason for you to wear yourself out before we've even gotten started."

Vincent looked dubious. "I'm not sure you're as incapable as you claim. Your magic gave me more than just strength."

Raymond shrugged. "I've studied a lot of things in my life, but there's a difference between book knowledge and practical ability. I have the book knowledge. You have the talent. The combination should be quite effective, particularly when we throw Jean into the mix."

"Then I guess we should get started."

"This will be easiest if I'm touching you somewhere," Raymond said. "Your shoulders or your arm. Whatever will be most comfortable for you."

"Probably my shoulders," Vincent replied. "I'll need my hands free to work with the walls."

Raymond moved into position behind Vincent, his hands resting lightly on the other wizard's shoulders. A moment later, he felt Jean move behind him, his hands settling heavily on Raymond's hips. He smothered a smile, sure he knew exactly what was going through Jean's mind at the possessive gesture and the sudden, sharp pinch of fangs in his neck.

Jean tasted Raymond's amusement in his blood, but it did nothing to stifle his urge to stake his claim deeper and more visibly on Raymond's skin. The wizard was *his*, damn it! He pressed closer against Raymond, letting his groin brush the wizard's buttocks, just in case he needed that reminder. Raymond chuckled, making Jean roll his eyes. It was going to be a long day.

Chapter 11

WHEN THEY had all reached the limits of their magical abilities, Raymond thanked everyone, fully expecting the others to return to Paris. They all lingered, however, so he took their presence as permission and put them to work cleaning the old-fashioned way. Eric made a comment about thinking he had seen the last of a mop and bucket when he stopped working as a waiter. They all laughed, and Raymond breathed a sigh of relief that the tension seemed to have dissipated after a morning working together. Leaving Vincent, Thierry, and Eric to clean, Raymond took the two vampires with him in search of the best rooms to convert for the vampires who would live at l'Institut for the duration of the educational program.

"The smaller the windows, the better," Sebastien said as they walked into the first of the monks' cells. "We can install volets and curtains and the rest, but ultimately, unless they find a partner—and even for some time after that until they start trusting the partnership—the vampires will be most comfortable in a room with as little exterior light as possible. They can walk outside at night if they want fresh air."

"If we make absolutely sure the route from their room to a classroom is free of sunlight, will they attend classes during the day?" Raymond asked as he made a note on the floorplan of the abbey.

"They might," Jean said, "but they'll be far more comfortable and therefore far more attentive if the classes are at night. It's your call, of course. Most of the vampires you could call on as instructors would be willing to teach at night as well as during the day, and I would think the partnered wizards would feel the same, if only because they surely remember how hard it was for their partners at first."

"Are you planning on using primarily partners as instructors?" Sebastien asked.

"I think we have to," Raymond said. "We can discuss agendas for specific sessions all we want, but ultimately the people best able to discuss the ins and outs of a partnership are people who have lived it."

"That certainly makes sense," Sebastien agreed. "I haven't discussed it with Thierry, but I'd be glad to take on a session or two if that will help you out."

Raymond smiled. "Thank you. I hope to eventually have a full-time staff of people who can do both the teaching and the research, but like everything else, that will take time to put in place. A limited number of partnerships formed during the war, and many of those people had jobs to go back to when the war ended."

"What else needs to be done that the physical strength of two vampires can take care of while everyone recovers their magical strength?" Sebastien asked.

"Too much," Raymond said with a sigh, "but the first thing has to be clearing out the debris left from years of disuse. We can't bring in new furniture or fixtures until we get rid of the old."

"Then I guess we'd better get started lifting, Jean," Sebastien said. "Surely between the two of us, we can clear a few of these inner rooms so there will be space for a dozen or so vampires when Raymond's ready to start classes."

"If I can get a dozen total people for the first class, I'll be happy," Raymond admitted. "I want to start small, to make sure we have everything in place before we expand."

"Thierry said something about Alain doing some recruiting. Did he have any luck?"

"I haven't heard yet," Raymond replied. "He had already left for the day when we came back into the office last night, and he hadn't checked in this morning when we came out here to start the repairs. I'll try to catch him this evening."

"That's what phones are for, you know," Sebastien said as he gestured for Jean to grab one end of a huge, dilapidated armoire, the door swinging drunkenly on its one remaining hinge as the vampires picked it up. Raymond could not stop the jolt of surprise at how easily the two vampires moved the huge piece of furniture. He had seen evidence of their strength on too many occasions to count, but he had yet to grow accustomed to it.

"I... I don't think I have his number," Raymond admitted.

Sebastien rolled his eyes as he rattled it off. "You really have to stop thinking like you're still an outcast. You're the president of l'ANS, in case you've forgotten."

Raymond hadn't forgotten, but it was far harder to take charge with Thierry and Alain than it was with those outside the organization who had no history with him. "I'll add it to my phonebook when we get back to the office."

"YOUR APARTMENT used to be easier to get into."

The phantom voice and the threat the words represented sent tension racing through Raymond's body. His wand jumped to his hand almost without his being aware he had reached for it.

"Relax," Jean murmured at his side. "Céline is an old friend."

Not entirely reassured, Raymond lowered his wand nonetheless, knowing that even without it, he was hardly helpless. He would give Jean's "old friend" the benefit of the doubt for now. As long as she kept her distance.

"It's been a long time, Céline," Jean said, embracing the woman and giving her the traditional kiss on each cheek. "What brings you to Paris, and particularly to my house, now?"

"Cour business, if there's somewhere we can talk in private," Céline replied, casting a dismissive glance in Raymond's direction.

"If it's Cour business, then we should go inside," Jean agreed. "Raymond and I will be happy to discuss anything that needs discussing with you."

"A mortal?" Céline scoffed. "This is Cour business, Jean. He doesn't need to be involved."

"Not merely a mortal. A wizard. The president of l'ANS. And my partner," Jean enumerated. "If it involves me, it involves him. Now, shall we go inside?"

Céline followed the two men inside, her surprise clear on her face when Raymond instructed the wards to allow her admittance. It was a petty gesture on his part and he knew it—a wave of his hand would have admitted her—but he wanted her to realize exactly how fully he fit into Jean's life.

When they entered the salon, Jean gestured for Céline to have a seat and offered her something to drink, making Raymond smile again. Even for vampires who needed no sustenance other than blood and could barely register the taste when they did ingest other things, the formulas of hospitality remained unchanged. Jean returned a moment later, two glasses of cognac in hand, one for Céline and one for Raymond. "I thought you'd enjoy a drink to relax."

Raymond shot Jean a quick smile, appreciating the gesture even as he recognized the subtlety of the game Jean was playing in handing him his drink before giving Céline hers. Perhaps he was finally beginning to understand le jeu des Cours.

Returning to Raymond's side on the loveseat near the fireplace, Jean waited while Raymond and Céline sipped their drinks. "Ah, Raymond, I forgot to introduce you to our guest," Jean said after a moment. "Raymond Payet, this is Céline Girardot, chef de la Cour dijonnaise. Céline, Raymond Payet."

"Enchanté," Raymond said with a nod in the woman's direction. He reminded himself not to assume all the vampire leaders would be male simply because the few he had met were.

"C'est mon plaisir," Céline replied.

The formalities complete, Jean relaxed against the back of the couch and waited for Céline to begin. She had shown up on his doorstep. The next move was hers.

"Renaud called me yesterday," Céline said after a few moments. "He heard about your involvement with a project in le Morvan, and he thinks you're trying to impinge on his territory."

Jean rolled his eyes. "First of all, his territory is Autun. There isn't a Cour in any of the villages in le Morvan because there aren't enough vampires in any of them to support one. And secondly, *I* haven't done anything. L'ANS has purchased land in Dommartin for a project that will benefit any wizards and vampires who choose to be involved in it. Not my Cour, not his. All of them. Or none of them, if the vampires choose not to participate."

"And yet here you sit with the president of l'ANS," Céline pointed out. "You're splitting hairs, Jean. What do you want me to tell Renaud?"

"If he's so determined to meet with me, why didn't he come or call himself?" Jean asked.

"Because his reaction to you is the same as your reaction to him. You're oil and water, and you have been since he took in the vampire you banished from your Cour. That was his choice as it was yours, but he's not about to lose ground in le jeu des Cours by coming to you now, and he knows you won't come to him, so he called on me instead because the last thing I want is a war on my turf. Say what you want about le Morvan and its lack of Cours, we both know all of Burgundy looks to me when there's a problem," Céline said.

"So what are you suggesting?" Jean asked. His voice was even, but Raymond could feel the tension investing the slender frame next to him. He doubted Céline could see it, which made him realize how far he had come in the past year in regards to his lover.

"Saturday night at ten o'clock," Céline said, "in the crypt of St Bénigne. The priests won't disturb us, and neither will anyone else."

Jean rolled his eyes. "Could you be any more stereotypical, Céline? The crypt? Really? Surely we can find somewhere comfortable to meet. A private room in a restaurant, the cave of a café, somewhere... civilized."

Céline glared at him. "Could you be any more condescending, Jean?" she mocked. "When you broker a meeting on your territory, you can pick the setting." She rose and set the glass on the table. "Be there on Saturday. Monsieur Payet, I'd say it's been a pleasure, but we'd both know I was lying."

Jean sucked in a sharp breath, on his feet almost faster than Raymond's eye could track, but the woman was already across the room and out the door. "Salope," Jean muttered, turning back to Raymond. "I should refuse to go just for that comment."

"But you won't," Raymond said, "because whatever this Renaud wants to talk about, you need to hear him out. We have too much riding on the success of l'Institut to make an enemy of him if we can help it."

"He made an enemy of me twenty years ago," Jean muttered.

"You want to tell me about that?" Raymond asked. "You were stubbornly vague when we talked about it before."

Jean shrugged. "There isn't anything to tell. I banished a vampire because she had seduced another vampire's lover after they made a commitment before the Cour. Renaud chose to take her in. I didn't appreciate his choice."

Jean chose not to dwell on the scene in front of the Congrès des chefs, the insults that had flown back and forth as Renaud accused Jean of favoring mortals over his own kind, as Jean warned Renaud of the folly of trusting a pretty face. Renaud had stalked out in anger and had not returned to the Congrès des chefs since. The meeting in Dijon would reignite those old insults, he was quite sure, because once again Jean had chosen to ally himself with mortals—even if that was the best decision he had ever made. Renaud would not see it that way, and the fact that the alliance was now impinging on what Renaud would consider his territory would only exacerbate an old argument.

Raymond's arms encircled Jean from behind, the wizard's lips nuzzling beneath Jean's dark hair to find the sensitive patch of skin behind his ear. "Not many people approved of Marcel's decision to take me in after I defected from Serrier's ranks. Maybe all she needed was a chance."

"I doubt that. The last I heard, she'd left Autun as well, although I don't know the circumstances, since Renaud has chosen not to return to the Congrès des chefs since then," Jean replied, leaning back into Raymond's embrace. "It doesn't matter. She isn't the issue. The issue is his continued disdain for anyone and anything outside the world of vampires. It's the same kind of supremacy issues that Serrier espoused, only for a different race of beings. Renaud was a peasant before he was turned, at the mercy of a cruel local landowner, and so he despises anyone with power because he fears they'll gain power over him. What he doesn't realize is how many allies he loses in the process and how much stronger we all are together than we could ever be on our own."

"You're preaching to the choir here," Raymond joked, licking a stripe up the side of Jean's neck. His lover was not usually this difficult to seduce. The visit from the other chef de la Cour had obviously rattled him more than he was letting on. "We'll deal with that on Saturday. Tonight we have other things to deal with."

"Like what?" Jean asked, turning in Raymond's embrace, a suspicious expression on his face.

"Like the fact that you've neither fucked me nor fed in three days. That's entirely too long."

Jean groaned at the sinful image conjured by Raymond's words. Raymond spread out on his bed, skin winter pale against the dark sheets, legs wrapped around Jean's hips or perhaps draped over his shoulders....

"In the bedroom," he said, his voice gravelly with desire. "Now."

Raymond's stomach flipped at the tone of Jean's voice. He may have only heard it a few times since they had become lovers, but he knew exactly what it portended. He was about to get ravished.

Releasing his grip on Jean, he all but ran for the bedroom, shedding clothes as he went. The moment he was naked, Jean's arms closed around him, lifting him easily from the ground and tossing him onto the bed. Raymond gasped, his heart pounding at the feral look on the vampire's face. Jean maintained an affable façade, a civilized man despite the requirements of his existence—but a far more primal creature existed beneath the surface, strong enough to take and hold power in the largest Cour in France. Strong enough to break a man in two if he chose. Raymond shivered at the thought of being at the mercy of that creature. "Come on," he goaded. "Fuck me already."

The sound that left Jean's throat should have left Raymond paralyzed in fear, something between a hiss and a growl and all beast, but Raymond already knew he had nothing to fear from his vampire. He simply bent his knees and spread them wide, offering his body to Jean.

The submissive posture snapped the chains of Jean's control, the monster within breaking free. He fell on the body beneath him, needing to taste blood like a drowning man needed to breathe. Raymond tilted his head to the side, offering his neck, but tonight that would not be enough. Tonight, Jean needed more. Even mindless as he was, though, he would not take Raymond unprepared. He fumbled for the lube, his coordination failing in the face of this overwhelming desire. Getting the cap open, he coated his fingers, stabbing hard and deep into Raymond's quivering opening. The wizard thrashed beneath him, but Jean knew his lover well enough to recognize the movements as pleas for more. His fingers probed quickly, stretching with far less finesse than usual, but Jean had no more patience left. The moment he felt the guardian muscle give beneath his fingers he pulled them free, stroking his hand over his cock and plunging into the throbbing heat. His elbows caught Raymond's knees, lifting them as he moved forward so that Raymond's calves rested on his shoulders.

Raymond cried out, but the sound only drove Jean on, the demon within him responding to the desperation in his lover's tone. He turned his head, finding the smooth patch of skin behind Raymond's knee where his blood pulsed near the surface. He licked over it once, drawing a gasp of breath from his lover, before biting hard, blood rushing out to fill his mouth with all the richness of Raymond's heart. Jean's eyes closed against the nearly unbearable need to claim the man beneath him in every way possible. He wanted his brand on Raymond's neck, his claim as public, as visible, and as binding as magic and tradition could make it. He knew all the reasons Raymond resisted, and in his sane moments, he could accept them, but there was nothing sane about the way he was feeling now. Tearing his fangs free, he turned to the other side, biting the other leg as well as his hips pounded into his lover's body. Raymond tossed like a rag doll beneath him, totally submissive to Jean's demands. And even that was not enough. "Come for me," he demanded, his fangs leaving their current sheath as his hand closed around Raymond's cock. "Now."

Raymond's body responded mindlessly to the order, his cock twitching within Jean's grasp.

His need for blood even greater than his need for climax, Jean pulled out, releasing Raymond's legs and pouncing on his stomach, licking away the semen coating it before biting deeply into his lover's abdomen. Raymond cried out again, but Jean could taste only a matching need in the wizard's blood, so he sucked harder, drawing more and more of the life-giving fluid into his mouth. Raymond's hands found his hair, eliciting a deep growl from Jean's throat at the thought of even such illusory control. He grabbed Raymond's wrists, pinning them in an implacable grip as he bit his way higher, his fangs penetrating the heavy muscle of Raymond's chest, directly above his nipple. As he drew blood into his mouth once more, his tongue swiped across the sensitive bud, reigniting Raymond's flagging passion.

"Harder," Raymond pleaded. "Putain, Jean. Bite me again!"

Jean would have said he had no control left to lose, but hearing Raymond begging for more triggered something unprecedented inside him. He could no longer keep track of how often he bit or where his fangs scored his lover's flesh. His only connection with reality was the hot rush of blood over his tongue and the spiraling desire he could taste within. Mind and body spinning out of control, he pounded into Raymond, his cock plundering Raymond's passage as his fangs plundered Raymond's flesh.

When his climax finally overcame him and rationality returned, he could feel the cooling strands of Raymond's release against his belly and knew his lover had found pleasure in what they had done, but the sight of the bleeding tears all over the wizard's torso were a knife to his heart. He did not act this way. He had sworn he would never again give in to the beast within him. Grégoire Casile, his maker, had taken him to feed the night he was turned, and in his ignorance he had lost control, killing the man he fed from. The death itself had left him chilled to the bone, but only after he realized what had happened. As he had fed from his willing prey—for the man had been willing not only to feed him but to assuage the sexual desire that feeding had raised in the newly turned vampire—he had lost all awareness of anything but the powerful feelings of taking a lover for the first time and of the heady rush of blood into his system. When he had drawn back finally, replete, glassy eyes stared up at him from a lax face and a body that looked as savaged as Raymond's now did. Jean had determined to walk into the sunlight the moment it rose rather than risk becoming the kind of monster who could do such a thing, but Grégoire had stopped him, promising to teach him control. The older vampire had been true to his word, and Jean's beast had not slipped its leash since that night.

Until now.

"I'll get a rag to clean you up."

"Don't move," Raymond ordered, his voice brooking no argument. He had no idea what was responsible for the odd look on Jean's face or the unaccustomed withdrawal, but he was not about to let it go unchallenged. "You'll stay right here in bed and hold me. You can clean me up later."

Jean subsided onto the sheets, but while his arms opened for Raymond to move into his embrace, he did not cradle the wizard close the way he usually did, nor did he react to the tender kisses Raymond pressed along the line of his jaw. He had no idea why Raymond was not angry with him, but he could not help but be glad.

"What brought that on?" Raymond murmured huskily. "You've lost control before, but never like that."

Jean flinched. "It won't happen again. I swear. I don't know why I couldn't control myself tonight, but you don't need to worry. I won't hurt you again."

"Who said anything about being hurt?" Raymond asked, pushing up on one elbow so he could peer into Jean's face in the low light from the lamp on the bedside table. "Ravished, maybe. Desired beyond my wildest imaginings, certainly, but I'm not hurt."

"How can you not be hurt?" Jean protested. "You're covered in bite marks, every one of them bleeding. I don't act this way. The first thing every vampire learns is how to control the beast within him, the one that would rampage and kill if he didn't control it. That beast got loose tonight, and that hasn't happened to me since the night I was turned."

"And yet you didn't kill me," Raymond pointed out reasonably. "You covered me in love bites and you pounded me through the mattress just like I asked you to do, but you didn't kill me, and you didn't hurt me. I'm not saying I'd want it that rough every time we make love, but I certainly wasn't complaining tonight, and I won't complain if it happens again occasionally. The only reason I'm not slumped on the bed, all but asleep, is that you tried to leave. Now, will you hold me and let me sleep in your arms?"

Jean had no idea what he was supposed to say to that, so he simply nodded and drew Raymond down so that his head rested in the hollow of Jean's shoulder. He stroked the short, dark hair tenderly, trying to atone for his earlier roughness. He had no idea what had short-circuited his control tonight, but he did not intend for it to happen again.

Chapter 12

"SOMEBODY HAD a good night last night," Sebastien said with a grin when he saw Raymond and Jean the next evening. "I so rarely see even one bite mark on your neck."

Raymond flushed and lifted his hands to his neck, hiding the plethora of marks. "It was a rather enjoyable evening," he admitted, "but I probably ought to get these taken care of before the press conference tonight. It's one thing to appear with a single mark—I've been doing that since the alliance began—but nobody seeing me right now would have any doubt Jean was far more than my partner."

Sebastien shook his head. "It's not about being more than your partner. It's that they don't understand what it means to be partners the way we use the word. It's a deceptively simple word for so complex a relationship."

"It is," Jean agreed, voice tight. He could not decide which upset him more: the reminder of how completely he had lost control last night or the fact that Raymond felt the need to hide it. "And it's going to get more and more difficult to cover up that fact as l'Institut makes the partnerships more prevalent."

"Speaking of that, Alain said he had some interest from a few wizards, but has anyone met with the vampires?" Thierry asked.

"Not yet," Jean replied. "Orlando volunteered, but I'm not sure how well that will be received nor how well that truly represents what we're offering."

Sebastien nodded. "The Cour turned out in force for Couthon's *judicium*. There isn't a vampire in Paris who isn't aware of the brand on Alain's neck. If Orlando goes, at least if he goes alone, everyone will equate a partnership with an Aveu de Sang. I'd offer to help, but I need to be with Thierry at the abbey."

"I know," Jean replied. "I thought perhaps Mireille would be glad of a chance to interact with the Cour again. Between helping Caroline cope with her blindness and working for monsieur Lombard, she has very little time for herself these days."

"That's a good idea," Sebastien agreed. "I'd bet she'd be glad to help. Orlando could go with her. There's no reason they couldn't both represent l'Institut. If nothing else, it might not hurt to remind people that the partnerships have the potential to become very personal. We've said it a hundred times, but people don't always listen."

"Don't we know it," Jean muttered, thinking of Paul and Guillemin, the wizard and vampire who provoked the current push for l'Institut. "In the meantime, Raymond and I have a press conference to prepare for. If you see

Orlando, would you ask him to talk to Mireille and see if she'd be willing to go with him? If she says yes, they can start tonight. Hit the goth clubs, maybe go by Sang Froid—which reminds me that I need to talk to Angélique as well—some of the cafés. All the usual places."

"I'll tell him if I see him," Sebastien promised. "Go do what you have to do."

"We're for Dommartin to see what else we can accomplish today," Thierry added. "Even if it takes us weeks, we can still work faster than stonemasons who aren't using magic. Between us and them, we'll have the abbey usable in no time."

"Thanks," Raymond said. "Before you go, though, Thierry, could I avail myself of your wand? I can't go into the press conference with my neck looking like this, and I didn't think about it when I got dressed this morning."

"Of course," Thierry said. "If you'll excuse us, gentlemen, Raymond and I will just be a minute."

Jean's face tightened, but he did not protest as Raymond and Thierry disappeared into a nearby office.

When the two vampires were alone, Sebastien let out a low wolf whistle. "You did a number on him last night. I'm surprised he's walking straight."

"His self-mastery is beyond compare," Jean said, knowing it was no explanation.

"I know we haven't always been the best of friends, but I have to admit I wouldn't have expected to see one of your lovers looking that way. Leighton's, yes, but yours, not so much," Sebastien said.

Jean flushed, striking the wall angrily. "Don't remind me. I don't know what happened. I'm never like that, but I couldn't seem to stop. His blood is like a drug."

Sebastien nodded. "I understand that feeling. Every time I feed, I curse the magic that prohibits an Aveu de Sang from working twice. What I have with Thierry is like nothing I've ever known, not even my bond with my Avoué, which I would have sworn could not be surpassed. I can only imagine what it's like for Alain and Orlando, who have both the Aveu de Sang and the power of a partnership."

Jean could imagine all too easily, because he had spent far too much time dwelling on something he knew would not come to pass while Raymond had any leadership within l'ANS. "Another one of those things we'll probably never understand," Jean agreed. "The list seems to get longer, not shorter, each time we talk about it."

Sebastien laughed. "There's a reason I was never good at science and the like. The more you understand, the more you realize how little you know. Et voilà Thierry. We'll let you know what we get done today."

Jean watched as Sebastien joined his partner, his arm going easily around Thierry's waist as they walked toward their offices. He envied them their easy rapport. In private, he and Raymond were every bit as at ease with each other as Thierry and Sebastien, but Raymond pulled that damnable reserve around him like a cloak each time they left their apartment.

"It should be an interesting evening," Raymond said when he reached Jean's side. "We've been getting more questions recently about l'Institut, and now we actually have some answers for people."

Jean was not sure "interesting" was the word he would have chosen, but he let it go. Raymond had always been a master of understatement.

THE PRESSROOM was packed. The last time Raymond had seen it so full, he was giving his acceptance speech for his new position as president of l'ANS. That had been news, but the weekly doings of l'ANS rarely brought more than the reporters from the wizarding newspapers. "What have they heard?" Raymond murmured to Jean.

"I don't know," Jean replied, "but be on your guard. Don't let them trick you into revealing more than you're ready to say."

Raymond nodded, straightening his tie and rubbing idly at a spot on his chest where Jean had bitten him particularly deeply last night. It throbbed slightly, reminding him of how thoroughly he had been loved. He almost said something to Jean, but the final moments before a press conference were hardly the ideal time for personal declarations. He had waited this long. He could wait for the right moment.

Jean saw the gesture and flinched, thinking the bite must be bothering Raymond even with Thierry's healing spell. The marks on Raymond's neck were completely gone, even the bruising around the bites. If the spell had not healed Raymond's chest, he must have done far more damage there. Feeling sick to his stomach, he summoned a wan smile for Raymond as the clock rang out the hour.

Taking a deep breath, Raymond straightened his jacket and walked onto the dais. "Bonsoir, mesdames et messieurs. Welcome to our weekly press conference. I'm not sure what's brought so many of you out tonight, but I hope I'll have something of interest for you all."

"What are you hiding out in the provinces?" one of the reporters yelled.

"I wasn't aware of hiding anything," Raymond replied coolly. "A little less than a month ago, we announced our intention to purchase the old monastery in Dommartin with the plan of turning it into an institute for magical research and study. I'm sorry you weren't here when that announcement was made, but if you'll check the November editions of your colleagues' papers, you'll find a note of it in several of them."

"Why not have it in Paris then?" the reporter shouted back, clearly unperturbed by Raymond's sharp response.

"Have you looked at real estate prices in Paris?" Raymond scoffed. "L'ANS has a budget, yes, but not that big a budget. We couldn't locate a property in Paris that fit both our size and budgetary needs. The monastery in le Morvan fit both, and we think it will be a great economic resource to the community as well, since we hope to have a staff in residence there within the next six months."

"And what exactly will this staff be doing?"

"Addressing questions of magical importance and offering an education program to wizards and vampires who have an interest in the kinds of partnerships that formed during l'émeute des Sorciers," Raymond answered evenly. "What did you think they would be doing?"

"Why do they need a school for that?" the reporter demanded, ignoring Raymond's question. "Is that really the best use of l'ANS funds?"

"I don't like your insinuations, monsieur. L'ANS is a private nonprofit organization that receives no public funding," Raymond said, "so we are only accountable to our donors for how we spend our money. As for the reasons for the school, the partnerships are far more complicated than the simple exchange of blood between a mortal and a vampire. It's only fair to the people involved to make sure they understand the commitment they're making so they can choose whether to get involved. You wouldn't expect a doctor to start practicing medicine without some experience with the requirements of the field. The same is true of the partnerships."

"How difficult can it be? You let a vampire bite you."

Raymond took a deep breath, reminding himself not to be baited. "I think this line of questioning has gone far enough. My plan tonight was to announce that l'Institut Marcel Chavinier will begin accepting applications for its first educational seminars next week. The first seminar is currently scheduled to begin on January fifth. Any interested wizards or vampires should apply at the offices of l'ANS by the twentieth of December. We already have four wizards signed up. We will be accepting a maximum of ten wizards and ten vampires for the first session, which will last one week and require participants to live at l'Institut for the duration of the program."

"Why is it a residential program?" another reporter called.

"Because it's a very time-intensive schedule," Raymond explained, "and having everyone on site will allow time for discussion among the participants. Finding a partner is not simply a question of knowledge but of compatibility. Any vampire can bite any wizard, but only the right combination creates a partnership with long-lasting positive benefits. It would do neither of us any good if monsieur Dumont's partner bit me instead of biting him, for example."

In the wings, Jean bit his lip to hold back the hiss of displeasure evoked by the thought of any vampire biting Raymond. He would destroy any who tried. He consciously forced down the beast inside him. He had given in to it last night, but he would not let it rule his every action. Concentrating on Raymond helped, so he focused on his wizard and the continuing verbal sparring between him and the press corps.

"What about the vampires?" the reporter from *Libération* called. "Even I know they have to feed more often than that."

"Arrangements are being made," Raymond said vaguely. "You forget that distance is no object for a wizard. It is no more of a problem for those in the company of wizards. We will not starve them while they are with us."

"And if the citizens of Dommartin are not willing donors?" the reporter challenged.

"Then we will take them somewhere where there are willing donors or find donors willing to come to them," Raymond said. "Now, unless there are other questions—"

"I've heard the partnerships are sexual, not just practical," the reporter who had first hassled Raymond shouted. "Are you opening a brothel, monsieur Payet?"

Raymond rolled his eyes, eliciting laughter from the reporters who knew him from the weekly press conferences. "I don't think that question deserves an answer. Good evening, mesdames et messieurs."

He left the dais without looking back, despite the questions shouted in his direction.

"Nice dodge," Jean murmured when Raymond joined him again. "You know the question will come up again."

"And my answer will stay the same," Raymond replied. "Until we know definitively that the partnership bond can only function when the partners are also lovers, I will continue to reply that way. We will be upfront with the participants in the seminars about the possibility—"

"The likelihood," Jean corrected.

"The likelihood," Raymond allowed, "of the partnerships becoming personal, but forewarned is forearmed. We resisted even the wild magic working on us. Yes, that was temporary, but it was far more powerful than the day-to-day pressure of our partnership. We won't make the same mistake that led to the wild magic breaking free last time, so we don't have to worry about that pushing people into uncomfortable situations. I know that was the first time Adèle and Jude had sex. Do you remember her reaction the next day?"

Jean remembered all too clearly. Adèle had stormed into Milice headquarters with bite marks still oozing blood, demanding to know what spell had compelled her into bed with a man she hated. Far more troubling to Jean was the fact that they had continued to have sex after the wild magic was contained. He wanted to know why she had not gone back to resisting once the Piège-Pouvoir was complete. "I wonder how many other people fell prey to the wild magic and never 'recovered'. It might be worth asking. Not to mention asking if any who didn't give in to the bond at that point have continued to relate only on a magical level rather than a personal one."

"That assumes we can find anyone else who resisted that night," Raymond said.

"Angélique did, although I'm fairly sure she and David are also lovers as well as partners now," Jean replied, "but if she resisted and we resisted, others may have as well. Like you keep saying, this is why we need l'Institut—to help us find answers to all our questions."

"Good news, Raymond," Fabienne called as Raymond and Jean neared Raymond's office. "I just spoke with Luc Cabalet, the chef de la Cour in Amiens, and he's willing to come to l'Institut with his partner to help with the repairs. They've even offered to stay on site for a week so we don't have to worry about transporting them back and forth, although they have a few commitments over the next two weeks. They just need two rooms to be ready."

Raymond and Jean glanced at each other with raised eyebrows. "Two rooms?" Raymond verified. "I think we can have two rooms ready by then, particularly if we tell Thierry we need to focus on getting them done."

Fabienne handed Raymond a slip of paper. "That's Thierry's number. You can call him and tell him now."

Raymond looked down at the scrap of paper. "How did you know I didn't have his number?"

Fabienne smirked at him. "Because you never have anyone's number unless I've given it to you. Since he gave me a new number last week after he lost his cell, it stands to reason you didn't have it either."

"We'll need to arrange food for Magali," Raymond began.

"I've already checked with several restaurants in the area," Fabienne interrupted. "They've all said they'd be more than happy to help provide meals for anyone living at the abbey until we can get the kitchen staffed. I've also put help wanted ads in several local and regional papers and online. There's no reason we need to employ wizards to cook or to maintain the property. We'll have far more support from the locals if we hire from the surrounding villages than if we bring people in. Not to mention that locals won't have to live on the property so we won't have to worry about having space for them before we start the seminars."

"You're brilliant," Raymond told her with a smile, grateful not for the first time that Jean had suggested the African vampire as his admin. He would be lost without her.

"I know," she replied. "Just remember that at the end of the year when you're considering my bonus."

Raymond laughed and shook his head. "I won't forget. I promise."

Fortunately for Jean's peace of mind, Fabienne let them go after that. Jean was not sure how much longer he could contain his jealous reaction to the easy banter. He knew Raymond was faithful to him and that Fabienne had no more interest in Raymond than Raymond did in her. Usually he could listen to them with amusement, but today everything seemed to provoke his inner demon. He wondered desperately what it would take to appease the fiend.

"I've been thinking about the issue of the vampires needing to feed during the seminars," Jean said, choosing to ignore his reaction and focus on practical matters. "For the short term, we could make an arrangement with Angélique to either bring the vampires to Sang Froid or bring some of her employees to the abbey every few days. But if the classes grow larger, that's going to get unwieldy after a while."

"Do you have a suggestion?" Raymond asked.

"I do, although it's up to Angélique to agree," Jean said. "If l'Institut grows the way we hope it will, it might be worth it to her to consider opening a branch of Sang Froid in Dommartin or Château-Chinon. It wouldn't be as large or as profitable as the one in Paris, but we'd have a steady supply of customers for her once we go through the first trial seminars and start doing them continuously."

Raymond chuckled. "We'd have to be very careful how we explain it to local officials. I can see a few of them balking at what appears to be a brothel opening in their sleepy village."

"A restaurant," Jean insisted. "All Angélique sells is blood—and it's been that way for many years—and she pays her employees generously."

"I know that," Raymond assured his lover. "I went with you when the police came to investigate a complaint against Sang Froid last summer. They didn't find any evidence of it being an illicit sex shop despite the allegations. It wouldn't be any different in Dommartin. We just have to make sure we address any concerns upfront."

"If Angélique is even interested," Jean added. "I haven't actually talked to her about it yet." He hesitated before adding, "Have you thought any more about who you might want to name director of l'Institut?"

Raymond sighed. "No. The problem is finding someone who can handle the administration side and the research as well. And someone who would be willing to relocate to Dommartin. I know I said distance is a nonissue for wizards, but I feel like someone needs to be on site in case something happens."

"And you want that someone to be you."

Raymond wanted to deny it—but even if he did, Jean would see right through him. "Yes. I don't want to give up our apartment here, but a part of me wants to be there too."

"Could you hire someone to live there full time so you could commute during the day?" Jean proposed. "It wouldn't be quite the same, but even at boarding schools, the headmaster gets to leave occasionally. As you keep saying, you're a wizard. If the caretaker called you with an emergency, you could be there in a matter of seconds, barely slower than if you lived there. It wouldn't even have to be a wizard. Just someone to keep an eye on things and notify you of anything that came up during the night."

"If I hadn't made a commitment to l'ANS, I'd jump at it in a heartbeat," Raymond said, "but I already have a job and a half with l'ANS."

"So you have a decision to make. You have to decide what's best for you and for the organizations involved. What you can delegate or give up that will best serve the magical community and your own heart. I know Marcel spent the bulk of his life in the service of l'ANS, and I know you were the right choice a year ago—but could someone else do your job as well now, to free you to take on the responsibilities of l'Institut? Or is there someone else who could do that as well as you could, despite your desire to be involved, while you stay on with l'ANS?"

Raymond let out a deep breath. "I wish I knew."

"You don't have to decide right away, but you will have to decide soon." He did not mention that the director of l'Institut would be less in the public eye and would not risk his credibility by also being the Consort of the chef de la Cour.

Chapter 13

THE SIGHT of Raymond's strong back appearing from beneath his jacket and shirt never failed to rouse Jean, particularly the scar that ran parallel to his spine, but Jean turned away from the surely unintentional show when they returned home that night. His fangs dropped the minute Raymond reached for his tie, and it had taken far too much concentration to force them back for his peace of mind. He had savaged Raymond the night before. He did not need to feed, and he had every intention of giving Raymond time to heal before making love to him—carefully and tenderly this time—again.

"Jean?" Raymond said, his voice breaking into Jean's pensive thoughts. "Are you coming to bed?"

Jean turned, intending to make some excuse about not being tired, an excuse he was sure Raymond would have seen right through, when he saw his lover's chest. "You kept them."

Confusion marred Raymond's features for a moment as he looked down at himself. "What, the bites?" Jean nodded. "Of course I kept them. I only asked Thierry to heal the visible ones because I had the press conference tonight. If we had simply been working at the abbey or in the offices, I wouldn't have done even that. I certainly wasn't going to ask him to heal the ones no one can see." Raymond crossed the room to Jean's side. "Or did you not believe me last night when I told you I'd never been so thoroughly ravished?"

Jean had believed that part, but he had not believed Raymond would not regret it later. Tenderly, he drew Raymond into his arms. "You are a marvel to me," he said softly. "Let me show you?"

"You show me all the time," Raymond demurred, but Jean refused to take no for an answer. Keeping his fangs firmly withdrawn and his beast totally in check, he scooped Raymond into his arms, giving no heed to the differences in their size, and lay his lover on the bed. He took a moment to stroke Raymond's hairline, admiring the breadth of his forehead, lightly creased now by the lines of worry that came from the stress of his job. He smoothed them with his fingers, wanting irrationally to lift every care from his lover's shoulders. Lowering his head, he ghosted butterfly kisses across the bridge of Raymond's nose, his high cheekbones, and finally over his lips. He was tempted to linger, but he had other goals in mind, namely the bite marks all over Raymond's body.

Jean kissed his way down Raymond's neck, lingering momentarily where he knew he had bitten the night before, sucking lightly on the skin so as not to raise new bruises. The desire to mark and claim was no less intense than the night before, but this time Jean was ready for it, consciously keeping his touch light and loving rather than letting it turn feral as it had the night before. When he reached Raymond's collarbone, he no longer had to remember where the bites had been because the incisions remained. He tarried over each one, laving it with his tongue to help it heal since he had not taken as much time to lick the wounds closed as he would normally have done. Each mark provided proof of the unfathomable, as far as Jean was concerned. Raymond wanted him, every part of him, even the beast that lurked beneath his control. Working his way down his wizard's body, he found and worshipped every mark he had left the night before, on Raymond's chest, on his belly and hips, on his thighs and calves.

His cock throbbed in his trousers, but he ignored it. He had given in to his darkest desires yesterday. Denying himself now seemed a fitting penance.

Raymond lay quiescent beneath the tender assault, nearly as overwhelmed with tenderness as he had been with savagery the night before. His heart swelled almost to bursting as Jean kissed and licked every bite mark, his lips and tongue teasing around Raymond's nipples without ever actually touching, Jean's fangs not having pierced him there. When his lover moved lower, he held little hope his cock and balls would receive any more attention, but he barely missed it, so caught up in the feeling of being cherished that the arousal simmering in his blood took a back seat. He closed his eyes and let himself drift on the tenderness. Jean was always an attentive lover, but this felt different. Usually when they made love, even without Jean feeding, there was an edge to their interactions, a need to find their release. Raymond felt none of that urgency this time, content to lie still and let Jean take care of him.

Raymond had relaxed so much that the sensation of Jean's tongue on his sac surprised him, adding a sudden layer of need to the welter of emotions running through him. He gasped, lifting his head to stare down at Jean's head between his thighs. Jean looked back at him, his eyes glittering, as he extended his tongue and lingered over Raymond's groin the same way he had lingered over the rest of his body. Raymond's head fell back with a deep groan as Jean licked and sucked his most sensitive flesh, working his way from root to tip and then taking him inside.

The head of his cock bumped the back of Jean's mouth. Raymond tried to pull back so he would not choke his lover—but the vampire's hands stilled his hips as his head lifted for a moment, only to slide back down, taking Raymond's length down his throat. Raymond tossed his head from side to side, his fingers scrabbling in the sheets, trying to ground himself against the upsurge of lust and love that took him totally off guard. His control should have lasted far longer than this, but the need for release snuck up on him, building beneath the surface until it was suddenly undeniable. "Close," he warned.

Jean only sucked harder. Raymond gave up trying to resist and let his orgasm take him, welling out of him in long, slow waves. Jean's head ceased its bobbing, but the gentle sucking continued, drawing out Raymond's climax until he lay limp on the bed. He reached for Jean, only realizing when his hand encountered cloth that his lover was still dressed. "What can I do for you?" he asked sleepily.

Jean leaned down and kissed Raymond tenderly. "You can sleep in my arms and go with me to the meeting with Renaud on Saturday."

Raymond wanted to tell Jean that he would do those things anyway, but his climax had sapped his energy, leaving him too tired to insist. Tomorrow he would find a way to return the favor.

"ARE YOU sure Jean wanted me to be involved with this?" Mireille asked as she and Orlando left monsieur Lombard's house on île St-Louis. "Surely there are better choices."

"Who?" Orlando asked seriously. "If Jean goes, the recruiting has a more coercive feel to it. Sebastien is busy helping Thierry with repairs at l'Institut. Fabienne is all but running l'ANS right now so that Raymond can organize other issues with l'Institut. The advantage of having you come is that you aren't actively involved in any of the current projects. When you talk about your partnership, you aren't influenced by anything else."

"If you say so," Mireille replied, her skepticism still clear on her face. "Where should we start?"

"Jean suggested the goth clubs, since we know vampires go there to meet interested mortals," Orlando said. "Unless you have a different suggestion. I don't have a fixed plan."

"No, that's a good idea," Mireille agreed. "I don't have to hunt for myself anymore, but I often found people there who were willing to let me feed if I was willing to let them cop a feel. It seemed like a fair exchange, and I'm sure I'm not the only one who has come to that conclusion."

"Lead the way then," Orlando said. "I never frequented them before I met Alain, and I certainly have no reason to do so now, so I have no real idea of the protocol for approaching them."

"It's not hard," Mireille said with a laugh. "You go inside, sit where you can be seen, and smile so they can see your fangs. That's all the goth crowd needs to approach you. Of course, we aren't going to hunt, so we'll be the ones approaching the other vampires. Although, with you along, they might come to us."

Orlando shrugged, not comfortable with the attention his Aveu de Sang inevitably drew whenever it came to people's attention. His bond with Alain was a private matter. Unfortunately, it had become a matter of public interest—

perhaps because so few vampires made that bond—and it set him apart from the rest of the Cour. If that worked to their advantage tonight, he would live with it and then retreat to the safety of l'ANS, where the novelty of his bond had long since worn off.

"I'd honestly rather approach them," Orlando admitted. "I don't like being treated like I'm special."

Mireille did not reply that Orlando was special—that only he, of all the vampires in the alliance and all the vampires in the Cour parisienne, had taken the huge step of forming an Aveu de Sang. Only he had survived being captured and tortured by Serrier, and indeed any other vampire might not have survived, because Orlando's Aveu de Sang had given the alliance the means to find him.

They chatted about inconsequential things as they took the subway north to Montmartre and the clubs where they hoped to find vampires who might be interested in l'Institut's educational seminars.

The bouncer at the club recognized Mireille immediately, ushering her to the front of the line. "You haven't been here in a long time, Mireille," he chided. "We thought you'd forgotten about us."

"Not forgotten," Mireille assured him with a flirtatious smile, "but my responsibilities have changed, and I do not feed widely the way I once did. This is my friend Orlando. I'm hoping the club is busy tonight."

"With two such perfect vampires as yourselves on the prowl, we'll draw every interested mortal in Montmartre," the bouncer said fawningly.

Mireille thanked him and led Orlando inside, rolling her eyes at the bouncer's blandishments as soon as they were out of sight. "The management can say and do whatever they want. What brings in the customers is the presence of vampires in the club. We're royalty while we're here."

"You know I can't offer them anything."

"It isn't about whether we feed or not, because I have no interest in anyone's blood but Caroline's either. It's enough that we're here, that we might decide to pick one of them to feed from. Look around you. You'll see."

Orlando did as Mireille said, looking around the dim interior of the smoky bar at the young men and women dressed all in black with their heavy eyeliner and multiple piercings. Mixed among them were vampires in ordinary street clothes with none of the affectations the mortals adopted, but it was clear from the way the customers in the bar interacted with the vampires that they were thrilled simply to be in the same room. "I suppose I can see the appeal," he allowed, "at least for someone who is comfortable being in the spotlight."

"Or someone broke enough they can't afford to go across the street to Sang Froid," Mireille replied, thinking about the first months after she was turned, before monsieur Lombard took her into his employ. Being unable to go out during the day, she had promptly lost her job and had been unable to find another. She haunted the clubs at night, hoping someone would take pity on her and take her home with them. The clients at this sort of club considered it a real coup to have a vampire in their homes, even if only for one night. She had lived that way for what had seemed a very long six months before she had received a summons to the house on Quai d'Anjou that she now called home. "Let's see if anyone is interested in talking."

Orlando looked around the room, trying to read the vampires' potential interest from their body language. He doubted the ones who truly basked in the company of the young mortals would be interested in giving that up in favor of a long-term partnership, but perhaps he was underestimating them. Only time would tell.

"Over there," Mireille said at Orlando's elbow. "Natalie Bauche and Philippe Moreno. They're standing together and not talking with anyone else."

"You know them?" Orlando asked.

Mireille shrugged. "I know who they are. We aren't friends, but we're friendly at least."

"That's as good a place to start as any," Orlando decided.

They walked across the club to the two other vampires. They greeted Mireille with absent smiles and kisses on each cheek and Orlando with far more formality, making him uncomfortable again. He was definitely glad Mireille had agreed to accompany him.

"It's been awhile, Mireille," Natalie commented when the introductions were finished and Orlando and Mireille had taken seats at the small table. "What brings you back out tonight and in such august company?"

"I've spent most of the past year with my partner," Mireille explained.

"Oh, that's right," Philippe said. "You were one of the ones who found a partner in Bellaiche's alliance."

"The alliance wasn't his," Orlando interrupted. "It was the Cour's, for the benefit of all vampires. Or are you suggesting you haven't found some benefit in the antidiscrimination laws?"

Philippe looked like he had a sharp answer to that, but he bit it back.

"I did find a partner," Mireille said, turning the attention away from Orlando and back to the point of their conversation. "We meshed very well and have both benefited immensely from our association."

"How?" Natalie asked. "I thought the war was over."

"It is," Orlando said, "but the benefits of the partnerships had nothing to do with the alliance itself, or at least nothing directly. Our partners' blood didn't stop protecting us from sunlight simply because the war ended."

"Nor did the connection with them fade because we stopped having to fight for our lives," Mireille added. "I don't know whether you've heard, but Raymond Payet, the president of l'ANS, has set up a program for any wizards and vampires interested in exploring the benefits of a partnership. There's no guarantee you'll find someone, of course, since we have no idea what makes the matches happen, but if you do, you won't regret it."

"What, exactly, does a partnership entail?" Phillipe asked suspiciously.

"Feeding from a wizard on a somewhat regular basis," Orlando said, "or exclusively in my case, but that's a different issue entirely."

"Is it?" Natalie asked. "Your Avoué is also your partner."

"He is," Orlando confirmed, "or I wouldn't be able to have both, but our decision to make an Aveu de Sang was a personal one. As far as I'm aware, we are the only wizard-vampire partners to have done so. As I was saying, I know a fair number of vampires from the alliance who choose to feed predominantly from their partners, but it isn't a requirement."

"It's not a hardship, either," Mireille assured them. "There's something about magical blood, and especially about your partner's blood, that makes it appealing. If someone came up to me now, I wouldn't accept what they were offering even though I haven't fed in a couple of days, because why would I drink table wine when I have a Grand Cru waiting for me at home?"

"There can't possibly be that much difference!"

Orlando and Mireille exchanged knowing smirks. "Contact Jean at l'ANS headquarters, sign up for the first educational seminar starting in January, and find out for yourself if you don't believe us," Orlando said.

"And if we don't?"

"Then you'll continue hanging out here in the clubs, drinking substandard fare," Mireille said with a shrug. "The choice is yours. We've made—and benefited from—ours."

She rose from the table, Orlando at her side. "Bonsoir. The first group will be quite small, so don't wait too long to make your decisions."

Outside, Orlando grinned at Mireille. "That went far better than I expected."

Mireille laughed. "And all the other vampires in the room will wonder what we talked about. Natalie and Philippe will have to decide if they want to share the news and risk losing their place in the first class or keep it to themselves and possibly incur the ire of their friends later for not sharing now."

Orlando shook his head. "There are days I'm glad I never bothered with le jeu des Cours. I'd never master all the subtleties."

"You're outside it now anyway," Mireille said. "For as long as Alain lives, you have a status no one else in Paris can match."

The dual reminder of the public nature of a private bond and of Alain's mortality struck Orlando deeply. "Where to next?" he asked, changing the subject. "Jean said they were aiming for between five and ten vampires and wizards, depending on interest, for the first seminar. If those two decide to keep the news to themselves, we still have work to do."

"Laetitia Bastian owns a café near here, or there's Malika Robin, who owns an Internet café. It's a little farther away."

"Is there any reason we can't do both?" Orlando asked.

"No," Mireille said, "although I'd like to finish up quickly. Caroline has adjusted almost completely to losing her eyesight during the last battle, and she knew where I was going tonight, but if she wakes up alone in the middle of the night, she gets disoriented sometimes. I'd rather be there if that happens."

"Let's hurry, then."

Chapter 14

"THANK YOU for coming, Luc," Jean said when Luc Cabalet, chef de la Cour of Amiens, arrived at Jean's apartment.

"What's this all about?" Luc asked, taking the seat Jean offered with a respectful nod to Raymond, who joined them in the living room.

"You've heard about l'Institut Marcel Chavinier, obviously," Jean said. When Luc nodded, Jean continued, "The property we purchased is in le Morvan, as you know, an area uncontrolled by any Cour, but the closest Cour is Autun."

"Renaud," Luc said before Jean could go on.

Jean nodded. "And he's trying to stir up trouble in Burgundy, claiming I'm infringing on his territory or that I'm trying to do I don't know what. Céline Girardot from Dijon set up a meeting to hopefully resolve the issue before it results in problems for everyone."

"And by everyone, you suggest it will be a problem for me as well," Luc guessed.

"You have a partner. You stand to benefit from the research at l'Institut as much as any of the rest of us," Jean said. "Céline is… neutral, but not happy, particularly because I didn't insist Raymond leave the room while we discussed Cour business."

"Why would you?" Luc asked. "He's as much a part of this as you are."

"Having someone firmly on my side, someone Céline will know how to relate to, could tip the balance of the meeting in favor of l'Institut, both in a physical sense and in terms of recruiting vampires from the region."

"When is the meeting?" Luc asked.

"Saturday night, and of course your partner is welcome as well."

Luc laughed. "Something else to make Céline and Renaud uncomfortable?"

Something to take the focus off Raymond and the other vampires' need to pigeonhole him when Jean was not ready to apply a label to their relationship. He could not say that with Raymond sitting right there, however, so he simply smiled and let the other two men draw their own conclusions.

"I see no reason why we can't cause a little trouble in Burgundy this weekend. Shall Magali and I meet you here on Saturday?"

"It might be better to meet us at l'ANS," Raymond said. "Since we'll travel magically to get to the meeting, it might be easier to leave from there using the locator map. The meeting is at ten, so if you're there about quarter 'til, that gives us plenty of time to get there."

"We'll see you around nine forty-five on Saturday," Luc said.

After he had left, Raymond smiled at his lover. "For having a home without an open-door policy, we've had quite a few visitors in the past few weeks."

"I wouldn't exactly call them visitors," Jean said. "The chefs de la Cour may 'visit', but it's never just a social call. Our lives are too wrapped up in le jeu des Cours for that."

"All the more reason for them to come to the office during office hours," Raymond said. "You shouldn't have to deal with them at home."

"That would go over like a lead balloon," Jean sighed. "One does not make a chef de la Cour wait, even if one is another chef de la Cour. If I went to Amiens or Dijon or Autun, I would approach them the same way they approached me. It's the nature of the game."

Raymond rolled his eyes, annoyed once again at the sense of le jeu des Cours running their lives. "I'm more concerned about Saturday anyway. What's going to happen?"

"I have no idea," Jean replied honestly. "We'll meet at St. Bénigne and listen to Renaud's demands. If they're within the bounds of reason, we'll negotiate. If they aren't, we'll be back to the stalemate we have now, because he has very little legitimacy in any of the claims he's made so far, and we already have a legal investment in the property, so there's not much he can do except try to challenge me."

"Is that going to be a problem?"

"Not on Saturday. He won't violate Céline's hospitality that way because he can't afford to lose the goodwill of the one chef de la Cour who is still speaking to him," Jean explained. "If he decides to challenge me, it will be in a more public setting where his relationship with Céline is not at stake. He'll either come directly to Paris or he'll come to Dommartin."

"Adèle's wards will keep him out of the abbey," Raymond said.

"I know, but that would be perceived as hiding behind you if I used that as a way to refuse to meet his challenge," Jean said, "and I can't allow that perception any more than you can allow the perception that you're at the beck and call of a vampire. If he comes to Dommartin to challenge me, I'll face him the same way I would face anyone who challenged me on my own territory. Dommartin *is* my territory now, just as it is yours."

THE PHONE in their apartment rang as they were getting dressed the next morning, surprising both men. Jean answered it, face growing serious as he listened to the conversation on the other end. "We'll be there as soon as we can."

"What happened?" Raymond asked when Jean replaced the handset on the cradle and closed the dumbwaiter that kept the modern appliance from marring the historic perfection of their home.

"Thierry says a wall fell at l'Institut. It was one he'd labeled as being extremely dangerous, but it was in an area we weren't going to use right away. He wants us to come take stock so we can decide if we need to cordon it off, try to stabilize what's left, or look at our other options," Jean said. "Nobody was there, so nobody's hurt, but I got the impression he's worried about the walls around the collapse being destabilized and causing more damage."

"I'll call Marcel and Vincent," Raymond said, picking up his phone. "Can you check with Luc and Magali to see if they'll come if we send someone to effect the displacement?"

Jean nodded. "He didn't seemed panicked, like there was any immediate danger, so I think we can afford to all meet at l'ANS rather than you rushing there now."

"The others can go directly to l'Institut," Raymond reminded him. "It's only you and me and Luc and Magali who have to make arrangements for our displacement spells."

"They won't make any decisions until you get there," Jean countered. "Short of stopping another collapse, they'll defer to your authority, so there's no particular reason for them to rush out there either."

Raymond realized Jean was right. It was still a shock to him sometimes, even after a year, that people waited on his decisions to act. Particularly in something like this, where he was certain Thierry could make a more informed decision than he could. They made the phone calls and finished getting dressed quickly, Raymond eschewing his usual morning coffee in light of the urgency of Thierry's call. By the time they arrived at l'ANS, everyone but Luc and Magali were already there. Fabienne announced that Mathieu, her partner, had gone to Amiens and would be back momentarily. She had barely finished speaking when first Magali, then Luc and Mathieu appeared next to them.

"Thank you all for disrupting your schedules to be here," Raymond said. "I don't know all the details of the collapse, but you're the best people to deal with whatever needs to be done. Shall we go down to Dommartin and see what we find? Magali, will our magical signatures be enough for you to follow, or would you like one of us to take you the first time?"

"I haven't lost my skills simply because we're no longer fighting a war," Magali replied.

Raymond smiled. "I didn't think you had, but I felt it polite to ask. Luc, will you do me the honor of traveling with me?"

The other chef de la Cour nodded, moving to Raymond's side as Jean took his place next to Marcel. The four wizards who were familiar with Dommartin cast their displacement spells, Magali following seconds later. They arrived in the center of the cloister. Thierry and Sebastien waited at the entrance to the main building.

"So what happened?" Raymond asked, leading the group over to the two men.

"We got here this morning to start working before the workmen arrived, because it's easier to concentrate without the noise of their tools, and found a section of the exterior wall had collapsed during the night," Thierry explained. "It was a bad section, but I didn't realize it was this bad. I went into town and talked to one of the men at the café, and he said there was a strong storm in the area last night. The wind may have caused it, especially if the rain weakened the foundation. Or it might have just reached the point of not holding together."

"What needs to happen now?" Raymond asked.

"Minimally or best-case?"

"Both," Raymond replied.

"Minimally, the walls on either side of the collapse have to be stabilized so it doesn't continue to crumble on us," Thierry said. "I don't know how Adèle did the wards, so I don't know if those will need to be redone or strengthened. I was more concerned about the safety of people working on site than about the overall security of the building, since at this point we don't have anyone or anything of value here."

"And ideally?"

"Ideally we'd repair the wall completely now. If we can't do that, we're limited to propping up the walls on either side, because with that kind of hole in the middle, all we could really do on the walls that remain would be a containment spell rather than a repair spell," Thierry explained.

"Can you actually do a complete repair on the wall with this kind of damage?" Eric asked. "I mean, that's not a minor repair. That's rebuilding the wall."

"It would mean rebuilding the wall," Thierry agreed, "which would require more wizards than we have here, because we can't hold the stones in place and do the repairs at the same time. Ultimately it's what needs to be done, whether by magical or physical means."

"So it becomes a question of priorities," Raymond said. "Do we do it now before the wall collapses any more, or do we wait until we're ready to start the repairs on this section of the abbey?"

"I'd vote for doing it now," Thierry said, "but you knew that already."

"If we get enough wizards to hold the stones in place, can the four of you, supplemented by the rest of us here, complete the repair portion of the undertaking all at once, or would this have to be a multistage project?" Raymond asked.

Thierry looked at the hole and the surrounding wall critically. "It will be close. Sebastien and Luc will add quite a bit of power to my spells and to Magali's, but channeling magic through a wizard—even vampire-boosted magic—from outside isn't as effective for boosting power. If Marcel and

Vincent had vampire partners, I wouldn't hesitate to say yes, but I'm not sure we can supplement them enough to make it possible."

"We could ask monsieur Lombard if—" Raymond began.

"He won't come," Jean and Marcel interrupted at the same time.

"He came out of seclusion to help Orlando, but he's made it very clear since then that he has no intention of being dragged into the affairs of the wider world," Marcel continued. "It would be disrespectful even to ask. Whatever I can do to help, I will, but I will do it on my own."

"All right, the first thing to do is check the wards," Raymond decided, "and then to make this area as safe as possible, since there will be workmen arriving to work on the interior renovations. Once we've accomplished that, we'll see what we can do about getting enough wizards out here to work on more serious repairs in this area. I think we should also strengthen the wards around other areas that are dangerous, to make sure no one stumbles into those sections by accident."

"I can check the wards," Eric offered. "Adèle did them, right?" Raymond nodded. "Good. She and I worked together fairly extensively before the war. I should still be able to tinker with them without disrupting the magical signature too much, at least until she can come and reinforce them herself."

"If you'll do that, Marcel, Magali, and Vincent can work on securing things here while Thierry and I take care of things inside, since we're most familiar with the layout of the abbey," Raymond proposed. "Once that's done, we'll see where we are and decide if we're going to try to repair this completely today or wait a few days."

"If it makes a difference," Luc interrupted, "Magali and I were free today, but I have Cour business to attend to over most of the next week—so it would be the middle of next week or even the following weekend before we would be free to return. I'm trying to rearrange my schedule so we'll be free to come and stay for a block of time."

"Then we will do our best to finish today," Raymond decided. "Let's get started so we can get finished."

"MAKE A note in my schedule, please," Raymond asked Fabienne when they returned to l'ANS later that evening. "I'll be in a meeting on Saturday evening from nine thirty for an unspecified length of time."

"What meeting are you attending at that time on a Saturday night?" Fabienne asked, opening Raymond's calendar and marking the time slot as occupied.

"I'm going with Jean to a meeting with several other chefs de la Cour in Dijon," Raymond replied.

"You're doing what?" Fabienne asked, the pen clattering to the desk as she spun her chair around to gape at Raymond.

"I'm going with Jean to Dijon while he meets with the chefs de la Cour from Dijon and Autun," Raymond repeated, not at all sure how to explain Fabienne's reaction. "Luc Cabalet from Amiens is going as well, and his partner, I believe."

Fabienne shook his head. "You can't go to a meeting like that. You aren't a vampire!"

"What does that have to do with anything?" Raymond asked. "They're meeting because of l'Institut. It involves me."

"It doesn't involve you," Fabienne disagreed. "Nothing involving the chefs de la Cour involves anyone but them, except if one of them has a Consort. *I* wouldn't belong there. Orlando wouldn't. No one but the chefs de la Cour and their Consorts. The last time I checked, Jean hadn't summoned the Cour to declare you his Consort."

"Of course he hasn't," Raymond said. "I'm president of l'ANS. I wouldn't be able to do my job here if that were public knowledge. I'd have no credibility."

"Which is why you can't go with him on Saturday," Fabienne said. "You're a complete wild card. The moment you walk into that meeting, you put Jean at a disadvantage."

"Then why did he tell Luc to bring Magali to the meeting as well?" Raymond challenged. "Is she his Consort?"

"I have no idea," Fabienne replied honestly. "If she is, that doesn't help your position, and if she isn't, he won't bring her. Did you say something about going to Jean?"

"No, he brought it up with Luc," Raymond said. "I didn't see any reason to question it."

Fabienne sighed. "You can't go with him, Raymond. You'd go wanting to help and support him, but having you there would throw everything out of balance with everyone else. He needs to be strong at this meeting. If you're there without a reason or a role, it weakens him."

"I can't *not* go with him when he's asked me to be there," Raymond disagreed. "He's chef de la Cour. He knows the rules better than anyone. If he's choosing to break them, it's for a reason, and far be it from me to question that."

Fabienne looked like she wanted to continue the discussion, but she let it go. "If you have to go, keep your mouth shut and stay out of the discussion unless someone asks you a question. Whatever you think, whatever happens, let Jean handle it."

Raymond was only marginally happier about that, but at least he would be there, offering Jean his silent support. "If you really think that's necessary."

"You'll do your own thing, I know, but one of the reasons you wanted a vampire as an admin in the first place was to give you advice in exactly this sort of situation," Fabienne reminded him. "You don't have to like the inner workings of le jeu des Cours, but you made it my job to make sure you didn't trample them out of ignorance."

"And you've done your job." Raymond was not happy about the implications of it, but he could hardly fault her for doing exactly what he had hired her to do. "If anything bad comes of it, it will be on my head, not on yours."

"If that were true, I'd let you make your own mistakes," Fabienne muttered. "If anything bad comes of it, it will be on Jean's head and on the entire Cour."

Raymond sighed and nodded. "I'll talk to him about it before Saturday." He had no idea what he would say, but he would find a way to raise the subject and hope for the best.

Letting himself into his office, Raymond locked the door behind him, not wanting anyone to disturb him, even his lover. He slumped into his chair and stared blindly at the map on the wall, blank now because so few wizards carried their repères.

Consort.

Raymond had no idea what that meant in terms of him personally, but he was certainly well enough versed in history to guess at the implications. To be Jean's Consort would be to accept a position at his side publicly, as his partner, but probably not an equal partner, at least not in the eyes of the Cour. In this case Fabienne's objection to him accompanying Jean was about him not being a chef de la Cour, but on more than one occasion he had noticed a definite exclusion of mortals from activities that had included other vampires. The *judicium* at the end of the war when the Cour tried, and eventually executed, a rogue vampire came foremost to mind. Alain had immediately been invited to attend because he was Orlando's Avoué and Orlando was the vampire injured by Couthon—but none of the other wizards had been invited, even some who could have testified against the rogue. Only the intervention of monsieur Lombard had allowed Raymond and Marcel to attend.

Being Jean's Consort would eliminate the need to question whether he could attend this event or any other at Jean's side, but it would put a public title on a private relationship—and as long as he was president of l'ANS, he had to maintain the appearance of impartiality. Raymond ran his hand through his hair in frustration and wondered again how his life had gotten so complicated.

Chapter 15

RAYMOND DIDN'T wait for Jean before leaving for home. He had too much on his mind and no solution in sight. He saw no resolution for the conundrum Fabienne had pointed out to him, and until he had some solution to propose, he didn't want to bring it up with Jean. He would sleep on it tonight and they could talk in the morning.

To his surprise, Jean was already home when he came in the door, standing by the window and staring blindly out at l'église de la Madeleine. Crossing the room, he closed his arms around Jean's waist. "What are you looking at so intensely?"

Startled, Jean turned in Raymond's embrace, summoning a smile for his lover. "Nothing. I was just thinking."

"Thinking so hard you didn't hear the door open?" Raymond asked, surprised. Jean's hearing was as augmented as his physical strength.

Jean shrugged. "It's nothing to worry about. Are you ready for bed?"

Raymond smiled. "I was hoping I could talk you into a bath before bed." He slid his hands down Jean's back, squeezing lightly when he reached his lover's ass.

Jean almost refused. He had left l'ANS early, hoping he could use the solitude to strengthen his control over the monster that lurked beneath the surface, but the tension of the upcoming meeting with Renaud and of wanting Raymond to have a clearer place in his life had only fed the turmoil. And emotional turmoil could only lead to a repeat of his loss of control, something he was keen to avoid. It had been three days, though, and he would need to feed again soon. Even worse, Raymond knew he would need to feed again soon, and since they had become lovers, he had rarely fed from Raymond without making love to him. The more Raymond pressed him, the more likely he was to lose control again.

The hopeful look on Raymond's face kept him from refusing. He simply could not say no to his wizard, which was what had gotten them into this tangle in the first place. Smiling at the irony of that realization, he kissed Raymond tenderly. "A bath sounds wonderful."

They walked into the bathroom, shedding clothes as they went. The sight of the nearly healed bite marks on Raymond's torso shored up Jean's control, reminding him in vivid detail of the dangers of letting his beast slip its leash. Taking a deep breath, he forced down the monster within him and adjusted the bathwater to the temperature he knew Raymond liked, slightly warmer than

Jean preferred for himself. The warmer water would not hurt him, and Raymond was so often cold in the winter. "Go ahead, get in before you catch a chill," Jean urged, hoping that by focusing on his lover, he could maintain his own control. "I'll be right there."

Raymond sank into the tub, the hot water rising slowly around his hips. He waited, mostly patiently, as Jean finished undressing and set their towels over the radiator so they would be warm for later.

"Thank you," Raymond said, reaching for Jean's hand as his lover climbed into the tub behind him. When Jean was settled, Raymond rested his head on his lover's shoulder, tipped slightly sideways in offer. Jean kissed the smooth skin but made no move to feed, even though it had been three days. Raymond told himself to let it go, but a niggling voice in the back of his mind whispered that other things had changed in the past three days as well. Forcibly silencing the insecure musings, he focused on the present, sliding his hands down Jean's legs and back up again in silent encouragement.

To Raymond's relief, Jean picked up the washcloth almost immediately and began running it over the wizard's shoulders and then over his chest, spreading soap and warmth and desire. Raymond relaxed and let Jean bathe him, smiling when the rag lingered over the bite marks Jean had left three nights before. Raymond rather hoped he could persuade Jean to leave a few more before the night was over. He might not be Jean's Consort, but he could at least make it clear he was part of Jean's life.

Jean's fangs pierced his lower lip as he fought the urge to sink them into the vein that pulsed beneath the surface of the stubbled skin so close to his mouth. Raymond would not stop him. Every line of Raymond's body proclaimed his willingness, even his eagerness, to feel Jean's fangs again, but he held back. He had fed so fully the last time that he could afford to wait another day, maybe even two, one of the many benefits he had gleaned from their partnership. Instead, he focused on lavishing pleasure on Raymond's body, using the washcloth as an extension of his hand to tease his lover's sensitive places: the curve of his elbow, the inner face of his wrists, the backs of his knees. Little sighs escaped Raymond's lips with each pass of the warm cloth, bringing a smile to Jean's face as he tended to his lover. He could do this. He could be the tender, gentle lover Raymond deserved rather than the beast he had become the last time he fed. He simply had to focus completely on Raymond instead of giving in to his own needs.

Determined to hold to that plan, he ran the cloth over Raymond's chest, making sure to clean around the healing bite marks and then lingering over his wizard's nipples, the nap of the cloth providing an extra layer of stimulation. Beneath the surface of the water, Jean could see Raymond's cock beginning to fill. Hiding his smile against his lover's neck, he closed his fingers around one sensitive point, rubbing over it with the cloth until Raymond arched into his touch. Delighted by the reaction, he repeated it on the other side until Raymond was writhing against him, his ass rubbing repeatedly over Jean's cock. He ached to tip Raymond forward, brace his hands on the edge of the tub, and sink into his lover's tight heat, but he had promised himself he would act like a civilized man. He refused to break that promise the first time he was tempted.

Instead, he shifted sideways so Raymond was leaning against his leg and side rather than directly against his cock. The wizard murmured in protest, but Jean soothed him with a kiss and the swipe of the soapy cloth over his balls. "I can reach you better this way."

Raymond's eyes opened, whatever he might have said dying on his lips when Jean's hand moved deeper between his legs, cradling his sac and then rubbing behind it, over his perineum and into his crevice. "Please," he gasped.

"Please what?" Jean swiped the cloth directly over Raymond's entrance. The wizard's reply came out as a strangled shout, so Jean did it again.

Not able to catch his breath, Raymond grabbed the washcloth, pulling it out of Jean's grip so his fingers were in direct contact with Raymond's skin. "That."

Jean smiled and kissed Raymond softly, pulling back when his lover would have increased the depth and pressure of the kiss. He could not indulge that way with his control still so shaky. Not wanting to leave Raymond hurting, though, he circled the puckered entrance more deliberately, teasing the muscle into relaxing and allowing him ingress. It only took a gratifyingly few strokes before he could slip the tip inside and then the full length of his digit.

Raymond's eyes fluttered shut, sending a curl of need through Jean's stomach. He wanted to stay right there forever, Raymond pliant in his arms, body open for whatever Jean wanted, the rest of the world held far at bay. In this moment, titles did not matter. The chef de la Cour, the president of l'ANS did not exist. They were only Raymond and Jean, lovers, partners, perhaps soul mates.

"Can you take a second finger?" Jean asked, silently cursing the empty tube of waterproof lube on the edge of the tub. They had more, he was sure, but not within easy reach, and Jean really wanted to bring Raymond to climax now so he would sleep when they moved to bed.

Raymond nodded, sliding down in the tub so he could spread his legs wider, giving Jean greater access to his ass.

Tweaking at Raymond's nipples lightly to offset any burn from the stretch, Jean pulled his hand back and added a second finger, aiming for Raymond's prostate this time. He rubbed over the sensitive bump, smiling at the hoarse cry that wrung from Raymond's throat. Deciding he liked the sound, he did it again and again until Raymond was thrashing against him and the water was in danger of splashing over the edge of the tub. "Don't hold back," Jean whispered, blowing lightly in Raymond's ear.

"Bite me," Raymond begged, but Jean shook his head.

"Not tonight."

Raymond groaned in protest, but before he could say more, Jean's hand closed around his cock, sliding up and down the hard length, and that and the constant stimulation to his prostate was too much. His head fell back against the edge of the tub as his hips stuttered in release.

Jean's hands kept pace, continuing their stroking and probing to extend Raymond's climax as long as possible. When Raymond finally lay limp in his arms, Jean pressed a tender kiss to his lover's temple. "Don't move."

Raymond chuckled, not sure he could have moved even if he had wanted to. He watched in postorgasmic stupor as Jean rose from the tub and wrapped a towel around his waist, bending to let the water out of the tub. He almost protested when his lover scooped him up into his arms, but it felt too good to be held. Jean dried him quickly, the towel warm against his skin, and then carried him into the bedroom and into bed.

Burrowing under the covers, Raymond waited for Jean to join him so they could finish what they started in the tub. It took longer than he expected, the vampire taking the time to hang up the wet towels rather than simply dropping them to the floor the way he usually did when bathing led to lovemaking. Perplexed, Raymond pushed up on one elbow.

"Lie down. You'll get cold," Jean scolded.

Raymond frowned. "Come to bed."

"I will. I just need to take care of a few things first."

Raymond's frown deepened. "What's going on, Jean? It feels like you're avoiding me, and I don't like it."

"How am I avoiding you?" Jean asked, heart pounding as his mind scrambled to find a way to dodge this conversation. "We just made love in the bathtub. That hardly counts as avoidance, I would think."

"*We* didn't make love," Raymond countered. "You made love to me. Not that I'm complaining, but I'd like the chance to return the favor."

"I'm fine," Jean demurred.

"That isn't the point," Raymond insisted. "As good as you made me feel, it was one-sided."

"It wasn't one-sided. You have no idea the pleasure I get from seeing you come apart in my arms."

"Then why are you denying me that same pleasure? I want to see you that way too."

"Next time," Jean said.

"That's what you said two days ago when you blew me before bed," Raymond reminded him. "This makes twice in three days you've gotten me off without letting me touch you in return. What changed?"

Jean looked up, eyes blazing. "Look at yourself in the mirror and you'll know what changed!"

Raymond glanced down at his chest, at the plethora of marks still adorning his skin. "What? The bites?"

"Not the bites themselves, but what they represent. I lost control!"

"I know," Raymond said, his voice smug with satisfaction. "I remember."

"I hurt you!"

"You did not hurt me. I loved every minute of it." Deciding they were getting nowhere with Jean across the room, Raymond got up and crossed to Jean's side. "You were feeding from me the entire time. You know I loved every minute of it. I don't know how this has gotten turned around in your head, but there is nothing to feel guilty about here. Nothing."

"You're going to get cold."

"Then come to bed with me and keep me warm," Raymond said. "I'm not going to bed without you."

"You are so stubborn," Jean huffed, grabbing Raymond's arm and propelling him toward the bed. He climbed in after his lover, pulling the ties to release the bed curtains. "Haven't you learned by now that you can't out-stubborn a vampire?"

"And yet you're here in bed with me," Raymond pointed out smugly. "Now will you please tell me what's going on? Not that I'm complaining about the blowjob or the prostate massage tonight, but you're holding back on me, and I don't like it."

"You don't understand," Jean began, trying to find the words to explain without scaring Raymond away.

"Then help me understand," Raymond pleaded. "I don't want us to argue, but if you don't tell me there's a problem, I can't help you resolve it."

"I tell people vampires aren't monsters, that we can live in civilized society."

"They aren't, and you can," Raymond interrupted. "I've lived with you for over a year. I think I'd know if you were."

"That's just it," Jean said softly. "I am a monster. I've learned to control it, but it lurks beneath the surface, waiting for the opportunity to break free."

"Is that what you really think? That you're some sort of monster?"

"I don't have to think it," Jean replied. "I know I am. The night I was turned, I lost control and killed a man. I was drunk on the sweetness of his blood and the warmth of his body, so high on sex and feeding that I lost track of everything and drained him dry. My maker taught me control after that, but the beast still lurks, waiting for the right moment."

"And you think that's what happened three nights ago?" Raymond asked seriously. "You think it got the better of you?"

"How else would you explain the bite marks on your body?"

Raymond rolled his eyes. "I think you made love to me until I screamed. I think you made me feel like the center of your world, the one thing you can't live without. I don't know if I'd want it to be rough like that every time, but you didn't hurt me, you didn't scare me, and you certainly didn't kill me. I'm not belittling what happened back then, but I think you're underestimating yourself. It happened the night you were turned. Has it happened since then?"

Jean shook his head.

"Then why does it have to be the same thing? Why can't it be just what I said it was—a round of wonderful, rough sex?"

"Because I'm a vampire," Jean reminded his lover. "You probably outweigh me by twenty kilos, yet I carried you in here like I would a child. I take your life source every time my fangs pierce your skin. Rough sex with me will never be simply rough sex. I'm dangerous in a way no other lover could ever be."

"I've said this before, but maybe I need to remind you that you're not the only one who's dangerous. I might not be able to cast a spell on you directly, but if I needed to, I could stop you. I could spell the curtain ties around your wrists. I could force things between us to separate us. I could cast a displacement spell and simply be gone. Even if you turned on me the way you fear you might, I wouldn't be a helpless victim with no recourse," Raymond said.

Jean could hardly argue with that when he had watched Raymond in a fight and had seen him appear and disappear at will. "I don't like feeling out of control, and I felt like that the other night. It shook me because I thought I'd passed that stage."

"I can understand that, but unless you're planning on never feeding or having sex with me again—which I certainly hope is not the case—you're going to have to get past it," Raymond said.

Jean could not imagine giving up the man in his bed. "I'll do my best." He pulled Raymond into his arms, hoping he could relax enough to remain in bed with Raymond while he slept now that he had admitted the worst of his fears.

"Before we go to sleep," Raymond continued, "were you planning on telling me at some point that you were putting your position in le jeu des Cours at risk by including me in things I don't belong in?"

All the tension that had seeped out of Jean at Raymond's acceptance flooded back in. "Who suggested I was putting myself at risk?"

"I told Fabienne about the meeting on Saturday night, and she nearly took my head off when I told her I was going with you," Raymond said. "She claimed no one would be allowed but the chefs de la Cour, and that if you insisted on me being there, you would put yourself at risk unless I was your Consort. The last time I checked, I wasn't your Consort."

"The last time I checked, you didn't want to be my Consort," Jean retorted, "or has something changed in the past few days?"

"It has nothing to do with what I want," Raymond snapped. "You know I have to maintain some degree of impartiality or I'll lose all credibility as the president of l'ANS. We've been through this."

"And sharing my bed gives you so much impartiality," Jean snorted. "Put a title on it or not, you *are* my Consort. I've tried to have enough respect for you and your position not to put you in an untenable position, but I won't see you given less than the respect you deserve."

"That's just it," Raymond said, reeling internally at the revelation that Jean wanted him in a role he had not even known existed until a few hours ago. "Nobody understands why I deserve that respect, and so you are losing status because of it. You have to stop."

"Stop what?" Jean demanded. "Stop loving you? You can't ask me to do that."

Chapter 16

RAYMOND BLINKED, mouth opening and closing but no words coming out. He didn't doubt Jean's declaration. He simply had no idea how to react to it. They'd never talked in those terms. They were partners. Lovers, yes, but because that was part of their partnership. They shared an apartment because that made their partnership simpler. Love had never entered their equation, regardless of his own softer feelings.

Jean had just changed their equation.

He took a deep breath and tried to focus on the point of his conversation, but he could not let the declaration, unexpected and shouted though it was, go unanswered. "I love you too, but that doesn't change our situation. We have to resolve this problem."

Jean's eyes closed as he let out the breath he had been holding in fear of a negative reaction to his inadvertent declaration. Raymond loved him too. "There isn't anything to change. The situation is what it is, and I'm not willing to compromise more than I've already done."

"So I'll just refuse to come with you on Saturday," Raymond said. "You'll have protected my nonexistent position by insisting I be allowed to attend, and I'll protect you by staying away like I should."

"That's just it," Jean said. "You shouldn't stay away. Consort or not, this involves you. I wouldn't be in Dommartin, and we wouldn't be meeting on Saturday night, if you weren't involved. Céline and Renaud can say what they like about it being a question of territory, but it isn't. There's no dispute there that would stand up in any court of law, vampire or French. They aren't comfortable with the idea of partnerships, and so they're trying to use the issue of territory to keep l'Institut from going forward. They wouldn't be any happier with it if it was here in Paris. They'd just have less of an argument to do anything about it."

"And shoving your partner in their face helps how?"

Jean smiled wickedly. "It puts them off balance, which is always in my favor. Le jeu des Cours is a subtle game. I may appear to lose ground now. I may even actually lose some, but my position in Paris is secure—too many members of my Cour fought in the war and credit me with the alliance that led to the partnerships and equal rights legislation for any coup attempt to succeed As l'Institut grows and partnerships spread outside Paris and Amiens to the rest of the country and even to the rest of the world, Céline and Renaud and their ilk will be the ones standing in the way of progress. It may take a decade or more, but when the dust settles, I'll be the one still standing, and they'll be the ones who have lost the game. As my partner, as my lover, as my Consort, or simply as president of l'ANS, come with me on Saturday. I want you there."

"I swore to support your position as chef de la Cour. If going with you on Saturday truly does that, then I'll be at your side."

"I don't want you anywhere else," Jean said. "Ever."

"You know what that means, don't you?" Raymond asked, heart in his throat as he rolled Jean to his back.

Jean could think of all kinds of things he hoped it meant, from putting his brand on Raymond's neck and announcing him as Consort to the Cour to locking the door and not leaving for days on end. He doubted Raymond had any of those things in mind, though. "What does it mean?"

"It means you have to let me make love to you now," Raymond said. "You can't tell me you love me for the first time, even if you were shouting at me when you said it, and not give me that." He rocked against Jean's groin, feeling an immediate surge of interest from the vampire's body. His own cock was slower to awaken, but he knew it would take nothing more than Jean's fangs in his neck and he would be fully hard again. He only hoped he could convince his lover to bite him while they made love.

"What if I want to make love to you instead?" Jean teased, making no move to take control from Raymond. Hearing that Raymond returned his feelings had eased some of the immediate need to stake his claim. He still wanted his lover's position acknowledged by the Cour, but at least he now had the assurance that Raymond felt more for him than simply the partnership bond. The part of him that had fought to take and maintain control of his Cour would always crave dominance over his lover, but as he had told Raymond the first time they made love, he was a man as well as a chef de la Cour, and sometimes he wanted to receive as well as give. He would always crave proof of their commitment, but tonight he could let that proof come through Raymond's control rather than his own.

"You did that already, remember?" Raymond replied. "I'm still tingling all over from it."

Jean smiled, heart light from the compliment. "I remember. Every time we've made love is etched on my heart." He rested his arms lightly across the breadth of Raymond's shoulders, giving full control to his lover.

Charmed by the comment, Raymond mated his lips to his vampire's, kissing him thoroughly. Jean's mouth opened, allowing Raymond access. The wizard took advantage of it, his tongue darting inside to tease his lover's. He took his time, relearning every surface of Jean's mouth as if he had not kissed the vampire thousands of times since they had become lovers. This was the first time he had kissed—and been kissed by—the man he loved.

Jean's fingers traced the line of Raymond's spine, finding and lingering on the scar that paralleled it, sending shivers down Raymond's back. Raymond would never see the mark as something to be proud of the way Jean claimed he should, but he had reached the point of accepting that Jean saw it that way. He did not shy away from his lover's insistent touch, letting it add to his arousal instead. His ass clenched in anticipation of those fingers reaching the base of his spine and moving lower, but their progress stopped at the end of the scar.

Raymond recognized what Jean was doing in not pushing farther than that and leaving Raymond in control of their interactions, but he didn't want the vampire to hold back. Breaking the kiss, he scooted up Jean's body so he straddled his lover's hips rather than his thighs and guided Jean's hand to his buttocks. "You know I love having your fingers inside me. If nothing else, it'll get me ready again faster than anything short of you biting me. Not that you can't do that too."

"Not yet," Jean said. "I'll feed from you, I promise, but once I get my fangs in you, I won't be able to stop, and I don't want to limit your movement that much yet. I did say I'd let you make love to me."

"At least give me your fingers," Raymond repeated, sighing when Jean's hand moved over the globes of his backside, fingers delving into the crease between them. "Feels so good."

The words brought a smile to Jean's face, the thought of pleasing his love even more arousing and soothing than the thought of pleasing his lover. As he lay quiescent with Raymond's hands on his body and his fingers teasing his love's entrance, he realized he could hardly feel the beast within him, as if the knowledge that Raymond loved him had sent the creature back to the depths where it usually resided.

Letting go of that worry, he closed his eyes and let himself feel: Raymond's hands on his chest, palms kneading at his muscles, teasing his nipples; Raymond's weight over his hips, keeping him firmly in place on the bed; Raymond's balls against his shaft, rubbing over it every time he shifted. As Jean's fingers worked around the still-loose guardian ring, the vampire was tempted to tip Raymond forward enough that he could seat his cock in the snug passage—but he had offered control of their lovemaking to his partner. Regardless of how Raymond decided they would make love, it needed to be Raymond's decision, not Jean's. He had taken control out of his lover's hands too many times already in the past week.

Raymond shivered at the feeling of Jean's fingers teasing him. He wanted them deeper and harder, but he did not want to rush. Not tonight. Moving to one side so he could kiss his way down Jean's chest while staying within reach of his fingers, he lowered his head to lick at the pale skin, tracing the lines of muscle with his tongue. He loved the way Jean writhed beneath him, as if the sensation were nearly more than he could stand. It came, Raymond knew, from feeling he always had to maintain his position of authority, even with his lovers. In hindsight, Raymond should have known he was different the first time Jean asked him to top, but at the time, he had been too surprised to think it through, and later, he had simply accepted it because it had not been novel anymore. Lifting his head for a moment, he waited for Jean's dark eyes to open. Even in the low light that filtered through the breaks in the curtains, he could see the tenderness on his lover's face. "I love you," he repeated. "I just thought I'd say it again."

"You can say it as often as you'd like," Jean replied huskily. "I won't ever grow tired of hearing it."

Raymond smiled. "I can think of better uses for my mouth right at the moment." He shifted again so his head faced Jean's feet, his breath ghosting across Jean's cock.

Jean groaned, his hand dropping to the duvet as Raymond's mouth hovered over his shaft. "Please," he begged. "Take me in your mouth."

"Then put your fingers in me," Raymond said. "If you stop, I stop."

Jean groaned again, but their earlier lovemaking notwithstanding, he needed lube to do what Raymond asked. It took him a moment to find it on the nightstand, a long, torturous moment of feeling only Raymond's moist breath, imagining the heat of his mouth, while trying to concentrate on something else. The second he had coated his fingers, he plunged them deep, hoping Raymond would follow suit.

He did.

The moment Raymond felt Jean's fingers stabbing deep, he swooped down onto his lover's cock, deep-throating Jean on the first try, dragging a rough moan from his lover. Deciding he liked the sound and encouraged by Jean's rapid frigging, he lifted his head marginally and went down again, swallowing around the tip.

Jean's fangs dropped as Raymond worked his cock, the need for blood blindsiding him. He forced his mind to focus on Raymond, on his lover's pleasure, but the need grew until it pounded at him. "Raymond," he gasped. "Need you now."

Instantly, the wizard turned, straddling Jean again so that the vampire's cock bumped his entrance. He sank down in one push until his balls slapped against Jean's belly. Leaning forward, he offered his chest for Jean's fangs. "Right here," he said, rubbing the mark directly above his heart. "Bite me right here."

Jean didn't hesitate, the sight of the healing incisions from his fangs no deterrent now that he knew Raymond loved him. He lifted his head and bit into the muscle, the always-rich taste of Raymond's blood assailing his senses, the knowledge now that he tasted love as well as lust an added aphrodisiac. He sucked hard, pulling in the life-giving elixir, not even questioning what he had done to deserve a lover with such generosity in body and spirit.

He had expected Raymond to want to top, but this was perfect, his fangs piercing as close to his lover's heart as possible. Any other position would have made that impossible. Raymond's blood strengthened his body, flooding him with a sense of power and possibility that defied explanation. His hips matched the rhythm of his lips and tongue, filling Raymond each time he pulled blood into his mouth, retreating each time he paused to draw breath. Through it all, Raymond hovered over him, taking what Jean gave, giving what he needed, and Jean fell in love all over again.

Unable to say the words with his mouth busy on Raymond's chest, he tried to imbue the touch of his hands with all he was feeling as he stroked Raymond's scar repeatedly. He only hoped Raymond understood.

The feeling of Jean's fangs, the occasional brush of his tongue over Raymond's nipple, would have been sensation enough to make him feel desired. The push and pull of Jean's cock within Raymond's passage would have been enough to make him climax. Jean's hands caressing Raymond's scar so tenderly brought tears of joy to the wizard's eyes. His body seized and his cock twitched, spilling between their bodies. Within seconds he felt Jean's climax inside him.

Almost immediately, Jean rolled Raymond beneath him, pinning him to the bed as he sucked and sucked and sucked on the wizard's chest. Raymond cried out again as the drive of Jean's fangs into his chest drew out his orgasm, sending aftershocks along his nerves until his entire body felt hypersensitive. He could feel Jean drawing on his chest, feel the transfer of magical energy, but he could feel no weakening, physically or magically. He wondered idly if Jean could drink him dry. Before the thought was fully formed, though, Jean released him, licking the spot tenderly, repeatedly, until Raymond shivered. "How can you think you will ever hurt me when you take such good care of me afterwards? I never feel more loved than when you lick me like that."

Jean paused, looking up in surprise at Raymond.

"It's true," Raymond said, seeing the skepticism on Jean's face. "Even before we were lovers, even when you were trying to keep your feeding as perfunctory as possible, you always took care to close the wounds. But once we started sleeping together, you lingered, like it was suddenly more than just making sure the marks healed." He shook his head. "I should have realized a long time ago this was more than just a partnership, but I was afraid you didn't feel the same and wouldn't want a mortal pinning you down."

Jean bestowed one last lick on Raymond's chest. "Then maybe I should thank Fabienne for meddling in things that don't concern her, because I'd decided even before the war ended not to tell you. You were so prickly about anything that moved beyond the boundaries of our partnership that I decided I wouldn't say anything. I'd just treat you the way I would if you were everything I wanted you to be and let you make up your mind in your own time."

"It worked," Raymond said, shaking his head. "If you'd said something a year ago, I don't know that I could have accepted it. Not because I doubted you, but because I couldn't have understood how you—how anyone—could feel that way about me, with my past and my scar and—"

Jean silenced him with a kiss. "Don't ever say that. Don't ever suggest that your scar discredits you. I can accept many things, but not that. Not ever."

"I'm coming to believe that," Raymond promised. "You've dragged me there despite myself. A year ago, I couldn't conceive of it being anything other than a mark of shame. It's one more reason I love you." He draped his arms around Jean's shoulders. "So what happens now?"

Jean shrugged. "We go on as we have been. You still can't be my Consort, no matter how much I want you to be, so I'll go on treating you as if you were and you'll go on ignoring it in public and we'll keep bumping along. Vampires are many things, but we aren't fickle creatures. I can wait for you to be ready for more."

Raymond nodded, not entirely sure he would ever be ready for more—but then, he had not thought he was ready to tell Jean that he loved him, and now that he had, he could not imagine going back. He would have to give it some thought, and soon.

Chapter 17

RAYMOND COULD not completely hide his relief when Magali accompanied Luc into the foyer of l'ANS a few minutes before their scheduled meeting time of nine forty-five on Saturday night. He knew Jean had suggested Magali attend as well, but he hadn't known whether she would. He was nervous now in a way he wouldn't have been before his conversations with Fabienne and Jean, because he hadn't understood then how much was at stake tonight. Glancing at Magali, he guessed no one had informed her of the breach in protocol their presence would cause. He considered drawing her aside and telling her, but they didn't have time for her and her partner to hash out any differences that might arise from the revelation. He would have to hope Magali's customary astuteness continued through the night's wrangling.

"What's our plan?" Luc asked.

"I thought we'd arrive on place Darcy so we can stroll unnoticed down to the cathedral. If we happen to be a minute or two late, we can excuse our tardiness due to our unfamiliarity with the city," Jean replied.

"And yet you know the name of the main square and how to get to the cathedral from there," Raymond commented wryly.

Jean smiled slyly. "I didn't say I was unfamiliar with the city. I said it made a good excuse to make the other two wait on us."

"And if they're late as well?" Magali asked.

"They won't be," Luc assured her. "They won't be early, but they won't be late because they called the meeting. If we were on time and they were late, we could leave and accuse them of not showing."

"But they won't do that to us?"

"If we were fifteen or twenty minutes late, maybe," Jean replied, "but not if we're two or three minutes late, particularly because they set the meeting in an unusual location rather than one of the sites vampires usually use as neutral ground."

"Will they actually believe you didn't scope the area out ahead of time?" Raymond asked.

"They don't have to believe it," Luc said, "but it isn't something they can realistically argue with either. Shall we regroup on place Darcy?"

"Not on the place," Jean said. "There's a house on the place, number eleven, with an interior courtyard. We will make far less of a stir arriving there than out on the square—and the door locks automatically from the outside, but you can always leave from the inside, so we can simply walk out the front door, four friends going out for the evening, without drawing any attention to ourselves."

"In that case, I should follow you," Magali said, "since I don't know the exact location. I wouldn't want to end up on top of the building. Raymond, if you'll take Luc, I'll follow your magical signature."

Raymond nodded and looked to the other chef de la Cour for permission. Luc gave it with a sharp nod, and Raymond cast the spell, the two of them disappearing to reappear seconds later in a small stone courtyard in Dijon.

"Not the grandest of all buildings," Luc observed, looking around at the few winter-brown weeds and the collection of trash cans.

"There's a large park right across the street," Raymond replied, having examined the map with Jean when they planned this displacement. "The people who live in these apartments go there if they want some fresh air. This is purely practical, a place to store their garbage cans and bikes when they aren't in use."

Jean and Magali appeared next to them, forestalling the conversation. "We have a few minutes until we need to walk toward the cathedral," Jean said. "Would you like to take a walk around the square? It's not too chilly tonight."

They wended their way through the narrow corridor until they reached the heavy wooden door to the street. Luc opened it and held it as Magali and the others walked through, his arm immediately going around her to share his warmth as the wind rushed at them down rue de la Liberté.

"If we had come earlier, we could have enjoyed a drink at La Concorde," Jean said. "They have heat lamps so you can enjoy sitting on their patio even at night. Le Liberté isn't nearly as upscale, but its owner is an old friend who moved here a few years ago. As it is, we don't have time now."

"Maybe on the way back?" Raymond suggested, curious about Jean's "old friend."

"We have two minutes," Magali said, glancing at her watch.

"Then we should go down toward the cathedral," Jean said, indicating the way with a wave of his hand. "It will take about five minutes to get there."

They descended the rue docteur Maret toward St. Bénigne, passing the musée archéologique as they walked. They were about halfway down the hill when the church bells tolled the hour. "Perfect timing," Jean said as they reached the square in front of the cathedral. "Shall we go in?"

They entered the church by the transept gate, finding the door unlocked and one row of lights on. The gate to the crypt stood open to their left. "I'll go first," Jean said, "since I know they're expecting me."

Raymond stifled his protest that it also put Jean at risk for any kind of foul play. Even if his lover suspected that kind of intention, he wouldn't let Raymond go first on the grounds that Raymond's mortal body was more susceptible to injury or death than Jean's was. Then there was le jeu des Cours and the fact that Raymond entering first would diminish Jean's status. He slipped in front of Luc, though, having no intention of leaving Jean unprotected in the crypt for more than the few seconds it would take Raymond to enter after him. He had left his wand at home, not wanting to appear threatening, but that wouldn't matter if Jean were in danger. He hoped it wouldn't come to that.

"So good of you to grace us with your presence," Céline said the moment Jean stepped into the crypt. "We thought perhaps...." She trailed off when she saw the other three people enter the room behind him.

"We had a little trouble finding it," Jean lied. "We're not as familiar with the city as you are. I'm sure you know Luc Cabalet, from Amiens. He agreed to come with me tonight since our discussion will surely impact him as well."

"And how do events in le Morvan have anything to do with Picardy?" the other vampire—Renaud, Raymond assumed—demanded.

"I have no interest in what happens in le Morvan," Luc replied coldly. "My only interest is what happens at l'Institut Marcel Chavinier. You interrupted before I could introduce my guest. Magali Ducassé, my partner, this is Céline Girardot, chef de la Cour of Dijon and Guy Renaud of Autun, our hosts for the evening."

"Your... partner?" Céline repeated.

With a snap of her fingers, Magali snuffed every candle in the room. "His partner," her voice rang out in the darkness. A second snap reignited them. "Will that be a problem?"

"Of course it's a problem," Renaud roared. "She doesn't belong here. None of you do!"

"Why not?" Jean asked. "They have as much interest in l'Institut as I do, and that is why we're here, is it not? Dommartin is neutral territory. I haven't claimed it. I have no interest in claiming it for my Cour."

"You're building there," Céline pointed out, though she kept her voice level. "What are we supposed to think?"

"I'm not building anything," Jean said.

"He's not," Raymond agreed, playing his hand as boldly as Magali had done. Fabienne had advised him given her understanding of the situation—but secure in Jean's love and his place in the vampire's life, Raymond had already decided to follow his instincts tonight. "I am. If you have an issue with l'Institut being located in Dommartin, those concerns need to come to me."

"I said you have no part in this," Renaud repeated, advancing on Raymond. He took two steps and could go no farther. "What is this?" he demanded, beating his hands against an invisible barrier.

"A ward," Raymond replied. "It won't harm you. It will simply keep you over there and us over here, since you seem inclined to be threatening. Now, I will repeat myself. If you have an issue with l'Institut, bring it to me."

"Mortals have no business in the affairs of vampires," Renaud spat.

"Then I guess we're done here," Jean said, turning toward the exit. "Raymond will release the ward when we're safely outside the church."

"If you walk out of here right now, I'll denounce you both to the Congrès des chefs," Renaud threatened.

"On what grounds?" Luc demanded. "We came in good faith to a meeting you requested, prepared to discuss whatever concerns you have, and all we've heard is insults. We aren't the ones breaking the deal here. You are."

"Can we be rational about this?" Céline interrupted. "There has to be a compromise we can all live with."

"I have yet to hear a problem that requires compromise," Jean retorted, turning back as well. "Renaud thinks mortals shouldn't be involved in vampire business. This is not news, but it's not that something he can dictate or that the four of us can decide. You're both worried about my involvement with a research center being created by l'ANS in neutral territory that happens to be near your Cours. It's neutral territory, and it isn't vampire business. L'ANS is building it and will run it when it's finished."

"And do what there?" Renaud demanded.

"Research and education," Raymond replied succinctly. "The results of both will be available to anyone in the magical community, wizards and vampires alike, as well as anyone else who might benefit from what we discover."

"What kind of research?" Céline asked suspiciously.

"Research into the bond that can form between vampires and wizards," Jean replied, "among other things."

"And that is vampire business," Renaud crowed.

"How is who one vampire feeds from the business of anyone other than the vampire and his chosen prey?" Luc inquired. "If Magali had an issue with who I feed from, I could see discussing it, but I don't see how it's any business of yours if I feed from her or anyone else."

"You didn't say feeding, you said bond," Renaud countered, "and that is the business of the Cour."

"If the vampire and wizard choose to make a formal commitment, then yes, it's the business of the Cour," Jean agreed, "but you know as well as I do that many vampires have a preferred source of sustenance without ever declaring that preference publicly. This is no different, except that it benefits both parties."

"How?" Céline demanded.

Jean met Raymond's eyes and smirked back at Céline. "I could show you, but I think it might shock you."

Raymond shook his head, remembering his first meeting with Jean in Orlando's apartment in Paris. Orlando had ushered everyone out of the room after he and Jean had realized they were partners, giving them privacy for Jean to feed. Jean had explained later that feeding for a vampire was as intimate as having sex and that vampires preferred not to do so with an audience. That stricture had loosened considerably over the course of the war as they had discovered the benefits to be gained from a vampire feeding from his partner while the wizard performed magic, but Céline and Renaud had not been part of that and would still follow the older mores. He almost hoped they did insist on a demonstration. It would amuse him to see the shock on their faces when Jean's fangs sank into his neck.

"Then why don't you try telling us instead?" Céline said acerbically.

"To put it simply," Luc said before Jean could reply, "Magali's blood lets me walk safely in sunlight, and my bite increases her magic a hundredfold or more. It's what helped us win the war against Serrier."

"That doesn't mean wizards need to be in private meetings between vampires or involved in Cour business," Renaud insisted. "You weaken us all by relying on them."

"No," Jean said. "I strengthen us all by stretching out the hand of friendship to a community that has as much to gain through our cooperation as we do. If you have nothing else to add besides insults to our partners and friends, we will see you—or not—the next time the Congrès des chefs meets."

"You'll regret walking out like this," Renaud shouted, but neither Jean nor Luc turned back, so Raymond kept going as well.

"Release the spell," Jean said when they reached the top of the stairs down to the crypt.

Raymond dropped the ward, bracing for an attack from below.

"They won't come up until they know we're gone," Luc said.

"Then perhaps we should attend to our devotions," Magali said with a smirk.

Jean returned her grin and crossed himself, kneeling down in front of the altar in the side chapel and bowing his head piously. Though the comment had been meant in jest, he took a moment to say a prayer of thanksgiving for whatever divine intervention had led him to this moment in time and the man behind him, waiting patiently as he prayed.

When lingering longer would have made a mockery of his true piety, he crossed himself again and rose to his feet, his hand slipping into Raymond's as they left the church and the other two undoubtedly fuming vampires.

"Let's stop at the café for a nightcap," Magali proposed when they reached place Darcy again. "I want a rundown of what happened, because I know much of the subtlety of your game went over my head."

"That's fine with me," Raymond said. "Tomorrow's Sunday, and I only work then if there's an emergency."

They entered the café, taking a table as far from the other customers as possible. Raymond ordered coffees all around, even knowing the vampires would not drink theirs. If nothing else, he and Magali could each have an extra cup.

"So was tonight a victory, a defeat, or somewhere in the middle?" Magali asked after the waiter brought their coffee.

"With le jeu des Cours, it's always somewhere in the middle," Luc replied, "because even a victory carries consequences with the people who would want to see you brought down because of it."

"Where in the middle did it fall?" Raymond asked, already used to asking the same question in several different ways where le jeu des Cours was concerned. The answer was never straightforward.

"In our favor," Jean said. "We maintained control of ourselves and the conversation throughout the evening. We gave nothing away that we didn't intend to, and we pointed out the weakness of their position at the same time. They can try to make trouble for us—"

"And undoubtedly will," Luc interjected.

Jean nodded. "But ultimately they can't stop l'Institut because it's not in an area they control, nor is it in a domain they can influence. We don't want to alienate them completely because it would be nice to have relatively local vampires available in case we need support or advice, but the worst they can do to us at this point is refuse to allow anyone in their Cours to communicate with us."

"They could bring the issue up for wider debate when the Congrès des chefs meets, but that isn't scheduled for another eighteen months," Luc added. "By then it will be too late to do anything. L'Institut will have gained enough momentum that the disapproval of a few vampires won't matter at all."

"If they find enough supporters, could they shut us down by cutting off potential students for the school?" Raymond asked.

Jean shrugged. "Maybe, but ultimately any vampire is free to leave any Cour at any time. If vampires who live in unsympathetic Cours want to participate, it's a question of petitioning to join a new Cour. I don't accept everyone who asks to join, but if someone wanted to join because they wanted to participate in a seminar at l'Institut and their chef de la Cour would not allow it, I would grant them membership immediately."

"And some vampires choose to live outside any Cour," Luc added. "Didn't you have one like that in Paris?"

"Sebastien Noyer," Jean replied. "You met him the other day at l'Institut. Finding a partner has brought him into the Cour, but that was not the case until a year ago."

"Is there any way the Congrès des chefs could hinder our work?" Raymond asked.

"Or our partnerships, for that matter," Magali added. "I don't know that I'll be very involved with l'Institut, but I'd rather not suddenly be ordered to leave my partner."

Raymond's heart clenched at the thought, though he tried to hide any outward reaction. He had no sense of the level of personal relationship between Luc and Magali beyond the request for two rooms when they stayed at l'Institut to help with the repairs—but he knew, for himself and for the pairs he considered friends, that such an order would lead to another uprising, one he would fully support.

Luc and Jean stared at each other for several moments before Jean replied, "It is possible that they could declare association with a wizard to be a crime under vampire law, which would make any vampire who chose to continue with a partnership *extorris* under our law. I can't imagine they could gather enough support for that, particularly since we could have ten times the number of partnerships in the Cours eighteen months from now. And they would have to make the penalty extinction in order to actually dissuade anyone who already has a partner."

"Can they still do that with the new laws in place?" Magali asked. "The death penalty isn't legal in France."

"They can try," Jean said with a shrug. "They won't succeed. There have been attempts to change the laws before, and in all the time I've been a vampire, they've never succeeded. They won't succeed now, not with the number of partnerships already in place, two influential chefs de la Cour with partners, and, once l'Institut is open, more partnerships all the time, or at least vampires who understand what it means to have a partner."

"If this is a risk, though, isn't it to our advantage to actively approach other chefs de la Cour to persuade them of the rightness of our position before those two can spread their lies?" Magali asked. "I realize I'm no expert at le jeu des Cours, but I learned well in the war that the best defense was a good offense. If nothing else, once l'Institut is open, we could invite other chefs de la Cour to come for a tour so they could see what we're doing and understand that it isn't something threatening."

"Not threatening?" Luc said with a laugh. "Nothing in my memory has ever been as threatening to the fabric of vampire society. Even with our Cours, we're loners, used to living on the outside. Forming partnerships, creating those kinds of bonds... we're on the cusp of something extraordinary. It's a question of staying the course and seeing it through to the end."

"We aren't looking at another war, are we?" Raymond asked, uncomfortable at the very thought.

"No," Jean and Luc said simultaneously.

"There aren't enough of us for it to come to that," Jean said. "We may end up in two distinct camps, but our partnerships also make us stronger, so whatever it looks like ten or twenty years from now, we will prevail."

Raymond looked back and forth between the two leaders. "I hope you're right."

Chapter 18

RAYMOND'S CELL phone rang as he arrived in his office on Monday afternoon. He had given in to Jean's insistence that they not work on Sunday and that they keep their normal hours on Monday, so he was not at all surprised to find a pile of messages on his desk. "Hello?"

"Oh, good, I've caught you," Thierry's voice said from the other end of the line. "When you have time today, can you come out to l'Institut? I want to show you a few things."

"Let me check my calendar and make sure Fabienne isn't ready to quit on me and I'll come down. In about an hour?" Raymond suggested.

"An hour is fine. We'll keep working until then."

"I couldn't quit on you," Fabienne said, grinning at Raymond. "L'ANS would cease to exist without me here to run it for you."

Raymond chuckled, as he knew she intended, but he could not stop from flushing when he thought about how true that had become since he and Jean had started work on l'Institut. "Is there anything urgent for me?"

"A few things," Fabienne replied. "They're in the center of your desk, but more and more things are building up, waiting for your attention."

"That was Thierry on the phone. He needs to show me something at l'Institut. Let me take care of the urgent items, see what he needs, and then I promise I'll work on clearing my desk for the rest of the evening," Raymond said.

Fabienne did not look convinced, but she did not say anything, letting him go into his office to check phone messages and e-mails. He returned several calls from members of Parlement with questions about new initiatives sponsored or supported by l'ANS, and took care of in-house e-mails. He signed a fundraising letter and made himself draft a column for the member newsletter that would go out at the beginning of December, updating the readers on progress with various l'ANS programs.

When almost an hour had passed and he had emptied the urgent pile, he left his office. "I'm heading out to l'Institut. I have my phone, and I shouldn't be more than a couple of hours if anyone needs me," he told her.

"Jean came by a few minutes ago and said he'd meet you there," Fabienne replied. "He said something about needing to meet with Orlando first."

"Thank you," Raymond said. "I'll let you know when I'm back."

A quick displacement spell sent him to Dommartin. Despite the cold, he took a moment to savor the brisk breeze. He loved Paris, had lived there since he was a teenager, but there was something to be said for the purity of country air. If he walked down to the lake and dipped his fingers in, he was sure he would find the same purity. He had other things to take care of first, though. "Thierry? Sebastien?"

"In here," Thierry replied, sticking his head out of one of the windows on the upper floor of the abbot's house. "It's safe to come upstairs."

Raymond chuckled to himself as he wondered whether he needed to be more worried about the state of the building or walking in on Sebastien and Thierry in a compromising position. It had not happened recently, but more than once during the war, he had approached their office only to change his mind at the last minute because of the sounds he heard coming through the door. "What's going on?" he asked when he made it inside and up to the room where the two men waited for him.

"We've been working on getting the abbot's house ready for inhabitants," Thierry said. "You mentioned needing two rooms for Luc and Magali, so we focused on this area. It will be more comfortable for pairs coming to help run the seminars as well, because the rooms are more spacious on the whole. Once we know the main building is stable, we can look at some of the interior walls and possibly combine some of the monks' cells to make double rooms. For now, this is a better bet."

Raymond looked around the empty room. "Where are we in the process?"

"With Vincent's and Marcel's help, we've made this building sound," Thierry reported, "and the workmen have made sure there is heat and electricity in all the rooms and running water in the appropriate places. All we need is furniture, and people can start moving in. It will be shared restrooms and showers, unless you want to change the order of work that needs to be done to renovate the rooms in here."

"I think if we're upfront about the arrangements, most people won't have a problem with that," Raymond replied, "particularly while it's just Magali and Luc."

"Actually," Sebastien interrupted, "Thierry and I were thinking we might stay until the repairs are done as well. It's tiring to travel back and forth each day. If you're already arranging for food for Magali, you could easily arrange for food for two."

"I can do that," Raymond agreed. "We didn't have that set up for another week because Luc and Magali have commitments until then, but I can contact the restaurant again and see about moving it up."

"They don't need to deliver it for me," Thierry said. "Just see if they'll run a tab and bill l'ANS at the end of the week or something."

"I should probably go into Dommartin anyway," Raymond mused, "since we're about to be a very big employer in the area."

"The other thing that might be worth looking into," Thierry said before Raymond could leave, "is a car for the school. We're so used to popping in and out at will or hopping the métro that being out here in the country has been a real shock. Sebastien was going to come with me to get lunch the other day, but we were the only two here, and we ended up having to walk. It's not so far that we couldn't do it, but it definitely took more time out of our day than we had planned on."

"I won't find a car in Dommartin," Raymond said with a laugh, thinking of the tiny hamlet of perhaps two hundred inhabitants, "but I can see about finding one in Autun or Auxerre."

"Obviously, it doesn't have to be anything large or fancy or even particularly new," Thierry said. "Just something that will get us from here to there and back again."

"I'll look into it. In the meantime, I think I should go check in with monsieur Papot and make sure he doesn't need any reassurance about anything. I'll check with the restaurant while I'm there and get something set up for you. Jean was supposed to show up after he finished meeting with Orlando. I guess he can wait here for me."

"I'll send him on to join you," Thierry offered, "unless you'd rather I didn't."

"No, that's fine," Raymond said. "I didn't want to make more work for you."

"I'd be sending him with you now if he were here already," Thierry reminded Raymond. "It's no problem to send him later."

"Thanks."

Thierry inclined his head and shooed Raymond toward the door.

Raymond left, amused at the ease of the gesture. So many things had changed in the last year, and he owed it all to Jean. In his private moments, he could not stop smiling whenever he thought of his lover. He rubbed absently at the bite marks on his chest right above his heart. He fully intended for those marks to never completely heal.

"If you do much of that, people will start thinking you have heart problems."

Raymond spun around, relaxing when he saw Jean lounging against the wall to the abbot's house. "Jean, you scared me!"

"Then I'll have to make it up to you," Jean said with a grin, pulling Raymond into his arms and kissing him. Raymond's eyes darted around the cloister, wondering if anyone was looking, but Jean's hands caught his cheeks, keeping him from turning his head or pulling away. "No one's looking, and even if they did, no one cares. It's been hours since I've seen you, and I need a kiss."

Raymond relaxed into the embrace, unable to resist Jean's affection for long. Thierry and Sebastien would not care if they saw, and the workmen might not recognize either him or Jean to make the connection or to care about it.

When Jean ended the kiss several long, enjoyable seconds later, he smiled at his lover. "Were you leaving already?"

"Only to go into Dommartin," Raymond said. "I thought it might be worth paying a visit to the mayor and seeing what kind of waves our presence here is causing."

"Do you expect it to cause any waves?" Jean asked.

"Not really, but I didn't expect it to cause waves with the vampires either, yet it clearly did."

"About that," Jean said. "I was thinking about how to head off any problems Céline and Renaud, Renaud particularly, might try to cause. If Luc and I approach the chefs de la Cour of each region, a few at a time, and explain to them what we're doing and how it could possibly benefit them, I hope we'll at least get the typical vampire laissez-faire attitude, even if we don't get their support."

"I think it's a very logical plan," Raymond agreed. "Tell me what you need from me and I'll take care of it."

Jean grinned wolfishly. "Ask me that question again when we get home and I'll have an answer for you."

Raymond rolled his eyes. "That's not what I meant."

"Does that mean you aren't going to put out tonight?" Jean said with a pout.

Raymond snorted. "That expression makes you look about ten years old. Let's find Thierry. The sooner we can finish our meeting with the mayor, the sooner we can get back to Paris. And the sooner we do that, the sooner we can go home for the night and see about who's going to do what for whom."

Jean's expression brightened considerably, making Raymond laugh again. "Thierry! Jean's here!"

Thierry joined them in the open cloister a few moments later. "Go ahead and I'll send him after you," Thierry told Raymond. "Call me when you're ready to come back, and I'll come get you."

Raymond nodded and disappeared, reappearing moments later on what passed for a town square in Dommartin. The bistro stood to one side of the triangular commons, with the bakery and the préfecture on the other two sides. Raymond smothered a smile at the squawk of surprise his arrival elicited from children who were playing soccer in the square despite the cold. "Stay back a minute longer," Raymond warned. "I have a friend who should be arriving right... about... now."

As if on cue, Jean appeared next to him, the children oohing in delight.

"Now you can come closer."

The children ran up to Jean. "Are you a wizard?"

"He is. I'm not," Jean replied with a grin, careful not to let his fangs drop. "I just hang out with him."

The boys grabbed Raymond's coat sleeves. "Do something for us," they begged. "Cast a spell."

Raymond raised an eyebrow but drew his wand, an affectation he rarely bothered with in private. With a dramatic swoosh, he summoned water, sending it spouting through the air. The boys clapped in delight as the droplets froze into an elegant arc. Raymond met Jean's eyes over the children's heads and smiled.

"Can you tell us where we might find the mayor?" Raymond asked. "My friend and I need to talk to him for a few minutes."

"Will you do some more magic when you come back?" the oldest boy asked.

"One more spell," Raymond promised. "Think about what you want to see me do so you can ask for a good one. As long as it won't hurt or embarrass anyone, I'll do my best to show you what you want to see."

"He has an office in the préfecture, but at this hour of the day you can usually find him having a drink with the other men in the café," the boy replied.

"Thank you. We'll be back later," Raymond said. He joined Jean and headed toward the café. "'He is. I'm not'?" Raymond parroted. "You don't think they might have been interested in what you are?"

"They probably would have been," Jean said, "but I didn't want to make a spectacle of myself."

"So you made one of me instead."

"Exactly," Jean said with a grin. "Do you know which of those venerable gentlemen is the mayor?"

"No idea," Raymond said, "but I'm quite sure an introduction on our part will provide us with the correct information."

They crossed the threshold into the tiny café, every head turning at the sight of unfamiliar faces darkening their doorway. "Can I help you?" the man behind the bar asked.

"I'm Raymond Payet," Raymond said. "I bought the abbey outside of town. I thought it was time I came by to say hello."

"Monsieur Payet, I'm Claude Papot, the mayor of Dommartin," a portly gentleman said, rising and offering his hand. "Jacques, a drink for monsieur Payet and his friend. I'm sorry, I didn't catch your name."

"Jean Bellaiche," Jean said, "an associate of monsieur Payet."

"My partner," Raymond corrected. "We're working together to refurbish the abbey. We were hoping you would have a few minutes to talk with us. We wanted to share our plans with you and get your thoughts on ways we could be good neighbors."

"Please join us," monsieur Papot said. "You're looking at the city council, and this is about as formal as our meetings get. Jacques will get you something to drink."

"An espresso for me."

"Monsieur Bellaiche?"

"Nothing for me," Jean said with a shake of his head. "I appreciate the offer, but my needs are… particular."

The barman looked like he was about to take offense, so Raymond leaned in conspiratorially and whispered, "Monsieur Bellaiche is the leader of the vampires in Paris. He is quite limited in his diet."

The barman subsided, but the city council looked like they were ready to flee. "You needn't worry. He is a most civilized man," Raymond added, drawing up a chair and joining the town fathers.

"So what exactly are your plans for the old abbey?" monsieur Papot asked, looking far less at ease than he had before. Raymond was tempted to kick Jean beneath the table, but it would change nothing now.

"We intend to turn it into a research and educational institute," Raymond explained. "We will be studying the interactions between wizards and vampires that allowed us to win l'émeute des Sorciers, and we will be preparing wizards and vampires for future situations in which those interactions could be useful."

"Will the vampires need to come into town frequently?" one of the council members asked warily.

"They aren't children, so we won't be restricting them to campus or anything like that," Raymond said, inwardly shaking his head at the ignorance of some people, "but the wizards can, of course, take themselves wherever they want if they need to leave l'Institut for a few hours, and our intention is to either take the vampires into Paris when they need to feed or else arrange for willing company to come to them."

"We were actually looking into the possibility of buying or renting another piece of property," Jean interrupted. "One of my associates in Paris runs a restaurant for vampires and was considering opening a branch here for l'Institut."

"H-how do you have a restaurant for vampires?" monsieur Papot asked.

"It isn't a restaurant in the traditional sense," Raymond said with a quelling stare for Jean. "Madame Bouaddi employs a certain number of people who are willing to be blood donors for the vampires. The vampires come in, pick the person they would like to feed from, pay for their meal, and leave. The employees are paid for their time, just like the waitstaff at a restaurant. They're just on the menu instead."

"So there would be this… flesh house as well as your institute moving to town?"

"If you would prefer, we can send the vampires into town to hunt on their own," Jean snapped. "Madame Bouaddi has been in this business for over a century. She takes good care of her employees and makes sure nothing untoward happens. No one will be hurt or corrupted by having a branch of Sang Froid in town."

This time, Raymond did slide a hand beneath the table and put it on Jean's leg, rubbing soothingly. Jean glared at him but subsided somewhat. "As I'm sure you're aware," Raymond said, "the Parlement passed a hard-fought law in favor of the vampires a year ago. My partner gets frustrated still having to fight old battles. Now, as I was saying, we have already started renovations at the abbey and hope to have the first group of attendees for our seminars come through in early January. Our intention is to hire locally for all positions that can be filled by nonwizards or nonvampires. Should we post Help Wanted signs here in the café or at the préfecture, or both?"

"What kind of jobs are you talking about?" monsieur Papot asked.

"We'll need cooks, maintenance staff, custodial staff," Raymond said, ticking off each item on his fingers. "We may need grounds staff once the seasons change and we see what kind of garden the abbey has. There will probably be some administrative positions as well, to oversee deliveries and keep records of expenses, that sort of thing."

"You could employ half the town with that," monsieur Papot marveled, "and that's counting everyone, not just the ones who are of age to work."

"We intend to be good neighbors," Raymond repeated. "We're a nonprofit agency, so we won't have a taxable income at l'Institut, but we will put a decent amount of money into the local economy in terms of salaries and purchases we make if the town can supply those needs."

When monsieur Papot looked at the city council, Raymond swore he could see the man already counting the money. "I'm sure we can find a way to accommodate your needs. Perhaps you could put together a list of the kinds of supplies you expect to order on a regular basis so we can see where you can acquire those things in the area? That way, the next time we meet, we could have some clearer answers for you."

Raymond smiled and rose from the table, downing his espresso in one long swallow. "I'll have my assistant get you a list. It's been a pleasure, gentlemen. We look forward to doing business with you."

Jean rose at Raymond's side and followed him silently out into the darkening evening. "Mercenary," he muttered under his breath.

"At least they'll be predictable," Raymond said. "If money is what gets their attention, we now know how to gain their cooperation for future endeavors as well. Sang Froid will have an income, which will put taxes directly into the city coffers. They may make disapproving noises, but they won't make trouble. Now I need to stop by the restaurant, and then we can go home."

Chapter 19

WHEN THEY returned to l'ANS headquarters an hour later, a deep frown marred Fabienne's face. "You have a guest," she said, her voice pinched with displeasure. "I tried telling him I didn't know when you would be back, but he insisted he would wait for you."

"Who is it?" Raymond asked, trying to think who would elicit such a strong reaction from Fabienne.

"Jude Leighton."

Raymond rolled his eyes. "After dealing with the honorable city council of Dommartin, I've had my fill of ignorant idiots for one night."

"You can go work elsewhere and hope he leaves," Fabienne said.

"We could, but he'll just keep coming back, and in a worse mood tomorrow because we didn't see him tonight," Jean said. "It's easier just to deal with him now and send him on his way again."

"What could he possibly want?"

Jean shrugged. "I'm sure he'll tell us."

They opened the door and walked into Raymond's office.

"What's the point of having office hours if you aren't available during them?" Jude challenged the moment the door closed behind him.

"We don't keep office hours," Raymond said smoothly. "We keep working hours. Not all of our projects can be completed sitting behind a desk. I'm sure you didn't come here to upbraid us over our presence or absence from our offices. Did you need something in particular, or was this purely a social call?"

Jean smothered a smile. Leighton rubbed him the wrong way, but Raymond was handling the vampire like an expert at le jeu des Cours. That subtle condescension was guaranteed to send Leighton through the roof, giving Raymond a firm victory.

"I want to know where Adèle is," Jude demanded. "You've hidden her for a year now. You're starting this Institut whatever you call it to match vampires with their partners, as they should be, but you're denying me access to mine."

"First of all," Jean said, taking the reins of the conversation for the moment, "we aren't trying to match anyone with anyone. We're trying to educate everyone so that if people choose to form a partnership, they can do so fully aware of the benefits and risks associated with it. That's something something none of us had. Secondly, we haven't denied you anything since Marcel lifted the Ordre de restriction against you."

"If you hadn't treated Adèle so poorly, maybe she wouldn't have chosen to disappear at the end of the war to get away from you," Raymond added. "She doesn't want to see you, and as far as I'm concerned, that's far more important than your unreasonable demands. Having a partner is not a right, and feeding from your partner after you have one is even less so. You limited your options when you chose to maul her every time you fed from her even when you knew she didn't want it."

"She wanted it," Jude insisted. "I was feeding from her, remember? I know what she felt, little slut that she is."

"And that attitude is exactly why she returned to the country instead of staying here," Raymond said, opening the door. "We can't help you, monsieur Leighton. If you want to mend your fences with your partner, you're on your own."

Jude glared at both men as he exited the office, adding another glare in Fabienne's direction as he passed.

"Jean," Fabienne began when Leighton was gone.

"I know," Jean said. "I need to do something about him. The problem is that he's an obnoxious bastard who rubs everyone the wrong way, but he hasn't actually done anything wrong under vampire law. If Adèle would speak against him, we might be able to do something under French law, but she hasn't been willing to do that."

"She won't do it," Raymond agreed. "She is all too aware of being a woman in a man's profession, and she has a very strongly ingrained sense of needing to take care of things herself. Jude would have to hurt her so badly and so visibly that her colleagues started to pressure her to press charges before she would even think of doing it. And honestly, even then I'm not sure she would want the private details of their interactions made public."

"Was he really that bad during the war?" Fabienne asked.

"She didn't share details," Raymond said, "but when the wild magic broke loose, she showed us some of the marks he left on her, and she looked like she'd been savaged. And two days later, at the Piège-Pouvoir, he wouldn't stop touching her, even when she told him to and when so ignoring her demands caused her control of her magic to waver. He thinks she's his chattel, from what I can tell. Needless to say, she disagrees."

"So she's hidden herself away out near l'Institut in hope of avoiding him," Jean finished.

"She has a home there and did before the war," Raymond disagreed. "The speed of her return had something to do with Leighton, but I think she would have returned anyway. Her job was there, her home, her friends. It was always a point of pride for her that she went away to be educated and came back to her hometown to work. You saw Dommartin. Her hometown is somewhat larger, maybe two thousand people instead of two hundred, but it's still a small town in rural Burgundy."

In the hallway, Leighton slunk away on silent feet. He had heard enough to begin his search. One way or another, he would reclaim what was rightfully his.

"I can't imagine living in a town that small," Fabienne said with a shudder.

"We couldn't live in a town that small," Jean agreed. "We need the anonymity of a city to survive."

"You could live there now," Raymond said. "The antidiscrimination laws would keep you from being run off."

"But that wouldn't keep ignorance and disdain from making it impossible to find someone willing to let us feed," Fabienne countered. "We'd starve to death in a matter of weeks. There's a reason there's no Cour in that little town of yours."

"Prejudice is a terrible thing," Raymond agreed. "I suppose we need to get back to work."

Fabienne laughed. "Your inbox is fuller now than when you left."

Raymond sighed. "No rest for the wicked, I suppose."

Jean grinned at him and winked over Fabienne's head. "None whatsoever," he agreed. "I'm going to see if there's anything urgent I need to take care of. If there's not, I'll come back and help you."

Raymond grinned all the way back into his office. He knew exactly how much work he would get done if Jean joined him.

A LITTLE over a week later, Magali pulled her car off the narrow road onto the long driveway down to l'Institut. "This is going to be quite the complex when it's finished," she observed to the vampire sitting next to her.

"As long as it lives up to its promises where the research is concerned, it can be as grand or as simple as Payet desires," Luc replied.

Magali rolled her eyes. Her partner was such a vampire. He treated her with courtesy and respect and insisted everyone else do the same, but his priorities had been in no way affected by her intrusion into his life. She might be his partner and sole source of sustenance, but he still cared nothing for mortals as a whole aside from their liaison. In fact, she often thought he cared even less than before because he no longer had to worry about finding a willing donor when he was hungry. She could not complain too much, though. He had helped her get settled in Amiens, making room for her in his life and accepting her inability to fall asleep with anyone in bed next to her. He came to her room more days than not to feed, but when they were both sated, he left her in peace to rest.

"Raymond is many things, but before he was anything else he was a researcher and a historian. If anyone can make this happen, it will be him,"

Magali replied. "How would you feel about me coming down to help with the seminars during the day? I could commute and come home each night, so you could still feed as often as you needed to."

Luc's eyes narrowed, making Magali wonder if she would have a fight on her hands, but the vampire subsided after a moment. "As long as you are there when I need to feed, the rest of your time is your own. I told you that from the beginning."

They pulled up next to the grange and parked. "Shall we see what's going on inside? Raymond said they would have rooms for us in the abbot's house."

Luc nodded and took both suitcases from the trunk, carrying them toward the abbot's lodge. Magali rolled her eyes at his typical insistence on showing off. She grabbed her purse and the smaller bag and followed him, observing all the changes since the last time she had been there. The hole in the outer wall had been repaired completely as far as she could tell, and several of the markers on the exterior walls of the main building and abbot's house were gone as well. "It looks like they're making good progress," she commented. "I'm going to take a quick walk around. I don't like not knowing the lay of the land. Can you carry these inside as well?"

Luc grunted his reply and took the extra load. He didn't claim to understand all of his partner's quirks, but he had come to accept them over the past year. She had spent too long as a lone agent—the cleanup crew after a battle ended—to feel secure in an unfamiliar location until she had personally ensured their safety.

Magali started at the grange, walking the perimeter of the wards, inspecting them as carefully as she inspected the buildings themselves. She recognized Adèle's handiwork, which reassured her. She had not kept in touch with the other wizard after the war ended, so she had not realized Raymond was still in touch with her or that he had called on her to do the security of l'Institut. As she rounded the far corner of the compound, she smiled to see the object of her thoughts standing on the bank of the lake. "Adèle, what are you doing here so late?"

"I have a day job," Adèle said with a smile, crossing to Magali's side and kissing both her cheeks in welcome. "I didn't get off work until about an hour ago. I figured I'd come here and take care of this first, and then I could relax and think about some dinner."

"I haven't eaten either," Magali said. "Luc and I were going to drive into Dommartin and see what we could find after we got settled in the abbot's house. Would you like to come with us?"

"If you don't mind waiting," Adèle said. "I have another half hour's work here, probably, but you don't really want to go into Dommartin for dinner. If you're going to drive, you may as well go the extra ten minutes into Château-Chinon. You'll have far more choice and a far better meal."

"We can wait," Magali said. "Come find us when you're done. Unless you need some help here?"

Adèle shook her head. "It's honestly easier to do it myself. Then I don't have to worry about anyone else's magical resonances clashing with mine. It's bad enough Eric worked on them when the wall fell in."

"Then I'll let you work. Come get us when you're ready to go."

Alone again, Adèle turned her attention back to what she was doing, not entirely sure she wanted to spend an evening with a vampire-wizard pair. She had enough trouble with the longings she could not completely smother without having to watch people who had the kind of bond she had dreamed of and had been denied through her partner's irascibility.

Finished with the wards along the lake, Adèle stepped around the outer wall so she could reinforce the wards where the collapse had occurred. She closed her eyes, concentrating on the spell, picturing in her mind the layers of protection that would stop intruders, alert a wizard of someone's presence, and sound an alarm if magic troubled the wards.

The feeling of hands around her neck startled her out of her trance. Immediately she cast a stun spell on her unseen attacker, but the hands did not loosen. Cursing under her breath, she fell back on her police training, but the grip did not falter. "Hello, pussy."

Adèle cursed again when she recognized the hateful voice. Somehow Jude had found her. His hands tightened even more, cutting off her air. She relaxed in his grip, hoping he would not squeeze her throat until she lost consciousness. She could feel her vision blackening around the edges when his grip finally loosened a little. He chose that moment to puncture her neck with his fangs. She cried out sharply but did not struggle. She needed to lull him into complacency so she could get away.

One hand still on her throat, he moved the other hand to the front of her coat, opening the buttons so he could get to the body beneath. His fingers burrowed beneath the hem of her sweater, uncaring that the motion bared her skin to the frigid air as he sought the swell of her breasts. Biding her time, Adèle flicked her wand toward the wards, hoping the disturbance would alert Magali. Adèle was not particularly thrilled about the other woman seeing her pinned by her partner, but she was even less comfortable with what she knew Jude would do if she did not escape.

Jude's fangs left her neck, but his grip tightened again. "You have been a very bad girl, pussy, running away like you did." His fingers pulled the cup of her bra away from her skin, pinching roughly at her nipple. "You need to be taught a lesson about denying me what I want. I'm looking forward to teaching you." He released her neck, grabbing her hair and pulling her toward the woods.

Taking advantage of having her breath back, Adèle cast a displacement spell, fleeing to the safety of home.

"Hey! What are you doing here?"

The disappearance of the woman in his arms and the shouted question left Jude cursing. He turned to spring toward the woods and the car he had hidden there, but a spell caught him, sending him to the ground, unable to move.

"Who are you and what did you do with Adèle?"

Jude held his tongue until another person joined the woman demanding answers.

"Jude Leighton," the vampire said. "I should have known you'd come sniffing around."

"You know him?" Magali asked.

"Adèle's partner, or former partner, since she chose to come out here instead of staying in Paris," Luc replied. "You remember him from the Piège-Pouvoir."

Now that Luc had refreshed her memory, Magali remembered the incident clearly. In the middle of a powerful and dangerous spell to ground the wild magic that had escaped a Rite d'équilibrage, the vampire had started groping Adèle, causing her to nearly lose control of her magic and burn both of them. "What are you doing here?" Magali demanded.

Jude did not answer.

Scowling, Magali knelt down next to the prone vampire, her wand pressed to his breastbone. "You listen to me, vampire. You're used to dealing with Marcel and Raymond and the others. They have scruples. I don't. I don't have any qualms about using magic on you until you tell me what I want to know, and I can do it without leaving a single trace. And before you look to Luc, he'll turn a blind eye to what I'm doing because he's as addicted to my blood as you are to Adèle's." She sent a small tendril of magic through her wand, constricting his breathing. "Are you ready to talk to me?"

Jude nodded.

"Where's Adèle?"

"She disappeared," Jude gasped. "It's been over a year. I just want what's mine. You don't keep your partner from feeding. What gives her the right to deny me?"

"The fact that you treat her like she's worthless chattel," Luc said. "I'd say that gives her every right to do far more than simply leave. I'm pretty sure she could have you tossed in jail for assault."

"Stupid slut. She wanted it. I could taste it in her blood. She likes it when I'm rough."

"It will be your word against hers, and every woman on the jury would listen to the abusive way you talk about her and condemn you for that alone," Magali insisted. "I have no idea how you got here, but I know how you're leaving. Luc, if you'll excuse us for a few minutes, I need to take out the trash."

Jude started to protest, but Magali extended her binding spell so he could not speak. With a wave of her wand, she displaced them both to the offices of l'ANS in Paris. "I'm sorry to arrive unannounced," she said to Fabienne, "but I need to see Raymond and Jean."

"What's going on?" Fabienne asked, picking up the phone to buzz Jean's office.

"Leighton came skulking around l'Institut and attacked Adèle," Magali said.

Fabienne's eyes narrowed. "Where is he now?"

"In the hallway where I left him."

"Good," Fabienne said. "Stay here."

Magali followed, of course, in time to watch Fabienne plant a booted foot in Jude's stomach. "You know," Magali said with a smile for Fabienne, "I think he needs another one." She added a second kick to the first one, leaving Jude's face contorted in pain. "Maybe that will teach him a lesson."

"Probably not," Fabienne said, returning to her desk, "but it makes me feel better."

"Magali?" Jean said, coming into Fabienne's office from the other direction. "What are you doing here?"

"Get Raymond first," Fabienne said. "You both need to deal with this."

Jean rapped on Raymond's door and stuck his head inside, summoning his lover into the outer office.

"I found Leighton outside l'Institut tonight," Magali explained. "Adèle was nowhere to be seen, but it was her alert that summoned me, so my guess is that he found her and attacked her. She obviously got away, but that doesn't change his intentions."

"Where is he now?"

"In the hallway," both women replied, sharing a grin. "A little worse for the wear."

"Don't tell me anything you know I don't want to hear," Raymond warned.

They went out to the hall. "Undo the spell," Raymond told Magali, his own wand drawn and ready. The moment the spell was released, Jude sprang to his feet, lunging for Magali. Jean blocked him before he could reach her, pinning Jude against the wall with an arm across his throat. The difference in their sizes made little difference given the difference in their ages, Jean's greater age offsetting his slighter build.

"Don't do something you'll regret," Jean warned, pressing a little harder. "Even if you get away from me, you're still facing the wands of two of the deadliest wizards in France, and their spells will work on you. Now what the hell were you doing trying to find Adèle after she's made it very clear that she wants nothing to do with you?"

"I want what's mine," Jude growled. "You can't keep me away from her. I know where she is now. It's just a matter of time before I find her again."

"You'd be amazed what I can do," Raymond disagreed, "and if I can't—or won't—I can pretty much guarantee Magali can and will, so I suggest you return to whatever hole you crawled out of and forget about Adèle. You obviously can't behave like a civilized man, so don't expect any help or sympathy from l'ANS or l'Institut unless it's to give Adèle a way to end your partnership permanently."

"Is that possible?" Jude asked. "And if it is, would I be able to find another partner, one who might actually give me my due this time?"

"We have no idea yet if it's possible," Jean replied, "but don't hold your breath on finding another partner, because you have no concept of what a partnership is. If you did, you'd never treat Adèle the way you do. You don't want her to be your partner. You want her to be your property."

"She's a mortal and a woman. Is there a difference?"

Magali's spell hit him before anyone could react. "He'll wake up in a few hours with a pounding headache. Leave him somewhere nice and sunny and he won't be a problem anymore."

"You know we can't do that without a proper trial," Raymond sighed. "And I don't think we could do it even then. Having a bad attitude isn't a crime, however much we might wish it was."

"That's far more than just a bad attitude."

"Misogyny isn't a crime either, nor is xenophobia," Jean reminded Magali. "He hasn't harmed another vampire or done anything to endanger another vampire. That's all I can prosecute him for under vampire law. If someone can persuade Adèle to press charges, we might have a case."

"She was going to join us for dinner tonight, but I doubt that will happen now," Magali said, "but I'll call her. If she can be persuaded, I'll let you know." With a flick of her fingers, she was gone.

"Wake him up, Raymond," Jean said. "I understand why Magali cast the spell, but I can't just drop him somewhere."

Raymond didn't agree, but he reversed Magali's spell nonetheless. Leighton woke up slowly, his head clearly pounding.

"Get out of here, Leighton," Jean said, urging the other vampire toward the door, "and if you have the sense God gave a snail, stay the hell away from l'Institut and Adèle. I might not be able to convince her to press charges, but I know I can convince Raymond to charge you with trespassing if you're found at l'Institut again."

"In a heartbeat," Raymond agreed. "We'll post private property signs tomorrow."

Jude glared at them, but he left quietly if sullenly.

"Jean—"

"I know," Jean interrupted. "I have to do something about him. I just don't know what."

Chapter 20

"WE'RE ON schedule then?" Raymond asked Thierry at the end of the blond wizard's report on the repairs at l'Institut.

"Unless we have another collapse, we should have everything ready that we'll need for the first round of seminars by the second week of December," Thierry agreed. "That will give you three weeks to furnish the rooms—you should talk to Magali about that, by the way, she had a few choice things to say about the quality of the items in their rooms—and do any other preparations for the first group. I have some things in storage from the house in Versailles that I could donate if it will help."

"Alain, how many wizards do we have signed up?"

"Seven," Alain replied. "Three from l'Hôtel-Dieu and four from the police force. I think monsieur Sarraute will recruit more for us if the first seminar goes well. He said he'd been wanting to include some vampires on the force for help in dealing with situations that might involve vampires, but he hadn't known how to get around the issue of sunlight. He was intrigued by the idea of using paired vampires and wizards."

"And I have an equivalent number of vampires interested," Orlando said. "Actually, I have quite a few more than that, but I know you want to keep the groups fairly balanced."

Raymond nodded. "I don't expect there to be partnerships in every single group, especially not small ones like this, but I don't want to create the appearance of not giving everyone equal choice. Once people have completed the seminars, they're welcome to come back and look for partners among subsequent groups if they so desire."

A knock interrupted them. "Come in," Raymond called.

David's red head appeared in the doorway. "Good news!"

"What's that?" Raymond asked.

"Angélique went into Dommartin today after finding an old country estate she thinks will be perfect for Sang Froid's new branch," David reported. "She found the town council in session at the local café and charmed them into giving her the permits she'll need to open the business."

"Wonderful news!" Raymond agreed. "Not that I'm surprised. I'm pretty sure she could charm anyone into anything."

David laughed. "Yes, probably. She is most persuasive."

None of them said it, but they all remembered the argument between David and Angélique that had nearly ended their partnership. It had taken considerable groveling on David's part to convince Angélique to reconsider her decision to leave the alliance. Even after that, her business had continued to pose a problem for David until she had convinced him to look at it through a vampire's eyes.

"Where is she now?"

"She decided to stay in Dommartin for awhile," David replied. "Magali said something about looking in antique shops for better furniture and taking Adèle with her. Angélique offered to go along as well, and since her taste is exquisite, I expect they'll have l'Institut furnished by tonight."

Raymond groaned. "I don't want to get that bill."

"She's also an expert haggler," David reminded Raymond. "She may fill the building, but she'll do it for half the price it would cost if anyone else bought the same things."

"Then I'll just have to hope she's in top form," Raymond said. "Is there anything else we need to discuss for l'Institut?"

"Who's going to run it?" Thierry asked seriously.

"Are you offering?" Raymond joked.

"Don't do that to me," Thierry replied, completely seriously. "I'll spend as many hours as you want doing repairs. I'll give as many lectures as you want on any topic you give me, but don't ask me to be in charge of the place. I wouldn't have the slightest idea how to deal with the administrative side of it."

"So who would you suggest?" Raymond asked. "We can post a job opening and do a search, but we're talking about starting in five weeks. That's barely enough time to read resumes."

Alain and Thierry looked at each other and back at Raymond. "You," Alain said. "There isn't anyone in France more qualified, and if we start looking internationally for a researcher of your caliber, we'll be dealing with someone who doesn't have our experience with vampires or partnerships, not to mention the possible language barrier."

"What about l'ANS?" Raymond asked. "I can't do both."

Alain glanced at Thierry one more time. Thierry nodded and replied, "Neither of us can run it permanently, me because I don't have the patience and Alain because the brand on his neck puts him out of contention, but we could keep things going while we did a candidate search. Your replacement wouldn't have to have a partner as long as he or she shared the vision of l'ANS representing all the magical races. We can stay on here, along with Fabienne and others, to make sure everything continues smoothly and with the same focus on equality and integration that you've pursued this year."

Raymond took a deep breath, trying to steady his suddenly pounding pulse. He had not let himself think about it, had told himself he had a duty to l'ANS. To have his two most trusted advisors telling him now that the whole community would be best served by him following his heart was almost too much to bear. "I don't want to make a rash decision. Let's get the first group through and see where things stand. I want to make sure I'm leaving at a good time, if I do decide to go."

"Whatever you decide, you have our support," Thierry said. "We couldn't have asked for better leadership this year, and I know that will continue if you decide to stay. If you decide to take the position at l'Institut, we expect regular visits and updates. You don't get to disappear just because we won't be working together directly anymore."

"That's right," Orlando chimed in. "You're stuck with us now."

Raymond smiled. "I can live with that. Is there anything else we need to discuss before we adjourn?"

Everyone shook their heads.

"Then we'll meet back in a week and see how things look then," Raymond declared.

Alain, Orlando, Thierry, Sebastien, and David filed out, leaving Jean and Raymond alone in the conference room. Jean closed the door and turned to Raymond. "They're offering you your dreams on a silver platter."

"I know they are," Raymond replied, "but they're doing it because they know it's what I want. That doesn't mean it's the best thing for l'ANS, and I promised Marcel I would do my best for it when he asked me to take his place. I can't break that promise simply because something 'better' has come up. That isn't fair to anyone, nor does it speak very highly of me."

"I know," Jean said, "but promise me you'll consider it from every angle before you decide to reject their very generous offer."

"I promise."

"YOU THINK he attacked her?" Angélique asked Magali as they drove toward Château-Chinon and Adèle's house.

"I don't know what else to think and she brushed me off when I called to check on her," Magali admitted. "She was there working on the wards when I sensed an alert. There are two kinds of alerts in wards like the one Adèle built at l'Institut. One is like a doorbell ringing, just a way to let the wizards inside know that someone is outside trying to get in. The other is more of a warning. That's the one I felt, so I went outside to investigate. It could have been a test on her part, but I learned not to take chances during the war. I got to where I'd last seen her and she was gone, but Jude was there. I called out and he ran, so I stopped him. He wouldn't say whether he'd seen her, but he had no problem calling her all kinds of names and making it clear he wanted to see her."

"We'll see if she'll tell us more in person," Angélique said. "I've had centuries of experience in encouraging girl talk, even with reluctant girls."

"She needs to press charges against him if he did anything more than shout insults at her," Magali said. "We can bluff and threaten Jude all we want, but we haven't witnessed anything serious enough to press charges. If she doesn't do something to stop him, he's going to keep hounding her."

"And one of these days, she'll give in," Angélique sighed.

"Do you think so?"

Angélique nodded. "Between the partnership bond and her own attraction to bad boys, her resolve won't last forever. You're fortunate. You and Luc settled fairly quickly and comfortably into your partnership. David and I weren't so fortunate. Until the last week or so of the war, I expected to walk away from him when the war ended because we couldn't seem to agree on anything that mattered to me, but I couldn't do it. We worked out our differences, but I don't know how much longer I could have resisted even if we hadn't. I *needed* to be with him. Adèle is feeling that same pull, even if she's trying to deny it."

"Maybe it's gotten easier to manage while they've been apart?"

"Maybe it has, but then she saw him. Even if he didn't touch her—which I highly doubt—something happened to make her flee, or else she would have waited for you to come and help her," Angélique said. "I watched her fight. She isn't one to run unless there's no other choice."

The conversation paused as they reached Château-Chinon and had to follow Adèle's directions to her house. Adèle came out as soon as they pulled up. "Do you want me to drive?" she asked Magali. "It might be easier than me trying to give you directions the whole time."

"That's fine," Magali said, getting out of the car so Adèle could have the driver's seat. Adèle looked peaked, increasing Magali's concern, but if she brought it up right away, Adèle would either deny it or disappear before they could find out more. They had all day. They could bring it up later, when she had relaxed into a day of female camaraderie. "I'm not at all familiar with this area."

Adèle slid behind the wheel and started out of town along the winding country roads. "There are little shops scattered all through these hills. You just have to know where to find them and then see what they have."

"We need fourteen guest rooms, plus a few rooms for presenters who might decide to stay overnight before or after their portion of the seminars," Angélique said. "David called to let me know how many participants they have in the first seminar. The rooms don't have to be fancy, but they should at least have a bed, a table and chair, and an armoire."

"I can't promise we'll find fancy, but we'll see plenty of functional pieces," Adèle assured them. "The first place is just around the corner up here."

Magali bided her time, letting the atmosphere grow comfortable as the three of them looked through the first shop, discussing prices, comparing styles and matching pieces. When they finally settled on several items they thought would work, Angélique offered to discuss the price with the owner.

Magali and Adèle agreed and sat back to watch the vampire completely bulldoze the man behind the counter. By the time she was done, they had purchased all four pieces they wanted, plus one they had deemed too expensive, for less than the listed prices on the original four pieces.

"When do you want to take delivery of them?" the owner asked after Magali paid.

"We don't need delivery," she said. "We'll take them with us right now."

The man looked outside at the small car they were driving and back at the two armoires, two bed frames, and large table and shook his head. "How?"

Magali smiled and cast a displacement spell on the furniture. "Magic."

They left the shop with the man gaping behind them. As soon as they were outside, Magali gave in to her laughter. "Did you see the look on his face? I thought he was going to pop a vein right then."

"He did look pretty shocked," Angélique agreed.

"We don't get a lot of wizards out here in the country," Adèle explained. "They all go to Paris or Lyon to learn how to use their magic, and very few of them come back. This may be the first time that poor man has ever seen anyone actually do magic."

"Do I need to stop?" Magali asked. "I don't want to cause problems."

Adèle shook her head. "He'll get over it, and waiting for—and maybe paying for—delivery is ridiculous when we can take care of it with a wave of our wands."

They climbed back in the car, and Adèle continued toward the next shop. "I'm sorry we didn't get to have dinner earlier this week," Magali said, watching closely for a reaction from Adèle. "I came looking for you, but you weren't there anymore."

Adèle flushed. "I got called away."

"Nothing serious, I hope," Magali said. "I was surprised by who I did find, though. Your partner was skulking around in the bushes."

"I don't have a partner," Adèle snapped. "He forfeited that title when he wouldn't take no for an answer a year ago."

"I didn't realize it had gotten that bad," Angélique said sympathetically. "What happened?"

"He thinks that because my blood can protect him from sunlight, I should be at his beck and call seven days a week," Adèle complained. "He's disapproved of me from the moment we met at la Gare de Lyon, before we knew that a wizard's magic didn't work on her partner and the only way we could find each other was for the vampires to bite the wizards until they found the right one. By the time he approached me, my wrist was covered in bites, so somehow I was suddenly a slut in his eyes. Nothing I said or did ever changed that attitude."

"Did you sleep with him?" Magali asked, though she thought she knew the answer.

"I wouldn't call it that," Adèle replied, her voice heavy with sarcasm. "We fucked a couple of times, once after a battle, after the Piège-Pouvoir, a couple of other times, but it was always so twisted. My body reacted to him, but I hated every minute of it."

"So press charges against him," Magali said. "Even if you can't claim rape, you can certainly charge him with assault."

Adèle shook her head. "I can't do that. Not when I started it at least once."

"You also had the good sense to stop it," Angélique said quietly, "even if that meant leaving Paris to do so."

Adèle shook her head. "It wasn't like that. I came home, just like I'd always intended. I just neglected to mention to him where home is. I don't actually know how he found out, but it doesn't matter. He's found me again, so I'm sure I'll have more nighttime visits to look forward to."

The resignation in her voice tore at Angélique. "Why? Even if what happened before was both of you, why not do something about it if he starts stalking you now?"

"Because I don't want my private business drawn out in court," Adèle said. "I have to work with the people who would be investigating and prosecuting my case, and they don't need to know all the sordid details."

"Are they really that bad?" Magali asked.

"Yes."

Magali and Angélique waited for an explanation, but none came. Finally Angélique said, "Then what are you going to do?"

Adèle shrugged. "I don't know. I came home because that's what I'd always planned to do, so that didn't feel like running away and it certainly wasn't starting over. I could apply for a transfer within the department—but I'd have to sell my house and find a new one, get established in a new town, make a new name for myself there. I don't want to do that, but I don't know what else to do."

"You can't stick it out in Château-Chinon?" Magali asked. "Even if your wards won't work on Leighton, someone else could come add a layer that would. My magic works on him. Raymond's or Alain's or Thierry's would."

"As long as I didn't cave and let him in," Adèle said. "I heard his voice the other night and my brain screamed *run* while everything in my body melted into his arms. I got away from him because my brain is still capable of overruling my body, but for how long? How long before I'll hear that seductive drawl and think it won't hurt just once? Only once will never be enough. He's like a drug, and I'm a recovering addict. As long as I can stay away from him, I can live with the temptation, but I'm not sure I can fight myself and him."

"They are seductive bastards when they want to be," Magali agreed, flushing as she remembered Luc coming to her room the night before and ravishing her most pleasantly as he fed.

Adèle laughed, glancing at Angélique, who wore an amused expression. "Sorry, don't take that the wrong way."

Angélique shook her head. "Don't worry. I won't. Especially since I'm perfectly willing to admit I seduced my partner and continue to do so on a regular basis."

"If he'd ever bothered to seduce me instead of just demanding, I might not mind so much," Adèle admitted. "It isn't the rough sex that bothered me. It was his fucked-up condescending attitude, like I was somehow dirty because I enjoy sex in all its forms and because I'm woman enough to admit it."

"Vampires are a very traditional bunch," Angélique reminded them. "That doesn't excuse Jude's behavior—I don't condone the way he treated you in or out of bed—but it is something of an explanation. He has in his head a certain way mortals should act, a certain way women should act, and now a certain way his partner should act. They're wrong, but they're there. And because they're there, he reacts badly to anything that contradicts those ideas. You can argue with him all you want. He won't change his mind. It isn't in his nature."

"I've watched other vampires compromise," Adèle said.

"Every vampire is different, of course," Angélique agreed. "Some are not as set in their ways. Some have different ideas of mortals to begin with. Some come from different times or backgrounds that make them think differently. Jude is the unfortunate product of a specific time, place, and set of experiences. What can we do to help? Is there some spell we can use that will help you resist him? Something we do to him that will keep him away?"

Adèle smiled sadly. "Drop a wall on his head so I don't have to deal with him anymore. Other than that, I'll just have to do my best to resist him and live with the consequences if I can't. I thought about going to Paris to demand Raymond fix this, but there's nothing he can do about it either. I just have to hope something comes out of the research at l'Institut that will make it possible to break such a dysfunctional bond."

Chapter 21

THE MORNING of January fifth dawned cold and clear, making Raymond hope for an equally auspicious beginning to the first seminar at l'Institut. The seven wizards were scheduled to arrive that afternoon around three, with other wizards picking up the vampires after sunset to transport them to l'Institut. He glanced around the cloister, making sure everything was ready. Some of the areas were carefully cordoned off because repairs had not yet begun or were not yet finished. Thierry and Sebastien stood in the middle of one of those sections, discussing the next steps with the foreman of the remodeling crew that had done so much of the renovations after the repairs were complete on a magical level. Raymond suspected the foreman would have hired Thierry and Sebastien as part of his permanent crew if he could have lured them away. Thierry's and Sebastien's assistance, and the assistance of the other wizards with an affinity to earth, had cut the time needed for basic repairs down by at least seventy-five percent, maybe more. They never would have had l'Institut ready to open this quickly without the wizards' help.

The finished areas were as carefully manicured as a blustery January day would allow, the grass trimmed and the weeds cleared so the areas that would be flower beds later lay fallow beneath a layer of mulch. The villagers had come through, much to Raymond's surprise after the first meeting with the town council, providing assistance in a wide variety of nonmagical areas. The kitchen was fully stocked and staffed, ready to serve family style. The grounds had been cleaned by a group of five men who had been trying to start a landscaping company. Raymond intended to hire them to take care of the gardens when the weather warmed and they could begin fresh planting. A woman and her three daughters had offered to take care of all the cleaning and washing for the linens in the guest rooms. It made him realize how eager people were for living-wage jobs in their own towns, rather than having to drive several towns away for work. He was not sure Angélique would be able to staff her branch of Sang Froid locally, but he suspected she would be able to get all the extra help she needed with no problem.

"What are you doing here so early?" Thierry asked Raymond, crossing one of the construction zone barriers and joining Raymond on the grass. "Arrival time isn't scheduled for at least seven hours from now."

"I know," Raymond said, "but I needed to make sure everything was ready. I know the building is, but I wanted to check the guest rooms and see how preparations were going for dinner and make sure the materials were all copied and—"

"Stop," Thierry interrupted with a laugh. "I get it. Go do what you need to do. Just watch the barriers. Some of them are still only physical. Now that I've got Bertrand and his crew started, that's the first thing on my list for today so that no one will decide to get curious and ignore the warning signs."

"And we all know how curious wizards can be," Raymond agreed, thinking of the scrapes he had landed in during his youth because of his curiosity. Looking around the cloister, he hoped this would not be another of those "scrapes."

"We do indeed," Thierry laughed. "Let me get that taken care of and then I'll see if there's anything I can do to help you. Nothing else on my to-do list has to be done before the wizards arrive this afternoon or the vampires this evening."

"Thank you," Raymond said, heading toward the Hostellerie where the wizards would sleep. Despite feeling like he was giving the vampires second-class accommodations, he had given in to Jean and Sebastien's insistence that the vampires would be more comfortable in the monks' cells where no light came in during the day than they would be in the grander, airier rooms of the Hostellerie. He did not immediately see madame Naizot, but the eldest daughter, Aimée, was sweeping the foyer.

"Bonjour, monsieur Payet," she chirped when he walked in. "We have everything almost ready. Maman is making sure the flowers are fresh in all the rooms, and she has Chantal and Geneviève making sure all the linens are in place and all the hallways swept. I'm in charge of this level."

Raymond took a moment to wipe his feet so he would not traipse dirt or leaves across the immaculate floor. "Everything looks wonderful," he said. "I hope you and your family will join us for dinner tonight so I can introduce the full staff to our guests. I want to thank you all appropriately."

"I'm sure that's not necessary, monsieur Payet," Aimée demurred, "but I'll mention it to Maman and let her decide."

Raymond had already learned the futility of arguing with any of the Naizot sisters. Their mother was the final authority where their jobs were concerned. If Raymond wanted something done or not done, he went to madame Naizot or to no one. "I'll speak with her, then."

He found Chantal first, coming out of one of the rooms with an armful of towels. "How can you need to take those out of the room?" he asked. "No one has stayed there yet."

"There's a stain on one of them, and we don't have another set that matches these," Chantal explained. "I'll see if I can get the stain out, but for now, I've replaced it with a different set. Maman said everything needed to be perfect."

"Where is your mother?" Raymond asked.

"Upstairs," Chantal replied with a tilt of her head.

Raymond frowned. He had thought all the upstairs rooms were empty. The members of l'ANS who would be presenting the seminars had been assigned rooms in the abbot's house.

Climbing the stairs, he entered the first guest room to find it fully furnished and decorated. "Madame Naizot?" he asked in surprise, seeing her filling a vase with flowers. "What happened in here?"

"Those rooms in the abbot's house aren't fit to sleep in even for a night," madame Naizot insisted. "A couple of your wizards helped me find what we needed to set things to rights up here. I've set up a room down the hall for you, monsieur Payet. All you have to do is move into it. Let me show it to you so you can tell me if anything is amiss. I want it to be perfect for you."

"I already have a room in the abbot's house," Raymond said.

Madame Naizot tsked. "When the abbot's quarters are ready, you can move back over there, but until then, you'll stay here in a style befitting the president of l'ANS."

Raymond shook his head in amusement. "If that will make things easier for you and your daughters, that will be fine with me. Show me the room so I can move my things over here."

She led him down the hall to the room at the end under the eaves. It ran the full width of the building, making it easily the largest room in the Hostellerie, second only in the entire abbey to the as-yet unfinished abbot's quarters. She had decorated it simply, but he noticed the heavy drapes on the windows and the curtains on the four-poster bed. "My partner will appreciate the thought you put into providing for our comfort," Raymond said, fingering the quilt on the bed. "This is a lovely room."

"Monsieur Sebastien told me to make sure the rooms for the vampires had certain things," madame Naizot replied. "I don't have all the rooms as ready as I'd like, but yours is, and the ones in the main building where he said most of the vampires would be staying are ready as well. We'll get them all right and tight before too long, I promise."

"You have worked miracles already, madame," Raymond assured her. "Will you let me thank you and your daughters tonight by joining us for dinner? It won't be anything fancy, just a family-style meal in the réfectoire, but we would be pleased to have your company after all your hard work."

Madame Naizot ran a hand over her slightly disheveled hair. "If we can get everything done in time to make ourselves presentable, we'll join you."

Raymond smiled. "See that you make time."

JEAN JOINED Raymond an hour before the wizards were scheduled to arrive. "Have you driven everyone crazy yet?"

"I'm not driving anyone crazy," Raymond said. "I'm making sure everything is ready."

Behind Raymond's back, Thierry and Sebastien shook their heads adamantly. Jean smothered a smile. "Come inside with me for a few minutes."

"Jean, I have things I need to take care of before everyone arrives."

"I thought you wanted me to help you greet everyone," Jean said.

"I do," Raymond replied. "What does that have to do with going inside?"

Jean held out his hand, a perfectly healthy shade of pink. "It's been too long since I fed. I'm afraid I won't make it through waiting for everyone to arrive if I don't feed first. Your protection is wearing off."

Raymond could see no sign of graying on Jean's skin, but he was not about to take any risks with his partner. "Come on. Madame Naizot prepared a room for us in the Hostellerie. It's not quite our room at home, but it's nearly perfect."

Winking at Thierry and Sebastien as he passed, Jean followed Raymond inside and up to the top floor of the building. He had to admit that Raymond was right. The room Raymond led him into was everything a vampire could ask for. Raymond drew the drapes over the windows and switched on a lamp. "Why didn't you feed last night or this morning?" Raymond asked, shedding his coat and beginning to unbutton his shirt.

"Because we've both been so busy that I lost track of time," Jean lied, his hands catching Raymond's and pushing them aside so he could finish the job of baring his lover to the waist. "If I weren't worried about standing outside in the sun, I could have waited until tonight, but I want to be at your side."

"I want you at my side," Raymond agreed, kicking off his shoes so he could stretch out on the bed. Jean joined him immediately, straddling him and lowering his head to Raymond's neck. Raymond almost protested, but everyone coming to l'Institut would be a candidate for the same kind of partnership he and Jean shared. If they could not accept a bite mark on his neck, they would never be able to accept the rest. Even so, he caught his lover's face in his hands. "The bite on my chest is almost healed."

Jean grinned. "Then I'll have to make sure I take my time, won't I?"

Raymond groaned, his body tightening at the thought. They did not have time to make love. He had things he needed to do.

His libido, though, had no interest in anything outside the bed.

Hearing the sound of surrender, Jean lowered his head to Raymond's chest, licking at the healing bite mark right above his lover's heart. Other marks came and went depending on how they made love, but Raymond had refused to let this one heal completely since the night they had admitted their feelings for each other. Jean told himself he was imagining things, but he swore Raymond's blood tasted the richest from that spot, so he had no problem acceding to his lover's desire in this case.

Deciding he had time to tease his lover a little, Jean licked his way lower, across Raymond's left nipple.

"I thought you needed to feed," Raymond gasped in protest.

"I thought you'd grown tired of rushed, impersonal feedings a year ago," Jean retorted, licking the tightening nub again. "No one will be here for at least an hour. Lie back and let me help you relax."

As he spoke, he loosened Raymond's belt and undid his trousers. "These will get wrinkled if you don't take them off."

Raymond suspected that was a ploy to get him naked, but he was not entirely sure the entire setup was any more legitimate. It no longer mattered. Jean had sparked his desire, and nothing would do but to sate it with his lover's eager cooperation. He lifted his hips and helped Jean push his trousers down and off, leaving him dressed only in his open shirt. He started to pull it off, but Jean stopped him.

"You look completely wanton lying in bed that way, with your shirt still half on. Let me imagine I've dragged you off to bed to ravish you."

"Isn't that exactly what you did?" Raymond asked, but he smiled as he said it, subsiding onto the bed in tacit acceptance of whatever else Jean had planned.

"Who, me?" Jean teased. "I just told you I needed you. Not at all the same thing."

Raymond could not see any difference, but rather than discuss a moot point, he pulled Jean's head down to his to kiss his lover. Jean lingered on the kiss, drinking in the sweetness of Raymond's breath, twining their tongues together intimately. Before long, the simple contact was not enough. Jean kissed his way down Raymond's neck, pausing to nip at the smooth skin, letting the tension build until Raymond writhed beneath him in anticipation. Smiling, Jean licked swiftly at the patch of flesh he had chosen and bit down hard, letting his fangs penetrate deeply enough to draw fresh blood to the surface and to leave a lovely bruise around the incisions from his fangs. He sucked hard, taking what he needed to sustain himself, powerfully aware of Raymond's growing desire in the taste of his blood and in the press of his arousal against Jean's belly.

Suddenly the barrier of clothes between them was too much. Jean reared back, pushing off his own garments. He hovered over Raymond for a moment, eyes drinking in the vision of utter debauchery beneath him: the dilated pupils, the darkening bruise on his neck, the short, panting breaths that made Raymond's chest heave between the open plackets of his shirt, the shiny puddle of fluid on his stomach that leaked from the tip of his hard and reddened cock, the shameless spread of his legs parted wide in invitation. Jean's mouth watered with anticipation as he tried to decide what part of his lover to devour first.

The spot directly above Raymond's heart tempted him, as it always did, but he could bite his lover there when he slipped inside him later. If he started that now, he would not be able to pull himself away—and the thick, dripping erection lured him in with nearly the same power. Lowering his head, he licked along the shaft, relishing every sound that escaped Raymond's lips as Jean lavished attention on him. Pushing back the foreskin, Jean lingered over the mushroomed head, licking and sucking until Raymond was writhing beneath him and bucking into his mouth. "If I let you come down my throat, will you come again when I'm inside you?"

Raymond whimpered. "I want to, but I'm not eighteen anymore, Jean."

Jean grinned and wet a finger before sliding it between Raymond's cheeks to probe at his entrance. "Then perhaps I should stop. I want to feel you clenching around me, pulling me deeper and deeper inside you like you never intend to let me go."

"Then you'd better hurry," Raymond groaned, "or you'll miss it. And I don't intend to ever let you go."

Jean cursed under his breath as he realized the lube was in his trouser pocket on the other side of the room. He started to get up, but Raymond's legs went around his hips, stopping him. "Don't make me wait."

Jean spit in his hand, wetting his cock and hoping he would not hurt his lover too much. As often as they made love, Raymond would adjust quickly, he hoped. He rocked slowly against his lover's entrance, scooping up the fluid anointing Raymond's abdomen and using that as additional lubrication to ease his way. Raymond's body opened eagerly for him, calming his fears about hurting his wizard. When he was fully seated, he blanketed Raymond's body with his own, staying deep inside as he bent his head to find the spot above his lover's heart that begged for his attention. He teased Raymond a little more, licking across the puckered nipple several times before biting down directly above it. Raymond's desire hit Jean hard as he sucked blood into his mouth, leaving his own control shaky.

"Jean!" Raymond begged. "Harder… please… need…."

Raymond's broken pleas shattered what was left of Jean's control. He released Raymond's chest, pushing up on his elbows so he could pound into the eager body beneath him, giving Raymond what he needed. Within moments, Jean felt his lover's climax begin, the spasming muscles tugging at his cock, deep in the welcoming sheath, milking him for all he had. He gave it willingly, spilling inside the wizard's body, another silent claim on the man who held his heart.

When Raymond collapsed beneath him, Jean lowered his weight carefully onto his lover, licking tenderly at the two marks his fangs had left behind. He could feel the stickiness of Raymond's release between them, but he ignored it for the moment, preferring to concentrate on the thrill of being the one to reduce the most controlled wizard in Paris to this state.

Eventually Raymond stirred beneath him, turning his head to look at the clock. "I had work I wanted to get done before the first group of wizards arrived," he grumbled.

"You were driving everyone crazy with your 'work'," Jean disagreed. "Now you're relaxed and in a far better mood and you don't have time to do anything more than get dressed and go down to greet the first arrivals."

"I don't even have time for a shower," Raymond complained.

"I know," Jean replied smugly, even though he knew Raymond would do a cleansing spell to erase the worst of the mess and the smell before he went downstairs. "I like the idea of you feeling me inside you all day."

Raymond shivered. "It totally isn't fair to say things like that when I have to go out and deal with people for at least the next five hours before I can drag you back in here and do wicked things to you to make you pay for it."

Jean smiled and rolled to the side. "I'm looking forward to it already. I'll join you downstairs in a few minutes. It will take me a little longer to get cleaned up than it will you."

Chapter 22

DESPITE THE continuing distractions of his lover, Raymond managed to arrive back in the cloister at two minutes before three, in time to welcome the first of the wizards to arrive. He offered a quick welcome, an overview of where everything was, and an invitation to cocktails at six in the réfectoire before turning the first arrival over to madame Naizot to be escorted to her room so she could settle in.

Over the course of the next hour, the other six wizards arrived as well. Raymond watched in amusement at the varying reactions they had to the marks on his neck and the rather possessive way Jean hovered at his shoulder the entire time. They would have to get used to both if they had any hope of forming a successful partnership. Not every vampire hovered the way Jean did, but Raymond suspected that was more a question of practicality than preference given that all the partnered vampires he knew hovered when they could.

Once the wizards had all arrived, Raymond started toward the kitchens to make sure everything was ready for the evening. The vampires would not begin arriving until after sunset, around five fifteen, giving Raymond an hour to make sure the amuse-bouche were ready for the cocktail reception and dinner was ready for later. He made it as far as the réfectoire before Jean caught his arm, pulling him into a dark corner. "Am I going to have to hijack you again? You have to let people do their jobs. They all know what needs to be done, they all know this is important, and they all know to come find you if there's a problem. Come back to the office with me and tell me about the wizards who signed up for the seminar, and then I'll tell you what I know about the vampires."

Raymond gave in, knowing Jean was probably right. He followed his lover through the corridors to the office they had claimed as their own. It was not the director's office yet because Raymond was not quite ready to claim that position as his own, though with each day that passed he felt more and more certain he would reach that decision before long. Alain had taken over almost all the day-to-day business at l'ANS, leaving only the public appearances to Raymond, since the brand on Alain's neck and all it represented kept him from being a good spokesman for the association. After the way they had handled things over the past month, Raymond would have no qualms about leaving l'ANS with Alain and Thierry until a new president could be found. Raymond did not want to open himself to accusations of taking a position that was not his, though, so both the director's office and the director's quarters in the abbot's lodge still stood empty.

"So tell me about the vampires," Raymond said when they had closed the door behind them. "I don't think I've met any of them yet."

"No, you probably haven't," Jean agreed. "Two of them are from Paris, so you might have caught a glimpse of them when we had the first assembly at the Gare de Lyon, but since they didn't find partners, they weren't around much after that. Three of them are from Amiens, recruited by Luc, so I don't know them as well, and the other two are from Tours. They got word of l'Institut from friends, they said, and wanted to know more about the partnerships. I didn't ask which friends because it doesn't really matter, and having vampires coming from elsewhere in the country strengthens our position should Renaud and Céline try to make trouble later. The chef de la Cour in Tours seems perfectly willing to have people participating in the seminars, although if they pair with wizards from elsewhere in the country, they might be changing Cours before long. Either way, they're here, and that's a good start."

Raymond nodded. He had left it to Alain to arrange for wizards to go to each vampire's home to arrange an escort to l'Institut so the vampires would not have to worry about sunrise and sunset or making arrangements to travel after dark. They would start arriving in the scriptorium around five thirty, long enough after sunset for the vampires to be able to move outside even if there was still some daylight left. "How many men and how many women?" Raymond asked.

"Three women and four men," Jean replied, "the opposite of the wizards, I believe, not that gender seemed to have any role in the partnerships when they formed a year ago. And no, I don't know anything about any of their preferences. We've already established with Thierry and Sebastien that sexual preferences are irrelevant, so it doesn't actually matter. I did verify that they were all currently unattached."

"I did the same for the wizards," Raymond replied. "We don't know what would happen if one of the sides in a partnership was already married or involved with someone, but I'd rather not find out during our first seminar. There's too much at stake for that."

"I suspect a bond simply wouldn't form," Jean said, "especially if the relationship was in any way magical already, but I agree, there's no reason to run that risk at the moment. So tell me about the wizards. Are they all from Paris?"

"All but two," Raymond replied. "Monsieur Sarraute of the Gendarmerie nationale recruited two wizards from Lyon to participate in addition to the two from Paris, who are part of his office. Then there are three doctors from l'Hôtel Dieu in Paris, friends of a friend of Alain's, from what I understand. We'll find out more tonight when we have the cocktail party. I imagine it will be up to us to break the ice between the wizards and the vampires."

Jean chuckled. "I remember that first meeting at the Gare de Lyon. I wasn't sure we'd ever get the two groups to mingle."

"This won't be quite as awkward, I hope," Raymond said, grimacing at the memory of that night, "because we won't be asking the vampires to feed or the wizards to allow it. They'll still be strangers, but the expectations will be different."

"Sometimes I think it's a miracle anyone formed a partnership that night, as tense and awkward as the situation was. At least now we can use magic to determine a pairing. It's still trial and error, but it's less intrusive."

"I wish there were a way to have some of the seminars jointly," Raymond said with a sigh, "but I don't feel like I can ask the wizards to completely upend their normal schedules so they can have discussions with the vampires who can't come out during the day."

"I think the evening sessions will provide enough time for discussion," Jean replied, "and having some sessions separately will let each group ask questions without worrying they'll offend the other, either through their ignorance or through their reactions to whatever the presenter has said."

Raymond saw the sense in that, but he could not help the feeling that seeing those very reactions would help both sides learn sensitivity, something he knew he had not had in Jean's regard when they first started as partners. He would just have to encourage frank discussion during the evening sessions when everyone was together and hope that gave everyone what they needed. If nothing else, it could help everyone get to know each other so they could avoid a mess like the one Adèle and Jude were in.

"As soon as we get this group through, we have to start looking at how the bond works and whether there's a way to break it," he told Jean. "We can't leave Adèle open to Jude's attacks. She might not have complained to us, but Magali dropped enough hints for me to know it's a real problem."

"I know," Jean agreed. "Maybe if we get Paul and Guillemin to come down we can use them as guinea pigs, since they also want their bond severed. That way we don't have to put Adèle and Jude in the same room until it's time to actually do whatever needs to be done to end things between them."

"That's a good idea," Raymond said. "Let's get through this week, and then we can contact them and see what their availability is." He glanced down at his watch. "It won't be long before the vampires start arriving, and you should be there to meet them. They don't know me and have no reason to trust me. They may not all know you, but at least you're a vampire."

"Which only means I understand their unease with being out before full dark," Jean said. "It doesn't otherwise make me any more trustworthy than you. If anything, le jeu des Cours probably makes them warier of me than of you."

"May I just say 'stupid Jeu des Cours'?" Raymond asked. "How a group of otherwise intelligent creatures can let their lives be run by a game with no logic is beyond me."

"There is a logic to it," Jean insisted. "Maybe not an obvious one, but it's there."

Raymond rolled his eyes. "If there's any logic to it—or them—at all, they'll be glad to see another vampire in the midst of all the wizards who will have suddenly invaded their lives."

Jean decided it was easier to let it go than try to explain to Raymond the complicated balance that made any unknown vampire, sometimes even any vampire at all, foe as much as friend. If he were another unpaired vampire, he would be closer to their equal, but the marks on Raymond's neck, and the hidden one on his chest, set Jean apart from the majority of vampires now, even the ones in Paris, because he had a wizard in his life, with all the incumbent advantages of that relationship. If their guests found partners of their own, that would level the playing field again, perhaps even allying them more closely than anything other than a blood tie could do. Until that happened, Jean would be regarded cautiously. "Wizards aren't anywhere near as much of a threat as an unknown vampire."

Raymond shook his head again. "If you say so. I don't see how that makes sense when I know what wizards are capable of, but whatever. We should probably head that way. The wizards will be going to pick up the vampires soon, and we want to be present when they arrive."

They wended their way through the corridors, past the wing that still gave Jean cold chills every time they passed. Thierry had blocked it off with both magical and physical barriers, but it did not change Jean's reaction. He only hoped completing the repairs would ease his sense of dread.

The tables and chairs in the scriptorium had all been pushed to one side, leaving the main room open for the arrival of the vampires. Almost immediately after they entered the room, Alain arrived with a vampire in tow. Raymond stepped forward to greet the woman—Natalie, she said her name was—nodding his thanks to Alain, who disappeared after promising to be back with Orlando for the cocktail reception.

The introductions complete, Raymond looked around, finding Chantal Naizot waiting to escort the vampire to her room. The process repeated six more times, partnered wizards from l'ANS or the alliance acting as escorts to the other vampires. Despite the illogic of it, Raymond could see the truth in Jean's words as the vampires reacted when he introduced himself and Jean. Every one of them seemed more comfortable with Raymond than with Jean. "Okay, they're settled," Raymond said after the last vampire had arrived and been escorted to his room. "Shall we go be good hosts and greet everyone at the réfectoire for cocktails?"

"We could be bad hosts and show up fashionably late," Jean said.

"And what would we do in the meantime?" Raymond asked, a teasing light in his eyes. "You've already made love to me and fed today. What else do you want?"

Jean grinned. "You haven't made love to me. We could go back to the office and you could give me something to tide me over until tonight."

Raymond snickered. "You are insatiable."

"Is that a bad thing?" Jean replied. "I thought you liked that about me."

"Oh, I do," Raymond said, "just not when you're trying to distract me from my duties. Come on. I'll make it up to you after dinner."

Jean laughed. "You better believe you will."

Raymond grinned, amusement getting the better of him. "Be a good host during the party and dinner, and I'll do whatever you want tonight."

"*Whatever* I want?" Jean repeated.

"Whatever you want," Raymond repeated. "You can spend the next few hours imagining what you're going to ask for."

That was an offer guaranteed to put Jean off his game for the rest of the evening, but it also silenced his protests. He followed Raymond out of the scriptorium and into the réfectoire, where the kitchen staff had a selection of bite-sized dishes already laid out. "The champagne is chilling, ready to open as soon as the guests arrive, and dinner is well under way and will be ready to serve at eight as planned."

"Merci," Raymond said to Julien Moracchini, the man who had assured them he would manage the kitchen. It had only been a few days, but so far, the man was an absolute gem. Everyone but the town council had been since they arrived in Dommartin. "Everything looks delicious."

"Take a taste. There is plenty. Even if all the vampires decide to eat, I made enough. Anything that is left, I can take home to my family or save for later. Someone may come in wanting a snack, and I will have something."

Raymond picked up a miniquiche, popping it in his mouth. It was perfect, hot and fresh, the egg cooked to just the right firmness. Suddenly realizing he had skipped lunch, he tried a stuffed mushroom cap and then a bruschetta with artichokes and goat cheese. "What are you doing here in the country? Why aren't you in a restaurant in Paris somewhere?"

Julien shrugged. "Because Dommartin is home, and restaurant jobs are hard to find and even harder to keep."

"You have a job here as long as you want it," Raymond assured him, taking another bite of a prosciutto and cheese pinwheel.

"Raymond," Jean said softly, "our guests are arriving."

"I'll open the champagne," Julien said, disappearing into the kitchen and returning a few moments later with a bubbling bottle that he began pouring into elegant flutes.

"Welcome, everyone," Raymond said, the subtle reminder sending him into host mode. He shook hands with Olivier and Patrice, two of the wizards from Paris, and kissed Constance on both cheeks. "Come in and have something to eat. Our chef, Julien, has outdone himself tonight. I have a feeling we're going to eat very well this week."

"Always a plus," Patrice replied. "I've been to too many conferences where the food was edible at best."

"Take a taste and tell me what you think," Raymond insisted. "I was impressed."

The three wizards crossed to the table where the amuse-bouche were laid out and tasted the different dishes. "You're right," Patrice agreed. "These are fantastic. Wherever you found your chef, keep him."

"Right here in Dommartin, if you can believe it," Raymond said.

"I keep telling him there are gems to be discovered in the country," Constance said with a tip of her head toward Patrice, "but he never listens to me."

That implied a relationship Raymond had been unaware of. "You spend a lot of time together?"

"We work together," Constance said. "He has the office next to mine at the hospital, and he's always making comments about the provinces and what a dearth of anything worthwhile there is outside the capital."

Patrice shrugged. "So I like city life. That's not a crime, is it?"

"Of course not," Raymond soothed, excusing himself and leaving them to their bickering when he saw another group come in. "Natalie and Philippe, if I remember correctly?" he verified, greeting the two vampires.

They nodded.

"Welcome," Raymond said. "If you would like, there is champagne. Jean has assured me it won't do you any harm if you'd like a glass. I can introduce you around as well. You're both in Paris?"

"Yes, we both live in Montmartre," Philippe replied. "I don't know about Natalie, but I'll take a glass of champagne. It gives me something to do with my hands if nothing else."

Raymond ushered them over to the serving area and then introduced them to the wizards already present. "Your paths probably haven't crossed before, but you're all from Paris," he said. As he helped them break the ice, he noticed Alain and Orlando enter. They nodded across the room but left Raymond to his duties. When the next group of arrivals came in, though, Orlando met them at the door, greeting them like old friends and ushering them inside and into conversations, relieving Raymond's worry over how he would manage to introduce everyone on his own. He had no idea how Orlando knew the wizards, but it did not seem to matter. The young vampire acted the consummate host.

"Alain is good for him," Jean murmured, appearing at Raymond's elbow. "A year ago, he never would have been so outgoing."

"Orlando is good for Alain too," Raymond agreed. "Not that I was privy to all his secrets—but even outsider that I was, I could tell he was unhappy. Not anymore."

The arrival of the rest of the participants in the seminar forestalled their conversation as they separated to play host. There were a few awkward moments, but between them and the other paired vampires and wizards who made appearances over the course of the evening, they managed to keep everything running smoothly. When dinner had ended and everyone went their separate ways for the night, Raymond could relax and proclaim it a successful first evening. "Now we just have to hope the rest of the week will go as well."

"It will," Alain said confidently. "They've all chosen to be here, and I think they've all started to see hints of things between the pairs that were here tonight to intrigue them. I heard a couple of the vampires asking what it felt like to go outside in the sun again, and a couple of the wizards wanted to know how much of a power boost I'd experienced from Orlando. I didn't get into the Aveu de Sang, since we don't actually know if that affects the power boost anyway. I just gave them some examples of things I can do with Orlando's assistance that I can't do alone."

"Did the personal side of the relationships come up at all?" Raymond asked.

"Not in any great detail," Alain replied, "other than the observation that it was easy to tell who was paired with whom. Tomorrow is soon enough to deal with the rest. Now, if you'll excuse us, Orlando and I have the first panel tomorrow. We should get some rest."

Raymond thanked them and said good night. He turned back, intending to help with the cleanup, but Jean grabbed his arm. "You have a promise to keep, and I've had hours to plan. It's time for us to retire as well."

"But—"

"No buts. Julien has plenty of help in the kitchen, and you've already thanked him profusely. Everything else can wait until tomorrow. Except me."

The promise in those words did unspeakable things to Raymond's insides. "Let's go."

Chapter 23

RAYMOND WAS glad he was the first one in the réfectoire the next morning. He had no desire to endure the amused glances of the paired wizards or the confusion of the unpaired ones as he lowered himself gingerly into a chair. Jean had finally given in to his repeated requests and bitten Raymond's ass last night. Repeatedly.

He knew Jean had an oral fixation—he *was* a vampire, after all—but Jean had never been as single-minded in his focus as he was last night. Every inch of Raymond's body had been licked and nibbled on. Raymond sported an impressive collection of bruises from Jean's teeth as the vampire took a complete inventory of his body, looking for sensitive spots he had not yet discovered. Anywhere that got the slightest reaction from Raymond ended up with a bruise. The ones that got the most reaction felt Jean's fangs later.

The evening had ended with Raymond on his hands and knees, ass in the air as Jean licked and nibbled on his backside until he was begging. He had lost count, but Raymond was sure he had at least six or eight fang marks on his ass, culminating in Jean rimming him until he was begging for release.

Jean had finally made him come with his fingers and tongue before pushing inside Raymond and rocking slowly to his own climax. Raymond had fallen asleep with Jean still buried inside him, his lover's weight a reassuring pressure through the night.

In the morning light, Raymond wondered how a promise he had made when Jean complained about Raymond not having made love to him had turned into a night where Jean made all of Raymond's fantasies come true. Not that he minded. It just made him feel incredibly selfish. He did not expect to have much time today or even tonight, with the panels and discussion sessions scheduled to begin after breakfast for the wizards and to go through the evening and into the night for the vampires. He would have to find a way to make it up to Jean the next time they had a few private moments.

The arrival of Georges and Élodie, the two wizards from Lyon, forestalled his musings. He pointed out the coffee pot and hot water for tea along with the croissants and baguettes that were on offer for breakfast. They both thanked him somewhat sleepily, making Raymond smile in sympathy.

Armed with breakfast, they approached the table. "Do you mind if we join you?" Élodie asked.

"Please do," Raymond said, pushing out one of the chairs. "Were your rooms comfortable?"

"Very," Georges said. "I've stayed in hotels that aren't this nice."

"We've worked hard to make this a welcoming place for wizards and vampires alike," Raymond said, "so I'm glad you were comfortable. If you need anything, don't hesitate to ask."

"I'm embarrassed to say I forgot to bring a pen," Élodie said.

"Don't be embarrassed," Raymond said with a smile. "When you get your seminar packet, it will have pens and paper as well as Post-It notes and highlighters if you need those as well."

"Are the partnerships really that complicated?" Georges asked.

Raymond laughed. "No. And yes. On the one hand, it's as simple as casting a spell and seeing if there's a vampire it doesn't work on. That vampire is your partner. The mechanics are equally simple. The vampire feeds from the wizard. It's the implications that are complicated, because the more the vampire feeds, the more tightly bound the two become. That's what both sides need to consider before agreeing to enter a partnership."

"I noticed one of the wizards—I can't remember his name—had a scar of some sort on his neck," Élodie said.

"Alain Magnier," Raymond said. "You'll meet him again this morning, along with his partner Orlando St. Clair, but don't judge all partnerships on theirs. They chose to add a layer to their partnership that no one else has done. They're going to talk about the history of the alliance and the partnerships, since they were the first to form a partnership and to discover the protection a wizard's blood offers his or her partner. I'm sure they wouldn't mind if you asked about the Aveu de Sang. As you saw, the mark on Alain's neck announces their relationship to any vampire who looks, even if the rest of the world just sees a scar."

The other wizards came in as they were talking, getting coffee or tea and breakfast and joining Raymond and the other two at the table.

When they had finished eating, Raymond showed everyone to the scriptorium, where the chairs and tables had been spread back out for the seminars. Alain and Orlando were already there, setting out packets. "Do you need anything?" Raymond asked them.

"We're fine," Orlando said, "and if we think of anything, one of us will come find you."

"I'll be in the office getting ready for my session this afternoon," Raymond told them. "I'll see you all at lunch."

The seven wizards found seats. When they were all settled, Alain cleared his throat. "If we can get started, I want to make sure there's plenty of time for questions and discussion at the end of the session before you go to lunch. My name is Alain Magnier, for those of you I haven't already met. I work for l'ANS in Paris and have for twelve years. My partner is Orlando St. Clair, a vampire originally from London."

"I moved to Paris a little over a hundred years ago," Orlando added, "so I'm as much French as I am English at this point. I know some of you are from Paris, but I don't recognize any of you from the Milice. How familiar are you with l'émeute des Sorciers?"

The answers varied but averaged out to "not very."

"I won't give you a full history lesson, because the reasons behind the start of the war and even the unfolding of the war aren't really germane," Alain said. "It's enough for our purposes to know that in October a little over a year ago, the war was at a stalemate, and the time and energy we were expending trying to keep it that way had taken the wizards normally tasked with maintaining the magical equilibrium away from their duties dangerously often. I'm sure you all remember the typhoon in La Réunion about that same time, just one manifestation of the problems that would have grown more and more serious over time."

"I went to La Réunion after that happened to help with the relief efforts," Olivier said. "It was pretty catastrophic."

"So you understand why Marcel was desperate for a solution to preferably end the war, but to at least give us enough additional bodies in the field that he could spare a few wizards to attend to the magical equilibrium," Alain explained. "His idea was to approach the vampires, because while they were limited in their movements to nighttime, they were not prone to the erratic behavior of shapeshifters or some of the other magical races."

"Jean Bellaiche, chef de la Cour of Paris, was intrigued enough by the initial invitation to agree to a meeting," Orlando said, taking up the tale.

"Wait, chef de la Cour?" Patrice asked.

"It's the term given to the leader of the vampires in any given city or area," Orlando explained. "The Cour is the term we use to refer to any group of vampires in the same geographic area. So, as I was saying, Jean was willing to listen to Marcel's proposition. The two sides agreed on a meeting time and place, and Jean sent me as his representative. Alain was the Milice representative. The immediate result was an agreement that the vampires would help in the war effort in return for the introduction of equal rights legislation in Parlement. The less tangible result was that I tasted a wizard's blood for the first time. I know you're all sitting there wondering what that has to do with anything. The simple answer is that a sip of Alain's blood strengthened me more than what I would normally take as a whole meal."

"The rest of the answer is the reason we're here," Alain continued with a grin. "With some trial and error, we discovered that the effect is limited to the right combination of vampire and wizard. My blood would have no more effect on any other vampire than a random nonwizard's blood would. Any other wizard's blood would have no special effect on Orlando."

He left out the detail of the effect of other people's blood on Orlando for the moment because that was part of the Aveu de Sang, not something this group of wizards needed to focus on at the moment. His stomach clenched, though, at the memory of Serrier forcing someone else's blood down Orlando's throat and the terrible pain and nausea that had ensued. He might not have witnessed it himself, but the bond that let them sense each other's feelings had telegraphed the sensations with horrible vividness.

"So your partnership was the first?" Laure, another of the wizards from Paris, verified.

"It was," Alain agreed, "followed quickly by Raymond and Jean. Once we realized that the partnerships could protect the vampires from sunlight, it seemed imperative to form as many as possible as quickly as possible, so we gathered as many wizards and vampires as we could and let them loose in a room to try to find their partners. Out of a group of approximately four hundred people—about two hundred of each—over a hundred partnerships formed that night."

"How many more have formed since then?" Patrice asked.

Alain shook his head. "We don't keep that kind of data. I know of another dozen or so that formed later, but that number may or may not be representative. We had just begun to actively match vampires and wizards as new vampires joined the alliance, but about the same time we got that in place, the war ended. It seemed to take forever at the time because everything was happening at once, both with the partnerships and with the war, but it only took a little more than a month for the vampires' involvement to tip the scales in our favor and bring about Serrier's defeat. And if that isn't a testament to the incredible benefits of the partnerships, I don't know what is."

"Except that the war is over," Marguerite reminded him. "I'm not challenging your assertions that it made a difference in the war effort. I lived through the war in Paris even though my job with the gendarmerie kept me from participating with the Milice. What kind of benefits are we looking at now?"

"Every time a vampire feeds from his partner, it contributes to maintaining the magical equilibrium, for one thing," Alain said. "It also can boost a wizard's power astronomically at the moment when the vampire feeds. We also have some initial evidence that it increases the wizard's overall strength over time. Everyone will do a dépistage-pouvoir this afternoon so we can track any increases over time more deliberately if any of you decide to form partnerships. It was not an effect we predicted, and so it isn't one we set out to study a year ago. That said, though, we haven't found anything else that accounts for the experiences of a number of paired wizards."

"What does it feel like when a vampire feeds from you?" Constance asked. "And what about issues of safety?"

"To answer your second question first, vampires don't have any diseases you can catch. As long as you keep the bite marks clean, you shouldn't have a problem with that. Their saliva is particularly good for speeding healing, as well," Alain said. "As for what it feels like, it's a little pinprick at first, like giving blood, and then you can feel the vampire's mouth pulling on your skin as he sucks. It's very… intimate." He could not completely stop the flush of color that rose to his cheeks at the memory of Orlando's fangs in his neck last night or of the lovemaking that accompanied it. A quick glance in his lover's direction revealed a smug smile.

"How often would a vampire need to feed from his partner?" Marguerite asked.

"That depends on the vampire," Orlando answered, drawing attention away from Alain and giving him a moment to recover his composure. "The age of the vampire is one issue. Then there's the issue of whether the vampire feeds exclusively from his partner or whether he goes elsewhere. Finally, there's the issue of how much the vampire takes at any given time. Just like mortals, we can overeat and make ourselves sick. The average, though, would be every two to three days."

"Can the human body really support that?" Patrice asked. "We'd never let someone give blood that often!"

"I'm not the one to ask that question," Alain said with a shake of his head. "Orlando and I chose to form an extra bond that lets him feed from me as much and as often as he wants without it having any effect on me. Raymond or one of the other wizards could probably tell you, though. As far as I'm aware, Jean limits his feeding exclusively to Raymond with no apparent ill effects on either of them."

"The other thing to consider is the amount of blood we're talking about," Orlando said. "When someone gives blood, they give a pint at a time. A vampire drinks maybe a third of that at the most."

"It is still probably more than a person would donate if they were going to a blood center," Alain agreed, "but—and I know you're going to get tired of hearing us say this—there's magic involved, and that changes things in ways we can attest to without being able to explain."

"As l'Institut continues to grow, Raymond hopes to have more explanations," Orlando added, "but like everything else, that kind of research takes time."

"You said you found each other by chance, but surely there's a better way to go about it," Laure said.

"One of the things we've discovered since that first night is that a wizard's magic does not work on his partner," Alain explained. "A simple spell will reveal your partner because it won't work. At the end of the week, those of you who decide you want a partner, both wizards and vampires, will gather together, and we'll test it. A simple cleaning spell on dirty hands is enough to reveal it. If you find a partner, great. If not, you're welcome to come back for the day at the end of any seminar to see if you find a partner then."

"And if we decide we don't want a partner?"

"Then you'll have made an educated decision."

THE PRESENTATION that evening started the same way, giving the vampires the same overview that Alain and Orlando had given the wizards. Unlike the wizards, the vampires pounced immediately on the brand on Alain's neck.

"When did you make the Aveu de Sang?" Brigitte demanded.

"What does that have to do with anything?" Alain asked defensively. "It doesn't affect the origin of the alliance or the benefits we're discussing tonight."

"It affects everything you do," Philippe disagreed. "Everything you're telling us could be skewed by that bond."

"The factual events leading up to the formation of the alliance and the spread of partnerships have nothing to do with our Aveu de Sang," Orlando interrupted. "If you have questions about how it affects the benefits of the partnerships, we'll be glad to give you examples of other pairs who have had the same experiences we have. You will have other presenters over the course of the week who have not made an Aveu de Sang and so can address the question of degree with you from their own experience. Everything we're telling you now, however, is either provable fact or is universally accepted truth."

It took a moment for the grumbling in the room to die down, but Alain was able to continue his account of the formation of the partnerships at the Gare de Lyon. Anticipating the question about forming partnerships and feeding in public—for the vampires would surely realize how the first partnerships must have formed even if the wizards did not—Alain continued the story through Sebastien's arrival and the discovery that a wizard's magic did not work on his partner. He made a mental note to suggest that Thierry and Sebastien or even Raymond and Jean give the historical presentation next time, given the way the vampires had reacted to his mark. He should have grown used to it, but he never stopped expecting the next time to be different.

"Mireille said she chose to feed exclusively from her partner when she came to discuss the seminars in Paris," Philippe said when Alain was done. "Is that typical?"

"I can't speak for every single partnership out there," Alain began, "but all of those I work with closely enough to have some idea about have made that choice." He did not mention Adèle and Jude. He did not consider them partners, despite the vampire's continued claims. "It's a choice each pairing will have to make for themselves. It does appear, though, that regular feedings over time increase the effectiveness of the protection against sunlight."

"So it's to our advantage to feed from our partners regularly, not just each time we need to go outside, but as often as possible," Louis, one of the vampires from Amiens, commented.

"Within reason," Alain agreed. "We've seen that a vampire can feed from his partner more often than he could feed from someone else, but there are limits to what the wizard's body can take. If you weaken your partner so much that they can't support you, that isn't going to help either of you."

"And if the desire to feeds turns into the desire for sex?" Maurice, one of the vampires from Tours, asked.

"That will be up to each of the partnerships as well," Orlando replied. "The matches seem to form with no regard to either party's established preferences."

That sent a murmur through the room.

"If anything you hear this week is a deal breaker for you, if something a partnership could ask or offer is more than you're willing to accept, you can opt out of seeking a partner at the end of the week. No one is under any obligation here," Alain reminded them. "It's all about helping people make informed choices."

Chapter 24

THREE DAYS later, heads spinning with information, the wizards lingered over their aperitifs as the vampires came in before their evening session. The first night, the two groups had stayed strictly separate by race, the wizards clumped together on one side and the vampires on the other, but that had eased somewhat since then. When Natalie came in alone, Constance did not think twice about waving the vampire over to join her.

Natalie seemed a little surprised, but she joined Constance anyway. "You've lost your shadow," Constance commented after greeting Natalie. "Where is Philippe tonight?"

"I haven't the slightest idea," Natalie replied. "It's not my job to keep tabs on him."

"Maybe it'll be my job after the week is over," Constance mused aloud. "I could do worse than him."

"You could do a whole lot better than him too," Natalie warned. "He's nice to look at, but he's also cynical and occasionally condescending. It can be amusing when his wit is directed at random strangers or society as a whole, but he has a habit of cutting close to home that I wouldn't want to live with."

"I didn't realize," Constance said, revising her opinion downward. "How well do you know the others? Louis, Robert, and Maurice?"

"Not well at all," Natalie replied. "They aren't from Paris, and so my only contact with them has been our two nights of discussions. They seem reasonable enough. You should ask Brigitte about Louis. They're both from the same Cour."

"Do the members of a Cour really know each other that well?" Constance asked. "I mean, Amiens is not as big as Paris, but it's certainly not a small town."

"But the population of vampires even in Paris is fairly limited," Natalie explained. "There might be two hundred vampires in all of Paris, and that's a city of two million people in the city proper and more than eleven million in the greater metropolitan area. For a city like Amiens that's a hundred and fifty thousand people tops, you're talking fifty to a hundred vampires. That's not such a large number to get to know, given how long we live and how badly we were persecuted until a year ago."

"For what it's worth," Constance said softly, "I rejoiced when the equal rights legislation passed last year. I didn't know any vampires at the time, but I hate the thought of anyone facing discrimination."

Natalie smiled. "It's worth quite a bit, actually. So tell me about Olivier and Patrice. I think someone said you all work together?"

Constance nodded. "Yes, we're all doctors at l'Hôtel-Dieu. Patrice reminds me a little of your description of Philippe, honestly. Olivier is a quiet, gentle man who keeps very much to himself."

Natalie laughed. "I like that in a man. Far too many of them think they should be allowed to run a woman's life simply because they're men."

Constance chuckled. "In a male-dominated profession, that's even worse. I get it all the time, as if I hadn't sat through the same classes they did, passed the same exams, and spent the same number of hours in clinics along the way."

"Sometimes I think life would be easier if we simply locked the men in a room and visited them when we had needs another woman couldn't fulfill," Natalie mused aloud. "They could kill each other, sympathize with each other, or fuck each other silly if they wanted to, and all I'd have to worry about was which one of them I wanted to pick on the nights I wanted a man to play with."

"Let's see," Constance said, playing along. "Tonight I want someone with red hair and hazel eyes and—"

"And you'd better not let Angélique hear you describing her partner," Natalie warned. "She looks harmless as a fly, but I've watched her throw grown men—big men—out of her business when they made comments she didn't like."

"Then I'd better look at the vampires," Constance said. "I have no desire to be thrown anywhere. Maybe tall, dark, and handsome."

"As long as you're talking about Maurice and not Orlando, he's all yours," Natalie said. "Orlando is wrapped up in his Avoué body and soul."

"They've been pretty closemouthed about that," Constance observed. "I don't even really know what that means, except that, from the way you say it, it must be something pretty special."

"I think they aren't talking about it because they don't want to scare anyone on either side," Natalie said. "The bond they made is unbreakable, ancient magic that binds a vampire to one person for the rest of that person's life. Some even say beyond. I've known only two vampires over the course of my existence who have made that bond, because it's a double-edged sword. It's a promise of fidelity on every level for the life of the mortal—but the magic that allows that special relationship keeps the vampire from being able to turn the mortal, so it's also a guarantee of separation. A vampire who chooses to make an Aveu de Sang is elevated outside the normal fluctuations of rank within the vampire community for the life of his or her Avoué because of the rarity and the sacredness of the bond. One of the most heinous crimes a vampire can commit is to drink the blood of another vampire's Avoué."

"That's pretty intense," Constance agreed. "I guess they're afraid talking about it might make us feel like we're obligated to that kind of all or nothing commitment, which is silly since there are so many other partnerships around that haven't done it."

"Orlando was never one to seek the spotlight either," Natalie explained, "so having that much attention on his private life is probably uncomfortable for him."

"Why make the bond then? He had to have known it would draw attention to him," Constance asked.

"Now that's a question for which I have no answer," Natalie replied. "Not even a guess. It isn't something I've ever been tempted to do, so it's not something I can claim to understand except in theory, and even then, only in terms of its mechanics."

"I've fancied myself in love before," Constance admitted, "but what you're describing, it's a marriage with no way out, a contract that can't be undone. That's a little intimidating."

"On both sides," Natalie agreed. "If Alain were to decide to deny Orlando, Orlando would have no recourse but to starve. He'd eventually go into a sort of hibernation, but even that could be permanent if one of the vampires of his line isn't around to reanimate him."

Constance shuddered. "Talk about a lover's spat."

"I think that's one of the things that holds vampires back," Natalie admitted. "It's one thing to say you trust someone with your life. It's another thing entirely to actually do it. I've seen enough to realize that Jean and Raymond are very much together, whatever name they put on it publicly, but you don't see a brand on Raymond's neck. Jean has too much to risk, and I imagine Raymond does too."

"I can't even imagine what the reactions would be if he showed up marked like that," Constance agreed. "Let's just say I wouldn't want to be in his shoes if it happened. It would be political suicide."

THE FIRST seminar finished, Raymond gathered everyone together. "We've shared with you at this point everything we know about the partnerships, how they form, and what they entail once they've formed. We've been very upfront about what we don't know as well, sharing our personal experiences to try to make you as informed as we can prior to this moment. What you have to decide now is whether you're willing to take the next step. If you choose to leave right now, no one will think any less of you for it. You'll have made an informed decision not to be involved in a partnership, and that's a perfectly valid choice. If you choose to stay, we'll have the wizards take turns casting a spell to see if any of the vampires present is their partner. If a potential partnership exists, it's still up to the two people involved as to whether they want to take the next step. As long as no blood has passed between you, no bond will form. You can take your time and get to know one another before you go any farther. In fact, I encourage you to take the time to get to know one another and to make sure you're compatible, because once the bond forms, we don't know how to break it."

No one moved. Raymond hid a sigh of relief, having spent the week worrying that having heard all the details, everyone would opt out at the first opportunity.

"Then if our vampires will grab a pen and make a mark on your hands, we can begin," Raymond said. When that was done, he turned to the wizards. "You'll need to do a simple cleansing spell like you would do if you'd spilled ink on your desk or yourself. I'll have you do it one at a time. If anyone still has ink on their hand after you're done, that person is your potential partner. The rest is up to you. Volunteers to go first?"

"I will," Marguerite offered.

Raymond stepped out of the way and gestured for her to cast the spell. She did, her voice breaking nervously as she passed her wand across each of the vampires. The ink disappeared from each one's hands.

"I guess I wasn't meant to have a partner," she said.

"That isn't what it means at all," Raymond said. "It means your partner is not sitting in the room at the moment. We will continue to have seminars, and I hope you'll consider coming at the end to see if your partner is among the next group of participants. It may take some time, but that doesn't mean your partner isn't out there."

She summoned a smile. "I'll come back." She flicked her wand again and disappeared, not waiting to see if anyone else found a partner.

Without needing to be told, the vampires marked their hands again. "I'll try," Élodie offered.

The tension rose in the room as she stepped forward and lifted her wand. Once again, all the ink disappeared. The vampires shifted restlessly as the remaining wizards looked at each other with apprehension on their faces. Raymond issued the same invitation to Élodie that he had issued to Marguerite, but he could feel the tension building in the pit of his stomach as well. They had no idea what caused the partnerships to form between certain people and not others, and he knew not to expect every person who participated in the seminars to find a partner in their own group, but he could not stop the worry that l'Institut would be a failure if they could not facilitate any new partnerships.

"My turn," Patrice said, rising from his seat.

Raymond gestured for him to go ahead. His spell was equally unsuccessful. Raymond did not catch what the other wizard muttered under his breath as he cast a displacement spell, but he had a feeling Patrice would not be back. That was just as well, if the man was going to have that kind of attitude.

Laure and Olivier followed suit, neither one having any luck either. Laure chose to leave, but Olivier remained, wanting to see if either of the two remaining wizards had more success.

"I guess it's my turn," Constance said, heart pounding as she lifted her wand. She had come more because Patrice had persuaded her to than because of any real interest—but having listened to everything the presenters had to say over the course of the week, she had changed her mind about wanting a partnership. Taking a deep breath, she cast the spell.

"It didn't work!" Natalie said in surprise, holding up her hand with ink still staining the back of it. "Or maybe it did, I should say."

"The spell didn't work," Raymond agreed, breathing a sigh of relief that at least one match had occurred. It would be up to the two women to decide what that meant to them. "The attempt to find a partner did."

"So what do we do now?" Constance asked.

"You go in the other room and talk about everything you've learned this week and decide what you want to do," Raymond replied honestly. "You consider what relationship you're comfortable with having with each other now, whether that's open to change, and how you're going to know when the time is right to move beyond a potential partnership into an actual partnership. If you want someone to act as a facilitator in that conversation, one of us will be glad to help."

Natalie looked across the room at Constance. "I think we can handle it."

"Then I'll say good luck, and don't hesitate to call on l'Institut if we can help."

That left only Georges. "This probably isn't going to work, is it?" the wizard asked Raymond. "I mean, it's only worked once out of six tries."

"That doesn't matter," Raymond assured him. "If one of the vampires sitting here is your partner, the success or failure of all the other attempts doesn't matter. And if none of them is your partner, then it wouldn't matter how many successful matches had already been made. In the sense that six vampires is a small sampling, I'd agree that the likelihood of one of them being your partner is relatively small. But it did happen once, so it isn't impossible. You'll just have to try and see."

Georges looked at the six vampires waiting expectantly, suddenly nervous he would end up paired with one of the men. The presenters had assured him he did not have to form a partnership just because he matched with someone, that as long as he did not let the vampire drink his blood, they could both walk away, no harm, no foul, but Thierry had been very blunt about his own experiences and how the power of the bond had overridden his intentions. George swallowed around the lump in his throat. "I'll try, but only on the women. I can't have a male partner. I just can't."

Raymond frowned, not sure exactly how to respond to that. He could not force the other man, though, so he nodded. Only Joséphine and Brigitte marked their hands this time. Georges cast the spell, erasing the marks on both women's hands.

"Are you sure you won't try on the others?" Raymond asked, but Georges shook his head.

"Thank you all for participating in the seminar," Raymond said to the remaining vampires. "I hope it's been worth your time for the information, and I hope you'll be willing to come back as well at the end of subsequent sessions. There are wizards outside to take you home whenever you're ready to go."

"I'm going back to Paris," Olivier said to Philippe. "I can take you wherever you need to go, since it's on my way."

Philippe nodded. "Just let me get my bag."

Leaving the other vampires to gather their belongings as well, Raymond walked into the réfectoire to check on Constance and Natalie. They sat in the far corner on the same side of one of the long tables, their heads nearly touching as they leaned in to talk to each other. Raymond shook his head. He had not picked up on any particularly strong vibes between the two women during the evening sessions, but to see them now, he had no doubt they would end up partners. Maybe before they left l'Institut.

Deciding he did not want to intrude on their conversation when they obviously had matters well in hand, he went in search of his own partner to discuss the seminar as a whole and the results of the match in particular.

"Well?" Jean asked when Raymond came in.

"Well, we had one partnership form," Raymond replied. "And we had one wizard who decided he could only cast the spell on the female vampires because he couldn't bear the thought of a male partner."

Jean rolled his eyes. "Have we not done away with that kind of narrow-minded attitude yet?"

Raymond shrugged. "He has a choice. We may not agree with his choice, but the whole point of having l'Institut and doing things the way we're doing them is to avoid another situation like Adèle and Jude where they're partners, but truly aren't compatible. It might mean that he never finds a partner, and if his partner was one of the male vampires present tonight, the vampire might not find one either—although we don't know that for sure—but at least it means they won't form a partnership in ignorance only to regret it later."

"I've been going through the evaluations of the seminar," Jean said, holding up the stack of papers. "One of the things that came up frequently was wishing we had structured the days and nights so the vampires and wizards would have more time together. No one has specified whether they mean sessions together or unstructured time like the cocktail party the first night, but at least during the winter, I think we could change the schedule around a little, even if it means asking the wizards to stay up a little later and sleep a little later in the morning. That way we could do some joint sessions as well."

"The history session could be done jointly quite easily," Raymond agreed, "and since that's the first one, it would give everyone a chance to get acquainted. Alain mentioned the possibility of having someone else do that session for the vampires. They questioned the veracity of even the historical facts because of his Aveu de Sang. We could also see about getting new volets and heavier curtains on the scriptorium so the vampires could come to sessions even during the daylight hours if they're willing to."

"Some probably would," Jean said, "but I don't know that we could make that a requirement. Maybe during the summer when it stays light so late, but not right now when we have so many hours of darkness to work with."

"We don't have to decide that right now." Raymond picked up one of the evaluations and skimmed down it. "We have months until it will be an issue."

Chapter 25

RETURNING TO l'ANS headquarters a week later, Raymond smiled at the report he had to give Jean. He had gone to l'Hôtel-Dieu to check in with Constance and see how she was doing with Natalie and their partnership. He had found the two women in the break room, exhaustion clear on both faces.

"Sorry if we're not more talkative," Constance said. "We just spent the last eight hours in surgery."

"Did the patient make it?" Raymond asked.

"Thankfully," Constance said, "but it was touch and go for awhile. I couldn't have done it without Natalie's help. I had to restart his heart a couple of times during the surgery. We monitor it, but we'd have lost him if Natalie hadn't supplemented my strength toward the end."

A bite mark on Constance's neck proclaimed exactly how Natalie had helped. He noticed as well the protective way that Natalie hovered at Constance's shoulder. He did not know at what point in the past week they had moved beyond a match and into a partnership, but they had clearly crossed that line by the time he arrived that day. He did not ask for details—he did not need to pry to read all the little indicators in Natalie's body language that proclaimed the transition from a functional partnership to a true one. He had grown very familiar with those signs over the past year. "Make sure you get as much sleep tonight as your schedule will permit," he advised Constance. "Until your body has a chance to get used to the new demands of supporting yourself and Natalie both, you'll need extra rest. Your magic will compensate in a few days, as it gets used to supporting Natalie too. You just have to give it time."

As he left, he glanced back to see Natalie leaning over Constance. It brought a smile to his face as he thought of Jean and his protectiveness. He came out of the subway at l'ANS to find a crowd of picketers outside carrying placards accusing l'Institut of pandering. Frowning, he cast a displacement spell, getting inside without having to walk through the protestors.

"What is this?" he asked when he walked into his office.

"It started about two hours ago," Fabienne replied. "They aren't carrying any signs that indicate their affiliation, but all of their rhetoric is extremely conservative."

"The Front National?" Jean asked.

"It could be, although they usually identify themselves when they do a protest," Raymond said. "They want everyone to know they're working in support of their agenda."

"If not them, then who?"

"I haven't the slightest idea," Raymond said, "but we have to decide how we're going to deal with it, regardless of who it is."

"We ignore it," Jean said. "There's no truth to their accusations, and we give credence to them by denying them. What was it the English playwright said? Something about protesting too much?"

"'The lady doth protest too much'," Raymond supplied. "Are you sure that's the best plan?"

"Nothing we say will change their minds," Jean said with a shrug, "and the truth, that the partnerships that form as a result of the seminars at l'Institut probably will evolve into intensely personal relationships for the people involved, won't appease them. In fact, it's likely to give them more fodder for their protests. As long as all they're doing is waving signs and shouting, I don't see that it's all that important."

"It could be if it keeps people from signing up for the seminars," Raymond worried aloud.

"We didn't start l'Institut for money or for popularity," Jean reminded him. "We started it to educate people who want to form partnerships and to understand them better for the people who've already formed them. It doesn't hurt us if people don't sign up for the seminars. We're not trying to make money doing this, so if they don't come, we'll simply focus on our research and go on."

"What about the credibility of l'ANS?" Raymond said. "If people outside the association start to believe the accusations, it could endanger our work in other areas."

"If it comes up in other contexts, like in Parlement, then obviously we can address it there," Jean said. "I just think having a press conference, or anything similar, to deliberately debunk the rumors started by a bunch of protestors gives them too much power and makes us look guilty of something."

"Especially when we are?" Raymond laughed. "All right, I'll bow to your wisdom at the moment—but I'm going to prepare a statement that I can use at our regular press conferences if the subject comes up, which you know it will."

"Don't answer the claims," Jean insisted. "Simply reiterate the purposes and goals of l'Institut. After all, what the participants in the seminars choose to do after they leave, and the personal relationships of the existing partnerships, are not the business of l'Institut unless they choose to share them as part of our confidential research studies."

Raymond smiled. "You're good at this. Are you sure you don't want to take the next press conference for me?"

"I would," Jean offered, "but that also makes us look like we're hiding something, since I've only publicly attended press conferences when we have an announcement to make that's directly related to the Cours."

"You've been talking about reaching out to the other chefs de la Cour so they get accurate information before Renaud and Céline get to them," Fabienne interjected. "Jean could make that announcement so that he's visible at least, instead of hovering in the wings like he usually does."

Raymond frowned as he weighed his options. "The only problem I see with that is that it might serve to remind the press corps that Jean and I are partners as well as colleagues. If he isn't there, they may focus more in general terms instead of asking about our relationship in particular."

"Raymond?" Thierry's head appeared in the doorway.

"Bonjour, Thierry."

"The media is outside covering the protests, and a few of the reporters have asked if l'ANS has any comments," Thierry said. "I didn't want to issue a statement without checking with you first."

"We were just talking about that," Raymond said. "We're going to wait until our regular press conference."

"And give the protestors all that time to gather support?" Thierry asked. "Are you sure that's what you want to do?"

"It was," Jean said, "but the media hadn't shown up when I said that. I didn't want to draw attention to the protests, but if they're here and asking questions, that changes the game. The question now becomes how to best make the protestors look like they're unimportant."

"Do you have suggestions?" Raymond asked. "I don't want to go out there unprepared."

"My first suggestion would be that you not go out there at all," Jean said. "If you go out and address the concerns, it gives weight to the accusations because it's serious enough for the president of l'ANS to make a special appearance. It would be far better if Thierry or Mathieu went, someone 'unimportant' in the eyes of the media. If they know Thierry, they know him from the Milice, so that gives him credibility, but they have no idea of where he fits within l'ANS hierarchy. He has a partner, but they probably don't know who his partner is or maybe even if he has one, and he isn't currently sporting any visible bite marks—I won't ask about hidden ones—so there's no reason for them to try to make his relationship with Sebastien an issue." He winked at Thierry as he spoke.

"If you give me a prepared statement, I can read it," Thierry agreed, "but I'm not entirely comfortable with the idea of fielding questions. I don't want to accidentally reveal more than we want to say."

"If it isn't in the statement, you don't answer it," Raymond said. "They can ask all they want."

"That also comes off as a little underhanded," Jean disagreed, "but you're right about Thierry not having to make those decisions. The accusation is trivial to l'ANS, since it's clearly unfounded, but it's quite serious to the vampires, because if it were true, that would be an insult to our integrity."

"It would be to ours too!"

"Yes, but you know it's not true so you don't need to bother with such silliness," Jean explained. "I'll go with Thierry, a vampire and a wizard making a joint statement, an appearance of strength without any relationship between us but a professional one. If they have questions beyond Thierry's prepared statement, I'll answer them or guide Thierry's answers. The media will get the appearance they want, and we'll get our message out without giving too much away. And we might get an idea of who the ringleader is if the protestors choose to engage us while we're making our statement."

"If you think that's best," Raymond said. "Let's get our statement together. I just saw the accusation of pandering on one of the signs. Is there anything else in their protests, does anyone know?"

"Not that I've seen," Fabienne said. "I can go outside and blend in with the crowd to make sure if one of you will send me and bring me back in five minutes."

"While you do that, we'll start putting together our statement," Raymond said. "Get your coat. You want to blend in, not stand out because you're the only one not freezing."

Fabienne rolled her eyes. "Delicate mortals," she huffed, but they could all see the teasing affection on her face as she said it. When she was ready, Raymond sent her outside with a quick wave of his hand.

"She really is a jewel," Thierry said. "If you resign and go to l'Institut full time, you have to leave her here to keep Alain and me on the straight and narrow until we find a new president."

"That will be her decision, but I won't try to steal her away," Raymond promised. "Okay, let's think about what we want to say."

"I think the best tack to take is to simply and clearly restate the goals of l'Institut," Jean said. "That way we're informing the public of our reality instead of getting dragged down into an exchange of insults with the protestors."

"So we state that the two goals of l'Institut are to educate any wizard or vampire interested in forming a partnership and to research... research what?" Thierry asked. "I mean, I know, but how should I word it?"

"The magical causes and implications of existing partnerships," Raymond answered. "Everything we don't know falls under one of those two headings without giving away details."

"And if they ask for details of what those implications are?" Thierry asked.

"Then you talk about the protection from sunlight and the immediate and long-term increase in a wizard's power," Raymond replied. "Those are the universal results of partnerships, even in a case like Jude and Adèle where nothing else seems to hold true."

"Five minutes are up," Jean reminded Raymond. "Let's see if Fabienne has anything else to report."

Raymond summoned the vampire back with a quick spell. "Anything else worth noting?"

"Nothing," she said with a shake of her head. "The signs and slogans they're shouting are focused entirely on the sexual aspect of the bond and the fact that by promoting partnerships, we're acting as panderers."

"Then we're ready," Jean said. "Shall we go down, Thierry?"

"Yes, let's get this over with and get them off our steps." They stopped by Thierry's office to get his coat before going down to the front of l'ANS offices.

The moment they appeared, reporters swarmed them, shouting questions. Thierry held up his hand, requesting their silence so he could answer. "Mesdames et messieurs," he said, "it has come to our attention that some individuals have been casting slurs against l'ANS and its newest program. L'Institut Marcel Chavinier has two goals and only two goals. It was created primarily to provide information and education to any wizards or vampires interested in learning more about the partnerships that formed during l'émeute des Sorciers so they can decide for themselves if they wish to form such a partnership, and secondarily to research the causes and implications of those partnerships for those who are already involved, either from the war or since then."

"Why didn't monsieur Payet come out to answer our questions?" one of the reporters shouted.

"Because monsieur Payet is a very busy man," Thierry replied. "The accusations are so patently ridiculous that we saw no reason to trouble him with them when he's in the middle of important business elsewhere."

"Our source told us the partnerships were primarily sexual in a nature," one of the protestors shouted.

"Then you need to get a more reliable source," Jean scoffed. "The bond between partners comes from the exchange of blood between vampire and wizard. Anything beyond that is the personal business of the people involved, not of l'ANS or l'Institut."

"So you deny that the partnership bonds are sexual in nature?"

"The partnerships are what each pair chooses to make them," Jean replied coldly. "It is not the place of l'ANS, l'Institut Marcel Chavinier, or anyone involved with either institution to dictate how anyone leads their lives."

"Can the partnerships become sexual?" another reporter asked.

Jean laughed. "Any time you involve two people in a relationship, it has the potential to become sexual. That's human nature."

"And vampire nature?"

"Vampire nature as well," Jean replied, "but if that's all it takes to accuse us of pandering, then anyone who assigns two people to work together, anyone who merely introduces two people, could be accused of the same thing. Have we truly sunk to that level as a society?"

The reporters had no answer to that. Jean turned back inside, gesturing for Thierry to go with him.

"You know they're not completely wrong," Thierry said when they went inside. "Yes, there is a choice to form a partnership in the first place, but once the bond forms, I don't know that people really do have a choice about it turning sexual."

"That's the whole point of the seminars," Jean said, "so that people who aren't interested in forming a bond of that depth can choose not to go forward with it. As long as a vampire hasn't bitten his or her partner, the bond can't form, and the two are free to go on with their lives. If they choose to create something more, then they'll have done so knowingly, like any other couple that enters a relationship. We aren't forcing anything on anyone. In fact, we're trying to keep them from being forced unwittingly into something they don't want."

"Unfortunately, not everyone will see it that way," Thierry said. "They'll see the result and not care at all that the people involved chose their relationships."

"So we'll keep reminding them that nothing was forced, from enrollment in the seminars to participation in the matching to turning the match into a partnership," Jean said with a shrug. "There's nothing else we can do without giving in to the naysayers. And we've seen what happens when incompatible people form partnerships not knowing what they're getting into. The good news there is that Paul and Guillemin have agreed to come to l'Institut next month when we're ready to start our research so we can look into ways to break the bond for those who truly cannot function with their partners."

Chapter 26

"THANK YOU for agreeing to meet with us," Jean said, offering his hand to Roland Estrabaud, the chef de la Cour of Toulouse. The vampire had agreed to meet them in a café on l'île du Ramier that overlooked the Garonne and offered a spectacular view of la Ville Rose.

"You said it was important," Roland replied, shaking Luc's hand as well.

"There are rumors going around," Jean explained, "and we thought it would be to everyone's advantage to make sure the truth of the matter got out rather than letting everyone hear lies first."

"Who's spreading lies?" Roland asked, his face growing serious.

"Renaud," Luc said, "possibly Céline Girardot as well. Renaud is upset that l'Institut Marcel Chavinier is in le Morvan, even though it's outside his Cour. There are also rumors flying in the media about l'Institut and what its goals are."

"I've heard a little about it," Roland admitted, "but I honestly haven't paid much attention. It's not in my province, so it doesn't really affect me."

Jean wanted to shake the other vampire and ask how he thought something this important did not affect him, but he restrained himself. "It may not affect you directly unless you decide at some point to attend one of our seminars, but even if you don't, some members of your Cour might, and it's better for everyone if the chefs de la Cour have accurate information."

"So what do I need to know that Renaud and the media will try to hide from me?" Roland asked.

"Renaud will either claim we moved into his territory or that we're trying to force mortals into business that doesn't concern them," Jean said.

"We?" Roland asked. "Who is 'we'?"

"My partner, Raymond Payet, president of l'ANS and founder of l'Institut Marcel Chavinier," Jean said. "He could not join us tonight because he had a meeting with several representatives from Parlement that could not be rescheduled."

"Or in the case of forcing mortals into business that doesn't concern them, we would include my partner Magali," Luc said. "Both she and Raymond accompanied us to our meeting with Renaud and Céline, since the subject of discussion concerned them as well."

Roland raised an elegant eyebrow. "You're breaking all kinds of precedents with that, you know."

"We didn't invite them to the Congrès des chefs," Jean scoffed. "We invited them to a discussion about l'Institut."

"Still. So you, in some definition of that word, established this institute close enough to Renaud's Cour that he feels threatened," Roland summarized.

"Yes, except there isn't any threat," Jean said. "L'Institut is a research and educational facility designed to help wizards and vampires interested in forming partnerships and to study the inner workings of existing partnerships so we can better understand their personal and magical implications."

"That's quite a line," Roland said. "What does that really mean?"

Luc glanced at Jean. "It means that when we formed partnerships during the war, we opened a can of worms much bigger than we expected. Most of us who made that decision then don't regret it, but we're regularly surprised by it. The research aspect of l'Institut should help answer some of those questions. The education side aims to make sure people who might be interested in a partnership are aware of the potential ramifications before they do something that can only be undone with difficulty."

Jean's lips pursed at the disingenuous comment. He hoped they would be able to undo the partnership bond for the two pairs who could not function together, but they were certainly not at that point yet. "If at all," he added. "That's one of the research goals of l'Institut, to be able to help those who formed partnerships hastily and now regret their decisions."

"And what will the media say that I shouldn't believe?" Roland asked.

"There are a group of protestors claiming that l'Institut is a glorified brothel and that we're taking people's money in exchange for arranging sexual liaisons," Jean said bluntly.

Roland laughed in astonishment. "And they think vampires would go along with this?"

"As if the wizards would either," Jean said. "I didn't say it was logical. I said that's the line they're trying to sell. You know as well as I do that feeding always has a sexual thrill for vampires, and feeding from the same person over time adds to that, but we aren't forcing anyone into anything. We're actually telling people to make sure they're compatible with a potential partner before beginning to feed, because the exchange of blood creates a magical bond that grows over time and makes it less and less interesting to the vampire to feed elsewhere."

"And the repeated feedings lead to a desire for greater intimacy," Roland extrapolated.

"On both sides, apparently," Jean said, thinking of Thierry and Sebastien.

"Now that's surprising," Roland commented.

"It's the exchange of magic, we think," Jean explained. "Wizards are as sensitive to that side of it as vampires are to the intimacy of feeding. It's one of the things we're researching, though."

"Okay, so assuming everything you've told me is true, what do you want from me?" Roland asked.

"Ideally, your support should it come to a fight in the Congrès des chefs. At the very least, your agreement not to interfere with any of your vampires should they decide to participate in one of our seminars," Jean replied. "And to accept those vampires' partners if they find any and choose to return to Toulouse."

"I don't see any reason to keep members of my Cour from being involved," Roland said slowly, "but I don't accept just anyone into my Cour. Any wizard who wants to join as a vampire's partner will have to apply like anyone else."

"That's fair," Luc said before Jean could protest. Jean frowned, but Luc sent him a quelling look. "As long as you're open to the request. Would you be willing to talk to the other chefs de la Cour in your region? It will save us quite a bit of time if we only have to visit the chef de la Cour in the capital of each region."

"You don't have to try to answer all their questions," Jean added. "If they have questions, they're welcome to contact me, and I'll answer them. Just tell them you've talked to other chefs de la Cour and that l'Institut isn't a threat. The rest is up to each individual vampire."

"And if someone wants to participate in one of your seminars?" Roland asked.

"The February one is already full," Jean replied, "but we still have places for March. They can contact l'ANS in Paris to enroll."

"Jean?"

Jean looked up, surprised to see Orlando darkening his doorway. He rose, shaking Orlando's hand as his friend walked in. "How are you?"

"I'm well. I was more concerned about how you are," Orlando said.

"I'm fine. Why wouldn't I be?" Jean asked.

Orlando sat in one of the overstuffed chairs that graced Jean's office and regarded his friend seriously. "Because you're gambling with everything you have and everything l'Institut represents to try to get the chefs de la Cour on your side and to keep the media from giving too much coverage to the protestors while they're busy ignoring the truth?"

"It's nothing to worry about," Jean said dismissively.

"Stop giving me that line and talk to me," Orlando snapped. "I can tell it's wearing on you, and I hardly see you these days, which is reason to worry in itself."

Jean sighed, leaning back in his chair and closing his eyes. This was Orlando sitting next to him, the one vampire he trusted more than anyone else, if only because Orlando had always refused to even learn le jeu des Cours. His young friend cared nothing for intrigue or power or any of the things that made up the fabric of Jean's life. All Orlando cared for was Alain and their friends. That list was a little longer than it had been a year ago, when only Jean had a place on it, but Jean did not mind sharing. Orlando had needed someone to love who would love him in return, not as a little brother, but as a partner in life. Jean hoped Alain knew how grateful he was that Orlando had found his soul mate in the blond wizard. "Yes, I'm burning the candle at both ends and in the middle," Jean admitted, "but I don't know what else to do."

"I do," Orlando said. "Take Raymond and go somewhere hot and sunny and private for a few days. You would both benefit from the break."

"He'll never agree to that," Jean said immediately.

"He will if you tell him you need it," Orlando disagreed. "He won't do it for himself, but he'll do anything for you."

Jean shook his head. "I can't do that. That wouldn't be fair to him."

"It's not about being fair," Orlando insisted. "It's about taking care of the one you love. Or are you still trying to pretend you aren't as madly in love with him as I am with Alain?"

"I gave up that fight awhile ago," Jean said with a chuckle. "Was I really that obvious?"

Orlando rolled his eyes. "You treat him like your Consort. Even I, as clueless as I am, could see that. You never did that with Karine or with anyone else as long as I've known you. It's the only explanation that made sense."

"Yes, I love him, and yes, he knows it," Jean said, answering the next question as well. "But that doesn't give me the right to use his emotions to manipulate him."

"Even when it's for his own good?" Orlando asked.

"It won't help," Jean insisted. "Even if I convince him to go, he'll spend the whole time worrying about l'ANS or l'Institut or both."

"You mean to tell me you haven't figured out how to shut his brain off yet?" Orlando teased. "I know he's a thinker, but come on, Jean, no man is going to turn down sex, and if you give him enough of it, his brain will turn off for a few hours. And when it starts back up again, you start all over again too."

"That's easy for you to say," Jean grumped. "Your Aveu de Sang protects Alain from overdoing it. Raymond doesn't have that protection."

"Why not?" Orlando asked.

"Because he's president of l'ANS and—"

"Those are his reasons," Orlando interrupted. "What's holding *you* back?"

"The fact that he isn't ready," Jean said softly, "and may never be ready. It isn't something you force on someone. It can't be, or it will never work."

Orlando looked at Jean seriously. "You're right that it isn't something you force on someone, but it is something you ask for. Have you told him you want it?"

"It doesn't matter what I want," Jean repeated. "He doesn't even like going to a press conference with bite marks on his neck, no matter how happy he is for me to leave them anywhere and everywhere else. He isn't going to accept a brand on his neck that no spell will ever heal or hide."

"So don't put it on his neck," Orlando said. "Forget about le jeu des Cours and all the status games you play. I regularly wish I'd put my mark anywhere else *but* Alain's neck because I hate the way people treat me differently, as if my relationship with Alain were somehow their business. Choosing to love someone, choosing to commit to that person, is the most personal, private thing we can do."

"It's about protecting the Avoué," Jean replied automatically, "so no one else tries to approach him or her."

Orlando snorted. "And who exactly is going to get close enough to Raymond to feed from him or do anything else to him he doesn't want? He'd toss the vampire in question across the room, if he doesn't toss him all the way across France!"

Jean stared at Orlando, dumbfounded.

"We're not dealing with 'helpless' mortals anymore, Jean. We're dealing with wizards," Orlando reminded his friend, "and they are anything but helpless, as you well know because you fought beside them during l'émeute des Sorciers. You talk about moving into the future and all the possibilities it holds for us, and then you let yourself get trapped in a mindset that's even older than you are. Raymond is a wizard, yes, but he's also a mortal. He isn't going to live forever, and you're going to be so caught up in everything else that you let that time pass by instead of cherishing every minute of it." Orlando rose and looked down at Jean seriously. "Don't make that mistake. Now, if you'll excuse me, I have a vacation to plan. I hear Martinique is beautiful this time of year."

Orlando left before Jean could gather his thoughts enough to reply. "Beh, merde," he muttered as the full import of Orlando's tirade sank in. He had fallen into exactly the trap Orlando had accused him of not seeing. He had tried to move forward without ever seeing the centuries of blind tradition that held him back.

Raymond needed many things, to be loved not the least, but he did not need Jean's protection in any sense of the word. The man had defected from Serrier's ranks, knowing it would mean a price on his head and his death if he was captured by the dark wizards, without any promises from Marcel or the Milice or anyone else. Anyone who had enough courage to do that could handle anything the Cour of Paris or the assembled Cours of France could throw at him. Jean had watched his lover face down the media, the Parlement, and anyone else who stood in the way of his dreams, and yet he had still fallen into the trap of vampire society, thinking that anyone who was not a vampire would be lost and vulnerable there. Raymond might be vulnerable in private, but he had nothing to fear from the Cour, because they would never see his weak points. Only Jean and a few trusted friends would ever be allowed to see those.

If Raymond did not need Jean's protection, then that changed the rest of Jean's thinking as well. He could not introduce Raymond as his Consort as long as the wizard was also the president of l'ANS. However much Jean might resent that reality, he understood it. He also hoped it would not be their reality for much longer. Raymond spent more and more time at l'Institut, giving Alain and Thierry greater responsibility with each passing day. Until that became official, Jean could be patient in that respect, but an Aveu de Sang, if he took the element of protection out of it, did not need to be official. They could take that final step, bind themselves together in that most primal of ways, and no one would be any the wiser. A small mark on Raymond's inner thigh or his lower back, somewhere that would rarely if ever be visible outside of their bedroom, would be enough to seal their promises. And Raymond would be his for the rest of his life. He would lose Raymond at the end of it, but they had already learned that wizards could not be turned, so the bitter irony of the Aveu de Sang, that the very magic that bound a vampire and his Avoué kept the Avoué from being turned and ensured a separation at the end of the Avoué's life, would apply to them whether they made the bond or not.

He would belong to the wizard with equal depth, but he had no fear in that regard. He knew his lover to the depths of his soul. If Raymond made a promise of that magnitude, he would keep it, and the benefits would far outweigh any possible downsides. Jean would no longer have to worry about taking too much from Raymond when he fed. He would no longer have to second-guess his lover's moods when he was not feeding, because the bond would allow him to sense his lover's emotions. All he needed was for Raymond to agree.

Unfortunately, that was not a given, especially not right now. Not with all the stress of l'Institut and trying to run both it and l'ANS, not to mention the continuing protests. He thought Orlando might have the right idea, a more than amusing thought given how uncertain Orlando had been at the start of his relationship with Alain. And now, a year later, he was giving advice to Jean. Picking up the phone, he dialed the number for Frasques de Lune, a travel agency that specialized in arranging trips for vampires.

"Frasques de Lune, what kind of mischief can we help you get into tonight?"

"I need to plan a trip," Jean said, "but I don't have exact dates yet. It's a surprise for my lover, and I have to work with his secretary to clear his calendar."

"Where would you like to go?"

"Somewhere tropical," Jean said. "And we don't have to worry about traveling in the daylight. My lover is a wizard, so the ordinary concerns don't apply."

"In this season, la Réunion is an option, as is Martinique or Guadaloupe," the travel agent proposed. "How long would you want to stay for?"

"Four or five days," Jean replied. "I don't think we can get away longer than that."

"Then La Réunion is probably the better choice for you," the travel agent said. "You won't have to worry as much about time zone changes as much as you would if you were going all the way to the Antilles."

"We were there a year ago after the typhoon hit. It might be nice to visit it again under more enjoyable circumstances," Jean said.

"Let me put together a few proposals with flexible dates and I'll get back to you," the travel agent said. "Do you have a budget?"

Jean considered for a moment, thinking about what he hoped the trip would mean to both of them, and said, "No, I want this to be special. I don't want to waste money, but I can afford a proper vacation."

"I'm sure we can plan something that will be perfect. Your name, monsieur?"

"Jean Bellaiche."

"The Jean Bellaiche?" the travel agent asked. "The chef de la Cour?"

"Yes," Jean replied. "Is that a problem?"

"Not at all, monsieur Bellaiche," the travel agent said immediately. "I was surprised you had heard of us, that's all."

Jean smiled, though he knew the man on the other end could not see him. "You'd be amazed what I've heard of." He gave the agent his office number so he could keep the surprise from Raymond a little longer and hung up, feeling like he finally had his world back on track.

Now he just had to enlist Fabienne's assistance and convince Raymond to take a well-deserved vacation.

Chapter 27

"YOU WANT us to do what?" Raymond said that night when they got home from work and Jean sprang the vacation idea on him.

"I want us to take a vacation," Jean said. "A long weekend away where we can rest and be together and relax a little."

"Jean, that's crazy," Raymond insisted. "We can barely manage everything that needs to be done while we're here. How do you expect us to manage a vacation on top of that?"

"We have three weeks until the next seminar at l'Institut," Jean said reasonably, trying not to be hurt at Raymond's immediate dismissal of the idea. He steeled himself to make a rational argument in favor of his plans before resorting to emotional blackmail if he had to. "We've already taken care of the things we wanted to change based on the way the first seminar went. The repairs at l'Institut are under control, and Thierry can supervise anything that comes up while we're gone. All you do is agree to what he says needs to be done next anyway. If the president of l'ANS didn't need to be a wizard, I'd have nominated Fabienne months ago. She can handle things, with Alain and Thierry as spokesmen, for four days while we go relax. The protestors haven't gone away, but they haven't come up with anything new either, so that's not likely to be an issue while we're gone. Say yes, Raymond. Say you'll come enjoy a break with me."

Raymond looked like he was going to keep arguing, so Jean pulled out the big guns. "I need a break. I'm burning out, and I'm afraid I'll make mistakes that could hurt l'Institut, my Cour, or both, if I don't get a few days away. I can go without you, but I'd really rather not."

Raymond's stomach clenched as he thought of Jean on a tropical island without him. Visions of young nubile bodies entwined with Jean's as they offered him their blood and more assailed Raymond's mind. Intellectually, he knew the time Jean could go without feeding had stretched to four or five days since they had become partners if he had fed well, but such rationality had no place in the sudden fear of losing Jean to some nameless, faceless youth. He hated himself for the fear, but losing Jean would gut him. While he doubted Jean would leave entirely, if only because no one else's blood could protect the vampire from sunlight, he could not push away the image of Jean maybe finding comfort with another, even once, because Raymond had refused to accompany him on vacation.

"When are you planning on leaving?"

Jean's face fell. He had gambled on being able to persuade Raymond and lost. "Fabienne said the end of next week would be the easiest time to clear your calendar."

Raymond nodded. "I guess I need to find some summer clothes then. I'm not sure where they ended up packed away."

Relief flooded Jean as he realized he had misunderstood Raymond's question. "I know where they are. They're in with mine." He pulled Raymond into his arms. "We'll have a wonderful time and come back ready to face the next seminar and the rest of the challenges of l'Institut. You'll be glad you went with me. I promise."

Raymond smiled. He could not help it. Jean's happiness was catching. "When we get back, though, you're going to help me test how long the protection from sunlight lasts."

Jean grinned. "Then I'd better eat well between now and then, since you'll be cutting me off for however many days it takes for your magic to wear off."

Raymond ran his finger down the center of Jean's chest. "Just from feeding. We can still fuck all you like."

"You can't say things like that and expect me not to react," Jean warned, reaching for the button at Raymond's waist.

"Did I say I expected you not to react?" Raymond teased, shimmying out of his trousers and underwear with a little help from Jean. "I rather hoped you *would* react." He slipped from Jean's grasp and started toward the bedroom, fully aware of the image he presented with his shirttails brushing the top of his ass, the lower curve peeking out from beneath the fabric. The bite marks had faded to light bruises, but he suspected that would only arouse Jean more with the thought of refreshing the marks. He threw an inviting glance over his shoulder as he disappeared around the corner into their bedroom.

The playful side of Raymond's usually serious personality caught Jean completely off guard, so that his lover was out of sight by the time he recovered from the surprise of Raymond actually flirting with him. Not provoking him—that was very different. Raymond had actually flirted with him. Deciding he liked it, Jean stalked toward the bedroom, fully intending to reward his lover's unusual behavior with a night full of loving. They could start that portion of their vacation early!

"PAYET."

"Raymond, it's Thierry. I hate to bother you on a day you were planning on spending at l'ANS, but I think you need to come out to l'Institut, at least for a couple of hours."

"Of course," Raymond said, already rearranging his day's schedule in his head. "If you need me, I'll be right there. Just let me tell Fabienne to clear my schedule for the afternoon."

"It can wait for an hour or two if you need to finish anything up before you come," Thierry said across the phone lines. "It's serious, but it's not an emergency."

"Let me look at my schedule," Raymond said. "I'll be there as quickly as I can."

"Thanks. À bientôt."

Hanging up the phone, Raymond frowned at his calendar, wondering what could have happened that would make Thierry call him. Raymond had already told the other wizard that he trusted his decisions implicitly as far as the repairs were concerned. Unless a repair Thierry intended would disrupt a planned seminar, Raymond did not need the details.

That meant something else was wrong.

He had the press conference scheduled for that evening, but not until seven o'clock. It was only four, which gave him three hours to see what Thierry needed and get back. "Fabienne," he called into the next office, "have you seen Alain today?"

"He was in earlier," Fabienne replied. "Do you need him?"

"Thierry called and said he needs me at l'Institut. I hope to be back in time for the press conference, but I thought I'd see if Alain could take it if I don't get back in time," Raymond explained, coming to the door. "Everything else on my to-do list can wait until tonight or tomorrow if it has to. Thierry wouldn't have called if it weren't important."

"The sooner you leave, the sooner you'll be back," Fabienne said. "Go ahead now. I'll find Alain and see if he can cover for you. If he can't, I'll call you so you know you need to make it back on time."

"Thank you," Raymond said, making sure he had his cell phone before casting a displacement spell. He reappeared moments later in Dommartin.

"What's going on?" he asked Thierry when the other wizard came out to meet him.

"We had some guests sometime last night or this morning," Thierry reported. "I didn't get up until later than usual because we stayed up late trying to finish the repairs in the abbot's house so it would be ready for when we open the labs for research. I gave the workmen the morning off since they stayed to help well past their thirty-five hours for the week. Come outside."

Thierry led Raymond outside the walls of the cloister. The once pristine stones were now covered in graffiti. Some of it was of the generic "fuck you" variety, but other slogans were more chilling, spouting the kind of racial separatism that Raymond thought they had put to rest with Serrier's defeat. "I don't like this," he muttered, "particularly because they shouldn't have been able to get through Adèle's wards."

"I don't think they did," Thierry said. "The wards are on the walls themselves. As long as they held the paint cans outside the wards, the paint itself would go right through because it isn't harmful except in the words it spelled."

"If they can get paint through the wards, what else can they get through?" Raymond asked. "Gasoline? A match? A bomb? That isn't garden-variety graffiti. That's Serrier's rhetoric."

"Serrier's dead," Thierry reminded Raymond. "I saw his body, and he was very definitely dead. And we rounded up his supporters."

"His active supporters," Raymond agreed, "but that doesn't mean we got all his sympathizers. Merde. This could not be worse timing. Jean and I were supposed to leave on vacation at the end of this week. I'll have to tell him I can't go."

"Why can't you go?" Thierry asked. "This is just graffiti. We'll clean it off and get Adèle to adjust the wards so no one can get close enough to the walls to do it, or anything similar, again."

"Because this has gone beyond a few protestors waving signs outside our building now," Raymond said. "Whoever did this wasn't looking for media attention. They were trying to scare us off."

"And you're letting them succeed. How is that good for anything except giving you an ulcer?" Thierry demanded.

Raymond had no answer to that. He knew there had to be one, but he could not come up with it, so he shrugged and marveled again at the difference a year had made. Thierry was talking to him the same way he talked to Alain, something Raymond would never have believed possible. "I guess I need to call Adèle then."

"I already did," Thierry said. "She was in the middle of something, but she said she'd come out as soon as she could wrap it up. I don't expect her to find anything as far as investigating goes, but I haven't disturbed the scene other than to show it to you. You should probably stay around until she arrives, though, so you can discuss exactly what you want to do about upgrading the wards."

"Which means I have to figure out what I want to do," Raymond sighed. "There's a reason I had Adèle handle this in the first place."

"Come on. Let's go inside out of the cold and we can discuss it. Adèle should change the wards since she put them up in the first place, but I'm not half-bad at strategy," Thierry said. "If we can figure out what the taggers hoped to accomplish, maybe we can figure out who they are and how best to keep them from coming back."

They walked back inside. Raymond started toward the office he had claimed as his own, but Thierry drew him toward the other end of the building. "This is your office," he said, leading Raymond into a large, airy room with a south-facing window. "You can make your official decision in your own time, but we all know no one else will sit behind this desk."

Raymond knew he should argue, but he wanted that desk, that position, as his own, so he took the chair Thierry indicated. "So tell me what you think this is all about."

Thierry took a seat on the opposite side of the desk and considered the question seriously. "The insults on the walls suggest a couple of things," he began slowly. "There's the issue of racial separatism, like you mentioned. That was Serrier's line, but didn't you say some of the vampires shared that sort of superior mentality where mortals are concerned?"

"A few," Raymond said, "but one of them just happens to make his home in Autun, and he's made his disapproval of l'Institut and its location very clear to Jean and me. I suppose it's possible he or some of the members of his Cour could be behind this, although it seems petty for a vampire."

"Complaining about l'Institut being in le Morvan in the first place or worrying about whether other vampires have relationships with mortals is just as petty," Thierry pointed out. "So the vampire in Autun is one option. Then there are the protestors in Paris and the Front National, since they've made their opinions quite clear."

"But their protests so far have been all about getting media attention," Raymond disagreed. "The media will never hear about this because we'll have it cleaned up as soon as Adèle finishes her investigation."

"Yes, they want media attention," Thierry said, "but they also want our attention, and they haven't been getting it. Since they haven't said anything new, we haven't either. Whatever we say or don't say to the media about the vandalism, it's forced us to react, and that's what they want. If we leave it, their message stays visible. If we clean it up, we acknowledge that somebody did this. Either way, they get attention. Serrier started out this way too."

"I remember," Raymond said with a frown. "Would the Front National know how to find us here, though? We haven't exactly been open about the location of l'Institut."

"No, we haven't, but it isn't a huge secret either," Thierry said, "and we've garnered enough attention from the local population that if someone asked where we were located, people would know and not have any reason to keep it a secret."

"It wouldn't hurt to ask Eric and Vincent again if they can think of anyone we might have missed, maybe someone who supported Serrier's campaign financially but not physically, someone who wouldn't have broken the law necessarily but might still be around to spew his hatred," Raymond suggested.

"Ask Eric," Thierry agreed. "Leave Vincent out of it if you can. He's still very sensitive about having been on the other side of the war."

"I'm in no position to cast stones," Raymond reminded Thierry. "His scar might be in a different place than mine, but I bear the same mark of shame."

"Yeah, but you got out a hell of a lot earlier than he did, and you didn't capture Orlando," Thierry said bluntly. "I've worked with him enough to know he's a good guy and that his change of heart was genuine, but you dealt with people's prejudice—mine included—for two years. You know how hard that is."

"I'm fortunate people have seen past it now," Raymond agreed.

"Seen how blind and stupid we were, you mean?" Thierry joked. "Don't deny it. We were. At least I was. Vincent would probably be less bothered by you talking to him than by any of the rest of us bringing it up, but every time anyone says anything about the war or the alliance, he flinches. He's fine with current stuff, with Sebastien being my partner, with Luc and Magali being around, as long as nobody mentions the war or anything that transpired then. I'd just hate for him to feel we're only using him for his knowledge."

"Particularly since we really are using Vincent for his affinity to earth," Raymond said with a smile. "All right, I'll talk to Eric. If he doesn't know, maybe he'd be willing to ask Vincent in my place. That way, at least, Vincent wouldn't have to deal with me directly in that regard. Any other avenues you think we should consider?"

"You told me the town council of Dommartin wasn't terribly happy when you first went to meet with them. Could they have anything to do with this? Not directly, probably. I mean, they're probably all in their sixties, and I don't see them coming out to spray graffiti all over our walls, but could their influence have caused some of the local youth to decide to do it?"

"The local youth all work here at this point," Raymond laughed. "Dommartin is a town of two hundred people, and we probably employ fifty of them at the moment, between the cleaning, the cooking, the repairs, and the landscaping, and Angélique has probably hired another twenty to do the same at the branch of Sang Froid she's opening. The town fathers may not approve of us, but I don't see them doing anything that would rock the boat and make us reconsider our decision to locate l'Institut here."

A knock on the door interrupted their conversation. "Come in," Raymond called.

"Nice graffiti you've got out there," Adèle said, coming inside and shaking both men's hands. On another day, she would have kissed their cheeks, but she was here on business now.

"Did you see anything other than the obvious?" Raymond asked.

"Somebody can't spell," Adèle said with a shake of her head. "Your tagger spelled 'fous' wrong in 'fous le camp'. Other than that, there isn't really anything to see. The ground is too frozen for there to be footprints. They didn't leave the paint cans, so there aren't fingerprints."

"Does that tell us anything?" Raymond inquired.

"Only that it probably isn't the first time your tagger has done this, but that's not really any guarantee either," Adèle said. "They could be environmentally conscious, or they could watch enough cop shows to know not to leave anything behind. For all we shake our heads at stupid criminals, there are plenty out there who aren't dumb."

"So what do we do now?" Thierry asked.

"That's up to you, but as far as an official investigation, there's really nothing we can do," Adèle replied. "I can make all the suggestions about installing security cameras and that sort of thing, but you have to decide if it's worth that kind of expense. With a complex this big, it won't be a cheap system."

"What does the wizard suggest if the cop's hands are tied?" Raymond said, knowing all about the juggling of roles that Adèle faced.

"The first thing is definitely to change the wards," Adèle said. "I can move them back from the building, and I can make them somewhat thicker, but I'm not sure it's responsible on our part to make them so thick nothing can get through."

"Not to mention that we want certain people to be able to get through," Thierry added. "The people who work here, the people coming for the seminars, deliveries."

"It's a delicate balance," Raymond agreed. "Let's start by leaving the wards on their current level of exclusion but moving them out from the walls so that random people can't get close enough to tag or otherwise damage the walls."

"You know, this raises the question of whether the collapse a couple of months ago was natural or whether it had help too," Thierry said.

"There's no way to tell now," Adèle said. "With all the repairs completed on both a physical and a magical level, any evidence would be long gone. We'll just have to keep a closer watch now that we know somebody is targeting l'Institut."

Chapter 28

"ARE YOU sure you can handle everything while we're gone?" Raymond asked one last time as he signed the last of the papers that required his signature before he and Jean left for the airport for their trip to La Réunion. Alain, Thierry, and Fabienne had assured him repeatedly that they could keep things running while he was gone, but the vandalism had left him far less certain of his decision.

"Yes!" Fabienne, Thierry, and Alain answered in a resounding chorus.

"Get out of here or you're going to miss your flight," Alain added. "We'll see you in a week."

"It's only four days," Raymond replied automatically. "I'll be back at work on Tuesday."

The other three looked at each other in amusement at Raymond's assurance that he would be back at work after a ten-hour overnight flight, but they left him his delusions. "Go," Fabienne insisted. "Take your suitcase and work your magic. Jean will be thinking you changed your mind."

"No, I told him I had a few things to take care of before we left," Raymond said. "He's not expecting me for another half an hour."

"So surprise him by being early," Thierry said. "Just go or I'll send you myself."

Raymond huffed, but he grabbed his suitcase and cast a displacement spell, arriving outside the airport where he would not cause too much commotion with his arrival. He checked in quickly and made his way to the gate, finding Jean sitting there already, a cup of coffee and a newspaper in hand, looking for all the world like a casual traveler. "Ready for our escape?" Raymond whispered, coming up behind his lover.

"Now that you're here, I am," Jean replied, turning his head and kissing Raymond gently. "It wouldn't have been any fun going without you."

"I told you I was going with you," Raymond said defensively. "I keep my promises."

"I know you do," Jean said, pulling Raymond around to sit next to him, "but I also know things come up sometimes that are out of your control. You're here now, though, and that's all that matters. We'll go away for a few days, relax, recharge, and come back ready to tackle the world and all its problems."

Raymond smiled. "I like the sound of having nothing to do all day but sit on the beach soaking up the sun and nothing to do all night but lying in bed with you while you drive me wild."

"That sounds like heaven on earth," Jean agreed. "They're calling our flight."

Jean surprised Raymond by getting up when they called for first class to board. "First class?" Raymond asked. "But—"

"But nothing," Jean said. "I can afford it, and it's our first vacation together. I wanted us to be comfortable. It's a long flight. When was the last time you flew anywhere coach, much less for ten hours?" Raymond had no answer to that. "Come on. Let's get settled," Jean added.

They boarded and took their seats, greeting the stewardess who hovered in their section of the aircraft. Jean declined any beverages, but Raymond accepted a glass of wine, rationalizing that he needed to start unwinding and a decent glass of wine was the perfect way to start. "Don't drink too much," Jean whispered in his ear after the stewardess had gone on to other passengers. "I want to taste you when I follow you into the lavatory later in the flight, not the alcohol from the wine."

"Jean!"

"What?" Jean said with an innocent look on his face. "Everyone else will get a meal on the flight. Why shouldn't I get one too?"

"Because if you feed from me, even if you don't touch me except that, it will make me come," Raymond hissed.

Jean grinned. "And this would be a bad thing why?"

"Because everyone will hear and know what we're doing."

"But they won't know," Jean teased. "They'll think we're making love when all I'm doing is making sure I'm safe when we land tomorrow."

Raymond glared at his lover. "Like that's any better. Besides, you make love to me every time you feed. You have since the last time we were on La Réunion together."

Jean chuckled. "Back when you were still pretending you could resist me." He could joke about it now, knowing Raymond loved him, but the first time he had dared to bite Raymond's neck had been anything but a laughing matter. He could still remember how hard his pulse had pounded as he bit that tender flesh for the first time, having always fed from Raymond's wrist before that day.

"I wasn't pretending. I didn't want to give in. And then you bit me so carefully and yet so passionately. You were feeding, and yet it was all about my pleasure, not your hunger, and I was lost. I wasn't ready to admit it then, but that was the moment you won my heart."

"You weren't ready to admit it until a couple of months ago."

"Not out loud," Raymond agreed, "but I'd admitted it to myself by the time Marcel asked me to take over l'ANS. I didn't think you'd want to be saddled with a reformed dark wizard as a lover. You have to remember I can't read your emotions the way you can mine."

That would change if Raymond agreed to form an Aveu de Sang. Sitting on an airplane taxiing toward the runway was not the time to bring that up, though.

"Once we're airborne and can get up, go to the lavatory on the right, but don't lock the door," Jean said instead, nipping at Raymond's ear as he leaned close. "I'll join you after a moment so I can have my evening snack."

"Everyone will hear."

"What do you care? No one knows who we are. If you're really that worried, put up a silencing spell so the noise doesn't penetrate the walls. I know you can do it. You had one in your office at the Milice," Jean suggested.

Raymond grumbled more for form's sake than anything else. The thought of Jean feeding from him—not to mention doing who knew what else to him—in the lavatory had undeniable appeal. He simply had to be daring enough to allow it to happen.

The jet's engines roared to life as they took off, pressing Raymond back into the seat. With each second that passed, his stomach tightened more at the thought of getting up and going to the lavatory, knowing Jean would join him and knowing what would happen once the door closed behind him. Putain, he was so hard purely from thinking about it that he would probably come the minute Jean's fangs touched his skin. He squirmed in his seat, trying to hide his discomfort. He should have known better.

"Are you getting hard?" Jean whispered in his ear. "Are you thinking about what we're going to do and wishing we could start right now?"

"Yes," Raymond groaned, Jean's breath on his skin sending shivers through his body. "How do you do this to me? How do you make me want you even when I know I shouldn't?"

"It's a gift," Jean said smugly, unfolding the blanket in the seatback pocket and spreading it over them. Once he had it settled, he dropped his hand to Raymond's groin, squeezing lightly. "I could take you out right now and stroke you, and no one would be any wiser." He ran his hand down the cloth-covered length. "Although you'd have to be very, very quiet."

The captain turned off the fasten seatbelt sign, and Raymond was out of his seat like a rocket, flashing a look over his shoulder that promised retribution. Jean leaned back in his chair and relaxed for a moment before rising and following his lover.

Pushing inside the cramped space, he locked the door. "Do the spell, because I'm going to make you scream."

Raymond barely had time to cast the spell before Jean pulled open his shirt, biting deeply into Raymond's chest. Raymond cried out at the sharp pinch, but it dissolved quickly into the pleasure that only came from Jean's fangs in his body. He kept expecting his lover to open his pants or to caress him, but Jean's hands remained planted on the sink behind Raymond, only his fangs touching Raymond in any appreciable way. The wizard tried to press closer, to rub their bodies together in invitation, but Jean clamped his hands on Raymond's hips, holding them in place. Raymond mewled in protest, but he thought he understood. Jean wanted him to come from his fangs alone, the way he had done the first time Jean had bitten him with intent. It was both harder and easier now than it had been then. Back then it was all new, and the surprise realization that Jean was making love to him with his fangs had been nearly all it took to make Raymond come. The sensation was a familiar one now, after a year of being lovers—which took away the element of surprise but added a year's worth of conditioning that associated the vampire's kiss with mind-blowing pleasure.

Closing his eyes, Raymond consciously relaxed into the sensations, letting them push everything else from his mind until all he knew was the pull of Jean's fangs in his flesh and the ever-expanding magical connection between them.

Jean tasted the second Raymond surrendered to the moment, smiling against his lover's skin as he licked around the place where his fangs penetrated, adding layer upon layer of pleasure. He could taste the rising desire in Raymond's blood, and he set out to add to it, playing to their first connection. Within minutes, Raymond shuddered against him as he climaxed.

Jean could have left it at that. He had gotten what he wanted, but the sight of his lover leaning against the sink, head thrown back, eyes closed, damp spot staining his pants, was more than Jean's control could survive. He pulled open Raymond's trousers, coating his fingers in the stickiness of his lover's release so he could slide them into the relaxed opening behind the wizard's balls.

"Jean!" Raymond gasped.

Jean pressed the tip of one finger against Raymond's prostate and lifted his head, licking at the bite mark to close it. "Do you really want me to stop?"

Raymond shook his head. With Jean's fingers inside him teasing his sweet spot and the magical connection still buzzing between them, the last thing he wanted was for Jean to stop.

"Then turn around, because you can't sit on that sink and lean back enough to let me inside you."

Raymond turned immediately, shrugging his shoulders so his open shirt would fall down his back enough to bare skin to his lover's fangs. He had no doubt Jean would bite him again as he took him.

Jean's cock nudged his entrance, prompting Raymond to lean forward and shift his feet, opening himself to his lover's inward slide. When even that was not enough, he reached behind himself, spreading his cheeks wider to give Jean the space to take him. Jean's cock pushed home. Then his lips found the curve of Raymond's shoulder, his fangs penetrating seconds later. Raymond cried out at the overwhelming delight of being taken in love, his body seizing again.

"Not yet," Jean said, squeezing the base of Raymond's cock tightly. "Wait for me."

Raymond bit his lip, struggling to hold on and wait for Jean to catch up, but the combination of cock and fangs was potent, leaving him trembling on the cusp of release. "Please," he begged. "Hurry."

Jean thrust harder, sucked more deeply, his hand releasing its grip on Raymond's cock in favor of stroking it. Raymond gave a strangled cry, his climax tingling low in his back. He felt Jean shudder hard against him, felt hot cream coating his insides, and let go, collapsing forward against the mirror.

"Putain! What you do to me!" Raymond said when Jean released his neck.

"Good things, I hope?" Jean purred.

"You know they are. You can taste it."

"It's still nice to hear sometimes," Jean said softly.

"Yes," Raymond said, surprised at the vulnerability he heard in Jean's voice. "Very good things."

"Good," Jean said. "Clean yourself up and go back to our seats. It will take me a little longer, since I can't do magic. I'll be there once I'm done."

Raymond cast a cleansing spell with a flick of his wrist, erasing all the signs of what they had been doing except the two new bite marks on his body. Straightening his clothes, he leaned forward and kissed Jean tenderly. "I love you. Thank you for insisting we do this."

"Do what?" Jean asked. "Sneak into the lavatory to make love or go on vacation in the first place?"

Raymond grinned. "Both."

RAYMOND SLUMPED on the bed in mind-numbing repletion. The hours since their arrival in La Réunion had been one delight after another, from seeing how well the island had recovered from last year's storm to eating fresh seafood at a local beachside restaurant, from walking on the beach hand in hand with Jean to returning to their airy hotel room to make love again. Their lovemaking had been reminiscent of the night Jean had lost control, without the guilt afterward. Raymond was sure every sensitive spot on his body had a bite mark or four, and he was pretty sure he had discovered some new places he had not known were sensitive before now. His cock softened slowly in Jean's body, slipping free finally, making him wish they never had to be separated. Above him, Jean shifted as if trying to get closer—not that Raymond thought they could be any closer than they were—with Jean collapsed on top of him, having ridden him to oblivion.

"Are you trying to crawl inside me?" Raymond teased when Jean shifted again.

"I can think of far worse places to be," Jean quipped, lifting his head a little so he could meet Raymond's eyes.

"I can think of far better places to be," Raymond countered.

"I can't," Jean disagreed. "The little glimpses I get when I feed from you only make me want to know more. Your mind must be a fascinating place."

"I don't know any mind-reading spells," Raymond joked, not entirely sure where the odd turn of this conversation had come from. "Even if I did, they probably wouldn't work between us."

"I know one that would," Jean said slowly, "and it would work both ways, letting you sense as much about me as I could sense about you."

Raymond frowned. He was considered something of an expert on arcane and esoteric spells, but he had never heard of anything like what Jean was describing—much less something that would work on a vampire and his partner, at that. "What spell are we talking about?"

Jean rocked back on his heels, licking his way down Raymond's chest to his stomach, his groin, and his inner thigh. "A quick little burn right here," Jean murmured, sucking on an unmarked bit of skin, "in a place no one would ever see, and we could be linked in more ways than you can possibly imagine for the rest of your life, perhaps even beyond."

Every muscle in Raymond's body tensed. "I already wear one man's mark," he said slowly. "When I got free of Serrier, I swore I'd never belong to anyone else again."

"This isn't like that," Jean said, hurt that Raymond would even begin to compare the scar on his back with the vow Jean wanted to make. "For one thing, it would be a mutual commitment."

"But I would be the one marked again."

"No one would have to know," Jean insisted. "Orlando complained the other day that he hated the fact that everyone could see Alain's brand. It got me thinking—"

"Thinking that having a wizard for a partner isn't enough?" Raymond asked. "You need to mark him like a piece of livestock you're afraid someone will steal?"

"It isn't about the mark," Jean repeated. "Not between us. I know you don't need my protection. I've seen you fight. Even if another vampire tried to approach you, they'd never succeed, not even by force. You proved to me *I* wouldn't even succeed by force. It's about the relationship the mark represents."

"Then why do we need the mark in the first place?" Raymond demanded. "Why can't we just go on as we are?"

"Because I was hoping the fact that you loved me meant you'd be interested in discussing ways to deepen our relationship even more," Jean said. "If we make a private Aveu de Sang—I'm not talking about sharing this with anyone, not even our friends—it would mean I'd never have to worry about taking more from you than you could give. We'd never have to hold back while we're making love for fear of me draining you dangerously. We'd have a bond that nothing could break or challenge, no matter what."

"We already have that," Raymond said quietly. "Nothing you've said adds anything but an onus on you of not being able to feed elsewhere if the need arises."

"Our hearts would be linked," Jean offered. "You'd be able to read me the way I can read you when I feed. Not my thoughts necessarily, but my emotions. You'd be able to sense me the way Orlando and Alain can sense each other. Say you'll think about it."

"What's to think about?" Raymond replied. "We're perfectly fine as we are now. Why do we have to change things?"

"For the same reason people get married," Jean said, pulling away. "Because they love each other and want to make a commitment to each other."

"People get married because the Church told them they couldn't have sex unless they did, and it's become such a part of our society that nobody stops to realize they don't need a wedding or a marriage license to have that kind of relationship in this day and age," Raymond retorted. "A civil marriage gives couples certain rights under law, but again, that's a societal norm, not something that has any bearing on the commitment between the couple. If you want to make sure you're the heir to my estate or that you have the right to make medical decisions for me should I fall ill, then we need to be discussing a civil ceremony, but that's no more possible than it is for me to be your Consort, and for the exact same reason. If you want a private commitment, I'll give you one gladly. I will love you and stand by you for as long as you want me there. I don't need anything more than that."

Jean sighed and rose from the bed. "Maybe I do."

Raymond nodded slowly, feeling like his heart was breaking. "Then you'll need to find it somewhere else. I can't give you what you're asking for."

Chapter 29

JEAN STARED down at Raymond, heart pounding wildly as the beast within him fought for control. The rejection hurt. He had expected to need to persuade Raymond. He had not expected to be shot down completely. Feeling his control slipping, he turned, grabbing a pair of shorts as he stalked toward the door that led to the veranda and down to the beach. He had to get out before he did something he would regret. Like grabbing the nearest metal object and branding Raymond before he realized what was happening.

The door slammed against the wall in his anger, nearly smothering the small sound from behind him. The despair in the sound was enough to make him turn and look back. Raymond had curled onto his side, back turned, everything in his posture proclaiming his misery. That was more than Jean could bear. Kicking the door shut again, he strode back to the bed, tearing the shorts off, completely unconcerned that they came off in pieces. He grabbed Raymond's hips, pulling him onto his knees. "You don't get to do this," he growled as his hands steadied Raymond. "You don't get to drive me away."

Without waiting for a reply, he pressed against his lover's body, needing them joined again. The guardian muscle yielded immediately, the passage still slick from Jean's fingers earlier, before he had decided he wanted Raymond inside him instead. Jean's fangs dropped as if he had not fed minutes before, but he ignored them. He would not risk draining Raymond by feeding again, and he did not want to taste his lover's resistance.

Not that there was any in Raymond's body. The wizard bucked back against him with astounding ferocity, almost as if he had a beast to match Jean's inside him. "Mine!" Jean snarled as he pounded the willing body beneath him into the mattress. "You're mine. Never let you go."

Raymond moaned beneath him, but Jean was too far gone to care if it was pain or pleasure or something in between. Only his release mattered now, all finesse, all control incinerated by the heat of Raymond's body squeezing him tight and the knowledge of how close he had come to walking out on the best thing that had ever happened to him.

His orgasm burned through him, stealing his breath and his awareness momentarily, as he thrust mindlessly.

"Harder," Raymond begged.

Cursing under his breath, Jean flipped Raymond onto his back, his fingers replacing his cock as he went down on Raymond, drawing his lover deep into his throat. Raymond bucked and pleaded beneath him, needing just a little more. Lifting his head, Jean bit hard into Raymond's iliac crease, hoping the feeling of his fangs would be enough to push the wizard into release.

It worked. Within seconds, Raymond's cock twitched, disgorging creamy fluid across his belly. Jean tasted Raymond's release in his blood along with the bitterness of fear, a flavor he had thought long gone from their lives. It sobered him enough to reach for a towel so he could clean them both up tenderly. He tossed it toward the bathroom, intending to draw Raymond into his arms and convince him to tell Jean what had scared him so much, but Raymond had rolled to his side again, his back to his lover. With a sigh, Jean lay down next to him, not quite touching but not leaving either. Whatever damage he had done, he refused to give up on them.

Raymond lay motionless in bed, body tingling and heart aching. He had nearly screamed in protest when Jean started to leave. He had managed to smother it to a whimper, but even that had been enough to bring his lover back, all ferocious rage and passionate possessiveness. The rough coupling had reassured him on one level, but it only added to his fears on another. It would be so easy to give in and give Jean what he had asked for. The pain of the brand would be nothing compared to the pain of receiving the scar that still marred his back, but Jean was already so demanding, so possessive. A part of Raymond feared he would lose all sense of self if he accepted Jean's Aveu de Sang. He would never have another private thought or emotion, never have a moment without his lover's feelings influencing him.

He had always taken Jean and the needs of the vampires into his decisions as president of l'ANS, but it had been one consideration among many. If he made the commitment Jean had asked for, he did not know if he would be able to balance the needs of the many with the needs of his lover. Even if he gave up the position at l'ANS and became the director of l'Institut, he would still have decisions to make, decisions that would not always coincide with Jean's views. When that happened now, they discussed it rationally, Raymond explained his decision, and they moved on, even if Jean was not happy about it. If Raymond had to live with the pressure of Jean's displeasure in his mind, he feared he would soon start caving to the vampire's every whim simply to avoid that. He had fought too hard to reclaim himself after leaving Serrier's forces to put himself under another's control, no matter how loving.

Then there was the issue of their public relationship. Jean spoke of a private bond, a brand in a place no one but them would ever see, but Jean was also a public figure. Already the two had clashed over Jean treating him as if Raymond were his Consort without any announcement to that effect. If they formed an even deeper bond, that would grow a hundred times worse. A day might come when Raymond was willing to consider taking on that role, but he did not want to be pressured into it, intentionally or unintentionally.

Most deeply buried of all was the fear that Jean would change his mind, that Raymond would do something to make him change his mind. He had an abysmal track record with relationships because his fascination with his research had always been greater than his fascination with his lovers. The war and his current role as president of l'ANS had forced him away from that research and allowed his fascination with Jean to reign supreme in his life this past year, but if he took the job at l'Institut, that could change again. He knew how self-absorbed he became when he got a question in his head that he could not solve. Jean would never stand for taking a back seat to Raymond's research, something he respected about his lover, but Raymond could envision the fights that would ensue. It would be bad enough with their current relationship—but if Raymond accepted Jean's brand, it would mean Jean could not go elsewhere to feed if Raymond got busy, and Raymond feared he would come to resent Jean and vice versa to the point that living together would be pure hell.

With a stifled sigh, Raymond shifted to get comfortable with Jean's arms around him and tried to sleep. Maybe things would look better in the morning.

THE BUS ride from île St-Louis to the Cirque de Cilaos the next morning passed in tense silence, neither Raymond nor Jean willing to cancel their plans because of their fight the night before and yet both unable to move past the silent strain between them. When they descended at the end of the ninety-minute trip, the sight that greeted them took their breaths away. In the remnants of a prehistoric volcano, the town of Cilaos sat nestled among the steep gorges of the surrounding peaks. They wandered down the picturesque main street, side by side but not holding hands as they had done the day before.

The église Notre-Dame-des-Neiges rose brilliantly white against the green mountains with their cap of wispy clouds, bringing a sigh to Jean's lips.

"Do you want to go in?" Raymond asked.

"Do you mind?" Jean asked in reply.

"Of course not," Raymond said quickly. Yesterday, Jean would not have asked. He would have simply said yes—a fact that hurt far worse than any of the unyielding tension between them did.

The interior was both predictable and surprising. It was laid out in the shape of a cross with the altar at the far end, but instead of the high-vaulted naves and gothic architecture Raymond was used to seeing in France, the church had a lower ceiling with far fewer arches, a testament to a simpler place and perhaps a simpler faith. The décor, too, was simple, with none of the frescos or elaborate statuary so common in French churches. By the time this church had been built, the faithful had not needed to "read" the Bible in the images on the walls. Raymond did not know what Jean thought of the quiet effect because Jean had wandered to the front of the church, kneeling before the altar in prayer. Raymond told himself this was no different than any other visit to any other church, but the distance seemed to grow with each passing second. Feeling suddenly out of place, Raymond stepped back outside to give Jean his privacy and the other tourists a chance to see the church without him in the way.

When Jean joined him a few minutes later, Raymond could not decide how to interpret the look on the vampire's face. With a sigh, he looked at the map. "There's the Villa Soledad not too far away," he suggested. "It's supposed to be a prime example of the créole architecture of the area."

Jean did not say anything, falling in step beside Raymond with no further commentary. Raymond stifled a sigh and wondered what it would take to break the impasse between them. He could give Jean what he wanted, but that would cause as many problems as it solved. Surely there had to be another solution.

They wandered the town until lunchtime. Raymond was about to suggest trying one of the local cafés when Jean pointed to a small charcuterie with prepared sandwiches. "We could go sit by the lake," Jean added.

It was the first somewhat romantic suggestion Jean had made all day, so Raymond agreed, purchasing a sandwich and a bottle of Volvic from the local woman behind the counter. "Where's the best view of the lake?" he asked as she handed him his purchases.

"They're all good views," she said. "Nothing but good views in Cilaos."

Raymond smiled. "That's good to hear. We'll just wander until we find a likely place then."

They walked down to the lake and found a spot in the sun. It was warm, but not prohibitively so, and Raymond could feel some of his stress flowing away as they sat on the grassy embankment and listened to the breeze in the rushes. "I'm sorry we argued last night, but I'm not sorry we came to La Réunion," Raymond said softly between bites of his sandwich. "You were right about that break. I needed it too."

Jean nodded, not at all sure what to say.

They spent the rest of the afternoon much as they had the morning, wandering the outskirts of the town this time, even going up into the mountains a little before returning to catch the last bus back to île St-Louis.

After a delicious dinner that Raymond barely tasted because he was so worried about what would happen when they returned to the hotel, they wandered the beaches again. Raymond's heart clenched at the difference from the night before. Then, they had lingered on the beach to let anticipation build so that when they finally reached their bed, they were both already on edge. Tonight it was all about avoiding the source of their discomfort with each other.

Finally, though, sleep became a necessity for Raymond. "We should go back to the hotel. I'm exhausted from all the walking we've done today, and tomorrow is another busy day."

"We could change our plans and stay in if you need to rest," Jean offered.

Raymond smiled at the small olive branch. "I should be fine after a good night's sleep."

Jean nodded, following Raymond back to the hotel. They went inside together, but Jean made no move to join Raymond when the wizard gathered his toiletries for a bath. He would not be able to look at Raymond wet and naked and keep from begging the wizard to forgive him, to forget about everything he had said, to let things go back to the way they had been before he had opened his mouth last night and ruined everything between them. As much as the current estrangement hurt, he did not want to go back to the way things had been. He had asked for the Aveu de Sang because he felt deeply about it. He did not want to diminish his desire for that commitment by rescinding the offer.

When Raymond came back out of the bathroom, damp and disheveled, dressed only in his underwear, Jean rose and kissed him. "I love you," he said. "I'm not ready for bed yet, so I'm going to walk some more. Don't feel like you have to wait up for me."

"Jean, wai—" Raymond began, but Jean was already gone. He sighed and sank onto the bed in frustration. He could not seem to do anything right where his lover was concerned. He could only hope tomorrow would be better. It took a long time before he fell asleep.

RAYMOND'S PHONE rang the next morning as he was eating breakfast. "Payet."

"Raymond, it's Thierry. I'm sorry to disturb your vacation, but there was another incident at l'Institut, and I thought you'd want to know about it."

"What happened?" Raymond asked.

"Someone got through the wards—Adèle is still trying to figure out how—and set fire to the Hostellerie," Thierry reported. "No one was hurt, but there's some pretty substantial damage to the interior from the fire, plus the smoke and water damage once we realized and started trying to put it out."

"Merde," Raymond muttered. "Okay, give me a couple of hours to figure things out and I'll come home."

"I really am sorry."

"It's not your fault," Raymond said. "And you did the right thing calling me. This goes beyond a little bit of graffiti, especially since they got through the wards to do it."

"Okay, see you when you get here then. I'll start evaluating the damage when the arson investigator lets me in," Thierry said.

Raymond hung up with a sigh and stared down at his coffee and croissant.

"Did I hear the phone?" Jean asked, coming out of the bathroom.

"Yeah," Raymond said. "It was Thierry. There's been a fire at l'Institut. Someone got past Adèle's wards and set a fire in the Hostellerie. I'm sorry. I need to go back to Paris."

Jean nodded. "Can we find a wizard here who can send me back with you?"

Raymond's lips pursed. "It's not that simple. It's too far for one displacement spell. We'd have to find someone at each stop along the way, and I don't have time for that. We can call the airline and see if you can get on an earlier flight, or you could stay and take advantage of the rest of the vacation, since we already paid for it."

"I can't stay here relaxing while you're in Paris dealing with the fallout from this," Jean protested. "That's hardly fair to you."

Raymond shrugged. "None of this is fair to either of us, but that's beside the point. Call the airline and see what they say. I'm going to start packing. I told Thierry I'd be there as soon as I could."

Jean frowned, but he could hardly ask Raymond to stay, no matter how much he wanted to. He borrowed Raymond's phone and called Air Austral, explaining to the customer service agent that he had a family emergency and asking if it would be possible to change his reservation or even purchase a new one-way ticket back to Paris for that night. The agent was very courteous and very thorough, but in the end, no seats were available. "The best I can do is put you on standby for tonight's flight. You can go to the airport and if anyone doesn't show up, you can get a seat, but I can't make any guarantees."

"Let's do that," Jean said. "I would hate to miss the chance if something does become available." Hanging up the phone, he handed it back to Raymond. "I guess I'll see you in two days then," he said.

"Will you be okay until then?" Raymond asked. "We didn't check to make sure all the flight times would be at night because we were traveling together."

"I'll be fine," Jean said. "I fed the night before last."

"Are you sure? I don't want anything to happen to you," Raymond said, holding out his wrist in offering. "Even if it's not a full feeding, take a little to tide you over. I'll worry the whole time we're apart if you don't."

The offered hand was a slap in the face. With a roar, Jean tackled Raymond to the bed, his lips going to his lover's neck as his fangs dropped and penetrated, sucking deeply.

The taste of Raymond's blood calmed him almost immediately. No matter how he had taken the gesture, Raymond still loved him, was genuinely worried about him, and reacted to his bite with the same breathtaking desire he had felt since they became lovers. Gentling his feeding, he cradled Raymond's head in his hands, stroking the short, dark hair tenderly as he swallowed enough blood to hold him until he and Raymond could be together again.

When he was full, he lifted his head, licking at the wounds to close them. "Don't ever offer me your wrist like that again unless you're telling me you're done with me as anything but a casual partner," he said. "Even if we're arguing, don't push me away like that."

"I'm sorry," Raymond said immediately. "I wasn't thinking like that. I was thinking about speed, that's all." He kissed Jean tenderly, heedless of the blood still staining his lover's fangs. "I'll see you in Paris, either tomorrow morning or the day after at the latest. I love you."

"I love you too," Jean said, watching with a sinking stomach as Raymond and his bag disappeared.

Chapter 30

RAYMOND DETOURED by his and Jean's apartment only long enough to leave his bag before going out to l'Institut. He kept looking automatically for Jean, only to remember that the vampire was still in La Réunion.

Thierry met him in the cloister, the wards having alerted him to Raymond's arrival.

"Adèle has changed the wards again," Thierry said without preamble. "Approved people can still come and go, but any time someone comes through, the wards sound a notice. If nothing else, it should keep whoever is here aware of arrivals."

"Does she have any idea how the perpetrator got through the wards last night?" Raymond asked.

"None whatsoever," Thierry replied. "She's checked the entire perimeter and couldn't find any weakening or any evidence of tampering. She's completely baffled. Unless the person who did it had help on the inside."

"Someone from l'Institut?" Raymond gaped at Thierry. "You can't be serious!"

"According to Adèle, we're either looking at an inside job or someone who can cut through her wards like they aren't even there without her magic even recognizing the intrusion."

"Leighton?" Raymond postulated.

Thierry shrugged. "That was my first thought too, but she says her wards and other locking spells have worked on him before, though, because they actually affect the door handle or the wall or whatever instead of Leighton himself. But I still think it could be. I'd rather it was him than think we've got a saboteur in our midst or a rogue wizard or some other magical creature that can brush Adèle's wards aside like they aren't there."

"That would be… disconcerting," Raymond agreed.

Thierry smiled at the understatement. "Downright terrifying," he corrected. "Adèle's wards are second only to Marcel's. Serrier couldn't get through the ones she did at Milice headquarters. I'd rather deal with an inside job, as much as I hate to think of that kind of treachery."

"Let's take a look at the damage," Raymond said. "We can stand here debating all day, but we only have about ten days to get l'Institut back on its feet before the next seminar begins."

"I called everyone I could think of for help," Thierry said. "Angélique says she remembers where they bought most of the furniture. She's offered to take madame Naizot and any wizard who can help. They'll send pieces back here once they've made purchases to start furnishing rooms in either the abbot's lodge or the monks' cells for the wizards, since I don't know if we can get the Hostellerie usable again in time."

"I knew there was a reason I left you in charge," Raymond said, summoning a smile. "Thank you, Thierry. Seriously. Everything is all out of whack at the moment, so I really appreciate you being on top of things."

"Everything?" Thierry said, glancing pointedly at the bite marks on Raymond's neck.

Raymond sighed. "Everything. Jean wants more of a commitment from me than I feel prepared to make. It made for a tense day yesterday."

"That would be rough," Thierry agreed. "I'm not prying, but if you ever need someone to talk to, don't forget that Alain and I both have vampire partners in our lives, and while Orlando is different, Sebastien is every bit as stubborn as Jean is, and even Orlando has his moments. Alain has told me stories that certainly surprised me."

"Thank you again," Raymond said. "I might take you up on that."

"Careful when we go inside," Thierry warned. "Magali, Vincent, and I have stabilized everything as much as we could, but you might want to put up your shields just in case."

Raymond summoned a barrier of protective magic, sensing Thierry doing the same next to him. It was not something he could maintain indefinitely, but it would provide some protection during the tour of the damaged building.

"The fire started here," Thierry said, pointing to the remains of the curtains on the windows just inside the door. "The arson inspector found traces of gasoline dashed on the cloth here and on the rugs. The stone itself wouldn't burn, but the drywall the previous owners had used to cover the walls caught and helped the fire spread from room to room, as did the wooden beams. We may want to consider leaving the walls stone after we clean the rooms. The fire would not have done nearly the amount of damage it did without the drywall."

"We'll definitely keep that in mind," Raymond agreed, surveying the blackened walls and ruined furniture. "How much of it is like this?"

"The entire ground floor and most of the second floor. The third floor is mostly smoke and water damage. The arson inspector recommended a fire recovery service in Dijon that could help with the cleanup and restoration. I haven't contacted them yet because I want to make sure the structure is sound before we let anyone in."

"Not to mention that we have no idea who did this in the first place, and the more people we let in for whatever reason, the harder it will be to catch the person responsible," Raymond said. "I've seen enough. Unless there's something in particular you need to show me?"

Thierry shook his head. "It's more of the same upstairs. What are you going to do now?"

"Prepare a statement for the press, contact the participants in February's seminar and be honest with them about the sabotage in case they want to change their minds, and call in every favor owed to me by every wizard in France to get the repairs done here as quickly as possible," Raymond said. *And if I keep busy enough, maybe I won't spend every second expecting Jean to appear.*

"D'accord," Thierry said. "I'll be here doing what I can. Call if you need anything."

Raymond nodded and returned to Paris. Fabienne had not come in yet, so he went in his office and shut the door, trying to focus his mind on anything besides Jean's absence. He had not realized how used to his lover's presence he had become, but they had hardly been separated since they met, other than a few hours here and there for this meeting or that. He kept hearing Jean's voice playing in his head. "A quick little burn and we could be joined."

Heart pounding at what he was considering, he left a note on his door saying he had gone out and would be back shortly. Going home, he went into Jean's library, running his finger along the spines, trying to find anything that would tell him more about the Aveu de Sang. He could ask Alain about it from a wizard's perspective, or Sebastien, Orlando or monsieur Lombard from a vampire's perspective, but that would mean revealing his interest, and he was not sure he wanted to do that. The Aveu de Sang, if he and Jean made it, would have to be a secret. The more people he talked to about it in theory, the more people who would wonder, who might even ask, if they had made one.

The organization of tomes frustrated him, leaving him no closer to finding an answer to his questions. With a sigh, he leaned back in the chair and tried to decide what to do next. He had to make a decision, and he could not do that without all the information he needed. Deciding to bite the bullet and take Alain into his confidence, he pulled his coat back on so he could return to l'ANS.

He opened the door to his apartment in time to dodge Alain's knock, which would have hit him on the nose if he had been a little slower.

"What are you doing here, Alain?" Raymond asked, surprised to see Alain on the landing.

"Looking for you," Alain said. "Orlando was adamant that I find you right away."

"Why? What's wrong?" Raymond asked, concerned now that something else had gone wrong.

"He didn't say," Alain replied. "He just kept saying I needed to find you."

"Well, I'm glad you did," Raymond said. "Would you like to come in for a few minutes? I can make us some coffee, and I'd actually like to talk to you about a couple of things."

"Sure," Alain agreed, coming into the apartment. Raymond hung up his own coat and took Alain's as well.

"The kitchen is tiny, but you're welcome to join me, although I think you'd be more comfortable out here," Raymond offered.

Alain followed him into the small room. Raymond took comfort in the familiar ritual of making coffee as he searched for a way to ask his questions without revealing the depth of his interest. "It must be strange, having Orlando in your head all the time."

Alain frowned a little. "What, you mean because of the Aveu de Sang?"

"Yes," Raymond said. "How do you know what thoughts are yours and what are his, even?"

"It's not like that," Alain said quickly. "I can't sense his actual thoughts, first of all, just general emotions. I know if he's happy or sad or hungry, that sort of thing, but I can't tell what he's thinking. If I had been able to, it would have made the search for him much easier when he was missing. All I knew then was that he was in pain and that he missed me."

"But it's still always there, right?" Raymond said. The coffee pot hissed as it finished brewing, so Raymond poured them each a cup, setting one in front of Alain. He had watched the other wizard drink coffee often enough to know he liked it black. "How do you know what you're feeling is your emotion and not his?"

Alain took a deep breath, trying to figure out how to explain the connection he had with Orlando. "Yes, if we're fighting, I have to be careful not to let his anger trigger mine, but most of the time it isn't like that," he said slowly. "It's like hearing someone else's laughter. It's contagious, but you know you're reacting to something external. If you laugh with them, it's because you share their amusement, not because they've somehow forced you into it. I can feel Orlando's emotions, but I always know they're his, and most of the time, they're just there, in the back of my mind. I don't even think about it anymore, unless he deliberately projects something to get my attention."

Alain did not mention the occasions when Orlando would send a jolt of desire his way during a particularly boring meeting, a promise for later to tide him over until the end of the day. He had no idea what Raymond was driving at with his questions, but some things were meant to be private.

"And if you really need to concentrate? If having something like that happen would be a distraction?" Raymond pressed.

"It's possible to block it for a short period of time," Alain replied, "but honestly, I find it more disruptive to my concentration to put the block in place than I do to feel Orlando there. If I really need to concentrate on something, I let him know what's going on and he has enough respect for me not to disturb me. I would imagine that you ask Jean not to disturb you occasionally if you're in the middle of something. It's the same thing, just on a different plane."

"So you don't feel... I don't know, like you've lost a part of yourself because of the Aveu de Sang?"

"Does Jean want to mark you?" Alain asked. "Is that what this is all about?"

Raymond hesitated, but he could not make himself lie. "He mentioned it while we were in La Réunion. It caught me totally off guard, and I reacted... badly. If you had it to do over again, knowing what you know now, would you do it again?"

"In an instant," Alain said, his conviction ringing in his voice.

"You don't feel like his opinion influences you unduly?"

"Any relationship influences you," Alain reminded Raymond. "You think of things because of Jean that you wouldn't have considered a year ago. Is that unduly influencing you, or is that being sensitive to the needs and desires of the person you love? The Aveu de Sang isn't any different. Okay, maybe it's a deeper bond, but you have to remember that it goes both ways. Orlando is as aware and as influenced by my needs and wants as I am by his. You're thinking about it in terms of losing yourself, which I understand because I had the same reaction at first, but it isn't like that. I haven't lost anything by being Orlando's lover or by being his Avoué."

"Then I guess I have some thinking to do," Raymond said with a sigh.

"Don't overthink this," Alain counseled. "Do you love him?"

"Very much so," Raymond said. "I didn't think I would ever find someone who would want me with my checkered past, but he does."

"Would it bother you if he fed from someone else?" Alain continued.

"I'd almost rather he slept with someone else than fed from someone else," Raymond admitted.

"Then what are you worried about?" Alain asked.

"That I'll lose myself to his influence, that he'll regret being tied to me, that I'll somehow let him down," Raymond said in a rush.

"An Aveu de Sang won't give him any more influence over you than he already has," Alain said slowly. "I can assure you of that much. As for letting him down, that's a part of any relationship. I know I've let Orlando down at times, and there have been times I've been angry or disappointed with him. The Aveu de Sang isn't a cure-all. Sebastien told me something when Orlando and I were going through a rough spell. He told me the Aveu de Sang wasn't some exterior magical force picking two people who were right for each other. He said it was a promise. A magical one, to be sure, but still a covenant between two people. Fallible, imperfect people who make mistakes, but who come back together and work through their problems because they can't walk away. You've lived with Jean for a year now. Is there anything that makes you want to walk away? Not storm out of the room in frustration, but truly walk away and never come back."

"No," Raymond said softly. "Nothing like that."

"Then all you're doing is promising in another way to stay with him," Alain said. "It's that simple."

"Thanks, Alain," Raymond said. "You won't tell anyone we talked about this, will you?"

"Not a word, although I suspect Orlando already knows," Alain replied. "It would explain his insistence I come over here. Not that I know how he knew you hadn't jumped at the chance."

"Even if I had, I might have had questions," Raymond said. "He could have sent you in case I needed someone to talk to about my new bond instead of a potential bond."

"He has always been incredibly intuitive," Alain agreed. "And he seems to get more so as time passes. If he asks, I'd rather not lie to him."

"If he asks, tell him," Raymond agreed. "I don't want you to have to lie for me, but I'd rather you not tell anyone else."

"Your secret is safe with us," Alain promised. "And you can count on our support at any time. If you have questions, before or after you make your Aveu de Sang, don't hesitate to ask. We'll do our best to answer. Just remember this: a vampire is fundamentally incapable of hurting his Avoué. Orlando literally could not make himself do something that would injure me in any way. If either of you has to worry about losing yourself to the other, it would be Jean losing himself to you."

"You've given me a lot to think about," Raymond said slowly. "I appreciate it. If I have more questions, I'll call or come see you."

"You're welcome," Alain said, finishing his coffee and setting the cup in the sink. "I'll leave you to finish whatever you were doing when I interrupted. Will you be back at l'ANS later today?"

"Yes," Raymond said absently, "and then back at l'Institut tonight. I don't want to leave it undefended again. The damage from the fire was bad enough. If they try something else, they could put us months behind schedule."

"Just be careful," Alain exhorted. "A building can be repaired or rebuilt. A life lost can't be."

"I'll be careful," Raymond promised. "During the war, before the alliance formed, I didn't care if I lived or died, except that if I died, I wanted my death to help bring down Serrier. I don't feel that way anymore."

"You just answered all your own questions," Alain said, pulling his coat on. "See you later tonight."

Raymond said good-bye automatically, his mind racing as he took in Alain's parting words on top of everything else he had learned from their conversation. To listen to Alain, all his concerns were backward. He did not need to worry about losing himself but about "taking over" Jean. He was not sure that was any better except that, when he pushed aside his instinctual reaction and thought rationally about Alain and Orlando, he had never questioned whether Alain was acting under Orlando's influence or vice versa. So then the question was not whether it was possible to have an Aveu de Sang and maintain one's independence but whether *he* could do it. And if he could, did he want to?

A fluttering little piece of his heart he usually buried deep inside whispered *yes*. Instead of silencing that voice as he usually did, he let the thought bloom, exploring it carefully. He had always been a loner, never trusting anyone or anything that might hurt him. Then Jean had come along and changed everything. He could not keep the vampire at a distance, though he had tried at first. Little by little—bite by bite, if Raymond was honest—Jean had wormed his way into Raymond's life and heart. On the one hand, accepting an Aveu de Sang wouldn't change anything. He wouldn't love Jean more, wouldn't be more committed to him simply because he wore his lover's mark. On the other hand, it was a tangible, binding promise, a commitment he could truly, finally make to something—someone—who would never hurt him. Even after Raymond had rejected Jean's offer, Jean had not left, though Raymond would not have blamed him. He had stayed and loved Raymond as thoroughly, as possessively, as ever.

Raymond had never wanted a possessive lover. In the past he had ended relationships because his lovers had gotten too demanding, yet he regularly— intentionally—provoked Jean's possessive side. As much as he loved sex with Jean in all its forms, nothing curled his toes like Jean losing control and turning wild on him. He knew Jean held back most of the time for fear of hurting Raymond, of taking too much blood, or for other reasons Raymond knew nothing about. An Aveu de Sang would protect him from that. Jean could not take too much blood, no matter how much he drank. He would no longer have to hold back for fear of weakening Raymond too much. Raymond's stomach tightened at the thought, his cock twitching in his pants at the idea of Jean ravishing him repeatedly, with no concern for how often or how deeply he bit.

He took a deep breath, steadying his nerves, and glanced at the clock, willing the hours to pass by more quickly. No matter what happened, Jean would not be home before morning. Raymond did not want to tell his lover over the phone that he had reconsidered. That decision needed to be conveyed face to face, where the ritual could be carried out as quickly as possible afterward. Now Jean just had to get back so Raymond could tell him.

Chapter 31

JEAN PACED the aisle at the airport, waiting for his flight to be called. He had not been able to get on a flight the night before, even offering to downgrade to coach, and the extra day spent alone on La Réunion had been enough to leave him chomping at the bit with uncharacteristic impatience. He would have said he had banished that particular emotion soon after his turning, the reality of life as a vampire requiring a great deal of patience or at least the ability to bide one's time with grace. There had been nothing graceful about the way he had passed the two days of separation.

The airline employee called for Jean's flight to begin boarding. He pushed through the crowd to the ticket counter, handing over his ticket. "You're traveling alone, monsieur Bellaiche? Your ticket says for two."

"My partner had to return home early for an emergency," Jean said tightly. "I couldn't get an earlier flight."

The woman nodded and motioned for him to board. The reminder, as if he truly needed one, of Raymond's absence grated harshly on Jean's nerves. He took his seat, waving away the flight attendant who offered him a drink. With Raymond at his side, he often indulged for the pleasure of sharing the experience with his lover, but he had no interest in social niceties at the moment. He wanted the plane to take off so it could land and reunite him with Raymond. He did not really expect Raymond to meet him at the airport, although a part of him hoped his lover had missed him enough to want to make a romantic gesture. He did hope, however, to find Raymond still at home. He had gone two days without feeding before, even since he and Raymond had become lovers as well as partners, but this was the first time since the war had ended that they had been separated for so long. That combined with the tension between them at their parting left Jean anxious to feed again, if only for the connection it would give him to Raymond's heart.

He could give his lover the space he needed to make up his mind about an Aveu de Sang, as long as he could still taste the love in Raymond's blood. He chided himself silently for having rushed the discussion without sounding Raymond out about it first. He, who was known for his subtlety, had gone in with all the finesse of a bull in a china shop. With a sigh, he leaned his head back against the headrest, closing his eyes and pretending to sleep. He hoped no one would take Raymond's seat, leaving him in peace for the flight. He would never be able to make small talk in his current mood.

His thoughts circled repeatedly around to their flight to La Réunion and the teasing with Raymond about his meal. It had been so relaxed, so easy between them. *It will be again,* he promised himself. *I'll get home and we'll work this out. Even if it means no Aveu de Sang. I'd rather have that than this maudite tension.*

The flight finished boarding and they pulled away from the gate, the seat next to Jean still blessedly empty. All around him, he could hear conversations as people introduced themselves or finished phone calls or settled in with their traveling companions. The comfortable sounds highlighted his isolation. He reminded himself that he was alone because an emergency had called Raymond home, not because of their argument, but it made no difference to how lonely he was feeling. Regardless of why, he was alone, and they were fighting.

Except it had not really been a fight. Jean had asked. Raymond had said no. And neither of them had known what to do next. As beautiful as Cilaos had been, the day had been pretty much miserable, with none of the casual smiles and touches that were such a part of their usual coexistence.

The roar of the jet engines barely penetrated his musings as he played out scenario after scenario for how to fix the problems between them. At one extreme, he could force the issue, telling Raymond if he wanted them to continue as partners he would have to accept the Aveu de Sang, but Orlando was right. An Aveu de Sang could never work if both partners were not committed to it. Besides, he had told Raymond the day they became partners that he did not want a slave. He wanted a partner. To force Raymond into an Aveu de Sang now would make a liar of him and a mockery of everything they had shared.

At the other extreme, he could drop the idea entirely and go back to the way things had been before. They had managed very well over the past year building a relationship and a partnership that most people—vampires, wizards, and nonmagical folk alike—would envy. He could tell Raymond he had reconsidered, that he was wrong to have asked in the first place, and they could go back to being lovers in private and partners in public. Yet that would be a lie as well, and Jean suspected Raymond would recognize it as clearly as Jean did. He might accept it because it would give him what he wanted, but he feared it would not be long before Raymond started wondering what else between them was a lie. The answer at the moment was nothing, and Jean wanted to keep it that way.

A year ago, when he had been uncertain of everything where Raymond was concerned, Jean had resolved to treat Raymond as if they had the relationship he desired in the hope of seducing Raymond into that relationship. It had worked beyond his wildest dreams. Raymond had been the lover and partner every vampire desired, smart enough to play le jeu des Cours even without guidance most of the time, willing to push back when Jean became too domineering, yet giving in so beautifully when Jean needed to be the one in control. He had stood confidently at Jean's side whenever Jean asked, fulfilling the role of Consort without realizing it—and the Cour had responded, welcoming him as Jean's partner, as a hero of the war, as president of l'ANS. As one of them in every way except the one that would never be open to him anyway.

They had learned, to the great grief of one of the vampires, that a wizard's magic fought the magic that allowed a vampire to turn someone. That the wizard in question was dying anyway was no consolation to the vampire partner left behind. Jean still did not know how that reconciled with the fact that in every other case of a wizard being injured, the vampire feeding from his or her partner had sped up their recovery, but that was a question for l'Institut, not for Jean's random musings.

Jean could do again as he had done before, treating Raymond as he would an Avoué—not that there was any appreciable difference, given how besotted with and committed to his lover he already was. Most importantly, he could cherish every day they had together. As Orlando had so bluntly reminded him, even wizards, who lived twice as long as other men, would eventually die.

The stewardess came by with dinner, but though Jean's stomach grumbled hungrily, the rougail she was serving would not assuage his need. Only blood—Raymond's blood—would do that.

"Are you sure you don't want anything, monsieur?" the stewardess asked. "It's a long flight."

Jean knew exactly how long it was. Shaking his head, he let his fangs drop as he smiled up at her. "I'll be fine until we get to Paris."

She recoiled in surprise. "As you say, monsieur."

He knew it was petty of him to take such pleasure in the sight of her hurried retreat, but maybe she would leave him alone for the rest of the flight, leaving him to comfort himself with memories of making love with Raymond and dreams of doing so again soon.

The plane finally landed in Paris shortly before six in the morning. Jean waited for his suitcase at baggage claim, scanning the crowd for Raymond's broad shoulders and dark head, but he saw no sign of his lover. Telling himself it was just as well given that he could hardly feed from Raymond right there in the airport, he caught the RER back to Paris, hoping he was early enough to catch Raymond still at home.

He let himself into the apartment, finding it completely dark. He grinned. He could wake Raymond up in the most pleasant of ways. His fangs dropped as he slipped down the hall to the bedroom, only to find the bed empty and unslept in. If Raymond had been there, he had been gone for some time.

Frowning, Jean told himself Raymond's absence was not a rejection. He had no idea what might have happened to require his lover's presence at l'ANS or even at l'Institut. He could not help feeling a little hurt that Raymond had not left him a note, though. Surely he had not forgotten that Jean was coming home this morning.

Going back out, he glanced at the lightening sky as he walked to the subway stop, judging the Métro would be faster than a taxi at this hour of the morning. He arrived at l'ANS to find chaos.

"What's going on?" he shouted.

"An explosion!" Fabienne said, grabbing his hand and dragging him toward her office. "At l'Institut. Alain and Thierry are on their way. One of them can take you there."

"What? When?" Jean asked, heart pounding at the thought of Raymond possibly being hurt.

"Ten minutes ago," Fabienne said. "I made Mathieu go ahead, since Alain and Thierry weren't here yet. Now I wish I hadn't."

"Oh, thank God!" Thierry said as he and Sebastien ran into the office. "Come on, Jean. Let's go."

"Send Mathieu back!" Fabienne called as they disappeared.

They reappeared seconds later to find the scene at l'Institut in just as much chaos as the one at l'ANS. "Where's Raymond?" Thierry barked.

"No one has seen him," Mathieu replied, his face covered in dust as he came running up to them. "Julien, the chef who stayed last night as a watchman, called in the explosion."

"Where is he now?" Jean demanded. The wing they had completely condemned was nothing but rubble now, and Jean's heart clenched with fear. "Where is he?!"

"Over there," Mathieu said.

Jean ran to the man's side. "Tell me everything you know."

"Monsieur Payet woke me up, saying someone was on the grounds. He had someone else with him already, someone I didn't know, and he was dragging the man with him as he ran toward the main building," Julien recounted. "The man kept shouting about the sun rising, but monsieur Payet just ignored him, saying it was dark inside the building. And then I heard this awful noise, like a bomb, and the entire wing collapsed. I didn't know what else to do, so I called l'ANS."

"You did the right thing," Thierry assured him, having come up in time to hear the end of the conversation. "A vampire?" he asked Jean.

"It sounds like it," Jean said absently, his eyes fixed on the ruined wing.

"Merde. Julien, tell everyone we need all the blankets, sheets, tablecloths, anything you can find. If there's a vampire in there, we're going to have to protect him from the sun, or it will destroy him before we can get him out."

"Oui, monsieur Dumont. I'll take care of it."

"He's dead, isn't he?" Jean said dully.

"What are you talking about?" Thierry demanded.

"Raymond. He doesn't need a wand to do magic. He could just cast a spell and get out of there, but he hasn't. He's dead, isn't he?"

"You don't know that," Thierry insisted. "He could be unconscious. He could be trapped in such a way that he's afraid to try a spell. He could be injured badly enough that he can't do a spell. He doesn't have to be dead, so get your head out of your ass and use your senses to find him."

"I can't—"

"Yes, you can," Thierry interrupted. "They told me about the search and rescue in La Réunion. The vampires could smell the blood and used that to find the victims. I know you weren't there for long, but surely you can do that."

Jean took a deep breath, trying to calm his racing thoughts. If he had insisted, if Raymond had agreed, he would know right where his lover was. As it was, they would have to go by his nose and hope his senses were sharp enough to find Raymond in time.

Julien came running back with his arms piled high with blankets just as Alain and Sebastien arrived. "Mathieu," Alain snapped, "go back and get Orlando and anyone else who's arrived. We'll need all the help we can get here."

"Raymond is trapped somewhere in that mess," Thierry told them as soon as Mathieu disappeared, "and apparently there's a vampire as well."

"That's going to slow things down," Alain said with a low whistle.

"Yeah, I know. You've got the affinity with air. Can you keep the blankets shading whatever area we're trying to clear so we don't burn the vampire to ashes before we can help him?"

"Yeah," Alain said, his hands summoning the wind and lifting the covers from Julien's arms to form a tent over the closest section. "Get started."

"What's the fastest way to do this?" Sebastien asked Thierry.

"I haven't a fucking clue. Move the rubble. I'll try to keep the rest from collapsing, unless someone has a better idea."

No one did. Sebastien and Jean started grabbing stones, pushing them away and searching for any sign of the missing men. As more wizards arrived, Thierry put them to work, stabilizing areas, moving rubble, anything to speed up the search.

"Here!" Orlando shouted. "I see a foot!"

Everyone rushed to where he was working, combining their strength and magic to free the body buried in the remains of the building. "It's Jude."

"What the hell is he doing here?" Thierry demanded.

"I don't know," Jean said, crossing himself at the sight of the bloodied corpse, "but he won't be able to tell us. It looks like his neck was broken. I only hope it knocked him out before the wall crushed his skull."

The hopelessness in Jean's voice was palpable. "Hey," Orlando said, putting an arm around Jean, "he was only a vampire. Raymond's a wizard. Don't give up hope yet."

"What can he do against tons of stone crushing down on him?" Jean asked in despair.

"Put up a shield," Thierry replied. "Put the blanket over him, Alain, until we can deal with the body, so you can help search."

They worked systematically through the rubble, shifting enough to see underneath before moving on.

"Raymond!" Jean cried, catching sight of the wizard among the debris.

"Easy," Thierry said, grabbing Jean's arm. "Let me secure the area. You don't want to cause more to fall on him."

Jean waited impatiently for Thierry to give his permission before scrambling over the stones to the timber that had provided some protection for Raymond's head. He felt frantically for a pulse, finding a weak, thready beat at the base of Raymond's neck. Relief flooded through him. "He's alive!"

"Don't move him. We have no idea how badly hurt he is," Alain cautioned, pulling out his cell phone. "Let me see if I can get Constance down here. She's a doctor."

Jean stayed where he was, stroking Raymond's short hair, willing the wizard's eyes to open. "Don't you die on me," he muttered. "Don't you dare die on me and leave me with all this unresolved between us."

Orlando blinked at the prickle of tears that could never fall and went back to work trying to clear the rubble around Raymond's body. Jean could dictate to destiny all he wanted. Separation was a fate that awaited every partnered vampire.

"She's on her way," Alain said. "Can you get close enough to bite him? It helped during the war."

"His pulse is already so weak," Jean equivocated. "This isn't a magical injury."

"He isn't bleeding," Thierry said. "He's probably in shock, and feeding did help that. If you taste him getting weaker you can stop, but if it buys a few minutes for Constance to get here, it could well save his life."

Gulping past the lump in his throat, Jean scooted closer to Raymond until he could reach the wizard's arm. He bit carefully, ready to pull back at any second. The pain in Raymond's blood was nearly debilitating, but Jean forced himself to look past it, to find the kernel of self at his lover's core and to focus on it.

"What happened?"

Jean heard Constance's voice, but it was unimportant. All that mattered was maintaining the connection, however tenuous, with Raymond. He could hear Alain and Thierry explaining, hear Constance casting a spell, but he ignored it all.

"We need to get him to the hospital."

"Jean," Orlando said, holding his shoulder. "Let him go now. Constance needs to move him to Paris. She needs to operate."

Jean broke the connection with great difficulty. "Will he be all right?"

"I'll do my best," Constance said, using her wand to immobilize Raymond's body. "Come to l'Hôtel-Dieu when you can. We'll keep you updated on his progress." With a second wave of her wand, she and Raymond were gone.

"Did she say what was wrong with him?" Jean asked.

"She said she saw evidence of hemorrhaging in his brain, although it seemed like the bleeding had stopped, but she has to relieve the pressure so it won't cause brain damage."

"And I bit him!"

"And that probably stopped the bleeding," Alain said, grabbing Jean by the shoulders and shaking him slightly. "We didn't move him. We provided first aid. We did everything right. Constance and the staff at l'Hôtel-Dieu are some of the best doctors in the country. They'll help him."

"I need to go to Paris. I need to be there if...."

Alain looked at Thierry, who nodded. "Okay," Alain agreed. "Let's go."

Chapter 32

JEAN PACED the waiting room of l'Hôtel-Dieu, unable to sit still. Somewhere in the inner recesses of the hospital, Constance and a host of nameless, faceless doctors fought to save Raymond's life. No one had come out to tell Jean that the situation was dire, but he didn't need to see their faces to realize that he ran a very great risk of losing his lover before the day was over.

Flashes of Raymond's smile, his laugh, his face awash with passion tortured Jean's mind as he lost himself in memories, from the first time they had seen each other in Orlando's apartment to the last time they had made love in the hotel in La Réunion, the tension of the disagreement heightening their release.

He took consolation in the thought that the last words he had said to his lover were *I love you*, but it would be mist against the firestorm of his grief if Raymond did not survive. He wished again futilely that they had made their Aveu de Sang before this happened, because Jean could have shared his strength with Raymond through the bond that would have linked them. Even if that didn't help, he would have known if Raymond was still hanging on instead of fearing the worst.

"No news is good news," Alain said from across the room as if he could read Jean's thoughts. "As long as they don't come tell us he's dead, they're still working on keeping him alive."

"Constance said he was bleeding in the brain," Jean snapped, as if the wizard had not been the one to relate Constance's diagnosis to him. "That can't be good news."

"She also said the bleeding had stopped," Alain reminded Jean patiently, "which means they don't have to find broken blood vessels and repair them, just drain the blood that's already spilled. You gave Raymond that small advantage."

"I let him come back alone," Jean disagreed. "If I had insisted on finding a way to come home with him, he wouldn't have been alone when that corridor collapsed. He might not even have been in it to start with."

"He wasn't alone," Alain reminded Jean slowly. "He had a vampire with him, a vampire who is now destroyed. You don't know that you could have made any difference. In fact, worrying about you might have slowed down Raymond's reaction for his own protection. You can't second-guess this, Jean. I learned that the hard way when Orlando was missing. All you can do is pray for the best possible outcome now."

Jean nodded, looking up as the door opened, but the doctor called a different name. Taking a seat near the door, he leaned his elbows on his knees, folded his hands, bowed his head, and prayed like he had never prayed in all the long years of his existence.

"Jean? Alain?"

Jean rose to his feet at the sound of his name, searching Constance's face for any indication of the news she had to give him. "How is he?"

Constance gestured for them to come with her. "Let's go somewhere where we can talk more privately."

Jean's heart pounded as he followed her down the hallway into her office. "It's bad news, isn't it?" he asked. She would not have brought them here if she had good news.

"Not bad news," Constance said, "not bad at all. Somewhat guarded still, in part because we don't understand why the bleed in Raymond's brain presented the way it did, and therefore we don't know what that abnormality will do to his prognosis, but the surgery went well. The bleed had already stopped by the time we got him to the hospital here, so all we had to do was drain it. We did that by means of a small craniotomy directly above the place where the blood had pooled. He's in recovery now, but he will be in his own room soon."

"You said there was part of it you didn't understand," Jean said. "What part?"

"The fact that the bleed had repaired itself," Constance said. "With the kind of head trauma he'd had, we'd normally expect to find the bleed still gushing when we went in—but the arteries had closed on their own, which is highly abnormal."

"Jean fed from him as soon as we found him injured," Alain said softly. "That's what stopped the bleeding. We saw it time and again during the war, but it would seem to work on physical as well as magical injuries. It might be something for you to remember when you're dealing with injured wizards, especially if the partnerships grow more prevalent."

Constance's eyes widened. "I couldn't help but notice that he had more than a few bite marks. While we had him on the table, we checked for other injuries, but other than some scrapes and bruises, he got away with the bump to his head and a broken arm. He's very lucky."

Jean was sure he would not call lying in a hospital bed with a hole in his head lucky, but he knew it could have been worse. He could have been crushed like Jude was. "What happens now?"

"Now we wait for him to wake up," Constance replied, "and then we'll see if you stopped the bleed and we relieved the pressure quickly enough, or if there's some damage to his brain function. Just remember when he first wakes up that he's had a blow to the head, that he's been under anesthesia, and that he's on very strong pain medicine. If he seems a little out of it, that doesn't mean he's suffered brain damage. It means he's recovering from a double trauma and is doped up on meds to make that tolerable. It may be several days before we can truly determine if there's been a negative effect on his brain function, cognitive or magical."

"Can I see him?" Jean asked.

"It will be a few minutes," Constance replied, "but as soon as they have him settled in his room, you can go in."

"You do realize that he won't be leaving until Raymond does," Alain said with a smile for Constance.

Constance returned the grin. "I have a partner, even if our relationship is only a couple of weeks old. If it keeps getting stronger the way it has since Natalie first bit me, I can only imagine what it must be like for Jean."

"One other thing to consider," Jean said hoarsely, every fiber of his being aching to be with Raymond, "is that there have now been two, possibly three, cases of deliberate damage at l'Institut. We don't know who's behind it—well, Raymond might, but he isn't in any state to tell us if he does—nor what they hope to gain by it. I don't think Raymond himself is the target, but he's vulnerable right now. I think it would be a good idea to only allow a very short list of people to visit until we know he's capable of defending himself again."

"You, obviously," Constance said, flipping open her laptop and pulling up Raymond's chart. "Who else? I'll make notes in his file so the people in the ward will know who to allow."

"Alain and Orlando, Thierry and Sebastien," Jean said immediately, "and Adèle Rougier, once Raymond wakes up. She's investigating the attacks and will want to talk to him."

Constance nodded. "No one else will be allowed past the desk. Raymond will be in the ICU until he wakes up and we can determine if he's had any brain damage. Security is much tighter there."

"Would you mind if I added to it?" Alain asked. "My wards might not be as good as Adèle's, but they'll hold."

"I'll have to check with the hospital administrators about that," Constance said. "I understand your concern, but that's not a decision I can make."

"Tell them the other option is to have a wizard guarding Raymond's door round the clock," Jean said. "I think they'll prefer the simplicity of the wards."

"I'll check with them," Constance promised, glancing down when her pager went off. "Raymond is settled in his room. I can take you to see him now."

Jean jumped to his feet, impatience radiating from every line of his body as Constance led them through the historic halls to the Intensive Care Unit.

"Now just remember," Constance said, "he's bruised and he has tubes and cables running everywhere to monitor all his functions as he wakes up, and his head is swathed in bandages and his arm's in a cast. Don't let the sight of him throw you. Given everything he's been through, his condition is on the good side of expected."

Jean was not entirely sure that reassured him, but he appreciated her efforts. They stopped at the nurses' station so Constance could introduce Jean and Alain to the nurse on duty. To Jean's surprise, when they reached the door to Raymond's room, he hesitated. After having been so impatient to see his lover, he was nervous now that the moment had come.

"Do you want me to wait out here?" Alain asked.

"He's your friend too," Jean said, his protest sounding weak even to his own ears.

"That he is, but he's far more than that to you," Alain said, "and as soon as he recovers, he'll be even more."

Jean looked at Alain sharply, but Alain simply smiled. "Go see him. You'll feel better when you hear him breathing and feel his heart beating beneath your hand. I'll go let everyone know he made it through surgery and is recovering."

"Alain," Jean said, stopping the wizard's departure. "Please, come in with me. Raymond will need all his friends to get through this, not just me. The others can wait a few minutes longer to hear that he's going to be all right."

"If that's what you want," Alain agreed. He gestured for Jean to go in. "I'm right behind you."

Taking a deep breath and ignoring the odors of blood and disinfectant, Jean pushed open the door and walked inside. As Constance had warned, Raymond lay motionless on the bed, tubes running out of his mouth and nose, sensors attached to his forehead and chest in various places to monitor brain function and pulse and who knew what. The bandage that covered most of his head was pale against what remained of Raymond's dark hair. He had an IV in one arm that pumped fluids and probably drugs into his body. Bite marks covered his neck and chest, fresh ones and older, partially healed ones, scattered in and around the bruises that discolored his skin. The other arm was encased in a bulky plaster cast. Jean was tempted to lift the sheet to examine the rest of Raymond's body, as if he could somehow catch an injury the doctors had missed, but he would wait until Alain had left for that. Instead he listened to the hiss of the respirator and prayed it was a precaution rather than a necessity. Needing a connection to Raymond, he pulled a stool up to the side of the bed and clasped Raymond's fingers gently.

It was too much to hope that the touch would somehow be enough to pull Raymond from his drug-induced sleep, but Jean swore he could hear a change in Raymond's breathing—as if his lover had been on his guard, even unconscious, and could only now relax. "Rest," Jean murmured. "I'm here now to watch your back."

"Guard his dreams," Alain said, equally softly.

Jean looked up at him, his question in his eyes.

"It's something Orlando always says to me at night," Alain said, flushing a little at the realization that he had spoken aloud. "He promises to guard my dreams since vampires don't need sleep the way mortals do. When we got him back from Serrier, I knew everything would come right in the end when he whispered that to me after we got home. Even after he woke up, part of me feared he wouldn't remember, that he'd be changed somehow. He didn't recognize me right away, and that added to it, but when he told me to rest, he'd guard my dreams, I knew we'd make it."

"That sounds like Orlando," Jean agreed. He turned back to Raymond, thinking how much he wanted the same bond with Raymond that Alain and Orlando shared. "If you think it will make a difference, I'll guard his dreams and anything else he'll trust me with."

"Then you'll be guarding everything he is and has," Alain promised. "You scared him on the island with a commitment he didn't understand and wasn't ready for, but it doesn't make him love you less. And he understands a bit better now."

"He told you?"

Alain chuckled. "No, but it didn't take a genius to figure out where the questions were coming from. Don't worry. I won't tell anyone. If you choose to keep your vow private, I'll respect that."

"Merci. I seem to be saying that a lot recently," Jean said.

Alain shrugged. "I'm pretty sure there comes a point when such things are understood between friends. Are you okay now for me to go update everyone else? I know Raymond is used to thinking of himself as a loner and a recluse, but you both have more friends than you may realize."

"It's something we're coming to see," Jean said. "I'll be fine. Let everyone know we appreciate their concern."

"I'm going to send Thierry back until we get the hospital's decision on the wards," Alain said, "just so you know. He won't come in unless you invite him. He'll just make sure no one else disturbs you."

Alain disappeared before Jean could say thank you again. Jean turned back to Raymond, still motionless on the bed. "I told you they were our friends."

He fell silent after that, all the words he wanted to say stuck in his throat. Careful not to disturb any of the tubes or wires, he stroked Raymond's cheek, feeling the stubble of two days without shaving. He wondered if Raymond had slept in that time or if he had pushed himself as he had done during the war, subsisting on catnaps between shifts. "You don't get to do that anymore," Jean said softly. "You have to take care of yourself. If you don't, I'm going to take care of you, and you may not like that as much as you think you will. No more scaring me like this. No more running into condemned corridors. I knew that wing was evil from the moment we stepped foot in it, but of course you didn't listen. You had to go running down it like it was the safest place in the city."

His voice broke as he spoke, though no tears could ever fall, that sign of grief taken from him when he was changed. "You have to wake up," he went on, clearing his throat. "You have to open your eyes and let me tell you that I love you. I know I said it before you left to come home, but you can't keep me from saying it again."

A knock on the door drew his attention to Thierry standing on the other side, peering through the glass. Jean motioned for him to come inside.

"Any change?" Thierry asked.

"Alain only left two minutes ago," Jean protested.

Thierry laughed. "Yeah, but Raymond has been redefining the possible for so long that I figured he'd be awake and raring to go already. Adèle says Raymond brought Leighton in through the wards, but that the other person, the person who collapsed the wing of the abbey, came through on their own without changing the wards. Whoever it is, it's an inside job."

Jean's face tightened. "Then I'm glad only you and Alain and Orlando and Sebastien are on the approved list to see Raymond. Until we catch whoever it was, I don't trust anyone but the four of you, Adèle, and his doctor."

"That's probably wise," Thierry agreed. "Give him a few more hours and then make sure you feed from him again, even if it's just lightly. He'll get better faster that way. You remember what happened after the Rite d'équilibrage went wrong. They weren't sure I'd ever wake up or what shape I'd be in if I did, and I woke up right as rain the moment Sebastien's fangs broke my skin."

"They still had you on bed rest for a week to be sure," Jean reminded him.

"But I was awake when they weren't sure I would be... and my magic was intact when they were sure I'd burned myself out fighting the elemental magic," Thierry insisted. "In the grand scheme of possible outcomes, I couldn't have asked for better when I got Sebastien as a lover as well as partner out of the scare. I know you fed from Raymond at l'Institut, so give his body a few hours to recover from everything, but don't wait too long. Let your partnership bond help him heal."

Jean nodded and Thierry withdrew, leaving him alone with Raymond again. He looked down at the hand lying so still in his. It would be so easy to lift it to his lips and bite the skin at the base of Raymond's hand, where the artery pulsed so close to the surface. The thought that his bite might be enough to wake Raymond from his stupor tempted Jean at more levels than he cared to contemplate, but he resisted the urge for the moment. It had been only a few hours since he had fed before, and while it certainly had seemed to help Raymond at the time, his body had already undergone significant trauma. Jean could be patient a few more hours before he tried again. Closing his eyes, he started to rest his head against Raymond's thigh before realizing he had no idea if that would hurt his lover worse. Lifting the sheet, he saw only bruises and the bite marks he had left on Raymond's legs, reassuring him on that score. Relaxing again, he leaned his forehead against Raymond's thigh, inhaling the aroma of his lover's sweat beneath the smell of antiseptic and surgical soap. The scent was enough to calm his nerves and let him rest.

Chapter 33

JEAN HAD reached the end of his patience when Constance came in a couple of hours later, the latest in a string of medical personnel disturbing his peace. "They keep checking and checking, but nothing changes," Jean said.

"It's only been a few hours," Constance reminded him.

"I want to try biting him again," Jean announced. "It helped before, or at least we think it did, and we know it's helped in the past with magically induced injuries. You can stay and monitor him if you want—the researcher in him would probably appreciate it if you did—but one way or another, I'm going to feed from him and hope it helps."

"What kinds of injuries has it helped?" Constance asked, taking the seat opposite Jean. "Everything you can remember."

"Everything from magical overload to internal bleeding," Jean said. "I didn't always get all the details, but it goes both ways. It helped vampires as well as wizards on different occasions."

"It makes sense that it would help the vampires," Constance said, "but I don't understand why it would help an injured wizard."

"I don't either," Jean said, "but I know it has. Ask Thierry. He was in a coma from magical overload, and it snapped him right out of it."

Constance looked toward where Thierry stood in the doorway. "We don't understand it any better now than we did then," Thierry said, "but Jean's told you accurately what we know. The only instance I can think of where it didn't bring about almost a complete recovery was Caroline's eyes. They were shredded by flying glass during the final battle, and even her partner's feeding hasn't restored her sight."

"And you think that's why the bleeding in Raymond's brain stopped on its own this morning," Constance verified.

"We can't prove it, of course," Thierry said, "but it fits with what we've observed in the past."

"I'm going to try it again in the hope that it helps him," Jean said. "You can monitor him for both research and medical purposes or not, as you wish, but it's been long enough."

"Let's give it a try," Constance said. "If I see any signs that it's hurting his condition, I'll have to ask you to stop. I can't in good conscience let you do anything that will weaken him in his already precarious state."

"I don't want to hurt him," Jean agreed, lifting Raymond's hand to his lips. He glanced at Constance, who had her eyes fixed on the monitors behind

Raymond and was studiously not looking in Jean's direction. It seemed Constance's partner had educated her in the ways of vampires. Taking a deep breath, he licked the smooth skin, grimacing a little at the lingering taste of antiseptic, and bit carefully into Raymond's wrist.

The taste of the anesthesia and of the pain medication assailed his senses first, almost as oily as the pain he had tasted earlier, which was now blessedly absent. Continuing to suck lightly, Jean searched more deeply, seeking the connection he had felt earlier at l'Institut. Above his head, he heard a change in the rhythm of Raymond's breathing, as if the wizard was waking up. He sat a little straighter, keeping Raymond's wrist pressed against his lips as he studied his lover's face. The hazel eyes remained closed, but it seemed to Jean that his color was better. Not wanting to take so much that he could not try again later, he released his connection with Raymond, licking the wounds to close them.

"Well?" he asked, tearing his gaze from Raymond's face to look up at Constance.

"His breathing picked up," she said. "If it stays that way, we can take him off the ventilator. You were right. It seemed to help. How much did you drink?"

"A few milliiliters, not more," Jean said. "I don't think it's as much about the amount of blood as it is about the magical connection. I don't know if I can explain this since you haven't ever fed the way a vampire does, but it's like I can sense the core of his being, the part of his mind or soul that makes him Raymond. When I feed, especially if I really concentrate on that part of him, there's a connection. That connection strengthens both of us, regardless of how much or how little blood I actually take."

He looked over at Thierry. "I think that's what happened the first night with Alain and Orlando. I think in trying to read Alain's honesty in his blood, Orlando connected to his core, and that connection has never wavered."

"If you really took that little," Constance said, looking down at her notes, "let's give him six hours to recover and see how he's doing. If everything has stayed stable, let's try it again. The sooner he wakes up, the better it is for his overall prognosis. I'll send in a nurse to remove the breathing tube."

WHEN CONSTANCE returned six hours later, Orlando and Alain were sitting with Jean, the two men having arrived to give Thierry a break. She consulted Raymond's chart and the readouts from the various monitors. "Everything looks stable," she said. "He's continued to breathe fine without the ventilator, which means that his brain stem function is stable. His pulse has stayed steady, and his color has improved considerably. There's nothing to indicate any swelling or additional trauma in the brain, so from my standpoint, it's just a matter of him waking up so we can see how his higher brain functions are doing."

"And you want him to have higher brain functions with his partner biting him?" Orlando joked, elbowing Jean in the ribs. "I think that might be overestimating even Raymond's considerable abilities."

The levity broke the tension in the room. "Are you ready to try again?" Constance asked Jean, a smile playing around her lips.

Jean's reply was to reach for Raymond's hand again, looking for a different place on his arm to bite so he would not aggravate the already broken skin.

"Bite his neck," Orlando said before Jean could begin preparing Raymond's arm. "I know it isn't as easy with him in bed like this, but it's the freshest blood, the most intimate connection."

Jean shook his head, lowering the sheet to reveal the nearly faded bite mark on Raymond's chest. "That's the most intimate connection."

"Then bite him there. You want both his body and his spirit to respond to you. The more powerful the connection, the more likely that will happen, and it isn't going to happen if you bite his arm," Orlando insisted.

"Can you monitor the machines remotely?" Jean asked Constance. He had grown accustomed to biting Raymond's wrist or even his neck with others around, as he had participated in various magical rituals with his partner, but he could not bring himself to bite Raymond's chest with anyone else in the room.

"Of course," Constance said. "I should have thought of that. I'm going to turn the intercom on so I can get your attention if I see anything that suggests you need to stop, but otherwise you'll be alone."

Alain and Orlando rose as well, leaving Jean alone with Raymond. The vampire pulled the curtains over the window and returned to Raymond's side, stretching out alongside his lover as best he could in the narrow bed. "This better work, Raymond. Do you hear me? I'm getting tired of sharing our secrets with other people."

He lowered his head and licked over the healing mark, the one mark Raymond refused to let disappear, and matched his fangs to the existing incisions, biting down fully this time. If they thought a deeper connection would speed Raymond's recovery, then Jean would make the connection as powerful as he knew how.

He sucked hard, noticing in passing that the taste of the drugs had lessened since he last fed, which made him hope whatever had kept Raymond unconscious for the surgery was fading from his system. He delved as deeply as he had ever dared, finding Raymond's core and pouring himself into it. All his love, all his faith, all his hopes, all his desire, every positive emotion he possessed, he pushed it all through the connection, offering it to his lover, praying desperately that Raymond would feel it and respond.

He heard a gasp above him at the same time he felt a hand tangle in his hair, and suddenly the connection slammed fully into place, Raymond's desire growing to match Jean's own. Fearful of a sudden movement injuring Raymond and sure that Constance would burst into the room any moment, Jean released his fangs, surprised to sense the connection linger for a moment before it faded. "You're awake."

Raymond coughed a little as he nodded before looking around for something to drink.

"I don't know if you can have anything," Jean said. "Let me get Constance. Will you be all right for a moment?"

Raymond nodded. Jean opened the door to see Constance standing right there. "He's awake and thirsty."

"His throat is probably very dry from the feeding tube and the anesthesia and everything else," Constance agreed, coming into the room. "There's a pitcher of water by the bed. Raymond, you can have a few sips, but take it easy. Anesthesia makes some people nauseous. Not to mention that you have a head injury. I'm going to check your vitals and then I'll leave you to rest again."

Jean poured a little water into a cup and handed it to Raymond, who drank gratefully. "Easy," Jean said, catching his hand and drawing it away from his mouth. "She said a couple of sips. You can have more if this doesn't make you sick."

"So thirsty," Raymond said hoarsely.

"That's normal," Constance assured him. "Just wait a few minutes to let the water you've already drunk hit your stomach. If that goes well you can have more, and you can even have some soup for dinner."

"Do you remember any of what happened?" Alain asked from the doorway.

Raymond shook his head, wincing at the pain that caused.

"You probably won't want to move your head much," Constance counseled, seeing his expression. "You had a pretty serious bump, even before we had to do surgery to relieve the pressure on your brain from the bleeding."

"That explains the headache," Raymond quipped, summoning a smile for Jean. Ignoring everyone else, he stretched his good hand toward his lover—who was much too far away, as far as Raymond was concerned. Jean took his hand and perched on the edge of the bed, his hip touching Raymond's thigh.

"What's the last thing you remember?" Jean asked, echoing Alain's question.

"It's all fuzzy," Raymond admitted. "I remember being at l'Institut and hearing an alert because someone was nosing around the wards. I found Leighton outside, trying to get in. I don't really think he was responsible for the graffiti or the fire, but I dragged him inside to talk to him anyway. He denied everything, but I wouldn't expect him to admit it even if he was guilty." He looked toward the water. "Can I have some more, Constance?"

"Go ahead," she said. "All your vitals look good. Just a few sips of water at a time until you're sure you aren't going to get sick. I'll leave you to rest, and I'll order some soup for dinner."

Jean lifted the cup to Raymond's lips, steadying it as he drank. "Leighton's gone," he told Raymond as he set the cup back on the tray. "We found him buried in the rubble before we found you. His skull was crushed."

"Does Adèle know?" Raymond asked immediately. His immediate concern had to be Adèle and the effect the loss of her partner would have on her. He could deal with his own guilt for having dragged Jude with him into the explosion later, when his head was not pounding and he was not surrounded by people.

"She does," Orlando said. "She arrived shortly after Constance took you to the hospital. She kept looking around oddly until I finally asked her what was wrong. She said the pressure of the partnership bond was gone, so I told her what had happened. She looked like she couldn't decide if she was happy or sad. I don't really know her well enough to feel like I could press her to talk about it."

"Ask Magali to talk to her," Raymond said.

"What happened after that?" Alain asked. "Do you remember anything else?"

"Another alert, this one that someone had come through the wards," Raymond said. "I dragged Leighton with me as I went to investigate because I didn't expect anyone that early in the morning. I caught sight of a skirt or a cloak running into the wing we closed."

"The one I begged you not to go into?" Jean asked archly.

"That one," Raymond agreed, his voice meek. "I didn't think. I just reacted."

"Did you ever see who it was?" Jean asked again.

"It looked like Marguerite from the first seminar, but that can't possibly be right," Raymond said, releasing Jean's hand to rub at his forehead. "What reason would she have to do this?"

"I don't know," Alain said, "but I'm pretty sure Adèle will find out. I can't call her from here, so I'm going to step outside. I'll be back in a few minutes."

"No," Orlando said, joining Alain. "Raymond needs to rest. We'll come back in the morning and let you know if Adèle has learned anything."

The door closed softly behind them. Now that they were alone, Jean leaned forward and kissed Raymond gently. "I missed you," he said, his voice rough with emotion. "Every moment you were gone was like a year, and then to come back and find you buried alive.... Mon Dieu, Raymond, I almost lost you."

Raymond's good hand stroked through Jean's hair. "I'm harder to lose than that." He took a deep breath. "I did a lot of thinking while we were apart. We have some things to talk about."

"We'll talk," Jean promised, "as soon as you're well."

Raymond glanced down at the cast on his arm. "That's not likely to be for some time. My body aches in places I didn't know I had, but there's nothing wrong with my mind."

"You're making jokes, but we don't know that," Jean insisted. "You had brain surgery!"

"I didn't have brain surgery. They just let out a little blood," Raymond countered. "I'm fine."

Jean did not look convinced.

"If you don't want to talk, then just listen," Raymond said. "I had coffee with Alain the day I got back from La Réunion. He cleared up some things for me, some things I didn't understand about what it means to have an Aveu de Sang. I... I overreacted when you asked me about it because I was scared of how I thought it would change me."

"Why didn't you just ask me?" Jean asked.

"Because you couldn't know the answers any more than I did," Raymond explained. "You may know about it in theory, but you've never lived it, on either side of the relationship."

"The magic of the bond only works once," Jean said automatically. "If I'd already lived it before, I wouldn't be able to share it with you."

"See? You couldn't have answered my questions either. Alain could, and he did," Raymond said. "I probably would have asked you about my fears in time, but I'm not sure I would have ever been completely confident of the answers. With Alain, I am, because I see the truth of his relationship with Orlando every time I see them together. I just needed Alain to remind me of that fact."

"So what are you saying?" Jean asked.

Raymond smiled. "That it would be my great honor and pleasure to be your Avoué, just as soon as they let me out of here."

His face sobered. "It will still have to be our secret. Well, other than Alain and Orlando, who are on to us. I did a lot of thinking while we were apart, not just about the Aveu de Sang. When this all blows over with the attacks and things have settled down, I'm going to resign as president of l'ANS. Once that's done and a seemly time has passed, if you want to tell others, that's fine with me. If you still want me, that is."

"If I still want you?" Jean echoed, incredulous. "I've been going crazy the past few hours, sure you were dead or dying or hurt so badly you'd never wake up. Yes, I still want you."

"Then kiss me for now and promise you'll mark me as soon as we get home," Raymond requested.

"I promise."

Chapter 34

"IT'S FINISHED," Alain said as he came into Raymond's hospital room two days later. "Adèle brought Marguerite in and questioned her. It didn't take long before it all came out."

"What did she say?" Raymond asked.

"I wasn't there, but apparently she was a sleeper, one of Serrier's sympathizers who had stayed silent during the war but agreed with his ideas of magical superiority and keeping the magical races separate," Alain explained. "When she heard about l'Institut, she saw it as her chance to stop something so totally against her beliefs. The protests, the graffiti, the fire, and the cave-in that landed you here… she bragged about them all under Adèle's questioning."

"How could she have hidden all of that vitriol so completely during the seminar?" Orlando asked. "I wasn't there the whole time, but I never saw anything to suggest she was capable of this kind of violence."

"She's a trained police officer with a fair amount of investigative experience," Alain reminded them. "Not to mention she would have had to perfect the art of hiding her sympathies on the job during the war. She didn't want to do anything to draw attention to herself because she didn't want to be a suspect when she started implementing her plan."

"What happens to her now?" Jean asked.

"She's been charged with a variety of things, including voluntary homicide without premeditation because of Leighton being there at l'Institut and not surviving the blast," Alain said. "That seemed to be the only part that bothered her. She set the fire and the explosion spell when l'Institut, or at least those parts of l'Institut, should have been empty so no one would be hurt."

"That isn't any consolation for Adèle," Raymond said.

"Honestly, I think all Adèle feels is relief," Orlando replied, "but it doesn't change the fact that Marguerite ended Jude's existence. Her trial will be sometime in the next few months. Adèle didn't know how long the pretrial phase would last, although with Marguerite's confession, she said it would be a pretty cut-and-dried case."

"That wasn't the only interesting development either," Alain said. "We had another visitor last night, a vampire by the name of Denis Langlois."

Jean shook his head. "The name isn't familiar."

"It will be," Orlando said. "He is apparently the new chef de la Cour in Autun. Enough of the vampires there seemed to feel Renaud's leadership no longer represented their best interest. He's been replaced."

Raymond looked at Jean in surprise. "Is that done?"

"Not often because, as I'm sure you can guess, Renaud wouldn't have gone easily," Jean said. "I took my Cour when monsieur Lombard retired but even with him naming me his successor, I had to fight to keep my position. It hasn't happened recently, thank goodness, but in theory, it could happen at any time. We'll want to take a trip to Autun when you're well enough. Langlois came to us first, even if we weren't there to meet him. We should return the favor."

"We can certainly do that," Raymond said. "I'd rather have a positive relationship with our neighbors than the tension we had with Renaud." He would keep his eyes open, though, to make sure Renaud did not try to retaliate against Jean for his loss of position and status.

"How long until they spring you?" Alain asked Raymond.

"Constance won't say," Jean replied. "'A few more days' is her standard answer."

"Have you been home?" Orlando asked Jean.

"No. Raymond is here. I can use the shower, and his magic works on my clothes if I'm not in them," Jean replied.

Alain and Orlando snickered. Jean sent them a quelling look, which only made them laugh harder.

"Does your magic feel normal?" Alain asked when he stopped laughing.

"I don't have as much control," Raymond admitted. "I can do almost no wandless magic. Thierry brought my wand yesterday, and things have been better since then."

"Does Constance have any thoughts about that?"

"Only that the damage was to the area that would influence magical control. She says as I heal it will get better. I learned to do wandless magic once. I can learn to do it again if I have to. I'll give it another few days and then I'm checking myself out. As insistent as Jean is about how much I do, it won't be any different at home than being here except I won't have nurses poking at me every few hours."

Alain laughed, biting back his comment about Jean poking at him instead. "You've got an overprotective partner too?"

"I'm not *over*protective," Orlando replied, "just protective."

"What he said," Jean replied with a grin for Raymond. He leaned closer. "I have some promises to keep, and they require you being well enough to go home."

Raymond smiled tenderly at him before turning back to Alain and Orlando. "I'm going to resign as president of l'ANS. Not today or tomorrow, but as soon as I'm well enough and presentable enough to make the announcement. Would you ask Fabienne to start getting things ready for a candidate search? You and Thierry can help her with the requirements for the applicants, but I think that either having a partner or completing the seminar at l'Institut and agreeing to continue looking for a partner should be nonnegotiable. We have too much at stake to have someone like Marguerite slip through and try to take over."

"We'll tell her," Alain promised. "And while I don't think it will be too long before Thierry decides he'd rather be at l'Institut than at l'ANS, Orlando and I have already decided to stick around and make sure things keep going the way they should. Like you said, it's too important not to have someone keeping an eye on everything."

"You really think Thierry will want to come out to l'Institut?" Raymond asked, surprised. "But I thought they'd just bought a new apartment and...."

"Yes, I really think he will," Alain said. "He's flourished being out there, working on the repairs. Think about how you feel when you've spent the day doing a magical rite where you've worked intensively with water. You know that sense of balance that comes from it. You've given Thierry an entire complex of earth to play in and rebuild. He's in his element, no pun intended, and he positively glows with it. He'll stay at l'ANS, out of loyalty to the institution and to you, long enough to help the new president get settled in. But within six months, he'll be out there, offering to help with research in exchange for a place to stay so he and Sebastien can keep working on the repairs."

"You two are always welcome out there as well," Raymond said. "You don't need a reason or an invitation. I...." He looked at Jean helplessly. "I've never had friends, not really, until this past year, and I don't want to lose that just because we won't all be working in the same building on the same projects anymore."

"That's the beautiful thing about friendship," Orlando said. "No excuses or reasons needed. You just show up or send an invitation. We'll stay on at l'ANS, but we've both decided to cut back on the number of hours we spend there. The whole place-in-the-country thing is something we've talked about quite a bit too. We haven't found anywhere yet, but we've started looking. The urgency we all felt in the months right after the war has faded. We've done our duty, all of us, and it's time to do what feels right to us now. For you and Thierry, that's l'Institut, although for different reasons. We're looking at other things."

"What other things?" Jean asked, surprised this was the first he was hearing of Orlando's plans. Once, Orlando would have approached him first with any idea he had.

"We want to be foster parents," Orlando said. "I know it won't be easy, two men and one of them a vampire. But we've talked to Caroline, and she's going to help us get approved as soon as we have a place large enough to have an extra, or a few extra, around the house for the time it takes to find permanent placements or for them to be reunited with their families."

"Oh là là!" Jean exclaimed. "Where did this idea come from?"

"From my son's death, from news stories about kids who lost their families during the war, from a lot of things," Alain said. "Like Orlando said, it won't happen right away, but we're ready to start working in that direction as soon as everything is stable at l'ANS."

"I could wait," Raymond said, feeling guilty that his decision would put their plans on hold. "I feel bad now about dropping my responsibilities on your shoulders."

"Don't," Alain and Orlando said at the same time. "Our plans are flexible," Alain continued. "The work l'Institut will be doing is too important to delay. We were sharing good news with our friends, not asking our employers to accommodate our plans."

"Although I'm sure we'll do enough of that later," Orlando said with a laugh. "We should go and let you rest. Call us if you need anything."

"We will," Jean promised as Alain and Orlando departed, leaving him alone with Raymond once more. "I know I keep saying this, but what a difference a year makes!"

Raymond smiled. "For all of us."

"So Thierry and Sebastien at l'Institut full time and Alain and Orlando as foster parents," Jean mused.

"And you and me running l'Institut," Raymond finished, "if you're willing to help me, that is. I know you have the Cour to run as well."

"That's more of a general availability issue than it is a full-time job," Jean reminded Raymond. "I kept office hours at l'ANS for the convenience of it and because you were there. I never had an office or set hours before the alliance. I can go back to a more flexible schedule now."

"I'm ready," Raymond admitted.

"Ready for what?"

"For all of it. To go home, to resign as president of l'ANS, to take over l'Institut full time, to become your Avoué. Not in that order. Going home and becoming your Avoué definitely rank highest," Raymond said.

"Soon."

"ARE YOU sure you know what to do?" Constance asked Jean for what felt like the fiftieth time.

"Yes," Jean said, "and I have your cell phone number if I have any questions. Alain is waiting outside to take us home so Raymond won't strain himself doing that strong a spell yet, nor will he be exposed to anything in a cab or car. Everything will be fine."

Unable to think of any other objections, Constance relented. Jean helped Raymond to his feet, his arm around his lover's waist to steady him. "Alain," Jean called. "You can come in."

Alain walked inside and smiled at them. "It's good to see you on your feet again, Raymond, even if you do have a little help there."

"I don't want him to fall and hurt himself worse," Jean said. "No more delays. We're going home right now."

Alain glanced at Constance, who nodded her approval. "I'll come by and check on you in a couple of days. Call me if you need anything before then."

Jean nodded, and Alain cast the displacement spell, sending them to the landing outside Jean's apartment.

"The first thing I'm doing when I'm well enough is fixing these wards," Raymond grumbled as Jean unlocked the door and helped him inside.

"You've been saying that for a year," Jean laughed.

"This time I mean it," Raymond said, leaning on Jean as they walked inside to the couch. He sat down, careful of his injured arm, and sighed deeply. "Mon Dieu, it's good to be home."

Jean kissed Raymond's forehead. "It's good to have you home. Do you need anything? A blanket? Something to eat? To put your feet up? I don't want you to overdo it and end up back in the hospital."

"I'd like a bath," Raymond said. "I smell like antiseptic, and I feel like I have at least a centimeter of dirt caked on my skin from where the wall fell on me. And then, yes, something to eat would be nice."

Jean hurried to help him into the bathroom, determined to do everything he could to make the transition home and Raymond's recovery as smooth as possible.

"JEAN, KNOCK it off," Raymond said, summoning a glare for his lover. He had been home for twenty-four hours, and Jean had not stopped hovering yet. "All I need now is for you to sit down next to me and hold me close. I've missed being in your arms."

Jean hesitated a moment before settling on the couch next to Raymond and cradling him tenderly in his embrace.

Raymond hummed happily, resting his head against Jean's shoulder. "Tell me what happens now," he said.

"What do you mean? You rest and get well."

Raymond lifted his head, meeting Jean's eyes. "With the Aveu de Sang. I've been around vampires long enough to know there's a ritual of some sort surrounding it. Tell me what will happen."

Jean closed his eyes. "That's up to us. There's a ritual that's usually followed, but the Aveu de Sang is usually a somewhat public affair, in the sense that there are witnesses and that sort of thing. We don't have to abide by that ritual, because our Aveu de Sang is only for us."

"If you want that ritual, we could ask Alain and Orlando to be our witnesses," Raymond offered. "They already know, and they'll keep our secret."

"The magic that creates the bond will be no more or less powerful because of the ritual. Just look at Orlando and Alain. I doubt Orlando even knew there was a ritual. He certainly didn't follow it," Jean replied. "I don't need it."

"I don't need witnesses, but I want as much of the ritual as we can manage with just the two of us here," Raymond insisted. "Rituals are important. If one exists, it exists for a reason, even if only to impress on the people involved the seriousness of what they're doing."

"We need to decide what I'll use to mark you and where we'll do it," Jean said. "The location usually isn't in question, but since we want ours to be private, it can't be on your neck."

"On my back," Raymond said immediately. "Cover the mark of my shame with the mark of my joy."

"There is no shame in your scar," Jean insisted, though he knew he would never convince Raymond of that.

"Then cover the mark of my past with the mark of my future," Raymond said. "Either way, that's where I want it."

"That takes care of half of the question."

"What do vampires usually use to mark their Avoués?" Raymond asked.

"It varies from vampire to vampire, but it's usually something that will leave a mark others will recognize, not simply as the mark of an Aveu de Sang, but whose mark," Jean replied. "Orlando used the signet ring he took from his maker after Thurloe was destroyed."

Raymond considered. "Your medallion," he proposed. "If ever a symbol defined you, that would be it. The mark of your rank, the very thing that brought us together. If anyone does see it at some point, they will recognize immediately whose Avoué I am. More than that, it is the symbol that defines our relationship."

"Are you sure?" Jean asked. "The medallion isn't small. It's a good ten centimeters across. That's going to leave a painful burn."

"The size doesn't matter," Raymond insisted. "Symbolism is important in rituals. Can you think of something you could use that would represent you as well?"

Jean had to admit he could not.

"Then get the medallion. We've already waited too long to do this."

Jean shook his head. "Come into the bedroom. Location is as important to a ritual as the words or symbols. Where better to consecrate our relationship than in the bed where we regularly make love?"

"And will we be making love there again soon?" Raymond said with a grin.

"Most certainly," Jean replied, "just as soon as you are mine."

Raymond's grin broadened. "Is that part of the ritual?"

"Actually, it is. Once the brand is done, the witnesses leave the newly bonded pair alone and guard the door while the vampire feeds," Jean explained. "As you can guess, that inevitably leads to making love."

Raymond rose to his feet, taking a moment to ensure his balance before starting toward the bedroom. "Then let's go."

"Can you get undressed by yourself?" Jean asked Raymond.

"I can get the buttons undone, but I'm not sure I can get my shirt off over the cast without help," Raymond admitted.

Jean helped Raymond ease his shirt off his injured arm. "Can you do the rest while I gather a few things we'll need for the ritual?" Jean asked.

"Are all Avoués naked when they're marked?" Raymond teased.

"Yes," Jean said, "to make sure there is no deceit. If you had your shirt on, no one would know if you already bore my mark. While I know you would never do that, part of the ritual is for one of the witnesses to proclaim the future Avoué unmarked."

Raymond shrugged, toeing off his shoes and removing his trousers. "It's a good thing we won't have witnesses then, since I'm not unmarked."

"It's not the same," Jean replied immediately, stopping Raymond's undressing and pulling the wizard into his arms. "Serrier only marked your body, and it was a surface mark. The magic of the Aveu de Sang will mark both our souls."

"And does someone verify that the vampire is similarly unattached?" Raymond asked.

"The magic of the Aveu de Sang only works once," Jean reminded Raymond. "A vampire cannot complete the ritual if he or she has already had an Avoué, living or dead. I'll be right back."

Raymond sat on the bed in the soft light filtering through the closed volets and wondered if perhaps he was making a mistake becoming so embroiled in such a ritual-bound society, but he reminded himself that Jean had broken precedent after precedent to have Raymond at his side. Their Aveu de Sang would not bind him to anything except Jean because no one else would know about it. Jean returned a few moments later with a handful of candles that he lit and set at strategic places around the room.

Always sensitive to the ambient magic in his surroundings, Raymond felt the shift as soon as the last candle was lit. Stepping outside the circle, Jean undressed as well and hung the medallion that proclaimed his rank around his neck. "Normally the person presiding over the ritual would ask who brought the Avoué to be claimed," Jean said.

"Raymond Payet," Raymond replied immediately. "I bring myself to this place for this ritual with the full and honest intention of joining my life to yours for the rest of my time on this earth."

Jean swallowed down the lump in his throat. "Then the presider would ask who intended to claim this man."

"Who would bind with me?" Raymond asked, adapting the words to the absence of officiant or witnesses.

"I would," Jean said, stepping inside the circle. Raymond's breath caught as he felt the surge in power. "Then the officiant would ask the witnesses to confirm that the future Avoué was unmarked."

Raymond stood and turned slowly, so that Jean's gaze could caress every inch of his body—verifying that the only marks on Raymond's body, other than the scar on his back, were those left by Jean's fangs. "I bear no claim but yours. I want no marks but yours."

Jean lifted the medallion over his head, starting toward the candles.

"Put it on my back," Raymond said. "I can heat it far hotter, and far more quickly, than you can with a candle."

Jean hesitated for a moment before acceding to Raymond's request, centering the medallion over the scar that paralleled Raymond's spine. "When you're ready."

With unsteady hands, Raymond picked up his wand, pointing it over his back. "*Chauffez.*"

The metal glowed white hot, the smell of searing flesh assaulting their noses. Jean held the medallion for as long as he could, feeling the magic of the Aveu de Sang slam into place. The moment it did, he let the metal circle fall from his hand and drew Raymond into his arms. "With this brand, I claim you as my Avoué. I bind myself to you for as long as you live. Let no one challenge our bond."

The pain was intense, different from when Serrier had marked Raymond's back. His eyes watered, every nerve in his body shouting in protest, but he pushed the pain aside, seeking the awareness Alain had promised would be there. It took a moment, but then he felt the unfamiliar presence in his mind. Not an invasion as he had feared, but a companion. "It worked."

Chapter 35

"I KNOW," Jean said, turning Raymond in his arms. "I can feel you." He touched his hand to his heart. "Here."

Raymond smiled, sliding his good arm around Jean's waist and pulling the vampire's hips closer to his. "There's somewhere else I want to feel you," he said huskily.

"And where is that?" Jean teased, rubbing his groin against Raymond's, feeling the beginning of his lover's erection.

"Inside me."

Jean groaned. "Don't tempt me. I can't very well tumble you onto your back right now."

Raymond trembled at the bolt of desire he felt through the fledgling bond. "You just bonded with a wizard, remember?" he said with a grin. Bending to pick up his wand, he pointed it down his back. "*Soulagez.*" The spell was not as effective as if someone else had cast it for him, but it worked well enough. "Now you can tumble me onto my back."

Jean almost asked if Raymond was sure, but he realized with a jolt of surprise and pleasure that he did not need to. He could feel the decrease in pain and the increase in anticipation humming through their bond. He backed Raymond toward the bed, stopping when the wizard's back—the unmarked side—hit the post of the bed frame.

"I will certainly take advantage of that," Jean promised, "but not yet." He kissed his way down Raymond's neck and across his collarbone, lingering on every bruise and scrape that marred his wizard's skin. They would heal; he just had to remind himself of that frequently, since the sight of them also reminded him of how close he had come to losing his lover forever. Working his way lower, he licked at the already tightening nipples, feeling Raymond's reaction through their bond.

"Bite me," Raymond begged, arching his back in offering.

"I will," Jean promised, sucking on one taut peak before moving to the other, "but once I start, I won't be able to stop, and I have other things I want to do with my mouth first."

Raymond moaned in delight as Jean paid homage to his nipples. He had always been exquisitely sensitive there, but every sensation seemed heightened now. Perhaps it was the Aveu de Sang; perhaps it was the length of time since they had last made love and everything else that had happened in the meantime. Whatever it was, Raymond hoped it would not fade anytime soon.

With one last lick to each pink bud, Jean worked his way down Raymond's abdomen, tracing lines of muscle on the body that looked like it belonged to an athlete rather than a researcher. The marks there were more on the order of healing bites, bringing a smile to Jean's face as he kissed each one. He would open them again or leave others, but not yet. Not when he could smell the musky fluid leaking from the tip of Raymond's cock.

Raymond's good hand tangled in his hair, pushing him lower. Jean went willingly enough, but he dodged his lover's intended target, nuzzling the curls around the base of Raymond's cock and the iliac crease that tempted him so fully. Unable to resist, he bit lightly into the fold, the flavor of Raymond's love and lust exploding onto his tongue. He did not doubt what he was feeling through their bond, but he had a millennium of experience interpreting the flavor of a lover's blood and only a few minutes with the bond.

Drawing his fangs back up had never been so easy. He wanted to take Raymond in his mouth; his fangs would hurt his lover. Those two thoughts were all it took, rather than the force of will it had always required before if he let his fangs drop too soon. He took his time licking his way up the long shaft, starting at the base and making his way to the mushroomed tip that peeked out of its foreskin. Closing his lips around the flap of skin, he pushed it down, revealing the sensitive glans.

"Jean," Raymond gasped above him, "I need to lie down or I'm going to fall."

Immediately, Jean rose to his feet, steadying Raymond, helping him move to the edge of the bed. "Do we need to stop?" Every instinct he possessed rebelled at the idea, but his Avoué's health took precedence.

"Don't you dare!" Raymond said, glaring up at his lover. "I can lean back and you can go right back to what you were doing."

Jean smiled, feeling the truth of the words through the link between their emotions. "Make yourself comfortable then," he suggested, returning to his kneeling position, "because I intend to take my time."

Raymond shifted a little on the bed so his hips rested on the edge of the mattress. He draped his legs over Jean's shoulders, opening himself to his lover's attentions. "Take all the time you want."

The change in position put Raymond's balls front and center, so Jean lowered his head and sucked them into his mouth, rolling them with his tongue and drawing gasps and groans from his lover. He smiled and worked them with more determination, his fingers trailing teasingly up and down Raymond's shaft.

"Jean!" Raymond wailed, thrashing on the bed. "Don't tease!"

"I'm not teasing," Jean promised, turning his head and nipping at the smooth plane of Raymond's inner thigh. His fangs scored the surface, barely enough to sting, but Raymond's reaction suggested a far more potent effect. Tenderly, Jean licked over the scrapes before pushing up higher to lick away the fresh spurt of fluid pooling on Raymond's belly. When he had captured every drop, he returned to the source, his tongue probing the slit in search of more of the heady flavor. He had done this before, but the taste had never been as sharp, making Jean wonder if the Aveu de Sang had restored some of his mortal senses where Raymond was concerned.

Raymond rocked up into Jean's mouth, clearly wanting more contact, but Jean was too intoxicated by the taste to let the head slip deeper into his mouth. He closed his fist around the base, stroking in time with his sucking, but always keeping the leaking tip on the flat of his tongue. Raymond jerked beneath him, his climax catching Jean off guard. He swallowed reflexively, taking all Raymond had to offer.

"I'm sorry," Raymond said. "I should have warned you."

"Don't be sorry," Jean apologized, licking his lips to make sure he had not missed so much as a drop. "I'm not. Now I get to find another way to work you up again."

"I'm not eighteen anymore," Raymond warned, though he made no move to pull away from Jean's hands as the vampire lifted his legs to his chest and spread his cheeks with tender hands.

"No, but you're my Avoué now," Jean reminded him. "Did Alain not tell you that part?"

"What part?" Raymond asked.

Jean grinned lasciviously and licked a slow path up the crease of Raymond's buttocks. "That as long as one of us is aroused, the other one will respond and keep responding. All I have to do is not come at the same time you do, and we could go on for hours."

Raymond groaned and pulled his legs closer to his chest with his good arm. "I like the sound of that."

The sight of Raymond offering himself this way, legs splayed above his body, cock and balls and ass on display, made Jean's mouth water. He bit the lower curve of one muscular cheek, knowing the feeling of his fangs was as much foreplay for Raymond as anything else Jean could do with his mouth. He sensed an immediate renewal in Raymond's interest, so he lingered for a moment, swallowing mouthfuls of blood while his hand ghosted over the other cheek, fingers slipping in and out of the dark crevice.

Jean could feel his own desire rising quickly. Too quickly. He was not ready for this to be over, so he released his hold on Raymond's backside, licking the wounds carefully to close them. He could bite to his heart's content later. For now, he wanted to see how many times he could make Raymond come. He had loved Raymond for some time, but the Aveu de Sang had made Raymond the center of his world. Nothing was too good for his wizard now.

Knowing Raymond's preferences, Jean moved inward, finding the puckered rosette that hid between his lover's buttocks, flicking it with his tongue. Raymond's hips lifted instantly, a surge of need washing through Jean's mind. Since indulging his lover coincided with his own wants, it was easy to lean closer and lick and suck at the delicate flesh until Raymond was writhing above him, curses and pleas falling one after another from the wizard's usually eloquent lips.

"What do you want?" Jean asked, lifting his head so he could peer up at Raymond. "Tell me what you need."

"You inside me!" Raymond gasped.

"Too soon," Jean said with a shake of his head. "Anything but that."

"Then use your tongue," Raymond said. "Fuck me with that until I can't think of anything but you."

"My pleasure." Jean winked at Raymond before returning to the pleasurable task of seeing how far inside his lover he could stick his tongue.

The answer, of course, was not far enough. Never far enough in Raymond's opinion. He loved the hot, wet slide of Jean's tongue against his entrance, but no matter how wide he spread his legs, no matter how deeply Jean buried his face against Raymond's ass, Jean's tongue could never go deep enough. His eyes closed as he chased that elusive moment of nothingness where all he knew was the passion Jean inspired in him. Jean's thumbs joined the act, pushing in when Jean's tongue slid out so that Raymond was never fully empty, and he felt the walls inside him, the ones he had erected around that central core of himself that he shared with no one, crumble. He was no longer Raymond Payet, controlled speaker, analytical researcher, disgraced wizard, rehabilitated president of l'ANS. He was distilled to his purest form, emotion and sensation. He was Jean's Avoué, his lover, his love. Everything else was extra, outside, extraneous. He had everything that mattered right here in bed with him, licking and sucking and fucking at his willingly offered hole until he could do nothing but thrash on the comforter and climax again, the upswell of emotion so strong it left him gasping for breath as wave after wave of release crashed through him. The aftershocks continued longer than they ever had before because Jean's tongue continued its teasing, extending Raymond's orgasm until he could hardly move with the wonder of it all.

"My turn!" Raymond gasped when Jean gave every indication of wanting to rouse him a third time.

"I'm supposed to be making love to my Avoué," Jean protested.

Raymond shook his head. "You'll still be making love to me. You'll just be the one getting off this time."

Jean could hardly deny the appeal of that when his cock throbbed mercilessly. "How do you want me?"

Raymond turned around so his head rested near the edge of the bed this time. "Come up here where I can reach you. I'm sure I'll think of something."

Jean could think of plenty of things, but he would let Raymond decide. He climbed onto the bed, straddling his lover's chest and waiting for an indication of what Raymond had in mind. "Scoot up here where I can reach you," Raymond directed. "With one hand in a cast, you'll have to make do with my mouth."

Make do? Jean scoffed silently. The thought of Raymond's lips closing around his shaft as the head of his cock slid down his lover's throat was nearly enough to make him come right there, as worked up as he already was. He moved again, spreading his legs wider so he could straddle Raymond's shoulders, the tip of his cock bumping his wizard's lips.

"Not yet," Raymond said with a shake of his head, his good hand urging Jean to lift up higher on his knees. Jean complied, gasping as Raymond's tongue darted out to caress his sac, now hanging directly in Raymond's face. "You are the most beautiful thing I have ever seen," Raymond murmured between licks.

Jean shook his head. "I'm too thin and too pale and—"

"And perfect for me," Raymond interrupted. He sucked the heavy balls into his mouth to prove his point. "I love everything about you, from your deceptively slender body to your creamy white skin to the way I never know which lover I'll have in bed with me at night—the tender, playful one or the masterful, ravishing one. You fulfill needs I didn't even know I had."

Jean trembled at the words. Unable to express his emotions aloud, he pushed them out through the bond, flooding Raymond's mind with his absolute devotion. He knew the moment Raymond felt it because the wizard's hazel eyes darkened and he moved his hand to Jean's cock, guiding it to his lips.

Raymond licked the tip lightly in imitation of what Jean had done to him, but the time for teasing had passed. Releasing his hold on Jean's cock, he let his hand fall to his lover's hip. "Fuck my throat." Jean hesitated. "You know I want you to. You can feel it the same way I can feel your desire to do it. Come on, Jean. Let go for me."

Jean's control broke, and he surged into the waiting mouth.

Raymond tilted his head back, providing a long channel into which Jean could thrust. He had never considered himself a passive lover, but there was something about the feeling of Jean taking him this way—every inward slide cutting off his breath for a fraction of a second before each egress that let him inhale again—that left him trembling with need. He resisted the urge to stroke his erection with his good hand, remembering Jean's words about keeping the passion high in one of them even after the other came so the bond would let them continue to make love. On any other day, stroking himself to completion while Jean came down his throat would have been perfectly satisfactory, but today, with the Aveu de Sang fresh between them, he needed more than that.

He needed to feel Jean moving inside him, filling him, completing him. Today, only that would do.

He stroked Jean's buttocks and back instead, urging him to move faster, to find the release Raymond could feel building through their bond. He only hoped his own control would hold, because he doubted he would recover anytime soon once the magic between them erupted.

It only took a few thrusts for Jean to come, the accumulated desire of Raymond's two previous climaxes having battered his senses for too long. He shuddered through his release, loving the feel of Raymond's throat massaging his length.

"Enough foreplay," Raymond said when Jean pulled back. "I want your fangs in my chest and your cock in my ass."

Jean grinned somewhat shakily, but the magic of the Aveu de Sang was working, Raymond's need feeding Jean's own. He leaned over to gather the lube from the bedside table. "Then turn around the right way on the bed so I can get you ready for me."

"You rimmed me until I came," Raymond reminded him. "I think I'm ready."

Jean shook his hand, squeezing the gel over his fingers. "Not yet. You're still talking. If you can think, you aren't ready for me yet."

Raymond glared but moved so he lay on his back with his head on the pillows, knees bent to give Jean full access to his body once more.

Jean found the spot on Raymond's thigh where he had grazed the skin before, biting down fully this time as he slid slick fingers to the already loosened iris. Two digits penetrated easily, spreading the slippery gel and finding Raymond's prostate with the ease of experience. As Jean sucked life-giving blood into his mouth, he rubbed the bundle of nerves, determined that this orgasm, their mutual orgasm, when it came, would surpass the ones that had come before, forging their bond so deeply that nothing would ever shake that foundation.

Raymond undulated slowly beneath the ever-increasing intensity of Jean's caresses. He had known his lover was a master at driving him wild, but it felt different this time, as if Jean were drawing on some new skill or awareness. Then it occurred to him. Jean was gauging Raymond's reactions through their bond and basing his actions on that. He shivered, imagining what it would be like a month or a year from now as they became more and more in tune with each other. Now that they had formed the Aveu de Sang, he could not imagine why he had ever feared it. Nothing could be more right. Jean's fingers pressed hard against his prostate, and all thought fled Raymond's mind.

Jean felt the moment Raymond gave in, both through their bond and in his lover's blood. Drawing back from the bite, he licked the wounds and moved between his lover's thighs, adding a third finger to stretch Raymond wider as he nibbled his way up Raymond's stomach, leaving a trail of bite marks in his wake. When Raymond was stretched to his satisfaction, he withdrew his fingers and mounted his lover, his cock sliding home. The rush of pleasure from Raymond was so strong that, for a moment, Jean imagined he could feel himself being filled even as he felt Raymond squeezing around his cock. Knowing he would not last much longer, he bent his head to the spot directly above Raymond's heart, biting deeply.

The connection slammed into place with the dual joining, until they were no longer two bodies but halves of one paired whole. The energy cycled between them, growing stronger and stronger until they could not contain it, their climaxes tearing through them with the force of a gale. And even that was not enough. The magic summoned by their bonding and their lovemaking demanded an outlet. Mist coalesced around them, thickening until their bodies were soaked with more than sweat, as they continued to move together, needing that one final nudge to push them over the edge.

Jean worked a hand beneath Raymond's back, finding the scar from Serrier's magic first and tracing it upward until he found the new mark, the one he had left, the one that tied them together for the rest of Raymond's life.

That was all it took. Raymond's magic exploded out of him in soft showers of rain as his body gave in to his passion, clenching and releasing rhythmically, shaking him through the throes of a climax like none he had ever known. And through it all, he could feel Jean matching him breath for breath, heartbeat for heartbeat.

Collapsing into a sated heap, Raymond tried to summon the words to tell Jean how much he loved him, but he had no energy left for that kind of concentration. Trusting Jean would feel the depth of his love, he let his eyes close and let sleep overcome him.

Jean stroked the damp hair off Raymond's face, not even bothered by the unexpected dousing. He had fallen in love with a wizard. If the occasional rain shower in his bedroom was the price he had to pay, he considered it well worth it. He wondered how long it would be before Raymond announced his resignation as president of l'ANS. As soon as he did, Jean could start planning his presentation as Consort. And not before time. "Sleep," he murmured, kissing Raymond tenderly. "I'll guard your dreams."

A Partnership in Blood novel

Reluctant Partnerships

By Ariel Tachna

Thanks to the efforts of Raymond Payet and l'ANS, vampires now have the same legal rights as mortals, and research at l'Institut Marcel Chavinier is focusing on the mysterious partnership bonds between wizards and vampires. But the battle for public opinion rages on. When Detective Adèle Rougier encounters Pascale Auboussu, a shy young woman turned into a vampire against her will, Raymond and Denis Langlois, chef de la Cour nearest the crime, fear a public relations nightmare.

The vampire responsible for Pascale's turning must be brought to justice, but Denis is distracted by an unlikely potential partner—Canadian researcher Martin Delacroix, who is spending a year's sabbatical at l'Institut—and Denis's lingering feelings for his deceased lover prompt him to reject the bond. There's no denying the attraction between them, though, and the allure of companionship is nearly as strong as Denis's grief.

Growing familiarity and yearning for a true mate may induce Adèle and Denis to soften their stances against new partnerships, but Adèle will have to accept a deeper intimacy with Pascale when she has never considered a relationship with a woman, and it will take a near-deadly attack to make Denis admit his most hidden desires. Now he has to hope Martin will be willing to stay.

Chapter 1

PASCALE RUBBED at her eyes. She had enjoyed her visit with Stéphanie and Rémy. Dinner had been wonderful as always, and they had been as in love with each other as ever. Sometimes Pascale thought it would be easier to stop torturing herself instead of going to see them, so happy and snug in their little house when she was all alone, but she would never do that to Stéphanie. They had been friends for too long.

With a sigh, she pulled into her garage, dreading the empty bed that waited for her. Maybe tomorrow she would meet someone. Maybe the woman of her dreams was out there right now, as miserable as she was.

She snorted at the maudlin turn her thoughts had taken. All the wishful thinking in the world would not make those dreams a reality. She grabbed her purse out of the passenger seat and headed inside.

As she reached for the doorknob, hard hands grabbed her from behind, one covering her mouth, the other around her throat, constricting her breathing. She tried to scream, to fight, to flee, but her attacker was too strong. Panic roiled through her as he dragged her toward the other door, the one that led outside to her yard. She forced herself to go limp, hoping he would take what he wanted and leave her alone.

She shuddered when she felt lips on her neck and prayed he did not intend to rape her. Then his mouth opened, biting down hard, breaking skin and drawing blood. She struggled again despite her best intentions, but her feeble thrashing did no good against his strength. It became harder and harder to breathe, to keep her eyes open, to think, like a shroud being drawn across her senses.

Dear God, don't let me die.

ADÈLE ROUGIER took a deep breath and steeled herself for the evening to come before getting out of her car at l'Institut Marcel Chavinier.

"Adèle, I see you made it—if a little bit late."

Adèle summoned a smile for Thierry Dumont, an old friend and one of the faculty at l'Institut. "What are you doing out here?" she asked as she kissed both his cheeks in greeting. "I would've expected you to be inside with Raymond and the others."

"I was finishing up some repairs on the grange," Thierry explained. "I needed a shower."

"How's that coming?" Adèle asked. Even in the fading September light, Adèle could see the difference in the grange. She had watched Thierry, his partner Sebastien, and a dedicated group of craftsmen transform the old monastery in Dommartin from near ruins a year ago, when only part of the abbey itself and the abbot's lodge had been in any usable condition, to a thriving research institute dedicated to exploring the partnerships between wizard and vampire as well as other issues related to the magical community.

"We're making progress," Thierry said, starting toward the abbey. Adèle fell in step beside him. "We've patched the roof completely. Bertrand started laying pipe so we can get water to the grange as well. I'm not sure what Raymond plans to use it for, but he wants it solid, with heat and running water."

"You really like it here, don't you?" Adèle asked, struggling as she always did to reconcile the image of Thierry here at l'Institut, acting as primary caretaker and guardian of the buildings, with the shrewd, calculating captain he had been during l'émeute des Sorciers.

"I do," Thierry said, ushering her into the scriptorium, where twenty-five people sat around a large table.

"You've done fabulous work. Your affinity to stone really shines through." Adèle had seen the condition of the property before Thierry had begun making repairs, his magic fusing stone to stone once more. It made the beauty of the buildings around her all the more impressive.

"We all have our own strengths," Thierry replied with typical modesty. "Your affinity to fire gives you an edge when it comes to the excitement of your detective work. We all did what we had to during the war, but the pace of life here at l'Institut suits me in a way your job never would."

"How did this week's seminar go?" Adèle asked softly, hanging back by the door. If she went farther inside, Raymond Payet, director of l'Institut, would see her and ask her again if she wanted to try to find a new partner, the central purpose of the educational seminars and indeed of l'Institut itself. With everything they had learned about the partnerships they had created so swiftly and naively at the height of the war, Adèle agreed with the logic of explaining the commitment to people before they created such a bond. She even understood Raymond's insistence that she join them for dinner at least once a week, preferably on Sunday at the end of that week's seminar, so he could make sure she was not suffering any ill effects from the separation from her own late partner, Jude Leighton. Jude had been destroyed during an attack on l'Institut six months before.

If she went inside, Raymond would certainly try once again to convince her to form a new partnership. She had yet to convince him that her partnership had not been the deep, life-changing relationship most of the partnerships had become.

From just outside the door, Adèle watched as one of the wizards cast a cleansing spell on the hands of the ten vampires sitting on one side of the table. The ink marks on all ten hands disappeared, to some sighs of disappointment and perhaps one or two expressions of relief. None of the vampires was the partner of that wizard, nor of any of the others who might have tested their magic that night. If they had been, the ink would have stayed on their hands, untouched by the wizard's magic.

"Adèle, you've arrived just in time."

Adèle cursed under her breath. "Bonsoir, Raymond."

"Come see if any of the vampires is your partner," Raymond urged.

"Not tonight," she demurred.

Raymond looked like he was about to argue, but Jean Bellaiche, his partner and codirector of l'Institut, intervened. "Dinner will be ready in the réfectoire if everyone would care to adjourn. We'll join you there in a moment."

The wizards and vampires who had come to l'Institut for the educational seminar filed out, leaving Adèle alone with Raymond, Jean, and Thierry. "Leighton is gone," Raymond began. "There's no reason you couldn't form a new partnership."

Adèle sighed. "Besides the fact that I don't want another one?" she asked. "I had enough of that with Jude."

She knew Raymond did not believe her, but she felt only relief at not wondering when her bastard former partner would show up on her doorstep and grab her, demanding blood and sex and submission.

Raymond was too in love with his partner to understand that her own partnership had been the opposite. Even seeing how Jude had treated her at times, Raymond could not truly comprehend the depths of Leighton's cruel, crude, callous disregard for Adèle.

"Leighton was an anomaly," Raymond insisted. "A new partnership wouldn't be that way."

"I know you believe that," Adèle replied, "but that doesn't make me any more interested in taking the risk. Let's go. Dinner's ready and people are waiting on us."

Raymond pulled a face but gave in to her logic and Jean's guiding hand.

Adèle wished, not for the first time, that she could find a way out of the weekly dinners. Work had not cooperated this week, and with no case to use as an excuse, she had given in to the guilt she felt at brushing off Raymond's concern. They had all seen the grief that had overtaken Blair Nichols, the one vampire she knew of who had lost his partner during the war, after Laurent Copé's death. Their partnership had been more like Raymond and Jean's or Thierry and Sebastien's, a true match of hearts and spirits that would have developed into a formidable bond if Laurent had not died in one of Serrier's attacks. She had lost sight of Blair after the war ended, making her wonder if Raymond importuned the vampire the same way or if Jean had reined his partner in on that score.

"I worry about you," Raymond said as they took their seats at the head table where Raymond always insisted Adèle sit. She might not be on the faculty at l'Institut, but she was a veteran of l'émeute des Sorciers like Raymond and the others on the staff, not to mention their friend. "Are you well?"

"I'm fine," Adèle said as she did every week. She suspected it would be easier on Raymond if she was pining away from Leighton's loss. He would understand that emotion. It would be his own reaction if anything ever happened to Jean. She shuddered to think of that. She might have hated her own partner, but she recognized the devotion between the partners around her. "Are Alain and Orlando here tonight?"

It was a diversionary tactic, but it worked. "They should be, although they said they'd probably be late. They're in Paris at a meeting," Raymond said. "Did you need them for something?"

"No," Adèle said. "I just hadn't seen them in a couple of weeks. You're not the only one who likes to keep up with his friends."

Raymond flushed. "Am I really that intolerable?"

"I know you want what's best for me," Adèle replied. Now if they could only agree on what that was. Raymond wanted her to find another partner, or rather, the researcher in him wanted to know if it was possible for a wizard who had lost her partner to find another one. "Did you have any matches this week?"

"None," Raymond said with a frustrated grimace. "More weeks than not, we don't. It seemed so easy that first morning at the Gare de Lyon. Not the meeting itself—that was incredibly awkward—but the partnerships. I don't understand why we have so little success now."

"A smaller pool to choose from, for one thing," Adèle suggested. "Ten wizards and vampires a week instead of the nearly four hundred people we gathered at the Gare de Lyon. And not all of the wizards and vampires each week choose to try for a partnership. Even those who do decide to try but don't meet a partner leave with good intentions of coming back to try again in subsequent weeks, but you know most of them get busy with their lives and forget as many weeks as they remember. Without the pressure of the war to add urgency to the mix, people put it off. Or maybe they change their minds once they're away and have time to reflect. If we'd known then what we know now, I probably wouldn't have let Jude feed from me that first time."

"Really?" Raymond asked.

"Okay, maybe I would have because of the war," Adèle admitted, "but Jude and I rubbed each other the wrong way from the moment we first spoke. He looked at the bite marks on my arm and judged me for it even though he knew why they were there. He never stopped judging me." Out of habit, she ran her fingers across the upper swell of her left breast where even now she bore the scars of his fangs. Realizing what she was doing, she jerked her hand away quickly, hoping Raymond had not noticed. She had healed the other marks he left on her body, but she kept the one set of scars as a reminder of the mistake she had made so she would not make it again.

Sebastien Noyer, Thierry's partner, joined them at the table before Raymond could reply to that, his hand trailing across the back of Thierry's neck as he passed. Adèle smiled at the open gesture of affection between the two men. She knew partnerships could be positive and productive. She had only to look at Sebastien and Thierry or Jean and Raymond to see it. Unfortunately, her own partnership had been nothing but a nightmare.

"Bonsoir, Sebastien," she said, drawing Sebastien's attention from his partner to the social niceties he had ignored in favor of greeting the lover he had left perhaps ten minutes earlier.

"Adèle, I didn't see you come in," Sebastien said, greeting her as Thierry had done.

"I just arrived a few minutes ago," she said.

"You're late tonight," Sebastien teased. "Did a case keep you?"

"Paperwork," Adèle said. It was even mostly true. She could have done it earlier in the day, but she had been working on it at the time she normally would have left to come to dinner.

"You work too hard," Raymond said, drawing a snort of disbelief from Adèle. That was a case of the pot calling the kettle black if ever there was one. "You need someone to make you relax."

"I don't need anyone to *make* me do anything," Adèle retorted, hackles rising. "It was that kind of condescending attitude that made me hate Leighton so much. I didn't take it from him, even if I understood where his attitude came from. I'm certainly not going to take it from you!"

A reverent murmur went through the room, forestalling the rest of Adèle's rant, although from Raymond's contrite look, he would have apologized before it went any further. Alain Magnier and Orlando St. Clair had arrived. To Adèle, they were friends, fellow veterans, and more proof of how good a partnership could be, but she had spent enough time around vampires not involved in l'émeute des Sorciers to know how they were viewed by the wider vampire community. The brand on Alain's neck, proof of a different kind of bond, set them apart and gave Orlando near mythical standing within vampire society. As striking as they were together, Orlando dark and slender, Alain fair and broader through the shoulders, Adèle suspected they would turn heads even if they did not have the Aveu de Sang to set them apart.

When they reached the head table, they greeted everyone, ending with Adèle, before taking their seats. "How did the meeting with Anne-Marie go?" Raymond asked.

"She said to tell you that you could have your job back whenever you wanted it," Alain said with a grin.

"Oh, no," Raymond said. "I served my time as president of l'ANS. That's her problem now."

They all laughed, Adèle included. L'Association Nationale de Sorcellerie, the nonprofit organization that campaigned for the rights of all magical beings, had fallen into Raymond's hands at the retirement of the previous president, Marcel Chavinier. Raymond had, in turn, retired from the post with the opening of l'Institut six months earlier. Anne-Marie Valour, his successor, was doing a good job from what Adèle could see, but she tried to give Raymond the job back at least once a month.

YAWNING, ADÈLE drove toward home, her thoughts all in turmoil. So far she had resisted Raymond's blandishments to try her magic on the vampires who completed l'Institut's educational seminars, but sometimes, especially on nights like tonight, when the partners around her seemed in a particularly affectionate mood, she wondered what her life might be like now if she had paired with someone different. It would always be her choice. Raymond could not coerce her into creating a new partnership bond. The whole point of having the seminars was to make both sides aware of the commitment entailed in forming a partnership, but she also knew he could not understand—not really—why she would not want it again, knowing what it meant. How could he, when Jean worshiped the ground he walked on—a feeling he clearly returned?

In the darkness and silence of her own bedroom, she could admit that she had not hated every minute of it. Most of it, but not all of it. Leighton, damn his black soul, had known how to touch her like none of her previous lovers had dared. She had fought him—and left him—because his attitude toward her was intolerable.

Shaking her head at her wandering thoughts, she yawned again, focusing on the road in front of her. As she rounded a bend, the beams of her headlights caught the slender form of a woman perched precariously on the edge of a bridge across one of le Morvan's many ravines. Slamming on the brakes, Adèle grabbed her wand, jumping from the car and casting a spell on the woman to keep her from jumping. The woman's arms continued to move wildly. Adèle cursed under her breath. She had felt the magic leave her. The spell had gone where she intended, but it hadn't worked.

Stomach churning, Adèle recognized the irony that she had just been thinking of the only other person her magic hadn't ever worked on, but she did not have time to worry over the implications at the moment. She could not let the woman jump. Changing her tactics, she cast a spell on the bridge itself, raising a barrier between the woman and the ravine. "Come down," Adèle urged. "No matter what it is you think is so bad, it isn't worth killing yourself."

"I'm already dead," the woman shouted back. "The fucker killed me—then instead of letting me die, he forced his blood down my throat and made me into a monster."

"Who?" Adèle asked, walking slowly toward the woman. "Who hurt you?"

"I don't know his name. He appeared out of the darkness and grabbed me as I opened the door to my house." The words came out in short gasps. Adèle wished she could see better in the darkness, the headlights from her car creating crazy shadows.

"He dragged me behind the garage and bit me."

Adèle could sympathize with that feeling. Jude had grabbed her and dragged her into alleys, empty rooms, and any other private place he could find to feed from her whether she agreed or not.

"I could feel myself getting weaker and weaker, and then instead of letting me go, he tore open his wrist and forced his blood down my throat."

Adèle shuddered. She had seen the strength of the vampires during the war. This slight woman who barely passed Adèle's shoulder would have had no chance against one of them.

"When I woke up, he told me I was a vampire and I'd need to find someone to feed from so I didn't starve. I don't want to be a monster like him!"

"Calm down," Adèle said soothingly, hiding her shock. She had learned enough about vampires over the past two years to know the mysterious vampire's behavior fell well outside the norm of accepted behavior within that community. She had no idea what, under French law, she could charge a vampire with for a nonconsensual turning, but she knew without a doubt what the reaction of the vampire leadership would be. She moved closer, keeping her hands out in front of her where the other woman could see them. "You aren't a monster, no matter what he did to you. What's your name?"

"You don't know what he turned me into!" the woman wailed, completely ignoring Adèle's question.

"You told me he turned you into a vampire," the wizard said, struggling to hold on to her calm. "That doesn't make you a monster."

"But he drank my blood. He took my life!"

Adèle rolled her eyes. She wondered if the woman was always this melodramatic. "And gave you a different kind of life. Look, I know it's a change, a huge one, but I know some people who can help you."

"They can make me human again?"

"Nobody can do that," Adèle said apologetically, "but they can help you learn to live with your new situation. I have some friends who are vampires, decent ones, not like the one who turned you without your permission. I can take you to them if you want. We can be there in twenty minutes. At least listen to what they have to say. If they can't convince you, it will be dawn in an hour or so. A lot of what you hear about vampires isn't true, but that part is. If you really can't deal with your new existence after you've talked to Jean and Sebastien, all you have to do is walk outside once the sun is up. It will be over in a matter of seconds."

"They won't... hurt me?" the woman asked, stepping away from the edge of the bridge.

"What else can they do to you that you weren't going to do to yourself?" Adèle asked, stepping closer. "Come on. It's cold. You'll be warmer in the car."

"I don't even feel it," the woman said.

"There you go," Adèle joked. "An advantage to being a vampire, because I'm freezing standing out here."

"Why are you helping me?"

"It's what I do," Adèle said, pulling out her badge. "Detective Adèle Rougier at your service."

"Enchantée, Detective."

"And you are?"

"I'm sorry," the woman apologized. "I'm Pascale Auboussu."

Adèle had to suppress a shudder at hearing the first name of the dark wizard who had wreaked so much havoc in Paris before the Milice de Sorcellerie finally cornered and killed him. That wasn't this Pascale's fault, Adèle reminded herself. Here in the country, she had probably been only marginally aware of what many saw as a magical problem. Many people outside of Paris had never registered that the loss of the war would have disrupted everyone's lives and instituted an absolute rule the likes of which had not been seen in France since the days of Louis XIV. Taking a deep breath, Adèle let it go. She had more pressing problems. Like a potential partner who was newly turned and had no idea of anything. "Let's go, Pascale. Time's passing. We need to get you somewhere safe before sunrise."

In the dim glow of the car's dome light, Adèle got a better look at the woman she had rescued. Pascale was petite, blonde, and slender, the opposite of Adèle's height, dark hair, and curvaceous figure. Snarling at catching herself staring, she reminded herself firmly that she didn't want another partner, and even if she did, she liked men. Given her own experience and what she had observed, indeed what l'Institut was teaching during its seminars, anyone entering into a partnership needed to expect and accept it becoming personal, even sexual.

Even if she were interested—which she most certainly was not—asking Pascale to think about a partnership only hours after she was turned into a vampire was ludicrous. Better to leave her with Jean and forget she had ever laid eyes on the vampire. Pascale certainly would not know. Jean and Raymond would insist Pascale participate in a seminar, but she would either find another partner or else continue to function as an unpaired vampire, and Adèle could go about her comfortable existence much as she had the past six months.

Now if she could only believe that.

The wards at l'Institut parted easily to let her in, since she herself had set all of them when Raymond first hatched this crazy scheme. Adèle smiled at the memory. Despite her doubts as she had first prepared the wards, Raymond's "crazy scheme" had worked. More vampires and wizards flocked to l'Institut each week for the educational seminars, and the research they were doing had gained international attention.

Climbing out of the car, Adèle was surprised not to see Raymond. A moment later, a very rumpled Thierry came into the courtyard. "What are you doing back?"

Reluctant Partnerships

"Where's Jean?" Adèle asked. "I found a newly turned vampire trying to commit suicide on my way home tonight. I stopped that, but she's lost and more than a little upset at the moment."

Thierry ran his hand through his short, blond hair. "Let me get Sebastien. At least he can talk to her vampire to vampire."

"Where's Jean?" Adèle repeated.

"He and Raymond went back to Paris for the night and tomorrow," Thierry said. "Something about meeting with Anne-Marie Valour. Apparently she had questions Alain and Orlando couldn't answer."

Adèle nodded as Thierry went back inside the old abbot's lodge that had been converted into living quarters for the full-time staff at l'Institut. Jean and Raymond had the actual abbot's quarters. Thierry and Sebastien had rooms there, as did Alain and Orlando and a few others who presented regularly at the seminars. The participants stayed in the monks' cells in the main building, where they could interact more easily.

Thierry returned a few minutes later, Sebastien at his side. The dark-haired vampire could not have been more Thierry's opposite, slender where Thierry was broad-shouldered, dark where Thierry was fair, but Adèle had seen the strength of their partnership too many times to doubt they belonged together.

"What's this about a newly turned vampire?" Sebastien asked.

"She's in the car," Adèle said, "but go gently with her. Apparently her maker didn't give her a choice, and she's wishing she were dead."

"Didn't give…." Sebastien's face tightened. "There are names for people like that."

"What name?" Adèle asked.

"*Extorris* if he isn't careful," Sebastien said.

Adèle recognized the word, although she had been only peripherally involved in the trial and execution of Edouard Couthon, the rogue vampire who had killed several human victims before participating in Orlando's capture and torture during the war. Vampire justice had been swift and merciless.

"I thought that applied only in the case of a vampire hurting another vampire or an Avoué or something like that."

"The vampire turned her, then abandoned her," Sebastien said. "If you hadn't found her, she would have destroyed herself. That sounds like hurting a vampire to me. What's her name?"

"Pascale."

Adèle winced as she said the name, sharing a pained look with Thierry. It would take more than two years of peace to get used to hearing that name without reacting, when it had been a source of terror for the past four years. Two years of fighting, of watching people around her get hurt and sometimes die because of the evil of one man.

"He'll calm her down," Thierry said as Sebastien walked toward Adèle's car. "He's one of the most matter-of-fact vampires I know."

"It's Sunday night, "Adèle reminded Thierry. "There's no one here for her to feed from."

"We'll have to take her to Paris," Thierry agreed. "Angélique gives her local employees Sunday night off since we don't have seminar participants who need to feed. She'll help her, I'm sure. L'Institut can pay for it until she gets acclimated to her new situation."

At the car, Sebastien slipped into the driver's seat. "Bonsoir, Pascale. I'm Sebastien. Adèle tells me you had a bit of a surprise tonight. How long ago did the vampire bite you?"

"I don't know exactly," Pascale said, her voice heavy with emotion. "Sometime between ten and eleven, because I was coming home from a friend's house when he grabbed me outside my house. I didn't fight him, hoping he'd take what he wanted and let me go."

"He did," Sebastien said. "He just took more than you thought. So if that's the case, it's been almost seven hours, and you have to be starving."

"I won't do to someone else what he did to me!" Pascale protested.

"You don't have to," Sebastien assured her. "See that man talking with Adèle?"

Pascale nodded.

"That's Thierry. He's my partner. I've been feeding from him for getting close to two years now, and he's as healthy as ever. Healthier in some ways. He's certainly stronger than he was when we met."

"I don't understand."

"What the vampire who turned you did was unforgivable, but it doesn't have to be that way. With a bit of experience and a chance to learn control, you can feed as much as you need to without hurting anyone," Sebastien explained. "If you're willing, I'd suggest we go to Paris and see a friend of mine. She runs a restaurant for vampires. All the different flavors of blood you could possibly want."

"So... what?" Pascale said, her stomach churning at the thought of more blood in her mouth. Even upset as she was, she understood what Sebastien was trying to do—but nothing could make this new life appealing. "I give him what he wanted and live this way?"

"Your other choice is to end your existence," Sebastien said philosophically. "I've known a few vampires who made that decision, heard tales of a few more, but for the most part, we keep finding reasons to stay around a little longer."

"How old are you?"

"About five hundred years old," Sebastien said with a grin. "I'm told the years have been kind to me."

"We'll never get to Paris before dawn," Pascale said, "and Adèle said I couldn't be out in daylight."

"Adèle obviously neglected to mention a few things," Sebastien said with a short laugh. "Thierry, could you do me a favor?"

"Sure," Thierry said, coming to the car. "What do you need?"

"Can you send my new friend to place Pigalle? I'll get Adèle to send me too. Pascale needs to meet Angélique."

"Of course," Thierry said, drawing his wand. "Relax," he told Pascale. "This will feel a little odd, but it won't hurt."

With a flick of his wrist, she disappeared. Sebastien dropped a quick kiss on Thierry's mouth before calling for Adèle to send him to Paris as well. Moments later, he reappeared on place Pigalle, the Moulin Rouge to his left and Sang Froid, Angélique Bouaddi's establishment, to his right.

"I don't understand," Pascale said again.

"Thierry and Adèle are wizards," Sebastien explained. "Come on. Sunrise is getting closer. It won't hurt me, but the same isn't true for you."

"Why won't it hurt you?" Pascale asked, hurrying to keep up with Sebastien's long strides.

"Because Thierry is a wizard," Sebastien replied. "I promise to explain everything I can, but first you need to get inside and you need to feed."

Sebastien held open the door to Sang Froid for Pascale.

"Sebastien, what are you doing here?" Angélique asked, summoned by the chime above the door.

Sebastien kissed Angélique on each cheek. "You're looking lovely as ever, chérie. This is Pascale. Pascale, Angélique Bouaddi, proprietress of Sang Froid."

"Enchantée," Pascale said.

"Indeed," Angélique replied. "What's your pleasure?"

"She doesn't know," Sebastien said. "She was turned earlier tonight and then abandoned by her maker. Adèle found her and brought her to l'Institut—but Thierry is the only human in residence at the moment, and I didn't feel like sharing."

"Oh, ma pauvre," Angélique fussed, wrapping her arm around Pascale's shoulders. "Come inside and let me take care of you. Go away, Sebastien. This is girl talk."

"As if you wouldn't have the same talk with a male vampire," Sebastien laughed.

"Of course I would, but that doesn't mean Pascale wants you to hear her secrets," Angélique scolded. "Go away. I'll take care of her."

"Is David around, by any chance?" Sebastien asked. "Because if he isn't, I'm stuck here until Thierry sends someone looking for me."

"Don't terrorize my staff," Angélique said. "David is asleep, but I'll have him send you home when he wakes up. He had a bad case yesterday. I won't disturb him if it's not an emergency."

"Can I use your phone, then, so Thierry knows that I've been delayed? I left my cell phone at l'Institut," Sebastien asked. He respected Angélique's protectiveness. David worked as a child advocate in custody and abuse cases. Sebastien suspected all of his cases were tough ones.

"It's behind the desk," Angélique said with a wave of her hand as she guided Pascale out of the main room and into her parlor-cum-office. "Now that the men are gone, we can talk."

"Talk about what?" Pascale asked nervously.

"Which of my lovely employees will provide the blood you need tonight," Angélique said. "You are hungry, aren't you?"

"Ravenous," Pascale said, "but how am I supposed to choose? Does one person's blood taste different from another's?"

"You aren't supposed to choose," Angélique said. "Not without some experience. I, on the other hand, have centuries of experience to share with you, and over a hundred years of matching vampires with my employees. And yes, the taste of blood varies from person to person. I'm sure we can find someone who appeals. Male or female?"

"Female," Pascale replied immediately. "Well, as a rule, anyway."

"Female it is," Angélique said without blinking an eye. "Your age, younger, older?"

"How is this supposed to help?"

"Because what you prefer in a person generally carries over to what you will prefer in their blood," Angélique explained patiently. "Answer the question."

"Older," Pascale whispered. "Not a lot, but a few years anyway."

"Femme or butch?"

Pascale hesitated, not sure she was comfortable discussing such things with a woman she barely knew.

Angélique laughed at her shyness. "I lived in a harem, dear," she said, holding up her henna-covered hands. "There is nothing about sex and sexual preferences that I haven't seen and probably lived. You don't need to be embarrassed with me."

"Not butch," Pascale said. "I don't want someone masculine, but someone who can take charge and take care of me. I'm not the aggressor."

"That may change a little now that you're a vampire," Angélique said, "but for now, any preferences in coloring?"

"Dark," Pascale said. "Someone like you, if you weren't a vampire."

Angélique laughed. "Oh, darling, they stopped making them like me centuries ago, but I'll find someone who suits. Let me show you to a room."

"A room?"

"Feeding is very personal, very intimate," Angélique explained. "As a rule, vampires feed in private. Since this is your first time, I'll be there to help you find your balance. Your maker should have done this, but since he… she?"

"He."

"Since he didn't do his duty, I will take his place gladly."

Angélique led Pascale to a finely appointed sitting room, furnished with two love seats and a chaise longue. "Make yourself comfortable. Take off your coat. Your shoes, too, if you want. I'll be back in a few minutes."

Angélique left Pascale alone, shutting the door behind her. Pascale started toward the shuttered window, wondering what time it was, but the heat coming through the closed volets nearly burned her. She jerked her hand away, seeing the grey cast to her skin and feeling the painful tingling along her arm. "What nightmare have I walked into?"

Angélique returned a few minutes later with a beautiful, busty woman in tow, exactly the kind of woman Pascale might have flirted with when she came to the city. Exactly the kind who never gave her the time of day. "Pascale, this is Isabelle. Isabelle, the vampire I told you about."

"Welcome to Sang Froid," Isabelle said, holding out her hand. Pascale took it uncertainly, her eyes fixed on the pulse at the woman's wrist. Her mouth watered. She could practically taste the blood flowing beneath the surface.

"Gently now," Angélique said. "You can't simply dive in. Have a seat on one of the couches where you'll be comfortable."

Pascale frowned. This was the part where her shyness always kicked in and she lost her nerve. She took a seat as Angélique instructed, wondering how she was supposed to make small talk while the urge to bite, anywhere she could, was nearly overwhelming.

"Take her hand again," Angélique instructed. "Lick the skin of her wrist. You should always prepare the place you intend to bite. Your saliva will numb the area a little so the bite hurts less, and afterward, you lick the whole area again to help her heal faster."

Pascale breathed a huge sigh of relief, lifting Isabelle's wrist to her mouth and licking over the lightly perfumed skin. The smell went to her head, evoking an odd tingling in her mouth, then a sharp pain.

"Look at me," Angélique said.

Pascale turned her head.

"Show me your teeth."

Confused, Pascale smiled.

"Good, your fangs dropped on their own. Sometimes new vampires have a problem with that, and then it gets complicated. You can bite her now."

Pascale looked up at Isabelle.

"Go ahead," Isabelle said with a friendly smile. "I'm a willing participant in this."

"You enjoy it?" Pascale asked, caught by the smile.

"Very much," Isabelle said. "It's a good job, and I've grown to crave the feeling of a vampire's fangs in my skin."

Bemused, Pascale lifted Isabelle's arm to her lips, biting into the skin.

"Harder," Isabelle said. "Your fangs are sharp, but you have to push them deep enough to draw blood."

Pascale pressed harder, feeling the sudden give in the other woman's skin as her fangs pierced deep. Blood flooded her mouth, surprising her. She almost choked as she tried to find the rhythm that would allow her to swallow.

Next to her, Angélique kept a close eye on Isabelle. The woman was one of her longest-term employees. She would know when she reached a critical level and Pascale needed to stop. The vampire herself would learn to identify that moment in time, but not tonight, with the need of her turning burning through her. Angélique suspected it would take two or three feedings to satisfy her completely.

When Isabelle nodded, Angélique tapped Pascale's shoulder. "That's enough," she said.

Pascale gripped Isabelle's hand tighter.

Angélique tapped a little harder. "Pascale, you need to let her go now."

Pascale ignored her.

Grabbing Pascale's hands, Angélique forced them away from Isabelle's wrist. The moment her hand was free, Isabelle snatched it back.

Pascale spun to face Angélique, her eyes wild. "I wasn't done."

"No, but Isabelle is," Angélique said mildly. Her superior age guaranteed she could restrain Pascale if she needed to, but usually her calm demeanor did the trick.

"I'm still hungry!" Pascale shouted.

"And Isabelle's sending someone else in," Angélique said, "but you have to get control of yourself. You said you didn't want to do what he did to you—but if you don't control the beast driving you to feed, you will do exactly that, intentionally or not."

"How?"

"You probably can't control yourself now," Angélique said honestly. "You're newly turned and the blood hunger is driving you hard. After you've sated yourself and rested, we will talk again and I'll teach you some techniques."

They repeated the process twice more before Pascale let go of a donor's wrist voluntarily. "There is a bedroom down the hall where you can rest today," Angélique said. "You'll be hungry again tonight, but we will talk some more before then."

"I don't think I can rest," Pascale said. "I'm on edge."

"That's a side effect of feeding," Angélique agreed. "With a willing partner, the fastest way to ease that restlessness is a round of hot, sweaty sex. Unfortunately, that isn't on offer here. I don't run a sex shop."

"So what am I supposed to do?"

"There's a vibrator in the drawer, still in its package," Angélique said. "It's yours if you want it."

"Why are you being so helpful?" Pascale demanded.

"Because Sebastien asked me to, because every vampire should have guidance when they're turned, because you remind me of a girl in the harem, because this is what I do," Angélique replied. "Take your pick."

"Are you sure you won't join me?" Pascale asked, the blood rushing through her system emboldening her.

"You are temptation itself, but I have a lover," Angélique said, "one whom I am not willing to give up. Before I can do anything, I would have to talk with him, and he will have already left for the day."

"A vampire?"

"No, a wizard."

"Another wizard? I'd never met one in my life until tonight and now they're everywhere!"

"You're a vampire now, a magical creature," Angélique reminded her. "Wizards are about to be a large part of your life, at least until you're ready to be on your own again, and perhaps even after that. I predict you have about twelve hours before Raymond and Jean descend on you, and that's only because they'll wait for sundown before they disturb you."

"Who are they?" Pascale asked.

Angélique laughed. "The two most charismatic men you'll ever meet. Either one of them is enough to turn a woman's head. Together…." She shook her head and laughed again. "More relevantly, they're the chef de la Cour of Paris and his Consort, as well as the directors of l'Institut Marcel Chavinier."

"None of which tells me anything," Pascale reminded her.

"Rest," Angélique insisted. "The sun is up and you're about to be very twitchy unless you're somewhere dark and enclosed. You'll be safe in the bedroom as long as you stay away from the volets, but you'll rest better if you close the bed curtains too."

Pascale wanted to argue, but Angélique was implacable, showing her into the small, well-appointed bedroom, offering her a nightgown if she wanted, and closing the door firmly behind her. Pascale checked the handle the moment she was gone. The door was unlocked. She could leave if she wanted, the room, anyway. The sun outside would keep her from leaving the building.

The thought surprised her. Sometime in the past hour, she had recovered her equilibrium and her desire to live, even in this altered state. She had no idea what it really meant to be a "magical creature" as Angélique had said, but she had fed without hurting the people who helped her. She could exist this way without becoming a monster. It would be different, but perhaps it would not be horrible. Suddenly exhausted, she climbed into bed, drawing the bed curtains as Angélique had suggested. Cocooned in darkness, she closed her eyes and let dreams take her.

Don't miss what
happens next in

Covenant in Blood

Sequel to *Alliance in Blood*
Partnership in Blood:
Volume Two

By Ariel Tachna

The wizards and the vampires have forged an alliance based on blood and magic, hoping to turn the tide of the war against the dark wizards. A few wizard-vampire bonds are as successful as Alain Magnier's and Orlando St. Clair's, but some are much less so, leading to arguments, resentment, and outright fights between the allies despite their mutual goals.

Following his best friend Alain's example, Thierry Dumont determinedly forms a partnership with vampire Sebastien Noyer, despite the wizard's discomfort with being so close to a vampire—a man—so soon after his wife's death. But they find that desperation may be the key to forming a covenant that works: Thierry and Sebastien are almost immediately devoted to one another's safety.

With new strength behind it, the Alliance's leaders move to announce its existence to the whole world, hoping to rally support against the dark wizards who threaten to destroy life as they know it. Struggling to find its way in the expanding war, the Alliance discovers that despite its advantages, the partnerships are affecting the balance of magical power in the world, which may be an even bigger threat than the war itself.

http://www.dreamspinnerpress.com

The story continues in

Conflict in Blood

Sequel to *Covenant in Blood*
Partnership in Blood:
Volume Three

By Ariel Tachna

As the Alliance wizard-vampire partnerships grow stronger, the dark wizards feel the effects and become increasingly desperate to find enough information to counter them, unaware of the growing strain of the blood-magic bonds on the wizards and vampires alike.

The conflict is spreading. The strife of uncomfortable relationships, both personal and professional, is threatening to tear up the Alliance from the inside, despite the efforts of Alain Magnier and Orlando St. Clair, Thierry Dumont and Sebastien Noyer, and even Raymond Payet and Jean Bellaiche, leader of the Paris vampires, who is fighting to establish a stable covenant with his own partner so he might lead by example.

As the war rages on and heartbreaking casualties mount on both sides, the dark wizards keep searching for clues to understand and counter the strength of the Alliance, while the blood-bound Alliance partners hunt through ancient prejudices and forgotten lore to find an edge that can turn the tide of the war once and for all.

http://www.dreamspinnerpress.com

A Partnership in Blood novel

Lycan Partnership

By Ariel Tachna

By the time the alpha of the Morvan werewolf pack approaches l'Institut Marcel Chavinier for help solving his people's fertility problems, pack numbers have dwindled and the remaining members are desperate. Though the wizards at l'Institut have no experience with werewolves, their lore, or their brand of magic, Raymond agrees to help.

At l'ANS headquarters, Raymond finds Marc Gourlin, a young wizard fascinated with werewolves. Marc agrees to visit the werewolves' home to study their rituals for the source of the problem. But when he arrives, he finds himself distracted by Adenet Silaire, the pack shaman. The attraction between them is powerful, but though Marc suspects he might be Adenet's mate, Adenet rebuffs him. Marc is a man, and Adenet's sense of responsibility will not let him take a male mate when the pack so desperately needs children.

Meanwhile, Jean and Raymond discover the Aveu de Sang allows a vampire's Avoué to calm his inner beast. For Jean and Orlando, this is wonderful news—but it only convinces Thierry how much Sebastien is missing out on because they cannot form an Aveu de Sang. Determined to give his partner everything he can, Thierry sets out to recreate the bond denied them by Sebastien's past.

A Partnership in Blood novel

Partnership Reborn

By Ariel Tachna

All his life, wizard Raphael Tarayaud has dreamed of a vampire—first as a friend, then as a lover. His search for his missing soul mate brings him to the attention of Sebastien Noyer, one of his childhood heroes. While Sebastien isn't his soul mate, he could be the perfect partner for Raphael's best friend Kylian Raffier.

As strange coincidences mount up, Raphael offers his research expertise to try and help Kylian and Sebastien understand what is happening to them, though the more he learns, the less he likes it. But it won't keep him from fighting with everything he has to secure Kylian's future.

When he finally meets Jean Bellaiche, former chef de la Cour and grieving widower, the meeting is disastrous, but Raphael can't let it go. He doesn't stand a chance with Jean—who could compete with the ghost of Raymond Payet?—but nothing can stop him from dreaming.

http://www.dreamspinnerpress.com

ARIEL TACHNA lives outside of Houston with her husband, her daughter and son, and their cat. Before moving there, she traveled all over the world, having fallen in love with both France, where she found her husband, and India, where she dreams of retiring someday. She's bilingual with snippets of four other languages to her credit and is as in love with languages as she is with writing.

Visit Ariel at her website: http://www.arieltachna.com or on Facebook: https://www.facebook.com/ArielTachna, or e-mail her at arieltachna@gmail.com.

www.ingramcontent.com/pod-product-compliance
Lightning Source LLC
Chambersburg PA
CBHW051532260626
47170CB00003B/903